PÈRE GORIOT [OLD GORIOT]

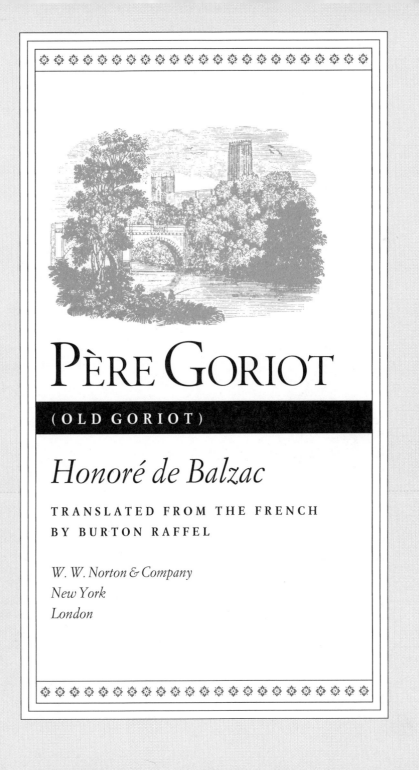

PÈRE GORIOT

(OLD GORIOT)

Honoré de Balzac

TRANSLATED FROM THE FRENCH
BY BURTON RAFFEL

W. W. Norton & Company
New York
London

Copyright © 1994 by Burton Raffel
Printed in the United States of America
First Edition

The text of this book is composed in Simoncini Garamond
with the display set in Adobe Titling
Composition by PennSet Inc.
Manufacturing by Courier Companies, Inc.
Book design by Beth Tondreau Design

LIBRARY OF CONGRESS CATALOGING-IN-PUBLICATION DATA
Balzac, Honoré de, 1799–1850.
[Père Goriot. English]
Père Goriot / Honoré de Balzac ; translated from the French
by Burton Raffel.
p.   cm.
1. Paris (France)—Social life and customs—19th century—Fiction.   2. Fathers
and daughters—France—Paris—Fiction.   3. Aged men—France—Paris—
Fiction.   I. Raffel, Burton.   II. Title.
PQ2168.A37   1994
843'.7—dc20   93-33216

ISBN 0-393-03620-0

W. W. Norton & Company, Inc., 500 Fifth Avenue, New York, N.Y. 10110
W. W. Norton & Company Ltd., 10 Coptic Street, London WC1A 1PU

1   2   3   4   5   6   7   8   9   0

to the memory of Professor Hélène Harvitt,
who introduced me to French literature
comme il faut

Translator's Preface

ACCORDING TO HENRY JAMES (EVERY BIT AS TORTURED AND BRILLIANT A CRITIC AS HE WAS A NOVELIST), THE BASIC LOCALE OF BALZAC'S *PÈRE GORIOT*, MADAME VAUQUER'S LODGING HOUSE, IS "ONE OF THE MOST PORTENTOUS SETTINGS OF THE SCENE IN ALL THE LITERATURE OF FICTION." The old widow's shabby, parceled-up house becomes, he goes on, "the stage of vast dramas, [and] is a sort of concentrated focus of human life, with sensitive nerves radiating out into the infinite." And the "vast drama" which Balzac lays out for us, says James, "easily ranks among the few greatest novels we possess."

James was writing in 1875, when Balzac had been dead only twenty-five years; the next year yet another novelist who cannot be accused of parochialism in saying such things of a French writer, Ivan Turgenev, scoffed that "if [Goncourt]'s being honest, he'll confess that French literature didn't exist before Balzac." André Gide, a French writer not naturally well disposed to Balzac, nevertheless said flatly that "it is important to have read Balzac, all of Balzac. Some writers have thought they could dispense with this; later on, they were not quite able to understand just what indefinable trait was missing in them; we realize it for them." And Gustave Flaubert, in theory at least virtually Balzac's exact literary opposite, exclaimed, "What a man Balzac would have been, had he known how to write! But that was the only thing he lacked." Much of what may seem to us, a century and a half later, most strikingly original in Flaubert's greatest book, *Madame Bovary*, were in fact lessons learned at Balzac's knee.

Published in 1834–35, *Père Goriot* began with the following authorial note: "A brave man—a middle-class lodging house—600 francs a year of income—being stripped by his daughters, both of whom have incomes of 50,000 francs a year, dying like a dog." Balzac saw his novel as something of a nineteenth-century French counterpart to *King Lear*, and its central figure as someone "who's a *father* as *a saint, a martyr is a Christian*." He vowed to "grasp paternity warts and all, paint it complete, just as it is." And because he was, as Ernst Curtius has said, "a great affirmer, . . . [a writer who] lived in the euphoria of creation," he gathered into his novel a wide swath of the living, breathing Parisian metropolis, its streets, its buildings, and above all its people. He told old Goriot's story, and a good deal more. "Our sense of life is heightened, our existence is intensified," explains Curtius, "when we see the world through Balzac's eyes."

The key to Balzac's vision, as it is the key to the unique impact of most great writers, is his style—much-maligned by the devotees of "l'art pour l'art" (Art for Art's sake), like Flaubert, but recognized by Théophile Gautier and others as "the indispensable, inevitable and mathematically correct style for his ideas" (le style nécessaire, fatal et mathématique de son idée). Balzac is perfectly capable, as we all are, of writing more effectively at one moment than another; he is even capable, again like the rest of us, of writing comparatively badly. But for the most part, though his is emphatically not the preciously honed prose we sometimes mistakenly think is the only sort worthy of praise, he writes both powerfully and beautifully. At his best, bluntly, he is a masterful stylist, a magnificent, eloquent, passionate and, in his way, elegant *prosateur* ["writer of prose"]. And since, as I have explained at some length in *The Art of Translating Prose* (1994), prose "is by its very nature woven much closer to the syntactic bone than is poetry," and syntax is "the basic component of prose style, as well as an important aspect of prose significance (meaning) . . . proper translation of prose style is absolutely essential to proper translation of prose, and close attention to prose syntax is absolutely essential to proper translation of prose style. In literary prose, the style *is* the man (or the woman), the very sign and hallmark of the mind and personality at work on the page."

It is said that comparisons are odious, but the only justification for a new translation of an old classic (as also the only justification for a translator's preface) must be that what has come before is less satisfactory than what we are now offered. That which is merely novel, and not better, has in my judgment no particular reason for existence: we do not need the sixty-fifth recording of Beethoven's Fifth Symphony unless it shows us a Beethoven significantly different from the sixty-four versions which have preceded it. *Of course* I think I have improved on the efforts of those who have preceded me, or I would not permit my translation to be printed. Just as there is a necessary *hubris* ("insolence/excessive pride") in presuming to tell the reader a story, by writing a novel, so too there is a necessary (though somewhat less commanding) *hubris* involved in translating one. Balzac is one of the supremely great novelists, and *Père Goriot* is one of his most important and impressive achievements. Believing that as I do, and also believing that neither he nor *Père Goriot* have as yet been given anything like an adequate representation in English, I have done everything I could to create at least some reasonable simulacrum, in my language, of the power and slashing, challenging emotion of what he has written in his. The translation neither is nor can be the original, but I have sought to make the translation breathe with at least some of that "euphoria of creation" for which, in French, Balzac is so justly famous.

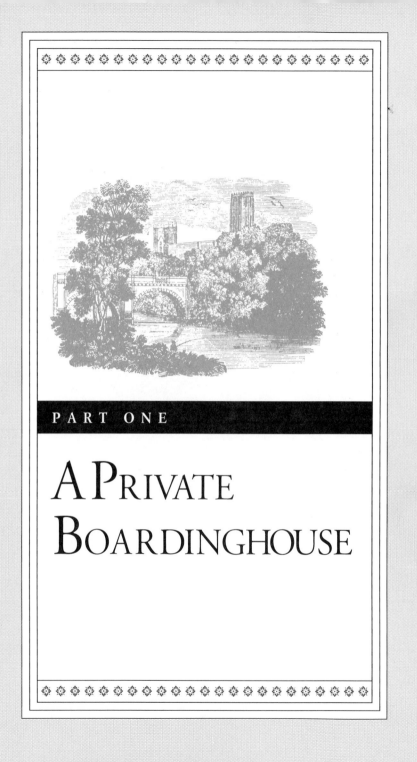

PART ONE

A PRIVATE BOARDINGHOUSE

MADAME VAUQUER (WHOSE MAIDEN NAME WAS CONFLANS, NO LESS) IS AN OLD WOMAN, FOR FORTY YEARS PROPRIETOR OF A PRIVATE BOARDING-HOUSE ON NEW SAINT GENEVIEVE STREET, BETWEEN PARIS'S LATIN QUARTER AND ITS SAINT MARCEAU SUBURB. Called "Maison Vauquer," the *pension* is open both to men and women, to young people and old dotards, but no breath of scandal has ever impugned the morals of so respectable an establishment. All the same, no young people have been seen in Maison Vauquer for thirty years, and any youngster who did live there would have had to be from a family that gave him an exceedingly meager allowance.

Nevertheless, when this drama begins, in 1819, there was a poor young woman living in the *pension*. And in spite of the disrepute into which the word "drama" has fallen, on account of the cruel overuse with which, in these days of heart-rending literature, it has been afflicted, the word must be used here—not that this story will be dramatic in the real meaning of the term but, once the whole tale has been read, a few tears may well have dropped, perhaps privately, perhaps even in public. You may well wonder: is that really likely to happen, outside of Paris? The specific details of this setting, so full of localized sights and colors, can truly be appreciated only between the rolling hills of Montmartre and the heights of Montrouge, along that famous valley where cracking plaster is always about to fall on your head and the gutters run black with mud; that valley full of genuine suffering, and of joys that often turn out to be false, and so incredibly tumultuous that it takes something God only knows how outrageous to cause a lasting stir. But here and there some immense heaping up of vices and virtues turns mere sorrow grand and solemn, and their very sight makes even selfishness and personal advantage stop and feel pity—though that notion of pity is much like some tasty fruit that gets gobbled right up. Civilization's high-riding chariot, like the believer-crushing car of the idol Juggernaut, barely slows down when it comes to a heart a bit harder to crack, and if such a heart gets in the way it's pretty quickly smashed, and on goes the glorious march. Which is what you'll do, too, you who are right now holding this book in your fair white hand, you who sink down in your soft easy chair, saying to yourself: Maybe this book is going to be fun. And then, after you've read all about Père Goriot's miserable secrets, you'll have yourself a good dinner and blame your indifference on the author, scolding him for exaggeration, accusing him of having waxed poetic. Ah, but let me tell you: this drama is not fictional, it's not a novel. *All is true*❁—so true you'll be able to recognize everything that goes into it in your own life, perhaps even in your own heart.

The *pension* occupies a house belonging to Madame Vauquer, located at the lower end of New Saint Geneviève Street, just where it slopes down toward Arbalete Street, dipping so suddenly and sharply that horses don't often come riding either up or down. This works out very well for the general calm and quiet prevailing in these close-packed streets, between Val-de-Grâce Cathedral and the Pantheon, two towering structures that change the very atmospheric conditions, jutting up into the air with their sallow spires, muddying everything with the glowering, harsh colors of their domes. In there, the pavement is bone dry, there's no mud in the streams, nor any water, and grass grows along the walls. In there, the most carefree man in the world is as depressed as everybody else walking those streets; the sound of a carriage or a cart going by becomes an event; every single building stands dark and gloomy; and the high, thick walls remind you of a prison house. A Parisian who gets lost, in there, would see only *pensions* and hospitals and private schools, only misery or boredom, old age sinking into the grave or happy youth forced into unhappy labor. There's no more hideous neighborhood in all of Paris, nor, in truth, one so little known. New Saint Geneviève Street, in particular, is like the bronze frame around a painting, and indeed is the only fit and proper frame for a tale like this, for which the reader cannot be over-prepared with too many shades of brown or too many somber ideas—just as, descending into the Catacombs, daylight fades further into darkness with every step, and the guide's

❁ In English in the original, borrowed from the alternative title to Shakespeare (and John Fletcher?)'s *Henry VIII*.

song turns hollow. What a realistic comparison! Who can tell us which is worse, to see dried-out hearts or empty skulls?

There is a small garden directly in front of the *pension*, making the house itself seem to drop away from New Saint Geneviève Street at a right angle, looking so deep down in the ground that it appears to be cut off from the street. All across the front facade, abutting on the garden, runs a cobblestone path, concave and a full six feet wide, next to which there is a gravel walk, bordered with geraniums, flowering laurels, and small pomegranate trees planted in great blue and white earthenware jars. The entrance to this walk, from the house, is through a narrow gateway, over which there is a sign, reading: "MAISON VAUQUER," and under that: "Private boardinghouse for both sexes and others." When there's daylight to see by, you can make out, through a latticework door armed with a shrill bell, that on the wall facing onto the street, down at the end of this little path, some local artist, making it look like green marble, has painted an arched passageway. And under the recess in the wall, which the painting pretends to create, there stands a statue of Cupid. The flaking green covering this figure might, if you were fond of symbols, make you see it as an allegorical representation of Parisian Love, which can be cured at the nearby Hospital for Venereal Disease. The half-worn-away inscription under the pedestal, with its enthusiasm for Voltaire (who had come back to Paris in 1777, and who composed these lines), will remind you of what things were like, back in the days when it was placed there:

Whoever you are, here is your Master:
Here is your destiny, shaped in plaster.

At night, the latticework grill is taken out and a solid panel put in. The little garden, just as wide as the width of the house, is enclosed both by the street wall and by the party wall belonging to the house next door, which shared structure is completely hidden by masses of ivy, creating—for Paris—an unusually picturesque effect which catches people's attention as they go by. Every one of these walls is draped with trellises and with vines, whose lean and dusty fruit Madame worries over, year after year, and constantly discusses with her lodgers. Each of these tall, heavy walls is bordered by a narrow walk, leading to an arbor of linden trees—"linden" being a word that, though she was born to the rank of a *de Conflans*, Madame Vauquer stubbornly insists on pronouncing "leenden," no matter how hard her grammatically-minded lodgers try to convince her otherwise. Between the two intersecting walks grows a square patch of artichokes, outlined by rows of sorrel, lettuce, or parsley, and flanked by fruit trees carefully grown into geometrical shapes. A round table, painted green, has been set under the lindens, and chairs placed all around it. There, on sultry days, any guests able to afford coffee come to sit and sip it, though the heat is intense enough to hatch eggs. The front facade, running up three storeys, and topped by a sloping mansard roof, is constructed of rough quarry rock and wash-painted in the same yellow tint which makes most of the houses in Paris so unspeakably ugly. The five casement windows set in each storey have small square panes and are furnished with awnings, no one of which is ever raised to the same height, so that the sight lines they create are all crisscrossed and uneven. The depth of the house permits no more than a pair of casement windows along each side, and, on the ground-floor level, these are decorated with iron bars, latticed with wire netting. Back behind the house there is a courtyard, approximately twenty feet across, where pigs, hens, and rabbits all dwell together in peace and harmony, and at one end of which there is a shed for drying wood. A meat pantry hangs between this shed and the kitchen window, and underneath it a pipe connects to the sink, from which greasy water spouts. This courtyard has a narrow doorway opening onto New Saint Geneviève Street, through which the cook gets rid of household garbage, washing it away with floods of water, to ward off infectious diseases.

Intended, more or less inevitably, to be used by lodgers, the ground floor consists of, first, a room into which one enters by a French window; it is lit by two smaller casement windows facing onto the street, and leads into a dining room, which is separated from the kitchen by a staircase, its steps fashioned of wooden squares, all painted and polished. You'll never see anything more woebegone than this chamber, stocked with chairs, some of them plushly soft, some covered in striped horsehair, one section dull, the next glossy bright. There's a table in the middle of the room, of gray-striped Saint Anne's marble with a round base, decorated with one of those white porcelain tea-sets you see everywhere these days, adorned with half-faded gold bands. This *salon*, its floorboards wildly uneven, has paneling running chest-high. Above, a kind of varnished wallpaper depicts the principal scenes of Fénelon's seventeenth-century didactic romance, *Telemachus*, with all the classical characters carefully colored. The panel just between the two barred windows gives the lodgers a glimpse of the banquet Calypso staged for Odysseus' son. For forty years, younger lodgers have been moved to make jokes about this picture, convinced that, by making fun of the dinners to which their poverty condemns them, they lift themselves above their stations. The stone chimney, with its perpetually clean grate to certify that fires burn there only on grand occasions, is decorated by a pair of vases full of artificial flowers, covered with glass and stiff with age, plus a marble clock in the worst possible taste. An odor rises from this *salon* for which, alas, the language has no word, so we must call it "the *pension* smell." It is a stale, musty, mouldy scent, rancid, and it makes you freezing cold, it makes your nose water, it bores into your clothes; it has the flavor of a room where people have eaten; it stinks of kitchens and servants and the poorhouse. You might be able to describe it, if someone had invented a technique for analyzing all the tiny, nauseating particles that each and every one of the lodgers, old and young alike, dumped into the air with their nasal effluvia, and all their other highly personalized bodily exhalations.

Never mind! In spite of these dull horrors, when you compare the *salon* to its immediate neighbor, the dining room, you'll think it truly elegant, perfumed as a lady's boudoir ought to be. Fully paneled, the dining room long ages ago received a coat of paint, the color of which is by now indeterminable, constituting no more than a background for bizarre patterns of dust and dirt. Sticky sideboards line these walls, bearing bespattered and well-nicked bottles and decanters, crystal tin-plate napkin rings, piles of thick, blue-bordered porcelain plates, made in Belgium. In one corner stands a box with numbered pigeonholes, which holds all the napkins, no matter how stained or wine-spattered. This room exhibits those utterly indestructible items of furniture, banished from all other houses, but deposited here just as civilization's wreckage is deposited at Hospitals for the Incurable. You can see a barometer furnished with a capuchin monk who pops out when it's raining; some engravings quite ghastly enough to take away your appetite, all with varnished wooden frames sporting gold stripes; a hanging wall clock in a scalloped case, inlaid in leather; a green stove; some of Monsieur Argand's eighteenth-century gas lamps (but with the oil heavily larded with dust); a long table covered with oilcloth so greasy that, if a waggish diner wanted to, he could write his name in it, using nothing more than his finger as a pen; an assortment of variously maimed chairs; some tattered reed mats, always falling apart but never finishing the job; plus some miserable charcoal foot-warmers, foot-holes broken, hinges destroyed, wooden fittings all charred away. But a truly precise accounting of exactly how all these furnishings were ancient, cracked, rotten, unsteady, pitted, gimpy, one-eyed, crippled, and moribund, would keep you from being involved in this story—and there would be people in a hurry who would never forgive me. The floor's red squares are ridged and dented, both from being walked on and from layers and layers of paint. In short: poverty rules, and there's no poetry to alleviate it—and it's a poverty that's tight-fisted, intense, grating. If it hasn't yet reached a state of utter filthiness, it's certainly showing the signs; if it's still not afflicted with holes and rags, it's clearly starting to rot.

This room truly comes into its own at the moment when, about seven in the morning, Madame Vauquer's cat appears, jumping up on the sideboards, sniffing at the milk standing in napkin-covered bowls and emitting his first purrs of the day. Soon the widow herself enters, decked out in her thin, netted cap, from which a twist of false hair protrudes at an unnatural angle; as she walks, she drags along her wrinkled slippers. Everything about her—her plump, withered old face, from the middle of which a parrot-beak nose juts out; her fat little dimpled hands; her body, as chubby as a church rat; her heavy, undulating breasts—matches this room where misery fairly oozes out of the walls, where futile fiscal speculation seems to lurk, and where Madame Vauquer manages to breathe in the warmed, fetid air without getting sick to her stomach. Her countenance, as cool and brisk as the first frost of autumn; her wrinkled eyes, which flit from the dancer's fixed smile to the moneylender's glum, bitter scowl; in short, everything about her seems to embody her *pension*, just as her *pension* invokes her image. You can't have a jail without a jailer, the one is unimaginable without the other. This tiny woman's pallid flabbiness stems directly from the life she leads, just as typhus comes from the foul effluvia in hospitals. Her flannel petticoat, hanging out beneath her outer skirt, cut down from an old dress, its cotton quilting protruding through the slits in the frayed, splitting material, is like a summary of the *salon*, and the dining room, and the garden; it proclaims the kitchen; it warns you what the lodgers will be. Given her presence, the whole spectacle is complete.

Now in her fifties, Madame Vauquer is very like all women who, as they say, have had a hard time. She has the hard, brittle eyes and artless expression of a female pimp, whipping herself to indignation so she can exact a higher price, ready to do anything to make herself a profit, prepared to sell out or inform on anyone she can find to sell or inform on. In spite of which, say her lodgers, she's "basically a good woman," because they hear her whimpering and coughing just the way they do, and think her luckless. What had her husband been? She's never said a word about the late Monsieur Vauquer. How had he lost his money? Through bad luck, she replied. And to her he had behaved badly, leaving her nothing but her eyes to weep with, and this house to live in, and the right never to feel sorry for anyone who experienced misfortune, because, she declared, she had suffered everything a human being could possibly suffer.

Hearing her mistress moving about, the fat cook, Sylvie, hurriedly began to serve the lodgers' breakfasts. Those who did not live but only ate at the *pension* usually contracted just for their dinners, at a cost of thirty francs per month. At the time this story begins, there were seven people actually living at Maison Vauquer. The two best apartments in the house were on the first floor. Madame Vauquer lived in the smaller, and the other belonged to Madame Couture, widow of a Military Paymaster who had served under the old French Republic. A very young girl, named Victorine Taillefer, lived with her; Madame Couture acted like the child's mother. The two women's apartment cost them eighteen hundred francs a year. Both the apartments on the second floor were rented, one by a graybeard named Poiret, the other by a man of about forty, who wore a black wig, dyed his side-whiskers, and called himself Monsieur Vautrin. There were four rooms on the third floor, two of which were rented, one by an old maid named Mademoiselle Michonneau, the other by a onetime manufacturer of vermicelli, starch, and Italian paste, who let himself be called Père Goriot. The two remaining rooms were reserved for birds of passage, usually unlucky students who, like Père Goriot and Mademoiselle Michonneau, could only afford forty-five francs a month for food and lodging together, though Madame Vauquer would rather not have had students at all, and took them only when she could not find anyone better: they ate too much bread. Just now, one of these rooms belonged to a young law student, come to Paris from somewhere around Angoulême, whose large family had to scrimp and save unmercifully for the twelve hundred francs a year they sent him. His name was Eugène de Rastignac; he was one of those young fellows forced by misfortune to work hard, knowing from the time they were small boys what hopes their parents had for them and, anticipating fairer fortune, already calculating what effect their studies should have and adjusting them in advance to the way the world was spinning, so they might be among the first to squeeze it dry. Without his careful observations, and his skill at making his way into Parisian society, this tale could not have been colored in those truthful hues which, without any doubt, it owes to his shrewdness, as well as to his interest in deciphering the secrets of a shocking situation, concealed just as carefully by those who had created it as by the man whom it crushed.

Up above this third floor there were a storeroom for stretching linen and two garrets, where the handyman, whose name was Christophe, and fat Sylvie, the cook, both slept. In addition to these seven live-in boarders, Madame Vauquer had, year in, year out, eight students of law or medicine, plus two or three regular habitués of the neighborhood, all of whom had contracted with her for their dinners. At dinner time there were eighteen people around the table (the room could have held twenty), but in the mornings there were only the seven lodgers, whose coming together over breakfast much resembled a family meal. They all came down in their slippers, allowing themselves confidential remarks about what had been set out for them, or about the appearance of those who merely dined there, as well as on the events of the previous night, expressing themselves with the self-assurance of intimacy. These seven were Madame Vauquer's spoiled children, and with the precision of a practicing astronomer she measured out what she did for them and the respect they deserved, each according to the sum total of their yearly rentals.

Though assembled under her roof by mere chance, they all operated on the same basis. The two lodgers on the second floor paid only seventy-two francs a month. Such a splendid bargain, only available in that neighborhood—Saint-Marcel, between Bourbe and Salpêtrière Streets—and to which Madame Couture was the sole exception, clearly indicated that these lodgers suffered, without much question, from fairly obvious misfortunes. So the distressing spectacle of the *pension*'s appearance was repeated in its lodgers' dress, the one just as dilapidated as the other. The men wore jackets of colors no longer identifiable, and shoes of the sort you find tossed in the gutters of elegant neighborhoods, with threadbare linen—clothes that had become soulless. The women's garments were old-fashioned, re-dyed, faded, with mended old lace, gloves shiny from use, muslin collars brown from re-ironing, and scratchy, worn-out shawls. That was how they dressed, but they were all solidly built, with constitutions that had resisted the storms and fury of life, their faces cold, hard, worn away like coins that have to be taken out of circulation. Their faded mouths were armed with greedy teeth. In these lodgers you could see the signs of dramas either finished or still working themselves out—not dramas played out in the gleam of footlights, against painted backdrops, but living dramas, mute, frozen dramas that make the heart beat faster, dramas which go on and on and on.

Old Miss Michonneau always wore, over her weary eyes, a dirty old green taffeta eyeshade, bound around with brass wire, which would have frightened off the Angel of Pity. Her skimpily fringed, miserable shawl might have been draped over a skeleton, so angular were the bony shapes it concealed. What acid had eaten away this creature's feminine characteristics? Surely, she had been pretty once, and well-made. Had it been vice, grief, greed? Had she fallen too deeply in love—had she been a peddler of used clothing—or had she simply been a whore? Or was she paying, now, for the triumphs of haughty youthfulness, wild with pleasure, by an old age that made passersby walk carefully around her? Her blank stare could chill you to the bone, her stunted face was frightening. She had the thin, high-pitched voice of a cicada, shrilling in the bushes at winter's coming. According to her, she had nursed an old man suffering from cysts in his bladder, abandoned by his children because they'd thought he had no money. The old fellow had bequeathed her an annuity of a thousand francs a year, which his heirs regularly contested, slandering her with all sorts of vile accusations. Although the forces of passion had marched across her face, leaving it in ruins, here and there her skin showed traces of a fine whiteness, suggesting that remnants of beauty might remain in her body, too.

Monsieur Poiret was more machine than man. Seeing him gliding along the pathways of the Botanical Gardens like a gray shadow, a limp old cap on his head, barely able to hold the knob of his yellowing ivory-headed walking stick in his hand, wind flap-

ping his wilted coattails so loosely behind him that they barely hid
trousers that seemed to have nothing in them, his blue-stockinged
legs quivering like a drunk, flashing a dirty white vest and a shriveled shirt-ruff of coarse muslin that seemed ready to part company
from the tie knotted around his turkey-cock neck—seeing him
thus, many people must have wondered whether this Chinese
ghost truly belonged to the bold white race, said to be descended
from Japthet, flitting up and down the Boulevard Italien. What
could have been the life's work that so shrunk him down? What
passion could have darkened a face so bulbous that, had it been
drawn by a cartoonist, no one would have believed it? What had
he been? But maybe he had worked at the Ministry of Justice, in
the office to which executioners report their expenses—how much
they'd spent on black veils for the eyes of parricides; how much
for straw and chaff, to line the basket where heads drop; how
much for twine to tie the guillotine's blades. Maybe he had been
the receptionist at a slaughterhouse door, or perhaps an assistant
inspector of health or sanitation. In a word, this was a man who
looked as if he'd been one of the mules who turn our great social
mill wheel, one of those Parisian Rats who pull other people's
chestnuts out of the fire but never even know who eats them, a
sort of spindle for public misery and filth to whirl around on—in
short, one of those men of whom we say, the minute we see them:
We can't do without fellows like that. Their cadaverous faces,
stamped by pain—psychological or physical—are unknown to the
Beautiful People of Paris. But Paris is as immense as an ocean.
Drop in your sounding line and it will never reach the bottom.
Have a look, try describing it! No matter how carefully you try to
see and understand everything, to describe everything, no matter
how many of you there are, trying hard, all of you exploring that
great sea, there'll always be places you never get to, caverns you

never uncover, blossoms, pearls, monsters, quite incredible things that every literary diver overlooks. And Maison Vauquer is one of those odd monstrosities.

Two faces stand in striking contrast to most of the lodgers and others who frequent the house. Mademoiselle Victorine Taillefer may have been so sickly pale that she resembled one of those yellow-skinned girls afflicted with anemia, and her habitual sadness, her pinched features, her poverty-stricken, miserable air may have stamped her with the sense of suffering lingering on everyone around that table, yet hers was by no means an ancient countenance, and both her movements and her voice were sprightly. She resembled, in her misery, a shrub with yellowing leaves, just replanted in a soil that disagrees with it. The faint hints of color in her complexion, her tawny blond hair, her extraordinary thinness, all spoke of that unearthly grace modern poets find in medieval statues. Her gray eyes, streaked with black, spoke of sweetness, of Christian resignation. Her plain clothes, obviously cheap, did not conceal her youthful body. She had a strange kind of juxtapositional prettiness. Had she been happy, she'd have been ravishing: happiness constitutes pure poetry, for women, just as rouge constitutes their dressing tables. Had the pleasures of a dance or a ball brought their rosy hues to her pale face; had the delights of elegant living reddened cheeks already grown faintly hollow; had love quickened those sad eyes, Victorine might have campaigned against the prettiest of young girls. She was missing exactly those things—fine clothes and lovesick letters—that bring women to life for the second time.

Her personal history would have made a good novel. Her father, having convinced himself he had good reason not to acknowledge her as his legitimate daughter, had refused to let her stay anywhere near him and allotted her only six hundred francs a year; he had altered the legal status of his estate so it could be left, lock, stock, and barrel, to her brother. Madame Couture (a distant relative of Victorine's mother, who had fled to her protection, long ago, dying of despair) had taken the orphan under her wing, as if the girl had been her own child. Unfortunately, the Republican Paymaster's widow had no worldly assets other than her marriage settlement and her pension: the day might come when, claimed by death, she would have to let this poor young woman make her own way in the world, without having accumulated either the world's wisdom or its resources. Every Sunday the good lady took Victorine to mass, and every other week to confession, so that—whatever else might happen—she would be a pious girl. And Madame Couture had been right. Religion offered hope to that unwanted child, who loved her father, who would regularly go to him, bringing her mother's forgiveness with her, but who found herself, year after year, stopped by her father's barred door, shut inexorably against her. Her brother, the only one who could have spoken for her, had now gone four years without once visiting or sending her help of any kind. She begged the Lord to open her father's eyes, to soften her brother's heart, and she prayed for them both, never once blaming them for anything. Neither Madame Couture nor Madame Vauquer thought there were enough words in the dictionary of human wrongs to describe such barbarous conduct. But though they castigated this infamous millionaire, Victorine spoke nothing but sweet-sounding words, like the song of the wounded wood dove, in whose miserable cries one can still hear the accent of love.

Eugène Rastignac's face was typically Southern: a fair complexion, black hair, blue eyes. His bearing, his manners, his habitual pose, all indicated the son of some noble family, whose basic education had been strictly governed by the traditions of good taste. Although he had to nurse his clothes along, and mostly wore only last year's fashions, still he could sometimes emerge dressed like a truly elegant young man. His ordinary outfit was an old jacket, a badly made vest, an absolutely ridiculous Student tie, black, faded, sloppily knotted, trousers to match, and patched-up boots.

Vautrin, the forty-year-old with dyed side-whiskers, stood somewhere between these two and the rest of the lodgers. He was one of those about whom ordinary people say: "Now that's really *somebody!*" He was broad-shouldered, with a well-developed chest and bulging muscles, and thick, square hands, the knuckles decorated with great tufts of flaming red hair. His face, scored by premature wrinkles, showed signs of a toughness that belied his good-natured, easygoing manners. His booming bass voice, which matched his loud cheerfulness, was emphatically pleasant. He was obliging and full of laughter. If a lock stopped working, he'd quickly take it apart, figure out what was wrong, file it down, oil it, and then put it back together again, observing, "I know all about such things." There were a lot of other things he knew about—ships, the sea, France, foreign nations, business, psychology, current affairs, the law, hotels, and prisons. When anyone complained too much, he'd immediately offer his services. More than once, he'd lent money both to Madame Vauquer and to some of her lodgers, but his debtors would sooner have died than not repay him, because for all his friendliness he had a look about him, deep, determined, that made people afraid. The very way he spat showed his unshakable composure; put in a difficult position, he'd obviously never hesitate to commit a crime, to get himself out of it. Like a stern judge, his glance seemed to pierce to the bottom of every issue, every conscience, every emotion.

It was his habit to go out after breakfast, to come back for dinner, to disappear for the rest of the evening, and then to return toward midnight, using a latchkey Madame Vauquer let him have. It was a favor he alone enjoyed. But he was so much in the widow's good graces that, putting his arm around her waist, he'd call her "Mama"—a hard to understand bit of flattery! It may have seemed perfectly straightforward to the good woman, but Vautrin was in fact the only one whose arms were long enough to encircle that ponderous girth. One revealing side of his character was a willingness to pay a generous fifteen francs a month for his after-dinner coffee and brandy.

Those less shallow than young people swept along by the bustling whirl of Parisian life, or than old people indifferent to anything that didn't directly affect them, would not have been satisfied to simply sense something doubtful about him. He knew or could guess at the private lives of those around him, though no one could figure out either what he was thinking or what he did with his days and nights. And in spite of the barriers he threw up between himself and everyone else, by means of his apparent good humor, his perpetual agreeableness, and his general gaiety, he'd sometimes give glimpses of the appalling depths within. Bursts of sharp-tongued wit worthy of Juvenal, apparently meant to take pleasure in mocking laws and lashing out at high society, convicting it of serious self-contradictions, might have led you to suppose he bore some hidden grudge against the whole social structure, and that deep at the bottom of his life there lay some carefully hidden mystery.

Attracted, perhaps without even knowing it, by Vautrin's power and Rastignac's good looks, Mademoiselle Taillefer divided her furtive glances and her secret thoughts between the forty-year-old and the young student, though neither of them seemed to be dreaming of her, even though—who could tell?—she might some-day find herself transformed into a woman of wealth. Nor did any of Madame Vauquer's lodgers take the trouble to learn if the misfortunes narrated by any of the others were true or only pretended. Their universal attitude, one to the other—caused in each case by their respective situations—was one of indifference mixed with suspicion. They knew themselves incapable of relieving their own troubles, and in telling and retelling them they had all poured forth everything their cup of condolences contained. Rather like old married couples, they had nothing left to say to one another. All the mutual contact of which they were capable was a kind of mechanical exchange, gears meshing without any oil. They would all of them walk unseeingly past a blind man in the street, would hear some unfortunate's tale without a trace of emotion, and would see death as a viable solution to the grinding poverty which left them, each and all, cold to the most ghastly agony.

Of all these ravaged souls the happiest was Madame Vauquer, who sat enthroned in that private asylum. The little garden, rendered vast and desolate as the steppes by silence and cold, by drought and by rain, was for her and her alone a laughing grove. Only for her did the yellowing, gloomy house, smelling as musty as an old shop, contain loveliness and delight. These dank cells belonged to her. She fed these convicts, sentenced to perpetual imprisonment, and exercised a respectable authority over them. Where would these poor folk have found for themselves, here in Paris, and for what they were able to pay her, a sufficiency of wholesome food, and rooms which, if neither elegant nor excessively commodious, at least could be kept clean and healthy? Had she been permitted some flagrant outrage, her victim would have endured it without complaint.

Such an assemblage should and in fact it does present us, though in a small compass, with the components of a complete social structure. Among these eighteen guests we find, just as we do in schools, just as we do in the world, a poor, defeated creature, both a whipping boy and a scapegoat, on whose back jokes fall like rain. For Eugène de Rastignac this person became, at the beginning of his second year among them, the most conspicuous of all those among whom he was condemned to live for another two years. This general butt and universal target was the onetime manufacturer of vermicelli, Père Goriot, on whose head a painter, like an historian, would have directed the full light of his picture. What mischance had brought such half-malignant scorn, such persecution mixed with pity, such disregard of the disregarded, down on the oldest of all the lodgers? Had it happened because he'd done something absurd, ridiculous, something strange and queer that the world tolerates far less than it does outright vice? Such questions underlie many social injustices. Perhaps it's simply human nature, whether out of weakness or indifference, to stand for whatever may be done to someone who, from true humility, allows anything and everything to be done to him? Don't we all love to prove our strength at the expense of someone or something? Even the puniest among us, the wandering street-urchin, will be out ringing doorbells when it's freezing cold, or climbing high on some unstained statue, just to scribble his name.

Père Goriot, a very old man of perhaps sixty-nine, had retired to Madame Vauquer's boardinghouse in 1815, after giving up his business. Initially, he had taken the apartment now occupied by Madame Couture, paying twelve hundred francs a year, in those days, like a man for whom a hundred francs, this way or that, meant absolutely nothing. Madame Vauquer had spruced up the three rooms of this apartment, on the basis of a cash advance large enough, it was said, to pay for its wretched furnishings: yellow calico curtains; varnished wooden armchairs, covered in cheap Dutch velvet; a couple of slapdash pictures; and wallpaper even suburban saloons wouldn't buy. It may have been the careless generosity with which Père Goriot—then known, respectfully, as Monsieur Goriot—let himself be fleeced that convinced her he was a fool and knew nothing of business matters. He had arrived with a well-stocked wardrobe, the magnificent clothing of a merchant who, retiring from all commercial activity, could deny himself nothing. Madame Vauquer had been struck by his eighteen shirts of fine cambric linen, not only beautifully made but seeming still more impressive because, across the row of ruffles that ran down each shirtfront, the former manufacturer of vermicelli wore a pair of pins, linked by a delicate chain, and on each pin there sat a fat diamond. His usual garb was a cornflower-blue coat, worn over a gleaming white vest, freshly washed and ironed, under which his pear-shaped, jutting belly rippled and heaved, causing his heavy gold watch chain, hung with tiny charms, to bounce up and down. In his snuffbox, also of gold, there was a locket crammed full of hair, making him seem for all the world like a regular Don Juan. When the proprietress accused him of being a fop and a dandy, he let his lips shape the happy smile of a bourgeois whose hobbyhorse has just been patted and stroked. His *storage-chesses* (he gave the word its lower-class pronunciation) were stuffed with all the silver plate that had lined his kitchen. The widow's eyes lit up when, obligingly, she helped him unpack and set out all the heavy soup ladles, the thick stewspoons, the placesettings, the rich cruets for oil and vinegar, the deep sauceboats, plus any number of platters, gilt breakfast sets—in short, items more or less lovely but solid, very solid, all of them things he simply could not do without. Seeing these presents from Heaven, he was reminded of the solemn domestic ceremonies of his former life.

"Now, this one," he said to Madame Vauquer, clasping a small porringer, with a lid fashioned like a pair of turtledoves billing and cooing, "this was the first gift my wife ever gave me, for our wedding anniversary. Poor thing! every cent she'd been able to save, before our marriage, went into that. And do you know what, madame? I'd rather be forced to scrape my living out of the ground with my fingernails than have to give that up. Thank God!

I'll be able to drink my coffee out of that, every morning for just as long as I live. I haven't got anything to complain about, I've got enough salted away to last me a long, long time."

And, with her magpie eyes, Madame Vauquer had also spotted some registered bonds that, quickly totted up in round figures, surely provided this excellent old man with an income of something like eighteen thousand francs a year. At that very moment, Madame Vauquer (whose maiden name was Conflans, no less), who was then really forty-eight but never admitted to more than thirty-nine, began to have ideas. Never mind that Goriot's eyes drooped puffily down, thick and swollen, so he was constantly wiping them dry: to her he looked altogether pleasant, exactly right. Besides, those remarkably fleshy legs, like his long, flat nose, suggested certain matching moral qualities which the widow apparently thought very important, attributes confirmed by the good man's guileless, moon-shaped face. Surely, he was a solidly put-together animal, unlikely to hold back his feelings. His towering hairdo, which the barber from the Polytechnic University came and powdered, every morning, fell in five points across his low forehead, nicely embellishing his countenance. He might be a bit of a boor, but he was so exceedingly well dressed, he helped himself to his snuff so lavishly, breathing it in like a man absolutely confident that his snuffbox would always be packed with the best Martinique could offer, that, from the day Monsieur Goriot came to live in her establishment, Madame Vauquer went to her bed every night fairly burning, like a partridge roasting in bacon, with the desire to throw off her Vauquer winding-sheets and be reborn under the name of Goriot. To be married, to get rid of her boardinghouse, to walk out on the arm of this fine flower of the bourgeoisie, to become one of the neighborhood's leading ladies, to go about collecting alms for the poor, to make jolly little Sunday trips to Choisy, Soissy, and Gentilly, to go to the theater whenever she felt like it, and sit in her own box, without having to wait for the free passes she sometimes got from her lodgers (but only in the stifling month of July)—she dreamed all the magical, golden dreams conjured up by every petty Parisian. She had never told a soul that, penny by penny, she had saved up forty thousand francs. With that sort of dowry she was certainly a good match, at least as far as money went. "And as for the rest of it," she assured herself, turning in her bed as if to prove all those abundant charms of which, every morning, fat Sylvie found the deep mould, "I'm worth as much as the old man is."

And so, for perhaps three months, Madame Vauquer took advantage of Monsieur Goriot's barber, and spent money on clothes, justifying these outlays by the necessity of maintaining, in her establishment, a decorum befitting the worthy gentlefolk who frequented those premises. She formulated all sorts of schemes for improving the level of her lodgers, pretending that, from now on, she would tolerate only those who were among the most distinguished in every respect. If a newcomer put in his appearance, she boasted about the preference shown her establishment by Monsieur Goriot, one of the foremost, most respectable merchants in all Paris. She distributed handbills, reading across the top "MAISON VAUQUER," and then "One of the oldest and most highly regarded private lodging houses in the Latin Quarter, with an exceedingly pleasant view (from the third floor) of the Gobelin Valley, and a truly *pretty* garden, at the edge of which there *stretches* a WALK of linden trees." And she also described her establishment's "fine air" and its "tranquillity." This advertisement brought her the Countess of Ambermesnil, a lady of thirty-six who was awaiting the final disposition and settlement of a pension, due her as the widow of a general *slain* on the battlefield. Madame Vauquer looked after her food, and for nearly six months fixed her a fire in the living room, and in general so thoroughly lived up to the promises in her handbill that, to fund them, she actually *dipped into capital.* The countess was always saying, addressing Madame Vauquer as "my *dear* friend," that she planned to bring her Baronness Vaumerland as well as Count Picquoiseau's widow, both of them close friends and just finishing up their residence at a more expensive *pension* in the old Marais neighborhood. These ladies too would be very well taken care of, once the War Department had completed work on their pensions. "Ah," said the countess, "but those bureaucrats never finish anything!" The widows regularly went up to Madame Vauquer's room, after dinner, where they had little chats and drank black-currant liqueur and nibbled on dainties and delicacies hitherto reserved only for the landlady's lips. Madame de l'Ambermesnil thoroughly approved of her hostess's approach to Goriot—an excellent plan—and something of which, to be sure, she had been aware from the very start. Monsieur Goriot seemed to her quite perfect.

"Ah, my dear lady, he's every bit as strong as he looks," the widow assured Madame Vauquer, "and so well preserved: he's certainly still capable of giving a woman a good time."

The countess commented freely on Madame Vauquer's clothing, which clashed, she observed, with what the landlady was after. "You must assume a warlike footing," she explained. After a good deal of discussion, the two widows sallied forth to the Palais Royal, where, in one of the little shops, they bought a feathered hat and a bonnet. Then the countess led her friend to that famous emporium, Jeannette's, where they picked out a dress and a silk scarf. With these weapons deployed, and Madame Vauquer fully prepared for combat, she was the spitting image of the sign hanging in front of the "Beef à la Mode" Restaurant. All the same, she considered herself so much improved that she felt distinctly obligated to the Countess and, by way of a small gratuity, asked her to please accept a hat, worth a good twenty francs. In point of fact, Madame Vauquer was planning to ask, as a favor, if she would sound out Monsieur Goriot and do what could be done for her. Madame de l'Ambermesnil was easily persuaded to try this little game and, hunting up the old vermicelli-maker, she managed to get herself alone with him, but once she saw how shy and modest he was, not to say deeply uncooperative, when she hinted that she might be interested in seducing him herself, she left him where he was, revolted by his coarseness and vulgarity.

"Ah, my angel," she said to her dear, dear friend, "you'll get nothing from *that* fellow! He's pathologically suspicious—a grasping old miser—a pure animal—an idiot. He'll bring you nothing but trouble."

Having to deal with Monsieur Goriot had been so excruciatingly unpleasant for Madame de l'Ambermesnil, indeed, that she could not remain under the same roof with him. She left Maison Vauquer the very next day, quite forgetting to pay the six months of rent she owed, and leaving behind only a castoff dress worth perhaps five francs. And no matter how carefully Madame Vauquer tried to find her, in all Paris there wasn't a trace of the Countess of Ambermesnil. She couldn't stop talking about this whole deplorable affair, moaning about how overly trusting she was, although in fact she was more suspicious than a cat; it was simply that, like a lot of other people, she was intensely mistrustful of those around her, while cheerfully surrendering herself to the first person who came along. This is a psychological fact, extremely odd, yes, but obviously true, and easy enough to trace to its roots in the human heart. It may be that, for certain people, there is nothing more to be gotten from those who live close around them; having long since exhibited all the emptiness of their souls, they feel as if they've been silently judged, and with well-deserved severity; still, feeling an irresistible need for the flattery they can no longer obtain, or else consumed by the longing to seem what they in fact are not, they hope to sneak up on the regard, or the very hearts, of those strange to them, even at the risk of someday falling flat on their faces. And then there are those who, born greedy and grasping, never do anything for their friends or for anyone close to them, simply because they owe such kindnesses, while in performing favors for absolute strangers they think they earn true self-respect: the closer you are to them, the less they like you; the more distant you are, the more obliging they become. Clearly, Madame Vauquer fit into one of these two categories, deeply mean-spirited, false, loathsome.

"Now if I had been there," Vautrin assured her, "you'd never have had that problem! I'd have damned well exposed that joker. I know all their little tricks."

Like all limited minds, Madame Vauquer never went beyond whatever actually happened, nor did she try to discover why it had happened. She dearly loved to blame others for her own shortcomings. Having suffered the loss just described, she held the honest old vermicelli manufacturer primarily responsible for the whole business, from which point on, as she herself said, she began to see him as he really was. Once she'd realized that he couldn't be tempted, and that all her finery had been a waste of money, it did not take her long to understand why. And what she understood, to use Monsieur Goriot's own words, was that he was and always had been an odd bird. Now, at long last, he'd shown her the futility of her pretty little plan: as the countess had rather forcefully phrased it—a woman who was surely a connoisseur in such matters—there was nothing to be gotten from a man like him. Her aversion, of course, was necessarily a good deal more intense than her affection had ever been. It was not love that led her to detest him, but disappointment. If the human heart is inclined to stop and rest, as it climbs the heights of affection, it rarely pauses on the rapid downward slopes of dislike.

Still, Monsieur Goriot was her lodger, and the widow had no choice but to stifle her explosions of wounded pride, smothering the sighs this deceit had caused her, choking back her lust for revenge, like a monk harassed by his prior. Petty minds ease their feelings, for good or for bad, by a constant stream of petty deeds. Drawing on her natural female spitefulness, the widow invented all sorts of underhanded persecutions for her victim. To begin with, she took back the extras that had sprouted on her table.

"No more pickles, no more anchovies! That's all just a lot of nonsense," she told Sylvie, the morning when she went back to her old way of doing things.

But Monsieur Goriot had always lived frugally, one of those self-made men who, forced to live close to the bone as they climb the ladder, end up being stingy as a matter of course. Soup, boiled beef, a plate of vegetables always had been and always would be his favorite meal. It was hard for Madame Vauquer to harass a lodger whose tastes she could not offend. So she set herself the task of ruining his reputation, thereby sharing her aversion for Goriot with all her other lodgers and enabling them, for their own amusement, to exact her revenge for her.

Toward the end of his first year under her roof, the widow had worked herself into such a state of mistrust that she kept wondering why this rich merchant, with seven or eight thousand pounds a year, who also owned a great deal of superb silver and lots of jewelry every bit as good as that of a kept woman, would be living in her house and, though he enjoyed so large a fortune, only paying her such an insignificant rent. For most of that first year, Goriot had usually dined out once or twice a week, but little by little got to the point where he would eat out no more than twice a month. His little private dinners had so well suited Madame Vauquer that she was pained to see her lodger dining more and more often at her own table. She attributed such changes both to a slow diminution in his fortune and to his interest in making life difficult for her. For one of the more detestable characteristics of such lilliputian characters is their habit of attributing their own pettinesses to others. Unluckily, toward the end of the second year, Monsieur Goriot gave them good grounds for their gossip about him, asking Madame Vauquer to let him transfer upstairs to the second floor, and to reduce his rent, correspondingly, to nine hundred francs a year. Indeed, he had to economize so severely that, all winter long, he did without a fire in his room. Madame Vauquer wanted him to pay in advance, and Monsieur Goriot—whom she thereafter christened *Père* Goriot—agreed.

Who could tell what had brought him down? It would have been a difficult bit of detective work! As the make-believe countess had said, Père Goriot was a sly one, he kept his own secrets. According to the logic of people with no brains—who are all by nature indiscreet, because they never speak about anything but trivialities—people who *don't* talk about their own business must be criminal types. And so this highly respectable merchant was transformed into a rascal; he might have been a dandy, but now he'd become a queer old fish. According to Vautrin, who at this point became one of Madame Vauquer's regulars, Père Goriot was one of those fellows who played the stock market and—in the vivid language used by financial people—first ruined himself and then set to gambling with whatever he had left. Another tale told about the old man was that he was one of those petty-ante poker players who can spend a whole night winning or losing perhaps ten francs. They also said he was probably a spy for the bigwigs in the police department, though Vautrin insisted Goriot wasn't smart enough to play *that* game. They gossiped that Père Goriot had to be a miser, making short-term loans, or maybe someone who kept betting, over and over, on the same lottery number, just waiting for his turn to win. They turned him into whatever vice, shame, and helplessness could make the most mysterious. But however awful he or his horrible way of life might be, their dislike never reached the point of evicting him: he paid his rent. And it was good to have him around, because they could all make fun of him, according to their mood, whether good or bad, tossing off jokes or insults.

The most likely explanation, and the one they usually held to, had been offered by Madame Vauquer. As far as she was concerned, this well-preserved old fellow, obviously so strong and capable of giving women a great deal of pleasure, was simply a libertine with queer tastes. And the facts on which she based her slander went like this. One morning, some months after that disastrous countess took off, having lived for six months at the landlady's expense, Madame Vauquer, not yet out of bed, heard the rustle of a silk dress on her stairs, and the soft step of some young fallen female slipping toward Goriot's room, and then Goriot's door opening to admit her, exactly as if she was expected. Fat Sylvie came right up to her mistress, telling about a girl far too pretty to be a decent woman, *and dressed like an angel*, with spotless twill slippers on her feet, who'd come gliding out of the street like an eel, and right into her kitchen, where she'd asked for Monsieur Goriot. The landlady and her cook set themselves to listening, managing to catch the old man and his visitor speaking a few tender words, for the visit was not a short one. And when Monsieur Goriot finally emerged, with *his lady* on his arm, fat Sylvie snatched up her shopping basket and pretended she was off on her errands, so she could follow the loving couple.

"Ah, madame," she told the landlady, when she got back, "no matter what, our Monsieur Goriot's got to be rich as the devil, if he's up to *that*. Just think, there was a superb carriage waiting, right at the Estrapade corner, and *she* got right in."

At dinnertime, Madame Vauquer carefully drew a curtain, to

keep Goriot from being troubled by the sun, which was shining in his eyes.

"You're the ladies' favorite, Monsieur Goriot: even the sun comes looking for you," she observed, alluding to that morning's visitor. "But you've got good taste, bless my soul! She was certainly a pretty one."

"That was my daughter," he told her, with a pride that seemed to his fellow boarders the foolish conceit of an old goat.

A month after this visit, Monsieur Goriot had another. Having come, the first time, in a light morning garment, this time his daughter appeared after dinner, and dressed fit to kill. Chatting among themselves, in the *salon*, the boarders could see she was a pretty blonde, slender, graceful, and obviously far too distinguished to be old Goriot's daughter.

"So now there are two of them!" exclaimed fat Sylvie, who did not recognize the young woman.

A few days later, there appeared yet another girl, this time a tall, well-made brunette with black hair and bright eyes and, like the first one, asking for Monsieur Goriot.

"And now there are three!" said Sylvie.

And this second girl, who also first visited her father in the morning, a few days later came back in the evening, dressed for a ball and riding in a carriage.

"So there are four of them!" exclaimed both Madame Vauquer and fat Sylvie, neither of whom could see in this great lady any trace of the girl in simple morning wear who had made the earlier visit.

At this stage, Goriot was still paying a rent of twelve hundred francs a year. It seemed perfectly natural to Madame Vauquer that so rich a man should have four or five mistresses; indeed, she thought him rather clever, pretending they were all his daughters. His bringing them to Maison Vauquer did not in the least offend her. All the same, since these visits explained the old man's indifference to her own attentions, as he started his second year under her roof she took to calling him an "old tomcat." Finally, when he was only paying nine hundred francs, she took the occasion, seeing one of the young ladies leaving his room, to ask him, insolently, just what sort of a house he thought this was. Père Goriot told her the lady was his oldest daughter.

"You've got three dozen of them, I suppose?" Madame Vauquer snapped back.

"I have only two," the lodger replied mildly, speaking with the air of a ruined man experienced in the gentleness of absolute misery.

Toward the end of his third year, Monsieur Goriot cut his expenses still further, moving up to the third floor, where he paid only forty-five francs a month. He stopped using tobacco, gave up his barber, and no longer powdered his hair. When he showed himself, the first time, totally without powder, the landlady gasped in surprise, noting the true color of his hair, which was a dirty greenish gray. His face, which had grown sadder day by day, etched by his hidden sorrows, had become the most ravaged of all those that decorated her table. Of that there was no longer the slightest doubt. Surely, only a doctor's skill had saved this old rake's eyes from the harsh effects produced, inevitably, by the medicines his various illnesses required. His hair's disgusting color most certainly came directly from his excesses and from the drugs he had to take, so he could continue them. And his physical as well as his moral and psychological state seemed to fully confirm all this nonsense. When he'd worn out the clothing he'd brought with him, he replaced his handsome linen by the cheapest calico, bought for fourteen cents a yard. One by one, his diamonds disappeared, and his gold snuffbox, the heavy watch chain he'd worn, his jewels. His cornflower-blue coat had vanished, along with all his other rich apparel, and now, in summer as in winter, he wore a coarse brown coat, a goat's hair vest, and trousers of thick gray wool. He grew steadily thinner; his legs became stick-like; his cheeks, plump with bourgeois happiness and success, shriveled almost to nothing; his forehead wrinkled up, his jaw be-gan to jut out.

By his fourth year on New Saint Geneviève Street, you would not have recognized him. The sixty-two year-old merchant who didn't look a day over forty, the stocky, stout bourgeois, as healthy as any animal, whose vigorous manners had delighted passersby, such youth glowed out of his smile, seemed to have become a bewildered dotard of at least seventy, wobbly, wan. His lively blue eyes turned a dull steel-gray, they'd grown pale, never watered any more, and their red rims looked as if they might weep blood. To some people, he was a horror; to others, an object of pity. There were young medical students who, after having made fun of him for a while and gotten absolutely no response, noted how his lower lip drooped, and measured the apex of his facial angle, and pro-ceeded to diagnose him as a cretin. After dinner, one night, Ma-dame Vauquer, pretending to be only teasing, said:

"What's happened? Your daughters never come to see you any more?"

"Sometimes they come," he replied in a quivering voice.

"Ah ha!" the students cried. "So you still get to see them! Ah, good for you, Père Goriot, good for you!"

But the old man didn't hear the jokes his reply had brought down on him; he'd fallen back into a meditative state that, to superficial observers, seemed a kind of senile numbness, caused by his severe intellectual deficiencies. Had they truly understood him, they might well have been fascinated by the problem his physical and psychological state presented—but for them nothing would have been harder. It would have been easy enough to determine whether Goriot had really been a vermicelli maker, and exactly how much he was worth, but the *pension*'s elderly inhabitants, though they were curious about him, never went out of the neighborhood, all of them holed up in their lodgings like oysters on some rocky coast. And as for the others, the special enchantments of Parisian life made them forget all thoughts of the old man of whom they made such fun, the very moment they left New Saint Geneviève Street. Both for those who lived their narrow lives entirely within the walls of Maison Vauquer, as for those who were younger and simply didn't give a damn, old Goriot's dried-out misery and dull-witted appearance were completely incompatible either with the possession of a fortune or indeed with any ability whatever. And as for the women he called his daughters, they all agreed with Madame Vauquer, who used to say, with that harsh logic common to old women who spend every evening in gossip, and who think they know everything:

"If our Père Goriot really had *daughters* as rich as all those ladies who've come to see him seem to be, he wouldn't be living here in my house, up on the third floor, at forty-five francs a month, nor would he be going around dressed like a beggar."

Such powerful reasoning was beyond contradiction.

Accordingly, toward the end of the month of November, 1819, at which time this drama burst into motion, everyone connected with Maison Vauquer had fixed opinions about the poor old man. He had never been married, he had never had any daughters; excessive self-indulgence had turned him into a snail, a human mollusk, as a Museum employee who ate his dinners there put it, of the genus *Cap-Wearer*. Compared to Goriot, old Poiret was a true gentleman who soared like an eagle. Poiret talked, used logic, answered when spoken to—in truth, he never actually said anything, when he talked, or used logic, or truly replied when spoken to, because he usually rephrased, in other terms, exactly what others had said to him, but all the same he took part in their conversations, he was alive, he seemed to be a sentient creature—whereas old Goriot, again according to the Museum employee, was stuck at zero on the Celsius scale.

EUGÈNE DE RASTIGNAC HAD RETURNED, feeling as all bright young men must feel, when a difficult situation obliges them to function, no matter how briefly, at the very highest level. The workload at the Law School, during his first year in Paris, was a light one, and he had been free to taste the obvious delights of the great city. Indeed, a student can't have too much time on his hands, if he wants to understand every theater's individual repertoire, study the Parisian labyrinth's intricate convolutions, learn how things are done, master the capitol's peculiar language, and grow accustomed to its special pleasures; he needs to explore both good and wicked neighborhoods, take all the interesting courses at the university, catalogue the treasures in all the museums. And a student needs to throw himself into endless idiocies, which seem to him immense and noble. He has his own personal idol, a great man, a professor, who's paid to be a crowd pleaser. He wears bright ties and struts about, catching the eyes of women seated in the Opéra-Comique's first balcony. And so, step by step, he strips off his babybark, raises his horizons, and in the end comes to understand the human layers of which society is composed. If, in the beginning, he's dazzled by the covered carriages trotting down the Avenue Champs-Élysées on a fine day, he learns soon enough to want one of his own.

By the time he'd taken his first two degrees (his B.A. and his elementary law degree) and gone off on his vacation, Eugène had, all-unconsciously, already served his apprenticeship. His childish illusions, along with his provincial notions, had quite disappeared. With his mind changed and sharpened, his heightened ambitions helped him pierce straight through to the heart of his paternal home, right into the very bosom of his family. The tiny Rastignac estate was inhabited by his father, his mother, his two brothers, his two sisters, and an aunt whose only fortune was a lifetime annuity. The property was worth perhaps three thousand francs a year, not allowing for the instabilities inherent in the wine trade, but somehow they managed to squeeze out twelve hundred francs a year for him. All the difficulties which this unfailing pressure involved had been generously hidden from him and, confronted by this, and by the comparisons he could not help making between his sisters, who had always seemed so beautiful to him, as a child, and the women of Paris, who had shown him at first hand a beauty of which, before, he had only dreamed, and faced with the uncertain future of this large family, which indeed rested entirely on his shoulders, and with the scraping, clawing niggardliness they exercised in even the most trivial tasks, the family table wine, squeezed out of the very leavings of the winepress—in short, confronted by a host of details it would serve no point to detail, here, doubled and tripled his longing to succeed, and made him hungry and thirsty for honor and eminence. Like all men of great spirit, he wanted to owe his success to nothing but his own abilities. But his was a supremely Southern temperament; when it was time to act, his decisions were attacked by the doubts and hesitations that always beset young men when they find themselves out on the open sea, not knowing toward which coast they ought to direct their energies, nor even at what wind-catching angle they should set their sails. If his first idea was to rush headlong into the task, pretty soon he'd find himself pausing, wondering about all the connections he surely had to make and, seeing how influential women could be, in social matters, deciding it would be best to jump in that direction and provide himself with female protectors—for could they be lacking to a passionate, idealistic young man whose spirit and dedication were heightened by personal elegance and the sort of nervous good looks which easily captured women's attentions? Thoughts like these would come sweeping over him, as he walked through the fields, tramping gaily about with his sisters, who found him very different from what he'd been. His aunt, Madame Marcillac, once presented at Court, had there become acquainted with prominent aristocrats, and the young man suddenly perceived, in the ancient memories his aunt had so often dreamily recounted, the fundamentals of social triumphs at least as important as those he had tackled in law school, so he questioned her about family ties which might still be renewed. After shaking the family tree's various branches, the old lady calculated that, of all those among the egotistical wealthy and powerful who might be of use to her nephew, the least reluctant was likely to be Madame la Vicomtesse de Beauséant. So she wrote a letter to this young woman, in the best old style, and handed it to Eugène, advising him that if he could get anywhere with the vicomtesse she'd also look up some other distant family members. Not long after his arrival home, Rastignac mailed his aunt's letter to Madame de Beausésant. And the vicomtesse replied with an invitation to a ball she was giving the very next day.

THIS, THEN, WAS THE GENERAL SITUATION at Maison Vauquer, toward the end of November, 1819. Two or three days later, at about two in the morning, Eugène returned to his rented quarters, having in the meantime attended Madame de Beauséant's ball. To make up for the time thus lost, the brave student had taken a vow, even as he was dancing, to sit and study until dawn. It would be the first time he had thus sat up, in this silent, dark neighborhood: the charm of all the worldly splendors he had seen gave him a kind of false energy. He had not dined at Maison Vauquer. Accordingly, the other lodgers might well have fancied that he would not be returning from the ball before breakfast, the next day, just as had been his habit after Prado student-quarter parties, or balls at the Odéon, coming in with his silk stockings dirty and his dancing shoes battered and worn.

The handyman, Christophe, was just peering out, to have a look down the street before bolting the door for the night. At exactly that moment, Rastignac came along, so he was able to go quietly up to his room, followed by Christophe, who made enough noise for the two of them. Eugène took off his formal clothes, stuck his feet into his slippers, pulled out a worn old jacket, lit his peat fire, and quickly got himself ready for work, so that the din of Christophe's great boots still masked the young man's infinitely less noisy preparations.

Eugène sat in silence for a few moments, before plunging into his law books. He had realized that Madame la Vicomtesse de Beauséant was one of the queens of Paris fashion, as her house was one of the most charming in the whole Saint-Germain district. Moreover, both by name and by family fortune she was an aristocrat among aristocrats. The poor student had been warmly received, thanks to his Aunt Marcillac, though he had not at that point understood what an immense favor was being accorded him. To be admitted into such golden rooms was as good as a certificate of high nobility. By appearing in such company, the most exclusive in all Paris, he had earned the right to go anywhere in the city.

Dazzled by the brilliant society in which he found himself, Eugène had barely managed to exchange a few words with the vicomtesse, more than satisfied to find, among the horde of Parisian deities who thronged here and there and everywhere, one of those women made for young men to adore. Countess Anastasie de Restaud, tall and singularly lovely, was said to have one of the most beautiful figures in all Paris. Imagine, if you will, a pair of great dark eyes, superb hands, a perfectly modeled foot, wonder-

fully animated movements—a woman the Marquis de Ronquerolles had labeled a true thoroughbred. Nor did this suppleness
deprive her of any advantage, for her figure was round and full,
but no one could have accused her of being plump. "A pure-
blooded animal, a thoroughbred, a classic beauty": these were the
latest terms of fashionable praise, replacing the "angels of
Heaven," the "Ossian-like" figures, and the whole ancient my-
thology of love the dandies were tossing aside.

But for Rastignac, Madame Anastasie de Restaud was quite
simply Woman incarnate. He had gotten himself two turns, on the
list of cavaliers written on her fan, and during the first quadrille
had managed a few words with her.

"Where am I likely to see you again, madame?" he'd said
bluntly, with that passionate strength so attractive to women.

"Oh," she'd replied, "in the park, watching the clowns, at
my house—everywhere."

And the bold Southerner made it his business to get to know
this delightful countess, at least to the extent that a young man
can strike an acquaintance with a woman during a waltz and a
quadrille. When he informed her he was Madame Beauséant's
cousin, the lady—and he took her for a very great lady indeed—
invited him to call on her, if he cared to. And after the final smile
she threw at him, Rastignac had no doubt about accepting the
invitation, though he did not know where she lived. Luckily for
him, he'd bumped into a man with no interest in making fun of
his ignorance (a fatal flaw in the eyes of all the famous fellows of
the time, like Maulincourt, Ronquerolles, Maxime de Trailles,
Marsay, Ajuda-Pinto, and Vandenesse, all of whom were there
and, in the full flight of their self-conceit, dancing attendance on
all the most elegant women of the day—Lady Brandon, the Duchess of Langeais, the Countess of Kergarouët, Madame de Sérisy,
the Duchess of Carigliano, Countess Ferraud, Madame de Lanty,

the Marquise of Aiglemont, Madame Firmiani, the Marquises of
Listomère and Espard, the Duchesses of Maufrigneuse and Grand-
lieu). Innocently, but happily, the student had stumbled on the
Marquis of Montriveau, lover of the Duchess of Langeais, a general and as straightforward as a child, and had learned from him
that the Countess de Restaud lived on Helder Street.

Ah, to be young, to be thirsty for society, to be hungry for a
woman, and to see opening in front of you not one but two great
houses! to have your foot in the Faubourg de Saint-Germain, at
Countess Beauséant's, and your knee in the Faubourg Chausée
d'Antin, at the Countess de Restaud's! to take one quick look and
then dive into the best houses in Paris, one after the other, confident you're quite handsome enough a young fellow to find help
and protection there, in a woman's heart! to feel yourself sufficiently ambitious to make a handsome figure, up on that highrope
where no one even attempts its superb maneuvers without the
assurance that falling is impossible, having found a charming
woman for your infallible balance-bar! Thinking such thoughts,
and seeing that very woman rise, sublime, right out of his sput-
tering peat fire, between his Code Napoléon and all the signs of
his poverty, who could have helped—not Eugène!—meditating on
a glorious future, a veritable parade of noble successes?

His wandering mind was so intent on coming delights that,
hearing the deep silence broken by a long, drawn-out sigh, the
young man first thought he was still with Madame de Restaud and
then felt his heart so caught that he wondered if he'd been hearing
someone's death rattle. Stepping carefully into the corridor, he saw
a bar of light etched under Père Goriot's door. Worried that his
neighbor might be sick, he peered through the keyhole and, looking around the room, saw the old man busy at so transparently
criminal an activity that Eugène could not help but perform a
service for society, were he to learn just what the so-called man-

ufacturer of vermicelli was plotting, there in the dead of night. Père Goriot had turned over a table and, clearly having tied a silver tray and a kind of varnished soup-tureen to the crossbar, was winding a length of heavy rope around these densely carved objects, tightening it so powerfully that he was actually turning them into ingots.

"My God! What a brute!" Rastignac said to himself, seeing the old man's arm muscles, which without any assistance but the length of rope were silently kneading so much gilt silver as if it were nothing but paste. And then he asked himself, leaning back away from the door: Could it be that Goriot was a thief, or a fence, pretending to be a helpless old clod and living like a beggar, the better to practice his trade? Eugène peered through the keyhole once more. Having peeled off the rope, Père Goriot had lifted off the mass of silver, set the table on its legs again, then spread out the tablecloth and now was rolling out the silver, rounding it into a smooth bar—an operation at which he was obviously a practiced, deft hand.

"He must be as strong as Augustus, King of Poland!" Eugène exclaimed silently, seeing how swiftly and easily the rounded bar was produced.

Goriot stood looking sadly down at his night's work, tears dripping from his eyes; he blew out the wax candle by the light of which he had wrung out the lump of silver; and then, sighing, he could be heard stretching himself out to sleep.

"He's insane," the student thought.

"You poor child!" Père Goriot suddenly declared.

Hearing this, Rastignac decided he'd better say nothing about the entire affair, nor ought he to thoughtlessly pass judgment on his neighbor. He was just going back into his room when he suddenly heard an odd noise, something rather like a number of men wearing felt slippers coming up the stairs. Listening carefully, he could make out the sound of two men breathing. No one had knocked at the door, nor had he heard footsteps, but suddenly he spied a faint light down on the second storey, where Monsieur Vautrin lived.

"This is a strange business for a private boardinghouse!" he told himself. He went down a few stairs, stopped to listen, and heard the unmistakable clink of gold. Then the light went out, he could hear the two men breathing once again, but there was no sound of a door opening or closing. Slowly, as the two men went back down the stairs, the sound of breathing got weaker and weaker.

"Who's up there?" suddenly cried Madame Vauquer, opening her window.

"It's just me coming home, Momma Vauquer," Vautrin's deep voice replied.

"But that's odd!" Eugène said to himself, going back into his room. "Christophe's already bolted the door."

Here in Paris, you had to sit up all night, if you really wanted to know what was going on all around you. These minor incidents having taken him away from his bold amorous daydreaming, he set himself to work. But though he'd been distracted by Goriot's suspicious behavior, he was even more distracted still by thoughts of Madame de Restaud, whose face kept flickering in front of him, like a messenger announcing some brilliant fate, so he finally went to bed and slept like a log. Out of any ten nights when young people decide to work, they end up sleeping through seven of them. You've got to be more than twenty years old, if you want to sit up late.

The next morning, Paris was covered by one of those fogs so dense that even the most punctual, in the midst of universal darkness and mist, lose track of time. Business appointments are broken right and left. People think it's eight o'clock just as midday rings out. By nine-thirty, Madame Vauquer had still not climbed out of bed. Christophe and fat Sylvie, equally off schedule, were sipping their café au lait, fixed with the creamy top layer meant for the lodgers, while Sylvie boiled the rest of the milk for a long, long time, to keep Madame Vauquer for knowing about this illegally levied tax.

"Sylvie," said Christophe, dunking his first piece of toast, "Monsieur Vautrin, who's a good fellow all the same, saw two people last night. If Madame Vauquer gets upset, you don't have to tell her nothing."

"What did he give you?"

"What he gives me every month, to keep me quiet."

"Except for him and Madame Couture," said Sylvie, "who aren't skinflints, all the others slip us something at New Year's, then keep trying to take it back."

"And all they ever do give us is a lousy hundred sous!" said Christophe. "Look at old Goriot, who even polishes his own shoes. Poiret, that tightwad, never has his shined—he'd rather drink the stuff than put it on those dirty old boots. And as for that baby-faced student, *he* comes up with forty sous. I can't buy my brooms for forty sous—and what's more he goes out and sells his old clothes. What a hole!"

"Bah!" snorted Sylvie, taking a few mouthfuls of coffee, "we've still got the best jobs in the whole neighborhood: we're doing all right. Anyway, Christophe, while we're talking about Sugar Daddy Vautrin, have you heard anything about him?"

"Yes. A couple of days ago, I met a man out on the street, and he asked me: 'Say, isn't there a big guy living at your place, a fellow with dyed side-whiskers?' So I told him: 'No, he doesn't dye them. A fancy guy like him, he doesn't have time.' I told Monsieur Vautrin about that, and he said to me: 'You handled that just right, my boy! Always give them answers like that. There's nothing worse than letting people know all about our bad habits. Stuff like that stops a lot of marriages.' "

"Hey, when I was at the market, somebody tried to get me to tell him if I'd ever seen Vautrin with his shirt off. That was a cute one! But wait a minute," she suddenly said, interrupting herself, "I can hear nine-forty-five ringing, over at Val-de-Grâce, and nobody's out of bed."

"Don't be silly! They're all long since gone. Madame Couture and that kid who lives with her went out at eight, to take communion at Saint-Étienne. Père Goriot went out with a package. The student won't be back till after his class, at ten. I saw them all leaving, while I was doing my stairs. Père Goriot clipped me with that package of his, and whatever it is, it's as hard as iron. What's that guy up to, anyway? The others keep spinning him around like a top, but he's a good guy, a good guy, and he's better than any of them. He doesn't give me much, but those ladies he sends me to, sometimes they come up with some first-class tips, and they're really dolled up."

"The ones he calls his daughters, eh? He's got a dozen of them."

"He's only sent me to two of them, the same ones who've come here."

"I can hear Madame Vauquer," said Sylvie, "and she's going to kick up a real fuss. I'd better get up there. Keep an eye on the milk, Christophe: watch out for the cat."

"What's this, Sylvie!" exclaimed the landlady. "Here it is, a quarter to ten, and you've let me sleep like a groundhog! I've never heard of such a thing!"

"It's the fog, madame, you could cut it with a knife."

"And what about breakfast?"

"Hah! Your lodgers are all possessed: they went hopping away as soon as the stars came up."

"Speak properly, Sylvie," replied Madame Vauquer. "You should say, as soon as the sun came up."

"I'll say anything you want me to say, madame. Fact is, though, you can serve lunch at ten o'clock. Mademoiselle Michonneau hasn't budged, and neither has old Poiret. They're the only ones still in the house, and they're snoring away like the tree stumps they are."

"Sylvie, Sylvie: you've got the two of them lumped together, almost as if . . ."

"Almost as if, eh?" Sylvie replied, laughing a great stupid laugh. "Well, it takes two to tangle."

"What's really strange, Sylvie, is how Monsieur Vautrin got in, last night, after Christophe barred the door."

"Oh, no, madame. He heard Monsieur Vautrin coming, and went down and opened the door for him. That's what made you think . . ."

"Just hand me my dressing gown, Sylvie, and then hurry and get lunch ready. Set out what's left of the mutton and potatoes, and those cooked pears, the nice cheap ones."

A few moments later, Madame Vauquer appeared downstairs, just as the cat, with a sudden swipe of his paw, pulled the napkin off a bowl of milk and lapped it quickly down.

"Mistigris!" she called. The cat jumped away, then came back and rubbed itself against her legs. "Yes, yes, I know all about you, you wheedling old coward!" the landlady assured her. "Sylvie! Sylvie!"

"Now what, madame?"

"Just see what the cat's been drinking."

"It's that stupid Christophe's fault, because I told him to watch out. Where's he gone to? But don't worry, madame: I'll use this milk for Père Goriot's coffee. I'll fill up the bowl with water, and he'll never notice a thing. He doesn't notice anything, not even what he puts in his own mouth."

"So where has he gone, that old Chink?" said Madame Vauquer, setting out napkins.

"Who knows? He's sold his soul to five hundred devils."

"I slept too long," declared Madame Vauquer.

"Ah, but you look as fresh as a rose, madame . . ."

Just then they heard the bell, and Vautrin came into the room, singing in his deep bass:

"I've been around and around the world
And everyone knows my name . . .

"Ah ha, Momma Vauquer," he said, spying his landlady, and giving her a great hug.

"Now that's enough of that."

"Tell me I'm too fresh," he answered. "Go on, is that what you're trying to say? Hold on, I'll help you set the table. Now, isn't that nice of me?

"I'm good to brunettes, I'm good to blondes,
I treat them all . . .

"But I've just seen something really strange.

. . . the same."

"What" asked the widow.

"At exactly eight-thirty this morning, our Père Goriot was on Dauphine Street, at the goldsmith's, the one who buys old silverware and lace. And Goriot sold him some sort of bowl, for a pretty good price, and it was very well rolled out, too, for a man who's not in the trade."

"No. Really?"

"Indeed. I was coming back here, after saying goodbye to one of my friends, who's going abroad by stage coach. So just for the fun of it, I followed along after old Goriot. He headed back to this neighborhood, over on Des Grès Street, and went in to see a well-known loan shark, a fellow named Gobseck, a really cool customer—a man who'd make dominoes out of his own father's bones—oh, he's a Jew, and an Arab, and a Greek, and he's a Gypsy, too, and no one's ever going to get anything that belongs to him, because every single penny goes right into the bank."

"So what's Père Goriot doing?"

"He doesn't *do* anything," said Vautrin. "He undoes things. He's such an old fool that he'll ruin himself for love of his daughters, who . . ."

"Here he comes!" cried Sylvie.

"Christophe," Père Goriot called, "come up with me."

Christophe followed Goriot upstairs, but came right back down.

"Where are you going?" Madame Vauquer asked her servant.

"I'm doing a job for Monsieur Goriot."

"And what have you got there?" said Vautrin, pulling out of Christophe's hands a letter on which he read: "To Madame, the Countess Anastasie de Restaud." "And where are you going?" Vautrin went on, handing the letter back.

"Helder Street. I've been told to give this to no one except the countess."

"What's in there?" wondered Vautrin, holding the envelope up to the light. "A banknote? No, no." He opened the envelope. "Ah, a receipt!" he cried. "I tell you! He's a real rascal, the old rake! Go on, go on, you lucky dog!" he exclaimed, giving Christophe such a poke with his huge hand that the man spun around like dice on a gaming table. "You're going to get yourself a first-class tip!"

They finished setting the table. Sylvie reboiled the milk. Madame Vauquer lit the stove, with Vautrin's assistance, he singing the whole time

I've been around and around the world,
And everyone knows my name . . .

When everything was ready, Madame Couture and Mademoiselle Taillefer returned.

"So where did you go this morning, my dear lady?" asked the landlady.

"We took communion at Saint-Ètienne, because today's the day we go to see Monsieur Taillefer," answered Madame Couture. "Ah, the poor girl," she went on, seating herself so close to the stove that her shoes began to smoke, "she's shaking like a leaf."

"Get yourself warm, Victorine," said Madame Vauquer to the girl.

"It was a good idea, mademoiselle, to pray that God might soften your father's heart," said Vautrin, pulling up a chair alongside the orphan. "But that isn't going to be enough. What you need is a good friend to tell that old miser the brass tacks—a monster who's said to be worth three million but won't give you a red cent. These days, even a beautiful girl like you needs a dowry."

"Poor child," said Madame Vauquer. "I tell you, my dear, that monstrous father of yours will have to pay for treating you this way."

At these words, Victorine's eyes fairly swam with tears, and the landlady held her tongue, seeing the sign Madame Couture gave her.

"If only we could see him, speak to him—if I could just

give him his wife's last letter," said the Military Paymaster's widow. "I can't risk sending it by mail; besides, he knows my handwriting . . ."

" 'Oh innocent, unlucky, persecuted ladies,' "✿ recited Vautrin, interrupting her, "what a mess you're in. Well, in a few days I'll stick my nose into your business, and it will all come out right."

"Oh, monsieur!" said Victorine, throwing him a damp but burning glance that did not move him in the slightest, "if only you did know some way of getting to my father and telling him that his affection, and my mother's honor, mean more to me than all the money in the whole world. If you could make him just a little kinder, how I'd pray to God on your behalf! Oh, you can rely on my gratitude . . ."

"I've been around and around the world," sang Vautrin softly, in a wry voice.

Just then, Goriot, Mademoiselle Michonneau, and Poiret came down, attracted, perhaps, by the brown sauce Sylvie was preparing for the leftover mutton. Ten o'clock sounded at the very moment when the seven guests were greeting one another and settling into their places, and then they could hear, out in the street, the student's footsteps.

"Wonderful, wonderful, Monsieur Eugène," said Sylvie. "Today you can dine with all the others."

The student greeted the other lodgers, and seated himself next to Père Goriot.

"I've just had the strangest adventure," Rastignac declared, as he helped himself to a generous serving of mutton and cut himself a slice of bread that Madame Vauquer seemed to measure with her eyes.

✿ Title of a popular comic melodrama by Balisson de Rougemont.

"An adventure!" said Poiret.

"Why not? Why should you be surprised, old top," said Vautrin to Poiret. "Our friend here is just made for adventures."

Mademoiselle Taillefer glanced shyly at the student.

"So tell us your adventure," urged Madame Vauquer.

"Yesterday I attended a ball given by Madame the Vicomtesse de Bauséant, my cousin, who owns a really magnificent house, with silk-lined rooms, and, in a word, we had a marvelous time, and I had as much fun as a king . . ."

"Let," Vautrin interrupted him, bluntly.

"What do you mean, monsieur?" asked Eugène.

"I say 'let,' because kinglets have more fun than kings do."

"Now that's true," said Poiret the echo-man. "I'd rather be that carefree little bird than a king, because . . ."

"In any event," the student went on, cutting him off, "I danced with one of the most beautiful women there, an utterly ravishing countess, the most delectable creature I've ever set eyes on. She had peach blossoms in her hair, and the loveliest bouquet of flowers, real flowers, and what a lovely scent—but you'd have to see her for yourselves! Who can adequately describe a beautiful woman with her color heightened by dancing? Anyway! This morning, at nine o'clock, I met this same divine countess, walking along Des Grès Street. How my heart began to beat! I thought that, maybe, . . ."

"She might be coming here," said Vautrin, giving the student a long, sobering look. "But surely she was going to see Papa Gobseck, the moneylender. If the hearts of Paris women could be looked into, you'd be more likely to find moneylenders in there than you would lovers. Your countess bears the name Anastasie de Restaud, and she lives in Helder Street."

Hearing her name thus pronounced, the student looked at Vautrin long and hard. Père Goriot suddenly looked up, too, and gave an intent, troubled glance at both men, considerably surprising the other lodgers.

"Christophe got there too late," Goriot said mournfully, his voice loud. "She'd already gone out."

"I've figured the whole thing out," whispered Vautrin in Madame Vauquer's ear.

Goriot ate his lunch mechanically, not knowing what he was eating. He had never seemed to them duller and more withdrawn than at that moment.

"Now how the devil could you know her name, Monsieur Vautrin?" asked Eugène.

"Ha ha, there we have it," answered Vautrin. "Père Goriot knows her name too, by God. And why shouldn't he?"

"Monsieur Goriot?" exclaimed the student.

"What!" said the poor old man. "She was really beautiful, yesterday?"

"Who?"

"Madame de Restaud."

"Just look at the old rascal," whispered Madame Vauquer to Vautrin. "How his eyes light up."

"Is she his mistress?" whispered Mademoiselle Michonneau to Eugène.

"Ah, yes, yes! She was fantastically beautiful," Eugène answered the old man, who was staring at him, avidly. "If Madame de Beauséant hadn't been there, my divine countess would have been the queen of the ball, none of the young men could look at anyone else, I was the twelfth to write my name on her fan, she danced every single quadrille. All the other women were furious. If anyone in the world was happy, yesterday, it was certainly her. One might well say that nothing in all the world is lovelier than a frigate under full sail, and a horse at full gallop, and a woman dancing."

"Yesterday at the top of the heap, at a duchess's house," said Vautrin, "and then, this morning, down at the bottom of the ladder, at a loan shark's. That's our Parisian women for you! If their husbands can't afford the wild luxuries they love, they sell themselves to pay for them. And if they can't figure out how to sell themselves, they cut open their mothers to find something that'll make them shine. They'll do absolutely anything. It's an old, old story!"

Père Goriot's face, which had lit up like the sun on a lovely day, listening to the student, turned somber at this cruel remark.

"Well!" said Madame Vauquer. "So what happened to your adventure? Did you speak to her? Did you ask her if she was planning to enroll in Law School?"

"She never saw me," said Eugène. "But to meet one of the prettiest women in all Paris, right here on Des Grès Street at nine o'clock in the morning, a woman who must have come home from the ball at two in the morning, isn't that pretty remarkable? Things like that could only happen in Paris."

"Bosh!" exclaimed Vautrin. "There are a lot of things a good deal stranger still."

Mademoiselle Taillefer had scarcely been listening, so absorbed was she in the plan she was formulating. Madame Couture signaled to her that it was time to go upstairs and get dressed. Once the two ladies had left the table, Père Goriot followed after them.

"So!" said Madame Vauquer to Vautrin and the rest of the lodgers. "Did you see him? Clearly, he's ruined himself for these women."

"You'll never persuade me that the beautiful Countess de Restaud belongs to Père Goriot!" cried the student.

"All the same," said Vautrin, cutting him off, "we don't have to persuade you. You're far too young truly to understand Paris;

you'll find out, eventually, that here in this town we have what might be called 'men of passion.' "

(At these words, Mademoiselle Michonneau gave Vautrin a knowing look. It was as if a regimental horse had suddenly heard the trumpet calling.)

"Oh ho," said Vautrin, pausing to give her a penetrating glance, "so we've had our little flings, too, have we?"

(The old maid lowered her eyes, like a nun looking at naked statues.)

"In any case," Vautrin went on, "once a man like that gets an idea into his head, he never lets go of it. Some specific water from some specific fountain is all they ever want to drink, or maybe wallow in, and in order to get it they'll sell their wives, their children; they'll sell their souls to the devil. For some of them that special fountain might be gambling, or the stock market, or a collection of paintings—or of insects, or music. For others, it's a woman who knows exactly what tid-bits they love to chew on. With men like that, you can offer them all the women in the world, and they'll laugh in your face, the only one they want is the one who satisfies their particular passion. Quite often that special woman can't stand them, she gives them a bad time, she makes them pay through the nose for their pleasures—well! These sporting types never give up, they'd drag their last blanket down to the pawnshop to bring her their last dime. And that's who Père Goriot is. The countess takes advantage of him, because he keeps his mouth shut—and there's high society for you! All the poor fellow ever thinks of is her. Apart from his passion, you see, he's a stupid animal. But get him started on this story, and his face lights up like a diamond. It's not a hard secret to ferret out. This morning, he sold some silver—I saw him going into Papa Gobseck's, over on Des Grès Street. Now listen carefully! When he came back, he sent that idiot Christophe to the Countess de Restaud's house: he showed us the address on the envelope he was carrying, and all there was in it was a receipt. Clearly, if the countess went to this same moneylender, it was a pretty serious business. And our Père Goriot gallantly supplied the cash. You don't have to be a genius to see what's going on here. And let all this prove to you, young fellow, that all the while your countess was busy laughing and dancing, and playing her little games, floating along under her peach blossoms, and holding onto her dress, she was, as they say, in it up to her ears, thinking about some checks that had bounced, hers or maybe her lover's."

"You make me desperate to find out the truth," exclaimed Eugène. "I'll go to Madame de Restaud's tomorrow."

"Yes, yes," said Poiret, "tomorrow it will be important to go to Madame Restaud's."

"And maybe you'll even find Goriot there, collecting on his gallant investment."

"But this Paris of yours," said Eugène with disgust, "it's just a mud pit."

"It's a strange mud pit," replied Vautrin. "If you get that dirt on you while you're driving around in a carriage, you're a very respectable fellow, but if it spatters all over you while you slog along on foot, then you're a good-for-nothing rogue. Make the mistake of grabbing anything out of the mud, no matter how insignificant, and they'll pillory you in the courts of law. But steal millions, and they'll point you out as a hero, in the very best houses. That's an ethical system you pay the cops and the judges thirty million a year to keep in good working order. It's just great!"

"Now just a minute," exclaimed Madame Vauquer. "Do you mean Père Goriot's been melting down his silver plate?"

"Weren't there two turtledoves on the lid?" asked Eugène.

"Indeed."

"It must have meant a lot to him," said Eugène, "because he

was crying as he crushed the soup tureen and the platter. I just happened to see him doing it."

"He loved it as he loved his own life," the landlady answered.

"So that's who he is, you can see how passion's got hold of him," exclaimed Vautrin. "That woman knows exactly how to get to him."

The student went up to his room. Vautrin went out. Not long after, Madame Couture and Victorine drove off in a cab that Sylvie fetched for them. Poiret offered his arm to Mademoiselle Michonneau, and the two of them went for a walk in the park, during these two loveliest hours in the whole day.

"Hey, there they go, they're almost married," said fat Sylvie. "Today's the first time they've ever gone out together. They're so dried up, both of them, if they bump into one another they'll flare up like charcoal."

"Mademoiselle Michonneau had better watch out for her shawl," laughed Madame Vauquer. "It'll blaze up like tinder."

When Goriot came back to the *pension*, at four that afternoon, he could see by the light of a pair of smoky lamps that Victorine's eyes were red and inflamed. Madame Vauquer was listening to the tale of the useless visit they'd made, that afternoon, to her father's house. Annoyed at having to receive his daughter and the old lady who'd come with her, he'd had them shown in so he could make himself perfectly clear.

"My dear lady," Madame Couture said to Madame Vauquer, "just imagine, he didn't even let Victorine sit down, he kept her standing the whole time. 'As far as I'm concerned,' he said to me, completely without emotion, just as cold as ice, 'please save yourself the trouble of coming to see me, for this young lady', and he didn't even call her his daughter, 'does herself no good by bothering him' (once a year, the monster!), 'since Victorine's mother had married him without a cent to her name, and therefore the young woman had no claim whatever on him'—and he went on saying the harshest things, all of which made this poor girl melt into tears. Then the girl threw herself at her father's feet, and she told him, as brave as brass, that she kept coming only because of her mother, and she'd do exactly as he wished and never complain, if only he'd read the poor dead lady's last letter, and then she took the letter and held it out to him, saying the prettiest things in the world, and the most beautifully phrased, I have no idea where she got them, it must have been God Himself dictating them to her, because the poor child was so absolutely inspired that as I listened to her, believe me, I cried like a baby. And then do you know what that horror of a man actually did, he was sitting there, cutting his nails, and he took that letter, watered with poor Madame Taillefer's tears, and he threw it into the fire, saying, "Fine, fine!" When he tried to lift his daughter off the floor, she took his hands and wanted to kiss them, but he pulled them away. Have you ever heard of such villainy? His great booby of a son came in, and never said a word to his sister."

"What kind of monsters are these people?" asked Père Goriot.

"And then," Madame Couture went on, paying no attention to the good old man's exclamation, "father and son left the room together, saying goodbye to me and begging me to excuse them, but they had some important business to attend to. And that was our visit. Well, at least he saw his daughter. I have no idea how he can deny her, she's as like him as one drop of water is like another."

The rest of the lodgers appeared, one after the other, both those who lived in and those who did not, wishing each other good day and murmuring those empty phrases which, among certain sorts of Parisians, constitute a kind of droll good humor of which stupidity is the main component and whose principal virtue consists only in how the words are pronounced or what gestures accompany them. This sort of jargon is always changing. The jokes that underlie it never last a month: some political event, some lawsuit or trial, a street song, some actor's comic routine, all serve to keep this joke going, since more than anything else it involves snatching up words and ideas as they go flying past, and then hitting them back, as if with racquets. That new invention, the Diorama, which carries optical illusion to an even higher level than did the Panoroma, has led a number of painters' studios to coin the jesting word "rama," the introduction of which term into the Maison Vauquer was effected by a young painter who often visited and had, as it were, innoculated the *pension* with it.

"Well, Mons-sieur Poiret," said the Museum employee, "how's our little *healtharama* going?" And then he went on, without waiting for an answer: "Ladies," addressing Madame Couture and Victorine, "have you had unhappy news?"

"Are we ever going to have *dinnerama*?" called out Horace Bianchon, a medical student and Rastignac's friend. "My shrunken stomach's fallen *usque ad talones* [down around my ankles]."

"It's incredibly *coltarama*," declared Vautrin. "Get out of the way, Père Goriot! Good lord! Your foot's taking up the whole front end of the stove."

"My illustrious friend Vautrin," said Bianchon, "why do you say *coltarama*? That's wrong, you ought to say *coldarama*."

"No, no," said the Museum employee, "according to the rule, it has to be *coltarama*, as in 'my feet are colt.'"

"Ah ha!"

"And here comes His Excellence, the Marquis de Rastignac," cried Bianchon, throwing his arm around Eugène's neck and making as if to strangle him. "Let's go in, you people, let's go in!"

Mademoiselle Michonneau came in, demurely, greeted the others without saying a word, and went to stand next to the other three ladies.

"She scares the blazes out of me, that old bat," Bianchon whispered to Vautrin, motioning toward Mademoiselle Michonneau. "I've been studying Gall's phrenology, and I think she has the bumps of Judas."

"So you've met the lady?" asked Vautrin.

"Who hasn't!" answered Bianchon. "I swear, that pale old maid reminds me of those long worms that can gnaw through a wooden beam."

"That's just how it is, youngster," murmured the forty-year-old, stroking his side-whiskers.

"Like a rose, she's lived like a rose,
only for a morning."❀

"Ah ha! Here comes a wonderful *souparama*," said Poiret, seeing Christophe come in, solemnly bearing their soup.

"Excuse me, monsieur," said Madame Vauquer, "but this is cabbage soup."

The young men began to laugh uproariously.

"That's the end of you, Poiret!"

"No more Poiret!"

"Score two for Momma Vauquer," said Vautrin.

"Anyone notice the fog this morning?" asked the Museum employee.

"Now that," said Bianchon, "that was a wild fog, unequaled, lugubrious, melancholic, green, wheezing—a positively Goriot fog."

❀ From a famous poem by Malherbe.

"A *Goriorama*," noted the painter, "because no one could see a thing."

"Hey there, my lord of Goriosity, it's you they is discussing."

Seated down at the end of the table, near the door through which the food was brought in, Père Goriot had raised his head, sniffing at a chunk of bread he had under his napkin—an old habit of his trade, which popped up from time to time.

"So!" Madame Vauquer exclaimed sourly, her voice rising over the din of spoons and napkins and voices, "is the bread bad, by any chance?"

"Not a bit of it, madame," he answered. "It's made of the very finest grade flour."

"And how do you know that?" Eugène asked him.

"By the whiteness, by the taste."

"The nose taste," said Madame Vauquer, "because you were smelling it, not looking at it. You're getting to be such a penny-pincher you'll end up living off the smells from the kitchen."

"And that's something you'll have to patent," exclaimed the Museum employee, "because it'll bring you a fine fortune."

"Forget it," said the painter. "He does that just to show us he used to be in the business."

"So your nose is a horny monster?" asked the Museum employee.

"A horny what?" said Bianchon.

"A horny whore."

"A horny hortator."

"A horny horse."

"A horny horoscope."

"A horny horary."

"A horny hormone."

"A horny horehound."

"A hornarama."

These eight responses, shot from all sides of the table as if fired from guns, seemed to them even funnier because poor Père Goriot was staring, dumbfounded, like a man struggling to comprehend some utterly foreign tongue.

"Horn?" he said to Vautrin, who was sitting next to him.

"Like a horn on your foot, old boy!" said Vautrin, flattening Père Goriot's hat with a slap that drove it down on his head, all the way to his eyes.

Stupefied by this sudden assault, for a moment the poor old man could not move. Christophe, thinking Goriot had finished his soup, brought him his napkin and took away the plate, so that when Goriot finally pulled the hat back up, and resumed plying his spoon, it banged on the table. All the diners burst into laughter.

"Monsieur," said the old man, "you've got a twisted sense of humor, and if you ever again allow yourself to handle me like that . . ."

"What, Papa, what?" asked Vautrin, interrupting him.

"You'll pay for it, that's what! Some day you'll pay for it . . ."

"That'll be in hell, won't it?" declared the painter, "in that special black corner where they put all the naughty children?"

"So!" Vautrin said to Victorine. "Mademoiselle, you're not eating. Was your father still reluctant?"

"A monster," said Madame Couture.

"He'll have to be set to rights," said Vautrin.

"Still," said Rastignac, who was sitting next to Bianchon, "Mademoiselle Taillefer might want to bring a suit against him, for support, since she's clearly not eating. Oh ho! Just look at old Goriot staring at her."

Indeed, Père Goriot was staring at the poor girl so fixedly, noting the profound grief her face vividly displayed—the sadness of an unacknowledged child truly loving its father—that he quite forgot to eat.

"My friend," Eugène said to Bianchon quietly, "we've been entirely wrong about Père Goriot. He's neither an idiot nor a weakling. Consider him according to your system of phrenology and tell me if you agree. Last night I saw him twisting silver plate as if it were made of wax, and just now his face registered the most extraordinary emotions. It seems to me there's some mystery about his life, something that can't help but be worth studying. But you're laughing, Bianchon, you think I'm joking, but I'm not."

"He's a sheer medical fact, that fellow," said Bianchon. "I do agree. I'll be glad to do a living autopsy, if he'll let me."

"No, just palpate his head."

"But just consider! His stupidity might be catching."

THE NEXT DAY, Rastignac put on his best finery and at about three in the afternoon went to visit Madame de Restaud, his heart filled with those foolish, aching hopes that swirl young men's lives into such states of noble sentiment: they never stop to measure the obstacles in their path, or to estimate the dangers, because all they can see is success, their imaginations casting over their entire existences the bright glow of poetry. Accordingly, they are plunged into sadness or even misery by the failure of projects that lived and breathed only in their wild desire; all that saves our society and its social life is their timidity and ignorance. As he walked along, Eugène took extraordinary precautions to keep himself from being mud-spattered, but his mind was busily rehearsing what he would say to Madame de Restaud, shaping witty observations, inventing clever rejoinders to imaginary sallies, readying a stock of noble expressions, words worthy of Talleyrand, conjuring up little details that might help along the declaration of love on which he was basing his entire future. But he was spattered all the same, and had to stop in the square to have his shoes shined and his trousers brushed. "If I were a rich man," he said to himself, as he changed a banknote he had brought along, *just in case*, "I'd have come in a carriage, and sat back at my ease and thought it all through."

At last he came to Helder Street and asked for the Countess de Restaud. He bore the scornful glances of her servants, who had seen him crossing the street on foot and heard no sounds of a carriage at the door, with the cold rage of a man who knows himself marked for success. But those glances made him sharply aware of his inferiority, an awareness he had already felt simply in appearing in such a place, where a sleek horse stood pawing the ground, handsomely yoked to one of those chic little rigs that bear witness to a life of dissipation and luxury, underlining all the casual enjoyment of Parisian pleasures. Without having spoken a word, still by himself, he felt a black mood sinking over him. All the open file cabinets in his brain, which he had counted on to carry him through, slid slowly closed and left him dull and stupid. Waiting while a servant went to present his name to the countess, Eugène stood balancing on one leg, in front of an antechamber window, supporting himself with an elbow against the frame, staring mechanically out into the courtyard. It took a long time and he might well have left, had he not been endowed with that Southern tenacity, capable of bringing forth prodigal things when it can move in a straight line.

"Monsieur," said the servant, returning, "Madame is in her dressing chamber and so occupied that she's given me no response. Still, if you'd like to go on into the drawing room, there are already others there."

Stunned by the ghastly power of such people, who can accuse and even pass judgment on their betters with a single word, Rastignac nevertheless opened the door through which the servant had reappeared, intending to show these insolent underlings that he was quite familiar with the house, but found himself confronted, ridiculously, with a small room filled with lamps, tables, a towel-warming bath apparatus, and which also led to a dark corridor and a half-concealed staircase. The stifled laughter he heard behind him, in the antechamber, completed his utter confusion.

"Monsieur, the drawing room is this way," announced the servant, with that insolent show of respect, obviously insincere, which seems even more mocking.

Eugène retraced his steps so rapidly that he bumped into a large wash basin, but luckily managed to grab his hat before it fell into the water. Just then, a door opened, down at the end of a long corridor lit by a single small lamp, and Rastignac heard, simultaneously, Madame de Restaud's voice, and Père Goriot's voice, and the unmistakable sound of a kiss. Then the servant led him away and he followed silently across the dining room into a small drawing room; noting that the window opened onto the courtyard, he went and stood in front of it, wanting to see if *this* Père Goriot was really *his* Père Goriot. His heart was beating queerly, and he was recalling Vautrin's shocking remarks. The servant stood awaiting him, at the door to the main drawing room, but suddenly an elegant young man came out through that same entrance, declaring impatiently,

"I'm leaving, Maurice. Tell Madame I've been waiting more than half an hour!"

This insolent fellow, who surely had the right to be insolent, then began to hum an Italian air under his breath, while he drifted toward the window where Eugène was standing, clearly as much interested in seeing the student's face as he was in looking out into the courtyard.

"You'd do better to wait just another moment, Monsieur le Comte, because Madame is no longer occupied," said Maurice, coming into the room.

At that moment, Père Goriot came down a little staircase and out onto the main driveway. Umbrella in hand, he was about to open it, not noticing the open gate and the gig, driven by a young man sporting a military decoration, that was just coming through. The old man barely had the time to step backward, to keep from being crushed. The umbrella's fluttering silk frightened the horse, who gave a kind of leap and lunged to the side. The young driver turned around, as if angry, but seeing Père Goriot greeted him with that obligatory respect accorded to loan sharks, who are necessary predators, or perhaps with the deference one cannot help showing to a black sheep, even though one regrets it later. Père Goriot replied with a pleasant nod, full of frank goodwill. It all happened with the speed of lightning. Too absorbed to realize that he was no longer alone, Euegène suddenly heard the countess speaking:

"Maxime, you were going away," she said, her voice reproachful but spiced, too, with a touch of resentment.

She had not noticed the gig driving up.

Turning sharply around, Rastignac saw the countess coquettishly garbed in a white cashmere dressing gown, ornamented with rose-colored knots, her hair carelessly done up, the way Parisian women wear it when they first awake in the morning; she'd put on perfume, so she'd clearly just taken a bath, and her heightened beauty seemed even more than usually voluptuous; her eyes were misty. Young men are capable of seeing everything: their souls blend with a woman's radiant beauty just as plants breathe in what the air brings them. Eugène could feel the fresh bloom of her hands without having to touch them. And he saw, through the soft cashmere, the rosy tint of her breasts, which the only lightly fastened dressing gown partially bared, and on which his glance focused. The countess had no need of a corset's help, the sash of her dressing gown showed her supple figure quite well enough;

her neck was like an invitation to love, her feet in their slippers were lovely. As Maxime took that beautiful hand, and raised it to his lips, Eugène suddenly became aware of him for the first time, as the countess for her part became aware of Eugène.

"Ah, it's you, Monsieur de Rastignac, I'm delighted to see you," she said with that tone to which lively souls pay close attention.

Maxime stood looking from Eugène to the countess, with an air more than marked enough to drive away any intruder: "This fellow, my sweet? I hope you're about to kick him out the door!" The impertinent young man, whom the countess had called Maxime, clearly said these exact words, though with a look rather than in actual speech, just as the way the countess stood looking submissively back at Maxime spoke volumes about her own sentiments, whether she meant it to or not. Rastignac was overwhelmed by a sudden violent dislike of the young man. Even Maxime's beautifully curled blond locks made him aware of how ugly his own hair appeared. But Maxime also had shining boots of the finest leather, while his own, for all the care he had taken as he walked there, were covered with a light film of dirt. And Maxime's jacket fitted him beautifully, almost as elegantly as a woman's frock, while at two-thirty in the afternoon Eugène was wearing a black suit. The son of the South felt how great an advantage his outfit gave this dandy, tall and slender as he was, with his bright eyes (capable of ruining an orphan without blinking), and his pale complexion.

Without waiting for Eugène to speak, Madame de Restaud made as if to slip quickly away, into the other drawing room, the movement making the skirts of her dressing gown flutter as if she'd been a butterfly; she moved away, and Maxime went with her. Angrily, Eugène too went into the other drawing room. The three of them found themselves face to face, in the middle of the great chamber. The student knew perfectly well he was annoying this unpleasant Maxime, but even at the risk of also annoying Madame de Restaud, he wanted to make the man's life difficult. He could remember having seen this fellow at Madame Beauséant's ball, and he suddenly realized in just what relationship to Madame de Restaud Maxime stood; with that youthful boldness which allows you either to commit the worst follies or to pull off the greatest triumphs, he said to himself, "This is my rival; I must defeat him." Utterly thoughtless! He did not know that Count Maxime de Trailles had no objections to being insulted: he simply fired first, and killed anyone who trifled with him. Eugène was a skilled hunter, to be sure, but he had not yet managed to hit twenty out of twenty-two clay pigeons in a shooting match. The young count dropped into an easy chair, to one side of the fire, picked up the tongs and stirred around the logs so violently, so dourly, that in an instant Anastasie's lovely face darkened. Turning toward Eugène, she looked at him with one of those cold, questioning glances that say, so terribly clearly: Why haven't you gone away? Any well-bred man of the world knows just the right words to excuse himself—words so familiar, indeed, that we call them "goodbye talk."

But Eugène only smiled pleasantly and said,

"Madame, I hurried to see you, because . . ."

And then he stopped. A door opened. The man who'd been driving the gig suddenly came in, hatless and, ignoring the countess, gave Eugène a thoughtful glance, then held out his hand to Maxime, saying, "Hello, hello," with an almost brotherly air that took Eugène aback. Young fellows fresh from the country don't yet know the sweet pleasures of a ménage à trois.

"Monsieur de Restaud," the countess said to Eugène, motioning to her husband.

Eugène made a deep bow.

Continuing her introduction, she went on:

"This is Monsieur de Rastignac, a relative of Madame the Vicomtesse de Beauséant, on the Marcillac side. I had the pleasure of meeting him at her last ball."

Relative of Madame the Vicomtesse de Beauséant, on the Marcillac side! These words spoken by the countess in a tone almost pompous (given that special pride by which the mistress of a house tries to show that, at *her* house, she receives none but distinguished people), worked like the chanting of a magic spell, and the Count de Restaud dropped his air of ceremonious frigidity and greeted the student warmly.

"I am delighted, monsieur," he said, "to make your acquaintance."

And Count Maxime de Trailles too suddenly looked at Eugène, concerned, dropping his insolent look as well. This waving of a magic wand, caused strictly and solely by the powerful intervention of a mere name, threw open thirty different doors in the Southerner's brain, restoring him to the bold, gallant mood he'd earlier enjoyed. The atmosphere of Parisian high society, still dim to his eyes, was suddenly pierced by a gleaming ray. And at that moment neither Maison Vauquer nor Père Goriot had any place in his mind.

"I'd thought the Marcillac line was extinct?" the Count de Restaud said to Eugène.

"It is, monsieur," answered the student. "My great-uncle, the Chevalier de Rastignac, married the Marcillac heir. But the only child they had was a daughter, who married the Maréchal de Clarimbault, Madame de Beauséant's grandfather. Ours is thus the junior branch of the family, and the poor one—and poorer still because my great-uncle, a Vice Admiral, lost everything in the service of the King. When it liquidated the West Indies Company, the Revolutionary Government refused us any standing."

"Your great-uncle, I believe, commanded the *Avenger*, didn't he—before 1789, of course?"

"Exactly so."

"Well then, he must have known my grandfather, who commanded the *Warwick*."

Maxime looked over at Madame de Restaud and shrugged, casually, as if to say: "If he ever gets to talking Navy with your husband, we're lost." Anastasie understood at once. Using those wonderful powers all women possess, she smiled and said,

"Come, Maxime; there's something I need to show you. Gentlemen, we'll leave you to sail alongside the *Warwick* and the *Avenger*."

She stood up, making a mocking, totally traitorous sign for Maxime's eyes alone; he followed her toward her boudoir. But this morganatic couple—what a lovely German expression! we've nothing like it, in French—had barely gotten to the door when the count interrupted his chat with Eugène.

"Stay here, Anastasie my dear!" he called out, irritably. "You know quite well that . . ."

"I'll be back, I'll be back," she said, interrupting him, "it will only take me a moment to tell Maxime what I want him to do."

And she returned promptly. Like all wives obliged to carefully study their husbands, so they can do exactly as they please, she had learned exactly how far she could go and still preserve that invaluable marital trust; she never collided with him over any of life's minor matters, and she had plainly heard in his voice that to leave the room and then stay in her boudoir would be a very risky business. Equally plainly, it was Eugène who was creating this difficulty for her. So she pointed at him, for Maxime's benefit, and with a gesture and an air of obvious annoyance, and Maxime responded by saying, to all three of them,

"I see you're all busy; I've no interest in bothering you; goodbye."

And he slipped out.

"Stay, stay, Maxime!" the count called after him.

"Come back for dinner," the countess instructed, leaving the count and Eugène once again and following Maxime into the smaller drawing room, where they waited a good long while, expecting Monsieur de Restaud to get rid of Eugène.

Rastignac could easily hear them, first one and then the other laughing, chatting away and then suddenly turning silent, but the spiteful student worked very hard at pleasing Monsieur de Restaud, flattering him, starting one discussion after another, so that, eventually, the countess would have to come back and he would find out what her relationship to Père Goriot was all about. She was clearly in love with Maxime, and knowing that, although she was easily able to get around her husband, she was somehow secretly connected to the old vermicelli manufacturer, struck him as a complete mystery. It was a puzzle he wanted to solve, hoping that in the process he would himself be able to rule this magnificently Parisian woman.

"Anastasie," the count called to his wife once again.

"We'll have to give it up, my poor Maxime," she said to the young man, "we can't help ourselves. I'll see you tonight."

He whispered in her ear:

"But I hope, Nasie, you'll be able to handle this young fellow, whose eyes glowed like charcoal when your dressing gown fell open a bit. He'll spout all kinds of love to you, and then he'll get involved with you, and you'll oblige me to kill him."

"Are you crazy, Maxime?" she replied. "It seems to me that these little students, rather than dangerous, are superb lightning rods. But don't worry: I'll be sure to make Restaud hate him."

Laughing, Maxime took his leave, and the countess went to the window where Eugène had stood, wanting to watch her lover climb into his coach and show off his horse, waving his whip merrily. Nor did she return to the larger drawing room until the great gate had been closed behind him.

"Just think of it, my dear," the count called to her as she re-entered the room, "Monsieur Rastignac's family lives very near Verteuil, on the River Charente. And his great-uncle and my grandfather actually knew each other."

"How pleasant to walk on familiar ground," said the countess absentmindedly.

"Even more than you think," Eugène murmured.

"Oh?" she said quickly.

"Yes," the student went on, "I just saw a man leaving your house who, as it happens, is my next-door neighbor in the *pension* where we both live: Père Goriot."

Hearing the name "Goriot," decorated with a word like "Père" [old], the count, who'd been poking at the fire, dropped the tongs as if they'd burned his hands, and stood up.

"My dear sir," he said brusquely, "you could at least have called him 'Monsieur Goriot'!"

The countess went white, seeing her husband's annoyance, then turned crimson, obviously embarrassed, and trying to seem unconcerned, and in a voice which she tried to make natural, she said,

"You could not possibly know anyone we love better."

Then she interrupted herself, stared for a moment at her piano, as if suddenly remembering something, and asked,

"Do you care for music, monsieur?"

"A great deal," replied Eugène, turning red and stunned to find that he'd committed some impossible stupidity, made some incredible mistake.

"Do you sing?" she cried, going over to the instrument and loudly striking key after key, from C in the bass clef all the way up to a high F. Rrrrah!

"No, madame."

The Count de Restaud was pacing up and down, back and forth, back and forth.

"What a shame," she went on, "you've deprived yourself of a high road to success. *Ca-a-ro, ca-a-ro, ca-a-a-a-ro, non du-bita-re,*"✿ the countess sang.

Eugène had worked some magic of his own, in pronouncing the word "Goriot," but this time the charm had gone in exactly the opposite direction. He found himself in the situation of a man who, graciously introduced to a lover of antiquarian curiosities, carelessly bumps into a cupboard full of statuary and makes three or four badly glued sculptured busts tumble to the ground. He wished he could drop into an abyss. Madame de Restaud's expression had become dry, cold, and the unhappy student could see that her eyes, utterly indifferent to him, were studiously avoiding his.

"Madame," he said, "I see that you need to discuss matters with Monsieur de Restaud, so please accept my best wishes, and permit me . . ."

"If ever you come again," the countess said hurriedly, stopping Eugène with a wave of her hand, "you may be sure that you will be equally welcomed by both Monsieur de Restaud and myself."

Eugène made them both a deep bow and left, Monsieur de Restaud following after him and, in spite of his protestations, accompanying him all the way to the antechamber.

✿ Part of a duet of secret love, from Cimarosa's opera *Il matrimonio segreto* (*The Secret Marriage*), which had been performed in Paris at the time of this story.

"If that man ever comes back," said the count to Maurice, "neither the countess nor I are at home."

When Eugène stepped outside the house, he realized that it was raining. "So that's that," he said to himself. "I've made some stupid mistake, and I don't know what I've said or what it means, and now I'm going to ruin my coat and hat into the bargain. All right, my job is to sit quietly in a corner, swotting up the law, not dreaming about being anything more than a plain and simple magistrate somewhere. How can I go out into society when, just to even move around, you have to have a pile of carriages and gigs, polished-up boots, all the equipment in the world, and gold watch chains, and expensive doeskin gloves for the morning and, at night, yellow gloves—oh, always yellow gloves at night! God damn you, Goriot, you old fool!"

When he started down the street, the driver of a hackney cab, who had probably just dropped off some newlyweds and wanted nothing better than the chance to pick up a few fares on his own (with nothing for his boss), saw Eugène walking in his black suit and white vest, yellow gloves and polished shoes, but without an umbrella, and signaled to him. Eugène was in one of those black rages that make a young fellow who's fallen into an abyss shove himself further and further down, as if that would somehow help matters. With a quick nod of the head, he accepted the coachman's suggestion. Though he had at most twenty-two sous in his pocket, he climbed into the cab, where a few fragments of orange-blossoms and some strips of gold braid bore witness to the bridal passengers just delivered.

"Where to, monsieur?" asked the coachman, who had already pulled off his white gloves.

"By God!" Eugène said to himself, "if I'm bound to sink anyway, I might at least let it do me some good! To the Beauséant Mansion," he added in a loud voice.

"Which one?" the coachman asked.

A metaphysical request, which staggered Eugène—this elegant new man of the world who hadn't even known there were two Beauséant Mansions, being totally unaware of how many rich relatives he in fact had, none of whom gave a damn about him.

"The Viscount de Beauséant, who lives on . . ."

"Grenelle Street," said the coachman, interrupting him with a nod of the head. "See," he added, as he yanked up the folding steps, "there's also the Count and Marquis de Beauséant, over on Saint-Dominique Street."

"I'm quite aware of that," replied Eugéne drily. "*Everybody's* having their fun with me, today!" he swore to himself, tossing his hat onto the front cushions. "This little caper's going to cost me a king's ransom! But at least I'll come to see my so-called cousin, looking like a real aristocrat. Oh, Père Goriot's already cost me a small fortune, the old scoundrel! Lord, Lord: I'll tell Madame de Beauséant the whole story, maybe it'll make her laugh. I'll bet she knows all about the ugly doings of this old rat without a tail, him and that damned gorgeous woman of his. I'll do a lot better amusing my cousin than whacking away at that lascivious female, which would pretty clearly be an expensive game. Now, if my beautiful cousin's name is so potent, how important must she be in the flesh? Try for the highest. If you're tackling something up in the sky, you've got to shoot for God!"

But this is just a brief indication of the thousand and one directions in which his mind went careening. He felt a bit calmer, a bit more confident again, watching the rain. He told himself that if he had to use up almost all the money he possessed, it would at least be well spent if it preserved his suit and boots and hat. Then he started, for a moment happy, as he heard his coachman calling, "The gate, open the gate!" A red-and-gold porter made the mansion gates wheeze on their great hinges, and it gave Rastignac a certain pleasure to see his carriage swing past the porch, then turn in the courtyard and come to halt under the canopied entrance stairs. The coachman, stuffed into his fat blue-and-white coat, bent and released the folding steps. But as he made his descent, Eugène heard stifled laughter. Three or four servants had already made little jokes about the vulgar marriage cart in which he'd arrived. The student understood their laughter, as he compared his carriage to one of the most elegant rigs in Paris, drawn by a pair of dashing horses with roses tucked under their ears, pawing the ground and gnawing at their reins, while a powdered coachman, sporting a handsome bow tie, stood holding their bridles, as if they'd been trying to escape. In Chausée-d'Antin, Madame de Restaud's courtyard boasted a young count's fine-looking rig. But here, in the Faubourg Saint-Germain, you saw the incomparable luxury available to a great lord, a carriage that couldn't have been bought for thirty thousand francs.

"So who's here?" Eugène said to himself, realizing—rather too late—that there would not be many Parisian women without their regular visitors, and that to conquer such queens you had to expend a good deal more than blood. "Damnation! My cousin's bound to have a Maxime of her own!"

His soul went dead inside him, as he went up the steps. The glass door swung open when he approached; inside, there were a group of servants looking as serious as a herd of donkeys being whipped. The ball he'd attended had been held in the mansion's huge reception hall, on the ground floor. Not having had the time, since that occasion, to call on his cousin, he had thus never set foot in Madame de Beauséant's personal suite: he saw for the first time all the wondrous things that bore witness to that great lady's elegance, all the signs and symbols of the personality and way of life of a woman of high distinction. It interested him still more, now that he had Madame de Restaud's apartments for a comparison.

At exactly four-thirty, the countess could be visited. Had her cousin come five minutes earlier, he would not have been received. Knowing absolutely nothing of these byways of Parisian etiquette, Eugène was ushered up a great staircase, almost white, its steps gilded, fairly lined the whole way with flowers, and into Madame de Beauséant's drawing room. He knew nothing whatever of how she led her life, though her personal history was one of those ever-changing tales that, in Parisian drawing rooms, always make the evening pass more pleasantly, as they're tossed from one ear to another.

For the past three years, the vicomtesse had been linked with one of the most famous, and wealthiest, of Portuguese noblemen, the Marquis of Ajuda-Pinto. It was one of those simple relationships that so well satisfies both parties that they cannot tolerate having anyone else around them. Even her husband, the Viscount de Beauséant, had given his public blessing—willy-nilly—to this morganatic union. When the affair had just begun, people who came to see the vicomtesse at two o'clock would always find that the Marquis of Ajuda-Pinto was already there. Not being able to simply close her door to anyone, which would have been positively indecorous, Madame de Beauséant would however receive visitors so coldly, sitting and studying the plaster on her ceiling, that no one could have the slightest doubt they were interfering. And once it was generally understood, all over Paris, that Madame de Beauséant did not like to be visited between two and four in the afternoon, she found herself left, during that time, in the most complete solitude. She went to the Opera and to the theater with both Monsieur de Beauséant and Monsieur Ajuda-Pinto, but like a true man of the world Monsieur de Beauséant always left them alone, as soon as he'd seen them settled in their seats.

But Monsieur Ajuda-Pinto was getting married. His bride was a Mademoiselle de Rochefide. And in the entire small world of

Parisian society, the only person who still had not learned of this marriage was Madame de Beauséant. A few of her friends had indeed spoken to her, but only in the vaguest terms, and she had simply laughed, thinking they were jealous of her happiness and wanted to spoil it. But now the banns were about to be published. And the handsome Portuguese gentleman, though he had come, that day, precisely to let the vicomtesse know about his marriage, had still not dared speak a traitorous word. Why not? Is there anything quite so difficult as issuing such an *ultimatum* to a woman? There are men who feel more comfortable on the dueling ground, facing a man who threatens their life with a sword, than having to deal with a woman who, after declaiming her misery for two solid hours, acts as if she's dying and calls for smelling salts.

At that very moment, then, Monsieur Ajuda-Pinto was on pins and needles, trying to make his escape, assuring himself that Madame de Beauséant would indeed be told, he would write to her, it would be better, far better, to deal with this romantic asassination by letter than in person. When therefore a servant announced the arrival of Monsieur Eugène de Rastignac, the Marquis of Ajuda-Pinto fairly trembled with joy. No matter how you hide these things, of course, a woman in love finds it easier to fathom your doubts than to vary your pleasures. Knowing she is about to be deserted, she understands the full meaning of even a simple gesture faster than that stallion, in Virgil, who could sniff right out of the air the very corpuscles that announce love's arrival. So too Madame de Beauséant was instantly aware of that involuntary but frightening, innocent little shudder, no matter that it was barely perceptible.

It had never occurred to Eugène that you never, never paid a call on anyone in Paris without having first heard, from your host's friends, the full tale of his affairs, and his wife's, and even his children's, to keep yourself from committing one of those stupid blunders which, in Poland, they so picturesquely call "pulling your carriage with five oxen"!—probably because that's what you'd need, to pull yourself out of the mud you'll get stuck in. If blunders like this have no name of their own, in French, it may be because we tend to think them simply impossible, considering how quickly and superbly we spread slanders in all directions. And having mired himself deep in the mud, at Madame de Restaud's (who never gave him a chance to yoke five oxen to his carriage), only Eugène would have been capable of pursuing a career as an ox-herder, blundering into Madame de Beauséant's house as he was. All the same, if he had seriously irritated Madame de Restaud and Monsieur de Trailles, to Monsieur Ajuda-Pinto he seemed like a guardian angel.

"Farewell," said that gentleman, rushing to the door as soon as Eugène walked into the little drawing room, all done in gray and rose, and so wonderfully elegant that it scarcely appeared luxurious.

"But I'll see you tonight, won't I?" said Madame de Beauséant, turning her head and looking straight at him. "We're going to the theater, aren't we?"

"I'm afraid I can't," he said, reaching for the door knob.

Madame de Beauséant rose and summoned him back, paying no attention whatever to Eugène, who, ignored, solitary, stunned by the glitter of such incredible richness, felt that the tales of the Arabian Nights were all strictly true; he wished he could have known where to hide, finding himself in the presence of this woman who did not so much as acknowledge his existence. The vicomtesse had raised the index finger of her right hand and, making a graceful movement with it, was pointing to the spot right in front of her where the marquis was to come and stand. This gesture expressed a passionate despotism so violent that, without a word, the marquis let go of the doorknob and came to her. Eugène was not unenvious.

"That," he said to himself, "that's the man who owns the magnificent carriage! But to make one of these Parisian women even look at you, do you absolutely have to have dashing horses, and servants in uniforms, and tons of gold?"

The demon of luxury gnawed at his heart, the fever of money-making seized him, the thirst for gold dried out his throat. All he had left for the semester was a hundred and thirty francs. His father, his mother, his brothers, his sisters, his aunt—all of them together didn't spend as much as two hundred francs a month. And this hasty calculation of the vast gulf between his present situation and the goal he needed to aim for helped stupefy him even further.

"And why *can't* you come?" asked the vicomtesse, laughing.

"Business! I'm to dine at the British Ambassador's."

"You don't need to stay."

Once you start lying, you're inevitably forced to spin out lie after lie. Monsieur Ajuda-Pinto laughed and said:

"Do you insist?"

"Most certainly."

"That's what I hoped you'd say," he replied, giving her a shrewd look which would have reassured any other woman. He lifted her hand to his lips, kissed it, and left.

Eugène ran his hand through his hair and, shivering a bit, prepared to make her a bow, expecting that, now, she would turn and acknowledge him, but she suddenly ran into the corridor and over to a window, where she stood watching Monsieur Ajuda-Pinto climb into his carriage. Bending to hear what instructions he gave, she heard the footman telling the coachman, "To Monsieur de Rochefide's house." These words, and the way in which he threw himself into the carriage, were like thunder and lightning to her; she turned slowly back, gripped by horrifying apprehensions. And, in the world of high society, horrifying catastrophes consist of exactly such fears. Walking directly into her bedroom, she seated herself at a desk and took up a sheet of beautiful notepaper.

"The moment you dine at Monsieur de Rochfide's," she wrote, "and not at the English Ambassador's, you owe me an explanation. I'm waiting for you."

Carefully, she corrected several places where the convulsive shaking of her hand had obscured the writing, then signed the note with a simple C, signifying Claire de Bourgogne, and rang the bell.

"Jacques," she told the servant, who came to her at once, "at seven-thirty I want you to go to Monsieur Rochefide's, where you will ask for the Marquis Ajuda-Pinto. If in fact he's there, you will see to it that he gets this note, to which I expect no reply. If he is not there, you will return and give me back my letter."

"There is someone in the drawing room, madame."

"Ah yes, that's true," she said, and shut the door.

Eugène was starting to feel very ill at ease when, at long last, the vicomtesse appeared and, in a voice so laden with emotion that it shook him to the very heart, said,

"Your pardon, monsieur, but I had a note to write. I am at your disposal."

She spoke automatically, not knowing quite what she said. What she was thinking, as she spoke, was, "Ah, he wants to marry Mademoiselle de Rochefide. But can he do it? By tonight, either that plan will be shattered, or I'll . . . But it will all be over by tomorrow."

"My dear cousin," Eugène began.

"What?" said the vicomtesse sharply, looking at him so haughtily that his blood froze.

He knew exactly what she meant. Indeed, in the last three hours he had learned so many things, that he fairly quivered with a new consciousness.

"Madame," he began again, blushing. He hesitated, then forced himself to continue. "Forgive me. I need so much assistance that any kind of kinship would be desperately welcome."

Madame de Beauséant smiled, but sadly, wearily, for she could already feel the misery lowering over her head.

"I think," he went on, "that if you knew how hard it has been, for my family, you'd be tempted to play the role of the good fairy who, with a wave of her magic wand, makes all her godson's troubles disappear."

"Well then, *cousin*," she said, laughing, "just what can I do for you?"

"But how can I tell you? To be related to you, even by the most obscure of lineages, is already a fortune in itself. My brain's been clouded, since I arrived; I no longer know what I came for. You are in fact the only one I know, in all of Paris. Ah, I wish I could ask you to let me be like a little child, tacking himself on to your skirts, and quite willing to die for you."

"Would you kill someone for me?"

"Two someones," answered Eugène.

"A child! You really *are* a child," she said, choking back tears. "You'd be a faithful lover, I know you would!"

"Oh yes," he replied, with a solemn nod.

His ambitious words strongly appealed to the vicomtesse. This was, in fact, the first time the young Southerner had ever truly measured what he said and did. Between Madame de Restaud's blue drawing room and Madame de Beauséant's rose-colored one, he had studied a full three years of that unwritten *Parisian* law—unwritten, but forming a social jurisprudence of the highest order and, when properly learned and accurately applied, able to accomplish anything and everything.

"And now I remember!" Eugène exclaimed. "I noticed Madame de Restaud at your ball, and this morning I paid her a call."

"You must have really upset her!" said Madame de Beau-séant, laughing.

"Indeed, indeed! I'm an ignoramus and, if you won't help me, I'll upset everyone. It seems to me immensely difficult, here in Paris, to meet a woman who's young, beautiful, rich, elegant, *and* unattached; I need someone to teach me what all you women obviously understand so very well: life. I suspect that wherever I go I'm going to find yet another Monsieur de Trailles. So what I came to ask of you was your help in solving a puzzle, and in explaining to me just what sort of stupidity I committed. While I was there, I mentioned an old . . ."

"Madame the Duchess of Langeais," announced Jacques, cutting him off, to the student's obvious displeasure.

"If you truly wish to get on," the vicomtesse said to him softly, seeing his impatient gesture, "you'll have to learn, first of all, not to be so demonstrative."

"Ah, welcome, good morning, my dear," she said in her normal voice, rising and going over to the duchess, whose hands she pressed with a show of the same warm, flowing emotion she might have lavished on her own sister, to which greeting the duchess responded with equal extravagance.

"Now here's a pair of true friends," Rastignac said to himself. "From now on I'll have two protectresses, because these two must think and feel alike, so this new one will certainly take an interest in me."

"What happy inspiration brings you here, my dear Antoinette?" asked Madame de Beauséant.

"Simply that I saw Monsieur Ajuda-Pinto being welcomed at Monsieur de Rochefide's, so I knew you'd be alone."

Madame de Beauséant neither bit at her lips or reddened, her face did not change in any way as the duchess spoke these fatal words.

"Of course, had I known you'd be otherwise engaged . . ." added the duchess, turning toward Eugène.

"Let me present Monsieur Eugène de Rastignac, a cousin of mine," said the vicomtesse. "And have you had any news of General Montriveau?" she asked her visitor. "Sérisy mentioned, just the other day, that no one had seen him in such a long time, and I wondered if, today, he'd happened to call on you?"

The duchess, who was said to have been thrown over by Monsieur de Montriveau, with whom she was hopelessly in love, felt the question like the point of a sharp knife, and could not keep from blushing as she replied,

"He was at the Palace, yesterday."

"On business?" Madame de Beauséant pressed on.

"Now Clara, I'm sure you know," the duchess responded, her glance emitting wave after wave of sheer enmity, "that the banns for the marriage between Monsieur Ajuda-Pinto and Mademoiselle de Rochefide are to be published tomorrow?"

This was so deadly a blow that, even as she answered with a laugh, the vicomtesse turned pale:

"One of those silly rumors that stupid people love to indulge in! Why on earth would Monsieur Ajuda-Pinto offer the Rochefide family one of the noblest names in all Europe? It was just yesterday, you know, that the Rochefides acquired their title."

"Still, they say that Mademoiselle Berthe will have two hundred thousand francs a year."

"Monsieur Ajuda-Pinto is far too rich to worry about such trifles."

"Yes, my dear, but Mademoiselle de Rochefide is truly charming."

"Really?"

"So, you see, he's dining there today, and everything's been settled. It does surprise me, my dear, to see you so poorly informed."

"So tell me, Monsieur de Rastignac," asked the vicomtesse, "just what stupidity you think you committed? This poor child, my dear Antoinette, has been so newly thrown into the world that, in truth, as he and I were just saying, he understands absolutely nothing. To keep from troubling him, my dear, shall we leave the rest of our discussion for tomorrow? By tomorrow, surely, everything will be official, and you won't have to worry about making any mistakes."

The duchess turned and leveled on Eugène one of those infinitely haughty looks which wrap themselves around a man, from head to foot, then squash him flat and reduce him to nothingness.

"Madame," he said, "without knowing it, I seem to have plunged a knife right into Madame de Restaud's heart. And that I did not know what I was doing," added the student, whose guardian spirit had let him sense the biting sharpness hidden beneath the affectionate words of the two women, "that was surely my own fault. One goes on seeing, and one perhaps learns to fear those who do damage, though they know perfectly well what they're doing, but a person who causes pain and hasn't the slightest idea what he's done—ah, there you have an idiot, a clumsy fool who can't learn from anything, and so everyone despises him."

Madame de Beauséant gave the student one of those soft, melting glances in which great souls are able to simultaneously blend both gratitude and dignity. It washed over Eugène like a balm, soothing the wound inflicted on his heart by the duchess, who had stared at him as if he'd been no more than a mere object presented to her for possible purchase.

"Think of it," Eugène went on. "I'd just managed to earn Count de Restaud's goodwill—because, you see," he explained, turning to the duchess with a humble air that managed, also, to express a degree of malice, "I must tell you, my dear lady, that I'm still nothing but a poor devil of a student, entirely on my own, utterly impoverished . . ."

"Oh, never say such things, Monsieur de Rastignac. Women don't ever want what no one else wants."

"Believe me," replied Eugène, "I'm only twenty-two, and a man must learn how to put up with the disabilities Nature has placed on him. Besides, you know, I must admit that I could not find a lovelier confessional to kneel in. In a room like this, after all, one commits the sins for which one must later beg forgiveness."

The duchess frowned at this antireligious skepticism, which seemed to her in the very worst taste.

"Your cousin," she said, "has just come . . ."

Madame de Beauséant began to laugh heartily at both Eugène and the duchess.

"He's just come, my dear, and so he wants an instructress to teach him good taste."

"Madame," Eugène said to the duchess, "isn't it natural that young men yearn for the secrets of that which so utterly charms us?"

(Lord, he said to himself! I must sound like a hairdresser!)

"Indeed," said the duchess, "but hasn't Madame de Restaud set herself to study such matters with Monsieur de Trailles?"

"I had not known that, madame," the student responded.

"And so, stupidly, I thrust myself right between them. But, as I say, I was getting on very well with her husband, and so I thought the wife could at least put up with me for a bit, when I happened to let them know that I was myself acquainted with a man I'd just seen leaving their house by a back staircase, and who, before leaving, had kissed the countess farewell."

"And who might that be?" both women asked.

"An old fellow who survives, by the skin of his teeth, in the same house in Saint-Marceau where I myself, a poor student, eke out my existence—a truly miserable old fellow the whole world teases, and who's known to us as Père Goriot."

"Oh, silly infant that you are!" cried the vicomtesse. "Madame de Restaud's maiden name was Goriot."

"Daughter of a vermicelli maker," the duchess went on, "a girl who was presented at court the same day as a baker's daughter. Don't you remember, Clara? The King actually started to laugh, and made a little joke, in Latin, about flour. 'We used to . . .' How did it go? 'We used to . . .'"

"*Ejusdem farinæ*," said Eugène. "'They're baked from the same flour.'"

"Exactly!" said the duchess.

"Then he's her father," continued the student, with a horrified gesture.

"Most certainly. The good man had two daughters of whom he was insanely fond, though they've both almost as much as disowned him."

Madame de Beauséant gave the duchess a look.

"The second one's married to a banker, I believe? Someone with a German name—Baron de Nucingen? Her name's Delphine, isn't it? She's a blonde, as I recall, who takes a box at the Opera, and goes to other theaters, too, and always laughs very hard so people will notice her?"

The duchess smiled.

"My dear, that was admirable! But what makes you bother about such people? You'd have to be crazy in love, as Restaud must have been, to lower yourself to someone like Mademoiselle Anastasie. But he can't have done very well, you know. She's fallen into Monsieur de Trailles's hands, and he'll be the ruin of her."

"They've disowned their father," Eugène repeated slowly.

"Oh yes," the vicomtesse echoed him. "Their father, their old father, their good old father, who they say gave each of them five or six hundred thousand francs to make sure they'd be happy, marrying as they did, and left himself no more than ten thousand a year, thinking they'd always be his daughters, and that he'd have manufactured two new homes for himself, two homes where he'd always be adored, and fussed over. It didn't take those people two years before they'd banished him from their sight, like the lowest, most miserable . . ."

Eugène could not restrain a few tears, for pure, holy feelings for the family had been recently quickened in him, and he was still young and idealistic, and, after all, this was still only his first day on the battlefield of Parisian society. Indeed, honest emotions have such an effect on others that, for some moments, all three of them remained silent.

"My Lord," said Madame de Langeais, "yes, I agree, it seems truly awful, but we see such things every day of the week. And isn't there a good reason? Tell me, my dear vicomtesse: have you ever stopped to think what a son-in-law *is*? He's a man for whom we raise—you or me, it makes no difference—a dear, sweet girl, linked to us in a thousand ways, who for seventeen years or so has been the joy and delight of our entire family, who as Lamartine says becomes its pure soul, and who will then become its plague and its pestilence. When this man has plucked her from our hands he begins, rather like someone wielding an axe, by snatching her love, but he ends by severing, deep in this angel's very heart (not to mention in her day-to-day life), all the feelings which link her to her family. Yesterday, she was all ours, and we were all hers; but the day after, she's become our enemy. Don't we see such tragedies, over and over? In one case, the daughter-in-law treats the father-in-law with infinite haughtiness, though the man has sacrificed everything for his son. In another, the son-in-law shows his mother-in-law to the door. I hear people asking: is there anything dramatic happening in today's society? But these dramas revolving around the son-in-law are positively frightening, and without even mentioning marriages that have turned into stupid, dull affairs. I can tell you exactly what happened to this old vermicelli maker. If I'm not mistaken, this Foriot . . ."

"Goriot, madame."

"Yes, this Moriot played a prominent role of some sort in the Revolution; he was in on the famous shortages, and began to accumulate his fortune by selling flour, at that period, for ten times what he'd paid for it himself. Of course, he could lay his hands on as much as he wanted. My grandmother's steward sold him some, at colossal prices. And I've no doubt whatever that this Goriot shared his profits, the way all those people did, with the Committee of Public Safety. I can remember the steward telling my grandmother she was perfectly safe, staying at Grandvilliers, because her wheat crop was good patriotic testimony. Ah well! Now, this Loriot, who sold wheat to the people who chopped off heads, had only one passion: they say he absolutely adored his two daughters. So he set the older one roosting with the Restauds, and grafted the other one onto Baron Nucingen, a rich banker who plays at being a royalist. You understand, I'm sure, that under the Empire these two sons-in-law didn't mind having this old Revolutionary around: that sort of thing was perfectly all right, under Bonaparte. But once the Bourbons were back in power, the old man began to bother Monsieur de Restaud, and bothered the banker even more. The daughters, who probably always loved their father, would have liked to fix things so the goat and the cabbage could still get under one roof—their father and their husband; they let Goriot come see them, when no one else was there; they gave some affectionate excuse. "Do come now, Papa, because it will be even nicer, we'll be all alone together!" That sort of thing. But do you know, my dear, I think that real feeling has eyes and a brain: the old Revolutionary's heart must have been bleeding. He could see his daughters were ashamed of him—that, since they loved their husbands, this sort of thing was annoying his sons-in-law. He saw he simply had to sacrifice himself, so sacrifice himself he did, because he's a father: he banished himself from both their houses. And when he saw his daughters were pleased, he knew he'd done the right thing. Father and children worked hand in hand, committing this little crime. We see this all the time. In their drawing rooms, wasn't this Père Doriot just like some dirty stain on the carpet? Besides, he wouldn't have had a good time, he would have been bored. What happened to this old fellow could happen to the prettiest woman in the world, with the man she loves best: if her love bores him, he'll leave her, he'll do some cowardly thing, anything, to get away from her. That's how it is with all emotions. Our hearts are treasure-chests: empty them out all at once, and you're ruined. We won't excuse you for showing everything you feel any more than we forgive a man for not having a cent to his name. The old man gave them everything. For twenty years he kept giving them his very bowels, and his love, but it took only one day to surrender his fortune. And once the lemon was well squeezed, his daughters tossed the peel into the gutter."

"The world is a horrible place," said the vicomtesse, pulling lightly at her shawl and never looking up, for she had been pierced to the very heart by the Duchess of Langeais's words.

"Horrible! No," the duchess continued, "it goes its own way, that's all. I tell you all this so you won't think I'm taken in. I feel just as you do," she said, squeezing the vicomtesse's hand. "The world's a mud pit, and we need to try to remain above it."

She rose and put her arms around Madame de Beauséant, saying:

"My dear, you're so very lovely, right now. I've never seen such a beautiful complexion."

And then she left, glancing at Eugène and giving him the faintest of nods.

"Père Goriot is sublime!" said Eugène, remembering how he'd watched the old man rolling out his silver, the other night.

Madame Beauséant was lost in thought and did not hear him. The silence hung, and the poor student was so embarrassed he hadn't the courage to leave, to stay, or to say a word.

"The world is horrible," said the viconmtesse after a long time, "and it's wicked. As soon as something bad happens, there's always a friend just waiting to come and tell you all about it, twisting a dagger in your heart and asking you to admire its handle. Always sarcasm, always nasty jokes! Ah, but I'll defend myself."

She lifted her head, like the great lady she was, and her proud eyes shone.

"Oh," she said, seeing Eugène. "You're still here."

"Still," he said pitifully.

"Well then, Monsieur de Rastignac, treat the world exactly as it deserves! You want to succeed; I'll help you. You'll learn what feminine corruption can sink to, you'll find out just how profound men's vanity can be. No matter how much I'd read in the book of this world, there were still pages I'd never come across. Now I know everything. The more coldly you calculate, the farther you'll go. Strike without pity, and you'll be feared. Think of men and women simply as post-horses to be discarded in a ditch, each time you change to a fresh team, and you'll get exactly what you long for.

"Understand, you'll never be anything, here in Paris, without a woman's backing. You need someone who's young, rich, and elegant. But also remember: if you have any genuine feelings, hide them like treasure; never let anyone so much as suspect them, or you're lost. Instead of being the executioner, you'll be the victim. And if you ever fall in love, keep that absolutely secret! Never breathe a word until you're completely sure of the person to whom you open your heart. And to protect that love, even before you feel it, learn to despise the world.

"Pay close attention, Miguel . . ." (Innocently, and quite unaware, she used her ex-lover's name.) "There's something even more ghastly than a father abandoned by his daughters, who'd prefer him dead. And that's the rivalry between two sisters. Restaud is of noble birth, so his wife's been taken up, she's been presented at Court, but her sister, her rich sister, the beautiful Madame Delphine de Nucingen, though she's the wife of a man of money, is dying of envy; jealousy is eating her alive, she's totally divorced from her sister; indeed, her sister is no longer her sister; these two women have disowned each other exactly as they've disowned their father. So Madame de Nucingen would lap up all the mud between her house and here, if she could only get into my drawing room. She expected de Marsay to do it for her, and she made herself his slave, but oh, how she bores de Marsay! He won't do a thing for her. If you bring her here, you'll be her Benjamin, her very, very favorite, and she'll adore you. Then you're free to love her, if you can—and if not, just use her. I'll let her come here once or twice, when there's a huge party and there'll be a regular mob; but I won't ever see her in the morning. I'll acknowledge her: that will be enough. Having mentioned Père

Goriot's name, you've closed the countess's door on yourself. Oh yes, my dear: you can call at Madame de Restaud's house twenty times, and twenty times she won't be at home. You've been banned. Fine! Let Père Goriot bring you closer to Madame Delphine de Nucingen. Our beautiful Madame de Nucingen will carry your flag. You'll be the man she singles out, and all the women will fight over you. Her enemies, her friends—her very best friends—they'll all try to steal you away from her. There are women who are drawn to a man someone else has already chosen, just like those stupid shopkeepers who put on hats like ours and think they'll start acting like us, too. You'll be a great success. And in Paris success is everything, it's the key to power. If women take to you, if women think you're all right, then men will believe in you, unless you teach them not to. You'll have everything you want, you'll be admitted everywhere. And you'll understand perfectly just what society is: a collection of fools and rogues. Don't be either the one or the other. I'll lend you my name, and you can use it like Ariadne's thread, to make your way through the labyrinth. But don't compromise it," she said, lifting her chin and staring at the student, "keep me unstained. So, now leave me. We women have our own battles to fight."

"But if you happen to need a man who's more than ready to light a fuse for you?" said Eugène.

"And if I did?" she replied.

He tapped on his chest, smiled back when she smiled, and then left. It was five o'clock. Eugène was hungry, he was afraid he might not be in time for dinner, and so being carried rapidly across Paris felt quite extraordinarily pleasant. This purely mechanical delight left him completely free for the thoughts that thronged through his mind. When scorn attacks a young man of his age, he becomes carried away, wild with anger, he shakes his fist at the whole world, he longs for vengeance even as he doubts himself. Rastignac felt himself overwhelmed by his cousin's words: "You've closed the countess's door on yourself."

"I'll go directly there!" he said to himself, "and if Madame de Beauséant is right, if I'm really banned, then I'll . . . I'll . . . Everywhere Madame de Restaud goes, she'll find *me*. I'll study fencing, I'll learn how to handle a pistol, I'll kill Maxime! And the cost of all this?" his reason reminded him, "where will you find *that*?"

All the riches displayed at Madame de Restaud's suddenly flared in front of his eyes. He had seen for himself the luxury for which Goriot's daughters so longed, the dazzling gilt, the costly this and the expensive that, all the typical mindless luxury of an upstart, all the squandering over-expenditure of a kept woman. And then this fascinating image was suddenly replaced by the immense Beauséant mansion. His mind went leaping about in the exalted regions of Parisian society, and his heart was driven to a thousand malicious feelings, as his mind and his critical faculties expanded to take it all in. He could see the world as it really was: neither law nor morality had any effect on the rich, and he understood that money is the *ultima ratio mundi*, the world's final authority.

"Vautrin is right," he said to himself. "Money is virtue!"

When the cab reached New Saint Geneviève Street, he quickly went up to his room, coming down with ten francs for the coachman, and then went into the foul-smelling dining room, where he saw Madame Vauquer's eighteen guests, like so many animals in a stable, gobbling their meal. The sight of these miserable souls, and the appearance of the room itself, seemed to him utterly ghastly. He had made too abrupt a transition, the contrast was too absolute: it made his ambitious striving fairly burst within him. On the one side there were fresh, charming images from the most elegant forms of social intercourse, young, lively figures framed in a setting of luxury and artistic wonders, passionate minds chock-full of poetry; and on the other, dark, ominous scenes surrounded by filth, and faces which passion had marked with nothing but scars and all its other ravages. All that Madame de Beauséant had taught him, lessons literally torn from her by the fury of an abandoned woman, surged back into his mind, along with her inveigling offers, and poverty passed judgment on them. Rastignac made up his mind to seek his fortune by digging two trenches at the same time, building dream castles both on his studies and on love, becoming a learned man but also a man of the world. He was still no more than a child! These are asymptotic lines, which can never meet.

"You're gloomy tonight, my dear count," Vautrin remarked, looking at him with one of those piercing glances by which he seemed to tap into a person's most deeply hidden secrets.

"I'm not in the mood for little jokes made by people who play at giving me titles," Eugène replied. "In Paris you need a hundred thousand francs a year to really be a count, and when you live in Maison Vauquer you're not exactly one of Fortune's favorites."

Vautrin gave Rastignac a fatherly and scornful look, as if to say, "Oh you little child! I could gobble you up in one bite!" But all he said was, "You're in a bad mood, because you haven't been able to get anywhere with our beautiful Madame de Restaud."

"She closed her door against me," Rastignac exclaimed, "for having said that her father eats at our table!"

They all stared at one another. Père Goriot lowered his eyes and turned his head to one side, wiping at his face with his napkin.

"You've gotten some snuff in my eye," he said to the person sitting next to him.

"From now on," declared Eugène, "anyone who annoys Père

Goriot will have to deal with me. He's worth the whole lot of us. But, of course, I was not speaking of the ladies," he added, turning toward Mademoiselle Taillefer.

It was a dramatic moment; Eugène's words had reduced them all to silence. Only Vautrin spoke, saying with a mocking air,

"To take Père Goriot under your wing, and set yourself up as his guardian, you'll need to be pretty handy with a sword and a dueling pistol."

"And I will be," said Eugène.

"And have you already started your campaign?"

"Maybe," answered Rastignac. "But I don't have to account to anyone, especially since I don't go around trying to find out what other people do at night."

Vautrin gave him a sharp look.

"My dear boy, if you don't want the puppets in the puppet show pulling your strings, you have to climb right in with the puppet master; you can't just peep through the holes in the curtain. Enough said," he added, seeing that Eugène was about to get excited. "We can have a little talk, whenever you like."

The atmosphere turned gloomy and cold. Père Goriot, overwhelmed with sadness because of the student's words, had not the slightest notion that, as regards himself, there had been a sudden change of attitude, and that a young man able to silence his persecutors had taken up arms in his defense.

Madame Vauquer spoke to Eugène, in a low voice,

"Then Monsieur Goriot is really the father of a countess?"

"And of a baronness," he replied.

"That'll be his only job," Bianchon said to the student. "I've examined his head. There's only the one bump, the one for paternity, so that makes him an *Eternal* Father."

But Eugène's mood was too serious, and Bianchon's joke did not make him laugh. He meant to take advantage of Madame de

Beauséant's advice, and asked himself how and where he could find the money he'd need. Seeing the fields of the world rolling in his mind's eye, simultaneously empty and full, he began to worry. No one in the dining room spoke to him again, as long as the meal lasted.

"So you've seen my daughter?" Goriot asked him, his voice trembling with emotion.

Roused from his meditation, Eugène grasped the old man's hand and, looking at him with a kind of tenderness, said,

"You're a brave and worthy man. We'll talk about your daughters another time."

He rose, not wanting to listen to Père Goriot, and going straight up to his room, wrote the following letter to his mother:

My dear mother, You must see if you can open me a third breast. I have a chance to make my fortune right away. I need twelve hundred francs, and I've got to have it, without fail. Don't say anything about this to my father, he might say no, and if I don't get this money I'll be so despairing I'll blow my brains out. I'll explain everything as soon as I see you, because I'd have to write you volumes to make you understand the situation I'm now in. It's not gambling, my dear mother, nor do I owe a cent, but if you want to save this life you've given me you'll have to find me the money. In a word, I'm putting myself under the protection of the Vicomtesse de Beauséant. I need to go into society, and I don't have a penny to buy myself the right gloves. If I had to eat nothing but bread, and drink nothing but water, even fast, I could, but I can't manage without the tools they work with, here. I'll either make my way or be stuck in the mud. I'm well aware of what hopes you've had for me, and I mean to make them come true right now. Oh, my good mother, sell some of your old jewels, I'll replace them soon enough. I understand our family's situation well

*enough to appreciate such sacrifices, so you must realize I wouldn't
ask them of you without good reason, because otherwise I'd be a
monster. And please, don't think I'm asking all this simply because
my own need is so great. Our entire future depends on this money,
which I need so I can start my campaign: life here in Paris is
indeed perpetual warfare. Even if you have to sell my aunt's old
lace, to get enough money, tell her I'll send her even more beautiful stuff. Etc.*

He wrote to each of his sisters, asking for their savings, and
to keep them from telling anyone else in the family about the
sacrifice he was sure they would joyfully make for him, he appealed
to their delicacy and to the ties of honor, always strung so tight
and resonating so powerfully in youthful hearts. And then, once
he had written these letters, he could not help feeling frightened;
he shook, he trembled. He was young and ambitious, but he knew
the pure nobility of all those souls, buried in solitude, he knew
what torments he was creating for his sisters, just as he knew how
happy they might someday be; he knew how happily they would
lie in the darkness and whisper together, just the two of them,
about their beloved brother. He could see them perfectly, he could
watch them secretly counting their little treasure; he could see
them making use of the conspiratorial powers all young women
possess, and sending him the money anonymously, trying to work
out some wonderful trick, making the whole thing absolutely sublime. "A sister's heart," he told himself, "is like a diamond of
purity, a bottomless well of tenderness!" And then he was
ashamed at having written to them. How powerfully they would
be praying, how virtuously they would yearn toward Heaven!
Theirs would be sacrifices of an incredible voluptuousness! And
his mother, how sad she would be, if she couldn't send him everything he asked! These noble emotions, these dreadful sacrifices,

would help spur him toward Delphine de Nucingen. How he wept—tears that formed the final incense he would throw on the sacred altar of the family. He strode about in an agony of despair. Père Goriot, who had left his door ajar, saw him in this state and came over to him, saying,

"Is there something wrong, my dear sir?"

"Ah, my worthy neighbor, just as you're still a father, so too I'm still a son and a brother! You're right to worry about Countess Anastasie, because that Monsieur Maxime de Trailles has gotten hold of her, and he'll ruin her."

Père Goriot stammered some words that Eugène could not understand, and left. The next day, Rastignac went out to mail his letters. At the last moment he hesitated, then he threw them into the post box, declaring,

"I'll win!"

The same words used by gamblers, by great magnates, helpless words which bring down many more men than they save.

A few days later, Eugène went to call on Madame de Restaud, and was not admitted. He returned three times, and three times found the door closed to him, even when he came at two o'clock, knowing Count Maxime de Trailles would not be there. The Vicomtesse de Beauséant had been right.

He was no longer a student. Oh, he came to the classes and answered the rollcalls, but once he had certified his attendance he left. He reassured himself as most students do: he'd wait to study until it was time to pass the exams; he'd made up his mind, it could all just pile up, the rest of his second year, the whole of his third, and then, at the last minute, he'd set himself to learning the whole thing. That way, for fifteen months he was free to navigate the Parisian ocean, to throw himself into the business of buying and selling women, or fishing for his fortune.

He called on Madame de Beauséant twice, that week, carefully arriving just as the Marquis Ajuda-Pinto's carriage was leaving. For a time this illustrious cousin of his, the most poetic figure in the whole Faubourg Saint-Germain, prevailed over all her antagonists, delaying the marriage between Mademoiselle de Rochefide and the marquis. But these final days, which the fear of losing her happiness made the most ardent of all, could not help but bring on the catastrophe. Both the Rochefides and the marquis had looked on the estrangement between the lovers, and then their reconciliation, as a very good thing, hoping that Madame de Beauséant would get used to the idea and, in the end, faced by the inevitable future that comes to all human beings, would sacrifice those long delighted-in hours. In spite of all the most fervent promises and vows, renewed daily, the marquis was simply acting out the comedy, for the vicomtesse relished the deception.

"Instead of making a noble final leap through the window," observed the Duchess of Langeais, her very best friend, "she's letting herself be rolled down the staircase."

All the same, these final flashes of light lasted long enough to keep Madame de Beauséant in Paris, where she was extremely useful to her young relative, for whom she had a kind of superstitious affection. At a moment when women are used to seeing nothing more than pity, genuine consolation but devoid of real concern, Eugène had shown himself full of devotion and tenderness. When men say gentle words to women, at such times, they are investing in the future.

Determined to know all there was to know about the chessboard, before making his first move toward the house of Nucingen, Rastignac set himself to digging out all the details of Père Goriot's earlier life, collecting some very precise information, which may be summarized as follows:

Before the Revolution, Jean-Joachim Goriot had been a simple vermicelli worker, skillful, thrifty, and sufficiently enterprising to have bought up his employer's business, when in 1789, by pure chance, the man became a victim of the first uprising. Goriot set up shop on Jussienne Street, near the Wheat Market, and had the great good sense to accept the presidency of his revolutionary section, which allowed him to draw on the influence of some of the most powerful men of that dangerous time, and thus protect his business. This wise stroke had been the foundation of his fortune, which began to accrue during the Great Hunger (whether it was a real famine or not), as a result of which wheat in Paris soared to enormously high prices. Some people fought and killed each other, on the doorsteps of bakeries, while others, making no fuss at all, hunted up spaghetti and macaroni in the grocery shops. This was the year when Citizen Goriot amassed the capital which, later, allowed him to conduct his business with all the advantages conferred on anyone thus richly endowed. What happened to him, indeed, was what happens to all men with no more than a certain limited ability: his mediocrity became his salvation. Besides, no one knew about the fortune he'd accumulated until there was no longer anything dangerous about being rich: he aroused no one's envy.

And his business had apparently absorbed every bit of his mind's capacity. What concerned him was wheat, and flour, and grain leavings, knowing what they were good for, where they came from, how to make sure they did not spoil, how to anticipate the market, predicting harvest surpluses or scarcities, how to obtain grains at a good price, how to lay in stocks from Sicily, from the Ukraine, and in all of these matters Goriot was second to no one. Had you seen him doing business, explaining the laws governing the export trade, and the import trade, penetrating to their very core, taking every possible advantage of their loopholes, you might have thought him capable of becoming a Government Minister. Patient, lively, energetic, stable, his commands flowing freely and rapidly, he oversaw everything with an eagle eye, he anticipated everything, he predicted everything, understood everything, concealed everything; he was diplomatic in conception, military in execution. Away from his speciality, however, from his simple, dark shop—where, when there was nothing to do, he stood on the doorstep, his shoulder leaning against the door—he became no more than a plain, stupid workman, the sort of man who could not follow a logical argument, deaf and dumb to all the pleasures of the spirit, who would fall asleep in the theater, one of those Parisian Dolibans,❖ powerful only in their stupidity.

All such people are very much alike. Virtually all of them treasure some sublime feeling, deep at the bottom of their hearts. The vermicelli manufacturer's heart was split between two mutually exclusive feelings, which between them had absorbed every bit of its vitality, just as his business had used up every shred of his mind. His wife, only daughter of a rich farmer from Brie, was for him an object of religious devotion, a love surpassing all bounds. In her Goriot had been struck by a nature simultaneously frail and strong, sensitive and beautiful, totally unlike his own. If the human heart possesses some innate feeling, surely it is the pride of being the perpetual protector of some weaker creature? And then, if you add to this powerful affection the vivid sense of gratitude, felt by all candid souls for the primary cause of their pleasure, you will have understood a host of psychological oddities.

After seven years of cloudless happiness, Goriot suffered an immense misfortune: he lost his wife, who had already begun to exercise total domination of him, quite outside the sphere of his affections. Perhaps she could have tilled the inert soil of his soul,

---

❖ M. d'Oliban, a stupid father in a 1790 farce, seemed to fascinate Balzac, who made him into the very model of a fool, even planning (but never writing) a novel about him.

perhaps she could have planted there some comprehension of the things of the world, some understanding of life. But as it was, Goriot's paternal feelings grew and grew, almost to the point of madness. His passionate love for his wife, defeated by death, was transferred to his two daughters, and at first they gave him all the emotional satisfaction he could want. He himself was determined to remain a widower, no matter what brilliant offers were made him by merchants and farmers, desperate to give him their daughters. His father-in-law, the only man of whom he was fond, pretended to remember Goriot swearing eternal fidelity to his wife, in death as in life. The men with whom he did business, unable to understand such sublime folly, teased him about it and tagged Goriot with a singularly grotesque nickname. The first one who dared to use it in his presence, while sharing a drink of wine one day, received such a blow on the shoulder that he went spinning out, head first, right into a signpost on Oblin Street.

Goriot's totally irrational devotion to his daughters, his touchy, ticklish love for them, was so well known that, once, one of his rivals, wanting to make him leave the market so the other man could have the field all to himself, told him that Delphine had just been run over by a taxi. Pale and wan, Goriot left at once. And then, for several days afterward, he fell ill from the mixture of feelings induced by this false alarm. If he didn't let this man have a murderous blow on the shoulder, he did drive him out of business, forcing him, at a critical moment, into bankruptcy.

His daughters' education, inevitably, was a preposterous affair. Having more than sixty thousand francs a year, and spending no more than twelve hundred on himself, Goriot's happiness consisted in satisfying his girls' every fantasy. He hired the very best teachers, charging them to endow the young ladies with all those abilities that indicate a good education; they had a live-in companion—luckily for them, a young woman of taste and spirit; they went riding; they drove about in a carriage; they lived as if they'd been the mistresses of some rich old lord; all they had to do was express a desire for something, no matter how costly, and their father would hurry to get it for them, never asking so much as a caress in return for his offerings. To Goriot his daughters were absolute angels, and inevitably far superior to their father, poor man! He loved them even when they were unpleasant to him.

When they were old enough to be married, he let them choose their husbands exactly as they pleased: each of their dowries was to be half their father's fortune. Wooed by Count de Restaud, for her beauty, Anastasie had aristocratic leanings which led her to leave the paternal home and throw herself into high social circles. Money was what drew Delphine: she married Nucingen, a banker of German origin who became a Baron of the Holy Roman Empire. Goriot went on being a manufacturer of vermicelli, but soon it offended his daughters, and his sons-in-law, to see him still carrying on his business, though it had always been his entire life. After enduring their objections for five years, he agreed to retire on what he could get for his business, plus the profits he had earned in those final years—a capital which Madame Vauquer, in whose establishment he had by then made his home, estimated ought to bring him in eight or ten thousand a year. The despair he felt, seeing how his sons-in-law obliged his daughters not only to refuse to take him into their own houses, but even to openly receive him there, led him to fairly throw himself into the *pension*.

This was all the information about Père Goriot available to a certain Monsieur Muret, who had bought out the old man's business. The assumptions Rastignac had heard the Duchess of Langeais making were thus confirmed. And at this point we have said all that needs to be said, in order to introduce this little-known but dreadful Parisian tragedy.

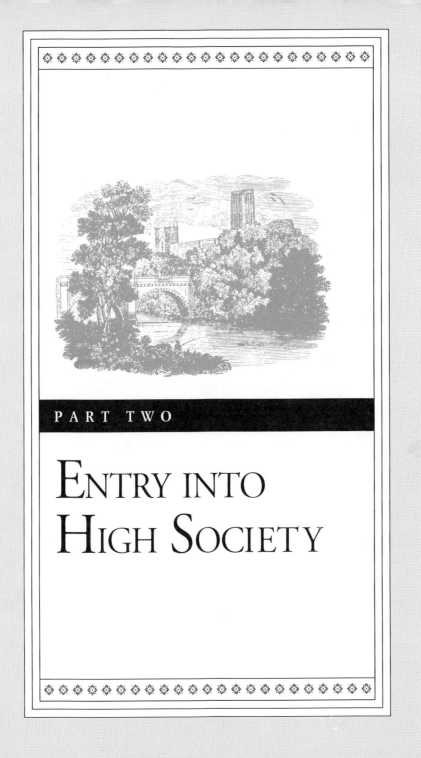

PART TWO

ENTRY INTO HIGH SOCIETY

T OWARD THE END OF THE FIRST WEEK OF DECEMBER, RASTIGNAC RECEIVED TWO LETTERS, ONE FROM HIS MOTHER, THE OTHER FROM HIS OLDEST SISTER. SEEING SUCH FAMILIAR HANDWRITING MADE HIM BOTH SHAKE WITH JOY AND TREMBLE WITH TERROR. Inside these two flimsy envelopes were warrants of either life or death for his hopes. But if he felt a degree of terror, reminding himself of his family's difficulties, he had long since too throughly tested their partiality not to also be afraid of having sucked their last drop of blood.

His mother's letter went as follows:

> *My dear child, I'm sending you what you've asked of me.*
> *Use this money well, because even were it to save your life, I*

*could not a second time lay my hands on so considerable a sum
without letting your father know, and that would damage the
peace of this family. Obtaining so much money would require us
to mortgage the very soil we live on.*

    *I cannot possibly judge the merits of projects about which I
know nothing, but what must they be, to make you afraid to tell
me about them? The explanation does not need to take up volumes
and volumes; all a mother needs is a word, and such a word would
have saved me from the anguish of uncertainty. I don't want to
hide from you the sad impression your letter has created. My dear
son, what must you be feeling to have conveyed such terror to my
heart? You must have been suffering desperately, when you wrote
to me, because that is how I have suffered, reading what you
wrote. Onto what career have you launched yourself? Your happiness, your very life, are they to be dependent on seeming to be
what you are not, so you can take part in a world where at every
step you'll have to spend money faster than you can afford, and
in the course of which you'll lose precious time from your studies?
My dear Eugène, take your mother's word for it: devious roads
never lead to anything noble. Patience and resignation are the
virtues required of young people in your position.*

    *I'm not complaining, I don't want you to receive this offering
of ours with even the slightest whiff of bitterness. I speak as a
mother, equally trusting and farsighted. You know your own re-
sponsibilities, yes, but I know the purity of your heart and the
wonderful goodness of your intentions. So I can also say to you,
absolutely without fear: go on, my well-beloved, do what you
must! I tremble because I'm a mother; but each and every step
you take will be accompanied, tenderly, with our prayers and our
blessings.*

    *Be sensible, my dear child. Young as you are, you must now
be wise like a man, for the destinies of five people to whom you
are very dear rest on your head. Yes, all our fortunes rest with*

you, just as your happiness is ours. We pray to Our Lord to help you with whatever you are doing. Your Aunt Marcillac has behaved extraordinarily well, in all of this: she even understood exactly what you meant about your gloves. She laughed and said she had a weakness for the oldest child. Be sure to love your aunt, my Eugène: I'll tell you what she has done for you, but only once you've succeeded, for otherwise her money would burn your fingers. You young people never know what it's like, sacrificing memories! But how can we not sacrifice them, for you? Your aunt has asked me to tell you that she kisses you on the forehead, hoping to send you, by that kiss, the power of being happy. That good and wonderful woman would have written to you herself, if she hadn't had gout in her fingers.

Your father is well. The harvest, this year, surpasses all our expectations. Farewell, my dear child. I'll say nothing to your sisters. Laurie is writing to you: I'll leave to her the pleasure of prattling about all our little family doings. May Heaven make you successful! Oh yes, succeed, my Eugène! For you've made me feel so vivid a sadness that I couldn't endure it a second time. I've known what it was to be poor and to yearn for fortune, so your child might have it.

So goodbye. Don't leave us long without news. Here is a kiss sent you by your mother.

By the time he had finished this letter, Eugène was in tears, thinking of Père Goriot as he'd bent his silver plate into ingots, to pay his daughter's bill. "Your mother has done the same thing with her jewelry!" he said to himself. "Your aunt has sold some of her memories, weeping as she handed them over! Have you any right to criticize Anastasie? For the sake of your own future you've just been selfishly imitating what *she* did for her lover! Which of you comes off better, eh?" He felt an unbearable fire eating at his bowels. He ought to give up society, he ought to refuse this money. He was filled with all manner of noble, beautiful remorse, hidden emotions rarely if ever understood when we judge our fellows, but which the angels in Heaven take into account, often, when they absolve a criminal of deeds judged criminal here on earth.

Then Rastignac opened his sister's letter, the graceful, innocent words of which refreshed his heart:

> *Your letter came at a good time, dear brother. Agatha and I had so many different plans for our money that we simply couldn't make up our minds what we ought to do. Just like the King of Spain's servant, when he re-set his master's clocks, you've set us in good order. Really, we've been constantly bickering about which one of us should have her way, and neither of us had ever once imagined, my good Eugène, this way to fulfill all our desires. Agatha was fairly jumping up and down with joy. Indeed, we've both been behaving like a pair of idiots, the whole day long, "so much so" (as our aunt likes to say) that my mother finally said, in her sternest voice, "But what on earth is wrong with you, young ladies?" If we'd been scolded a bit, I really think we'd have been even happier. Surely, a woman finds it enjoyable to suffer for someone she loves!*
>
> *All the same, I've been dreamy and disappointed, in spite of my joy. I've been a bad girl, no doubt about it—I've spent far too much money. I bought myself two belts, and a little awl for putting eyelets in my corset, and some other foolishnesses, so that I have less money than that fat Agatha, who is horribly thrifty and piles up her pennies like a magpie. She actually had two hundred francs! And I, my poor friend, I had only a hundred and fifty. I am well and thoroughly punished; I feel like throwing my belts down the well, it will be hard ever to wear them again. I stole them from you.*

Agatha's been charming. She said to me: "Let's send him three hundred and fifty francs, from the two of us!" But I promised to tell you exactly what happened. And I want you to know just how we obeyed your commands: we went for a walk and, the minute we got out to the highway, we ran all the way to Ruffec, where we just handed over the money to Monsieur Grimbert, who's in charge of the post office there! We felt as light as swallows, coming back. "Is it happiness that's pulling us along?" Agatha asked me. And then we said a thousand things I won't repeat to you, Mister Parisian, because you were what we were talking about.

Oh, my dear brother, we love you most dearly: that's the whole thing in two words. And as far as keeping quiet about it, well, as my aunt keeps saying, a pair of death-masks like us is capable of anything, even holding our tongues. Now my mother, together with that aunt of ours, has just made a mysterious trip to Angoulême, and both of them have been as close-mouthed as bishops about their trip, though they didn't make it without having a series of long discussions from which we were excluded—and not only us, but the lord of the manor, too.

Everyone in this Rastignac Domain is wondering all sorts of large wonders. The muslin dress all spangled with flowers, which the children have been busy embroidering for her majesty the queen, is progressing very nicely, though it's still a deep secret. There can't be more than two widths left. The wall along the Verteuil, it has been decided, will not be built, but a hedge-row planted instead. The common folk along the bank will thereby lose some fruit trees, and some trellises, but visitors will be supplied with some splendid views. If the presumptive heir to the throne happens to need any handkerchieves, we understand that the Dowager Marcillac, rummaging about in her treasure chests, one of which is known as Pompeii and the other as its twin city, Herculaneum, has dug up a handsome piece of Holland linen, *which she can't remember having, and the princesses Agatha and Laurie have agreed to place at the Crown Prince's disposal their thread, their needles, and their forever rather too reddened hands. The two young princes, Don Henri and Don Gabriel, have managed to check their fatal propensity for stuffing themselves with grape jam, and for driving their sisters wild, and for refusing to learn a blessed thing, and for entertaining themselves by stealing the eggs out of birds' nests, and for breaking and cutting willows, contrary to all the Laws of the Land, so they can make themselves switches. The Papal Nuncio, known to vulgar tongues as the parish priest, has threatened to excommunicate them if they go on neglecting the holy laws of grammar in favor of the rules of hand-to-hand combat with sticks.*

And so farewell, my dear brother: there's never been a letter laden with more prayers for your happiness, nor one dispatched with as great a sense of fulfilled love. How much you will have to tell us, when you come home! You'll certainly have to tell me everything, because, in case you've forgotten, I'm the oldest. There have been some suggestions from my aunt that you've not been doing too badly, out in the great world.

A lady's mentioned—and the rest is silence.❖

When you're talking to us, of course! But do tell us, Eugène, if you'd rather that lovely linen wasn't used for handkerchieves but for shirts. Tell us right away, please, because if you really need some handsome shirts, and need them quickly, we'd naturally make them for you one, two, three—and if there are some Parisian fashions we don't know about, you could just send us a model, especially when it comes to cuffs.

❖ Adapted from Corneille, *Cinna*, IV, 1290: "Water's mentioned, and the Tiber—and the rest is silence."

So: farewell, farewell! Here's a kiss on your forehead, on the
left side, because that temple belongs exclusively to me. I'll leave
the rest of the page blank, so Agatha can write in it: she's promised
me not to read what I've written. But just to be absolutely sure,
I intend to stay close to her while she's writing. And I remain
your sister, who loves you,

Laurie de Rastignac

"Oh yes, yes!" Eugène swore to himself, "a fortune—no matter what! No treasure could be reward enough for such devotion!
I want to make them all happy, all at the same time." He paused.
"Fifteen hundred and fifty francs!" he said to himself. "Every one
of them must do its work! Laurie's right, by God: all my shirts
are cheap linen. When it comes to making somebody else happy,
a young girl becomes as crafty as a thief. She may be naive for
herself but she's positively clairvoyant for me—like an angel, par-
doning earthly sins without ever understanding them!"

The world was his! He'd already sent for his tailor, sounded
him out, enlisted him. Having seen Monsieur de Trailles, Eugène
had learned all he needed to know about the importance of tailors
in a young man's life. But alas! there's no middle ground: a tailor
is either your mortal enemy, or else a friend bought and paid for.
And in his tailor, Eugène had found a man who understood the
genealogical function of the trade, a man who realized that, when
he played his cards right, he might well become a basic link between a young man's present life and his future one. And Rastignac, deeply grateful, had in turn made this fellow's fortune with
one of those deftly phrased remarks at which, later on, he so
excelled:

"I myself," he'd said, "am personally acquainted with two
pairs of trousers, made by his hands, which brought about marriages worth twenty thousand francs a year."

Fifteen hundred francs and all the clothes he wanted! At that moment the poverty-stricken Southerner could no longer doubt anything, but went down to breakfast with the indefinable air that a young man acquires from possession of any significant sum of money. The instant money comes sliding down into a student's pocket, it is as if some fantastic column sprouts up inside him, and on which he now securely rests. He walks more briskly than before, he feels as if he has a fulcrum on which he can lever anything; his glance is open, direct, his movements are quick; he may have been beaten, yesterday, when he was humble, timid, but tomorrow he'll triumph over the Prime Minister himself. Incredible things start to happen inside him: he hungers for everything, and is capable of everything, he feels impulses, desires over which he has no control whatever, he becomes perpetually cheerful, generous, expansive. In a word, he who a moment before was a bird that could not fly has suddenly recovered his wings. The penniless student snatches at a scrap of pleasure like a dog stealing a bone in the face of thousands of dangers, he splits it open, he sucks out the marrow, and then he goes off running, but the young man who can feel a few fugitive pieces of gold slipping and sliding in his pocket can savor his pleasures, itemizing them, delighting in them; he's walking on air, he no longer even understands the word "poverty." Paris quite simply belongs to him, lock, stock, and barrel. Oh, it's a time of life when everything gleams, everything shines and flares! a time of powerful joy from which, alas, no one profits, neither man nor woman! a time of debts and of vivid fears that intensify pleasures ten times over! If you've never walked along the left bank of the Seine, between Saint-Jacques Street and Saints-Pères, what can you know about life?

"Ah, if only these Parisian women knew!" Rastignac kept saying to himself as he devoured the nice, cheap cooked pears served at Maison Vauquer, "they'd come right here, looking for love."

Just then a Royal Mailman came into the dining room, having carefully rung the outside bell. He asked for a Monsieur Eugène de Rastignac, for whom he had two registered packages, and from whom he had to obtain a receipt. The profound look that Vautrin threw toward Rastignac felt like the stroke of a whip.

"Now you'll be able to pay for fencing lessons, and instruction in the use of dueling pistols," said that gentleman to Eugène.

"Your ship's come in," Madame Vauquer observed, looking at the packages.

Mademoiselle Michonneau was afraid even to look at the money, for fear of openly exhibiting her greed.

"Your mother is very good to you," said Madame Couture.

"You have a very good mother," repeated Poiret.

"Oh yes, his mother's been well bled," said Vautrin. "Now you can play your little games, and go out into society, and fish for fat dowries, and dance with countesses who wear peach blossoms in their hair. But just the same, young fellow, make sure you learn how to shoot."

Vautrin lifted his hand, as if aiming a pistol.

Rastignac wanted to give the mailman a tip, but there was nothing in his pockets. Vautrin dug into his and threw a coin to the fellow.

"Your credit's good," he said again, staring at the student once more.

Rastignac felt compelled to thank him, although ever since their bitter exchange, the day when he'd come back from Madame de Beauséant's ball, he'd not been able to endure the man. From that day to this, whenever Eugène and Vautrin had been in the same room, they had not spoken, though they exchanged glances.

Though he tried, the student could not understand what had happened. To be sure, the force with which we project our ideas is in direct proportion to the power with which they have taken hold of us, and they go hurling forth from our brains by laws of mathematics strictly comparable to those which govern shells fired out of a cannon. And their effect is necessarily a mixed one. There certainly are gentle natures which, when fired upon by ideas, can thereafter be utterly ravaged, but there are also stronger natures, lodged in craniums of solid brass, against which volleys may strike but by which they are blunted and tumble to the ground, exhausted, like bullets fired at a stone wall, just as there also are, finally, limp and cottonlike natures in which other people's ideas slow down and die, like cannonballs that get buried in a fort's thick, soft bulwarks. Rastignac's head was one of those, chock-full of powder, which go off at the least little shock. He was simply too energetically youthful, too liable to that infection by odd notions that can take hold of us, willy-nilly, not to be guilty of firing off ideas in all directions. His psychological awareness was as keen as the eyes of a lynx. His heightened senses were extended in that mysterious way, zooming easily in and out, that we marvel at in all superior souls, swashbucklers forever quick to take advantage of any errors their adversaries may commit. And besides, for the past month or so whatever deficiencies might have been revealed, in Eugène, had been balanced by increased capacities. Those deficiencies had been exposed both by the world and by the exigencies of his own desires. But among other new powers there was that prototypical Southern trait, a vigor and strength that would drive a man straight ahead, beating at a difficulty until it was beaten down, a restlessness which makes anyone from beyond the boundaries of the Loire absolutely unable to bear uncertainty, and this strength is one that Northerners are apt to label a deficiency, since, for them, if Murat's success stemmed from such qualities, so too did his death.❧ Which means that, if ever a Southerner can combine the clever trickiness of a Northerner with the audacity of the South he becomes a thoroughly integrated man who, if he likes, can easily become the King of Sweden.

Accordingly, the fire of Vautrin's heavy artillery was not something that Rastignac could endure for very long, without needing to find out if the man was in fact his friend or his enemy. Over and over again, it had seemed to Eugène that this singular man could cut right through his passions and read his very soul, although Vautrin himself remained so extraordinarily secretive that he might have been a sphinx, knowing everything, seeing everything, and saying nothing. And now, with his purse full, Eugène rebelled.

"Stay a moment, please," he said to Vautrin, as that gentleman rose from the table, having savored the last drops of his coffee.

"Why?" answered the older man, putting on his broad-brimmed hat and picking up a steel cane with which, often, he had been seen performing such effective fencing maneuvers that he was not likely to be afraid, even if attacked by four robbers at once.

"I propose to repay you," answered Rastignac, quickly undoing one of the packages and, first, handing Madame Vauquer a hundred and forty francs. "Paying your debts is the best way to make friends," he said to the widow. "We're all even, now, until the end of the year. Would you change this bill for me?"

"Good friends pay their debts," Poiret repeated, looking at Vautrin.

"And here's what you gave the mailman," Rastignac said to the bewigged sphinx.

❧ Murat was one of Napoleon's generals. As all Frenchmen know, his boldness won him his prestige, but his daring cost him his life.

"Are you afraid of being in debt to me?" Vautrin said brusquely, staring deep into the young man's soul while, at the same time, flashing him one of those wise, teasing smiles that, a hundred times over, had swept Eugène to the point of anger.

"Well . . . yes," replied the student, standing up, his packages in his hands, ready to go up to his room.

Vautrin left the room by one door and the student prepared to leave by the other.

"You know, don't you, Monsieur Count Rastignacorama," said Vautrin suddenly, slapping his cane against the door and walking over to the student, who was watching him coldly, "that what you said to me, just now, wasn't exactly polite?"

Rastignac continued out the doorway leading to the stairs, and Vautrin followed him; they stood in the space between the dining room and the kitchen, alongside a plain wooden door, inset with a small barred transom, opening onto the garden. Rastignac turned to Vautrin, just as Sylvie emerged from her kitchen, and declared,

"*Mister* Vautrin, I am not a count, and my name is not Rastignacorama."

"They're going to fight," said Mademoiselle Michonneau wearily.

"Fight!" repeated Poiret.

"Never," replied Madame Vauquer, who was sitting and caressing the stack of money Eugène had given her.

"But there they are, out under the lindens," called Mademoiselle Victorine, standing up and staring into the garden. "That poor young man was right, all the same."

"We'll go up, my dear girl," said Madame Couture. "We do not stand and watch things of this sort."

Madame Couture and Victorine rose, but fat Sylvie stood at the doorway, barring their way.

"What's going on here?" she said. "I heard Monsieur Vautrin

say to Monsieur Eugène, 'Let's settle this!' Then he took him by the arm and there they are, tramping all over the artichokes."

Just then Vautrin reappeared.

"Momma Vauquer," he said, smiling, "don't you worry about a thing. I'll just be under the lindens, testing my pistols."

"Oh, my dear sir!" cried Victorine, wringing her hands. "Why do you want to kill Monsieur Eugène?"

Vautrin stepped back a bit and stared at her.

"Ah ha," he cried in a teasing voice that made the girl blush, "another tale that needs telling, eh? He's a nice young man, isn't he, that fellow out there?" he added reflectively. "Well, you've just given me an idea. I'll make you both happy, my dear child."

Madame Couture took the girl by the arm and led her away, saying in a low voice,

"My dear Victorine! You're really quite unbelievable, this morning!"

"I want no one firing pistols on my property," announced Madame Vauquer. "Don't you go frightening all the neighbors and bringing the police down on our heads, first thing in the morning!"

"Now, now, be calm, Momma Vauquer," replied Vautrin. "There, there, it's all right, we're just going to have a little fun."

Then he stepped out and rejoined Rastignac, whose arm he took with a friendly gesture.

"Now, once I prove to you that, at thirty-five paces, I can hit an ace of spades five times running," he said to the student, "I know that isn't going to make you run away. I'm afraid you've got a bit of a temper, and you're quite capable of getting yourself killed like a complete fool."

"You're backing down," said Eugène.

"Don't try to make me angry," replied Vautrin. "It's rather pleasant out, this morning, so come sit down over there," he remarked, pointing out the green chairs. "No one will hear us. I need to have a chat with you. You're a nice young fellow and I don't wish you any harm. In fact, I like you, you know, or my name isn't Tromp . . . oh damn it, or my name isn't Vautrin. And I'm going to tell you exactly why I like you. So listen carefully, because I know you as well as if I'd made you, and I'm going to prove that. Put those packages over there," he directed, gesturing to the round table.

Rastignac set his money on the table and took a seat, feeling an extraordinarily heightened curiosity at the sudden change in this man who, having at first spoken about killing him, was now setting himself up as his protector.

"You're dying to find out who I am, and what I've done," Vautrin went on, "or what I do. Curiosity killed the cat, young fellow. Now, now, stay calm. There's a lot more you still have to hear. I've had my share of bad luck. Hear me out, and then it'll be your turn.

"So: here's my life, in three short words. Who am I? Vautrin. What do I do? Whatever I feel like. Which is enough of that. You want to know what sort of fellow I am? I'm good to anyone who's good to me, anyone whose heart speaks to mine. They can get away with anything, they can even kick me in the back or in the shins and I won't warn them, 'Okay, now watch out!' But God help me! I'm the very devil with anyone who crosses me, anyone I just don't fancy. And it's not a bad idea for you to understand that killing a man means as much to me as that!" he declared, spitting. "But I do my best to kill him properly, if I absolutely have to do it. You might call me an artist. I've read Benvenuto Cellini's *Autobiography*—me, yes, and in Italian, too! And what I learned from him, that rare son of a gun, was how to copy Fate, which bumps us off anytime it feels like it, and for any reason, and also to love goodness anywhere I can find it. Hey, but isn't that a great role to play, being all alone against the whole world, and having luck on your side?

"I've done a lot of thinking about this social disorder of ours. Young fellow, dueling is child's play, it's stupid. When one out of two living men is bound to disappear, the odds are so bad that you have to be a fool to play the game. A duel? It's heads or tails, that's what it is! I can put five bullets in an ace of spades, and I can make each shot go right where the one before it went, and still at thirty-five paces! And when you've got that kind of little talent, you can be sure of killing your man. So much for that! I fired at a fellow from twenty paces—and I missed him. The son of a gun had never touched a pistol in his life. And what happened?" exclaimed this strange man, undoing his jacket and exposing his chest, as hairy as a bear's, with a tawny ripple to it that made Eugène feel both disgust and fear, "hah! That baby-faced idiot put a hole in my hide," he went on, putting his finger on a deep indentation.

"I was just a baby myself, back then, about as old as you are now, barely twenty-one. I still believed in something, love for a woman and all that, some pile of dumb things like the ones you're going to fall into. We'd really fight, eh? Maybe you'd have killed me. And suppose you had, what good would it do you? You'd have to run away, maybe go to Switzerland, live off your father, who can't afford it.

"Well, let me set you straight, let me tell you just what you're up against, right now—but, mind you, every word I'm going to say comes to you freighted with the superior insight of a man who's carefully studied what the world's all about, and has understood there are only two sides you can be on: one is stupid obedience, and the other is mutiny. I obey nothing and no one, do you hear me? All right. Do you know what you need, the way you're going right now? A million francs, here and now. And without that, given your bullheadedness, you might just as well go strolling up and down Versailles, looking at the flowers and trying to figure out whether there really is a God. But, that million: I'm going to give it to you."

He stopped and considered Eugène.

"Oh ho, you're not making faces at Papa Vautrin any more! In fact, right now you look like a girl who's just been told, 'Until tonight,' and who'll get ready for the evening, purring like a cat drinking milk. All right then! Let's go! Ready, get set . . .

"Here's how you stand, young fellow. What we've got, back home, is a daddy, a momma, a great-aunt, two sisters (one of them eighteen, the other seventeen), two little brothers (fifteen and ten)—and here's how we handle the rudder. The aunt teaches your sisters. The priest comes and teaches Latin to the two brothers. The family eats more boiled chestnut porridge than good white bread, the father's careful with his clothes, momma barely lets herself have a dress for winter and a dress for summer, and our sisters, well, they do the best they can. I know the whole thing, I've been in your part of France. That's how it has to be back home, if your little place brings in three thousand a year and they send you twelve hundred. Oh, we have a cook, and a maid, we have to be respectable, our father has a title. And us, we're ambitious, we have a connection with the Beauséants but we still go around on foot, we want to be rich but we haven't got a cent, we eat boiled stew at Momma Vauquer's but we prefer fine dinners in the Faubourg Saint-Germain, we sleep on a straw bed and wish we had a mansion!

"That's fine, I'm not criticizing you for dreaming. Because, my fine young friend, it isn't everyone who's blessed with these longings. Ask women what sort of men they're looking for, and they'll tell you: the ambitious ones. Ambitious men have the strongest kidneys, there's more iron in their blood, their hearts beat warmer than other people's. Women themselves are so happy, and so beautiful, when they're strong, that they naturally choose powerful men, even if that power's so enormous there's a real risk it could shatter them.

"Now, I've given you this listing of your dreams so I can ask you a question. And this is the question I want to ask. We're as hungry as a wolf, our teeth are sharp, but how are we going to keep the pot boiling? First we have to swallow all the laws in the Napoleonic Code, and that's not much fun, and it really doesn't teach us anything, but it has to be done. All right. We become a lawyer, so we can get to be a chief judge and send poor devils, worth more than we are, to the prison colonies, so we can prove to the rich that it's safe for them to go to bed at night and close their eyes. That's not much fun, either, and it takes a long time. First, there's two years of cooling our heels in Paris, staring at all the goodies we love, without ever eating any. It's weary stuff, this wanting and wanting and never getting. If you're bloodless, with all the fire of a clam, it won't bother you a bit, but our blood's boiling like a lion's and we're hungry enough to gobble down twenty idiots a day. This agony will get to you, because it's the most terrible torture our good God's devised for his living Hell.

"Let's concede that you're sensible, you stick to drinking milk, and you write pretty poems, but noble soul that you are, you still have to start—after boredom and deprivation that would drive a dog mad—by being appointed assistant to some odd fish, off in some hole of a town where the government generously lets you have a salary of a thousand francs a year, just the way you toss a soup bone to a butcher's watchdog. Then you go barking after thieves, you argue cases for the rich, you send people who have anything in them to the guillotine. Wonderful! Thanks a lot! If there's no one looking out for you, they'll leave you in your provincial courthouse until you rot. By the time you're thirty, you'll get to be a judge, at twelve hundred francs a year, if you haven't long since given up on the whole business. And then, when you get to be forty, you'll marry some miller's daughter with maybe six thousand a year. Great. If you *do* have someone watching out for you, why, at thirty you can be a district attorney, at fifteen hundred a year, and you'll marry the mayor's daughter. If you get into political graft, like maybe reading a government candidate's name on an election report, instead of some unfriendly fellow (the alliteration ought to make your poetic soul feel a lot more comfortable), by the time you're forty you might get to be an attorney general, and maybe even get elected to Parliament.

"Now notice, young fellow, that along the way we've had to take some tucks in our little conscience, that we've endured twenty years of boredom, of hidden poverty, and our sisters will have taken the veil. It's also my pleasure to inform you that there are only twenty attorneys general in all France, and twenty thousand fighting for every appointment, among whom there'll be some jokers who'd sell their grandmothers to climb a single notch.

"If the whole business disgusts you, let's see what else we might try. Is Baron de Rastignac interested in being a barrister? Ah, lovely. It only takes ten years of suffering, the expenditure of a thousand francs a month, a handsome law library, an office, and then you plunge into society, you kiss a solicitor's feet so you get his cases, you lick the courthouse floor with your tongue. If this worked, I'd say go ahead, try it, but find me five barristers in all Paris who, at age fifty, are making more than fifty thousand a year? Bah! Before I'd shrink my soul like that, I'd go and become a pirate. Anyway, where would you find the money, in the first place?

"None of that's much fun. A dowry would help, of course. Are you interested in marriage? A wife's as good as a stone around your neck and, besides, if you marry for money, what happens to all our shining ideas about honor and nobility? Why not begin your rebellion against all social conventions here and now? It wouldn't be bad to go wriggling around like a snake, in front of some woman, or lick her mother's feet, or do stuff so dirty it would disgust a sow, no! If only it worked and you were happy. But when you've married a woman like that, you're bound to be as miserable as a stone in cesspool. Fighting with men is a lot better than fighting with your wife.

"So here's the crossroads for you, young fellow. Take your pick. But you've already made your choice: you've visited our Beauséant cousin, and you've gotten a whiff of luxury. You've been at Madame de Restaud's house, Père Goriot's daughter, and you've gotten a whiff of the Parisian woman. You came back, that day, with a single word written straight across your forehead, and I read it right off: *Succeed!* No matter what, succeed! Bravo, I said to myself: that's the kind of go-getter I like! You needed money. Where could you get it? You bled your sisters. Brothers always swindle their sisters, one way or another. They got you your fifteen hundred francs, though God only knows how, down where there're more chestnuts than gold pieces, but they'll slip away faster than soldiers going looting. And what will you do then? Will you take a job? A life of labor, if you understand it the way you now do, lets you end up in a room at Momma Vauquer's, if you're a strong as old Poiret.

"No. There are fifty thousand young fellows facing the same problem: how to make a fortune and make it fast. You're just one among many. So think how hard you'll have to try, and what a desperate fight it'll be. You'll all have to eat each other, like spiders in a chamber pot, because there aren't fifty thousand fortunes available. So how do you manage, eh? Simple. Either by a burst of genius, or by being a clever crook. Either you smash your way through that mob like a cannonball, or else you slide right into it, like the bubonic plague. Honesty will get you nowhere. People bow their heads to a genius, they hate him, they try to drag him down, because he only takes, he doesn't give, but as long as he keeps going, people yield, they have no choice—in a word, if you can't bury him in the mud, you fall on your knees, you adore him. Corruption's everywhere, but ability's scarce. So corruption becomes mediocrity's weapon, for mediocrity too is everywhere, and its slicing edge reaches in every direction. Consider the women with husbands who make six thousand a year, who spend at least ten thousand a year on clothes. Consider clerks with twelve hundred francs a year, who buy themselves estates in the country. Consider women who'll sell themselves, just to ride in a nobleman's carriage, so they can ride down the center lane in the Bois de Bologne. You've seen this poor numbskull, Père Goriot, making good on his daughter's debts, though her husband has fifty thousand a year. You can't take two steps, here in Paris, without seeing something dirty going on. I'd bet you my head, against a plate of that lettuce growing over there, that you'll get yourself into a regular hornet's nest with the first woman who interests you, no matter if she's rich, or beautiful, or young. Every single one of them's tied all around in some lawsuit, or fighting their husbands over everything and anything. If I had to tell you all the games they play to get lovers, to get clothes, to get kids, to keep their households running, or just for the sake of vanity—one in a million will do it for virtue—I'd never get to the end of it, believe me. So the honest man is everyone's enemy.

"But where do you suppose you'll find an honest man? Here in Paris, an honest man's the one who keeps his mouth shut and doesn't let anyone else in on the deal. I'm not talking about those poor peons, and they're all over the place, who never really get paid for all they do: they're what I call the lay brothers of God's Order of the Rundown Shoes. There's a kind of virtue in being that stupid, but it's the virtue of poverty. If God decides to play a bad joke on us, and stay away when the Last Judgment comes, oh, I can just see their faces!

"So if it's a fast fortune you want, you either have to be rich already or else look as if you are. Getting rich around here means you have to be a high-stake gambler, otherwise you're wasting your time, bye-bye baby! Just look at a hundred professions you might go into: if you find ten men who've made their fortunes quickly, everyone will tell you they're thieves. Draw your own conclusions. This is the way things are. Life's no prettier than a kitchen, it stinks just as bad, and if you want to get anything done you have to get your hands dirty: just make sure you know to wash them off: that's the beginning and end of morality, these days.

"Believe me, youngster, if I talk to you about the world this way, I've earned the right, I know what I'm saying. And do you think I'm critical? Not a bit. It's always been like this. The moralists are never going to change anything. Man's an imperfect creature. He gets either more or less hypocritical, depending, and then all the idiots say he's either gotten better or he's gotten worse. And I don't think common people are any better than rich ones: human beings are the same no matter where you find them. Take a million of these fancy cattle, and you'll find ten wide-awake fellows who climb right to the top, laws or no laws: I'm one of them.

"And if you're one, too, go straight ahead and keep your eyes open. Never stop worrying about jealousy, and gossip, and mediocrity: they're all around you. Napoleon ran into a Minister of War, a fellow named Aubry, who tried to ship him out to the colonies. Stay alert! See if you can't get up, every morning, more determined than you were the night before.

"I'll make you an offer you can't refuse. Listen carefully. I've got a plan, you know what I mean? My idea is to go live like a patriarch on some great estate, maybe a hundred thousand acres, in the United States, down in the South. I want to have a plantation, and slaves, make a couple of million a year selling my beef, my tobacco, my wood, living like a king, doing what I feel like, leading the kind of life you can't even imagine, here, where a man has to hide in a little plaster hole. I'm like a great poet, but I don't write my poems: my poems are what I do, what I feel. I've got fifty thousand francs, which wouldn't buy me more than forty Negroes. I've got to have two hundred thousand francs, because it won't be what I want unless I have two hundred Negroes. These Negroes, you know what I mean? They're like little children, you can make them do whatever you want, without some nosey district attorney snooping around. Then, with this black capital in hand, in ten years I'll have three or four million francs. And if I do, no one's going to ask me: "Who are *you*, eh?" I'll be Mister Four Million, American citizen. I'll be maybe fifty years old, still more than strong enough, and I'll have my fun, let me tell you. So here's my offer: if I get you a dowry of a million francs, will you give me two hundred thousand? Twenty percent commission—hey, is that too much? I tell you what, you make the lady really love you. And once you're married, you let her see you're worried, something's really bothering you, you're sad for two weeks at a time. So one night, after you've been fooling around, you tell her, between two kisses, and calling her "My love!" that you owe two hundred thousand francs. Some of the most distinguished young men in Paris play this little game all the time. No young woman closes her purse to a man she loves. Do you think you could lose anything? No. You'll cook up something to get the money back. With the money you'll have, and the brain you've already got, you'll pile up just as big a fortune as you want.

"Accordingly, in just six months you'll have made yourself happy, and your charming wife, and also your old man Vautrin, not counting your entire family, who sniffle all over their fingers, wintertime, for lack of wood. So don't be surprised either by what I'm suggesting or by what I want out of it! Take any sixty good marriages, here in Paris, and this is how forty-seven of them were made. Just the other day, the Chamber of Notaries forced Monsieur . . ."

"So what do I have to do?" asked Rastignac greedily, interrupting him.

"In fact, almost nothing," replied Vautrin, with an involuntary start of pleasure, like a fisherman who suddenly feels a fish on the end of his line. "Just listen! When a young woman is wretchedly miserable, her heart's like a dry sponge just waiting to fill itself with love, ready to swell up the moment a drop of emotion reaches it. Courting a young person who's all alone and solitary, overwhelmed by despair and poverty, a girl who has absolutely no idea she's to have a fortune—damn! That's playing poker with a straight flush in your hand, that's knowing in advance what numbers will win the lottery, that's gambling on the stock market after you get a hot tip. You're driving in the pilings for an indestructible marriage. When she gets her millions, she'll throw them at your feet as if they were pebbles. 'Here, my belovèd, take them! They're yours, Adolphe! They're yours, Alfred! They're yours, Eugène!' That's what she'll say, if Adolphe and Alfred and Eugène have been willing to make sacrifices for her. 'Sacrifices': that means selling an old suit so the two of you can have a bite to eat at a good restaurant, like the Blue Dial, and then maybe to a vaudeville show; it means hocking your watch so you can buy her a shawl. I won't tell you all about love-tricks, the cock-and-bull stuff most women gobble up, like, for example, spilling a few drops of water onto the paper, as if they were tears, when you're far away from her: it's my guess you know all about that kind of love-language.

"You see, Paris is like some great forest over in America,

where there are twenty different tribes of Indians, Illinois and Huron and the rest, each of them living a life that's structured by a completely different sort of hunting; what you're hunting is millions. If you're going to catch them, you have to use traps and snares, decoys and lures. There are all sorts of ways to hunt millions. Some go after dowries; some look for estates being settled; these fellows over here sniff after consciences, which means votes (and they're always for sale), and those over there set up an 'independent' newspaper and sell their subscribers like sheep to the market. Any hunter who comes back with his bag stuffed full is welcomed, celebrated, received by high society. We have to give credit where credit's due; Paris is a wide-open town, absolutely the most accommodating city in the world. Proud aristocrats all over Europe may refuse to open their doors to some millionaire rascal, but Paris takes him right into her arms, comes running when he gives parties and balls, eats his dinners and clinks his dishonorable glass."

"But where do I find such a woman?" asked Eugène.

"She's right here in front of you!"

"Mademoiselle Victorine?"

"Exactly!"

"But what are you talking about?"

"She's already in love with you, my dear little Baron de Rastignac!"

"She hasn't got a penny," replied Eugène, astonished.

"Ah, there we are! Two more words," said Vautrin, "and you'll understand everything. Daddy Taillefer's an old rogue who's said to have killed one of his friends, during the Revolution. When I mentioned people who don't give a damn about public opinion, I was talking about jolly fellows like him. He's a banker, senior partner in Maison Frédéric Taillefer and Company. He has just one son, to whom he'd like to leave his entire estate, cutting out

Mademoiselle Victorine. Now, I don't like to see anyone playing unfair like that. I'm a regular Don Quijote, I like defending the weak against the strong. Understand me: should God in His wisdom deprive old Taillefer of his son, he'd take up his daughter again: he's got to have an heir of some kind, any kind, because that's the kind of savage idiot he is—and he can't have any more children, I know that. Victorine is a nice, sweet girl, it won't take her long to twist her father around her finger; she'll have him spinning like a German top, he'll be so wound up with emotion! She'll respond far too well to your lovemaking to forget you, she'll marry you right off the bat.

"You see? I play the role of Fate, our good Lord's wishes are in my hands. I have a friend for whom I gave up a great deal—he's a colonel in the Army, until recently stationed in the Loire district, but now he's going to be in the Royal Guard. He'll do what I tell him; he's turned himself into a devout royalist, not like those idiots who just stick to their principles. If I've a piece of advice for you, my angel, it's this: honor your opinions no more than you do your promises. If they ask you to sell them, name your price. A man who boasts about never changing his views is a man who's decided always to travel in a straight line—the kind of idiot who believes in absolutes. But there are no principles, just things that happen; there are no laws, either, just circumstances, and the superior man espouses both events and circumstances, so he can guide them. If there really were fixed principles and absolute laws, people wouldn't go on changing them the way we change our shirts. No man needs to be wiser than a whole nation of men. The fellow who's been of less service to France than anyone else around has been turned into a kind of idol; people adore him because he's always seen everything colored bright red, but all he's really good for is to be exhibited in the Museum, somewhere in the machine section, with a label saying 'This is Lafayette,' while that prince everyone throws stones at, and despises most of humanity so fiercely that he'd cheerfully spit any oath they want, right in their faces, it was him, it was Talleyrand, who kept the Congress of Vienna from splitting France into little pieces: he deserves a crown, but they only throw mud at him.

"Oh, let me tell you, I know what's going on! I'm in on a lot of men's secrets! But that's enough. I'll get myself some unshakable opinions the day I run across three men who agree about what principles are good for—and I've been looking for those three men for a long time! You certainly won't find three judges in any court who agree about any article in the Code Napoléon. But let me get back to my colonel. He'd put Jesus Christ back on the Cross, if I told him to. All I need to do is say one word, and he'll pick a quarrel with that son of a bitch, that Taillefer kid who doesn't send a lousy penny to his sister. And then . . ."

Vautrin rose, assumed a fencing stance, and proceeded to act out the movement of a master swordsman making a fatal thrust.

"And he'll do it without any fuss at all!" he finished.

"Good Lord!" said Eugène. "You're joking, aren't you, Monsieur Vautrin?"

"Oh ho ho, take it easy," said the other. "Don't act like a child—but all right, if it makes you feel better, go ahead and get angry! Pitch yourself a regular fit! Tell me I'm a swine, a scoundrel, a dirty rascal, a gangster—just as long as you don't call me a swindler or a spy! Go on, go on, fire your broadside! I forgive you, it's natural enough, at your age! I've done the same thing myself! But then, stop and think. You'll do worse things, someday. You'll flirt with some pretty woman and she'll give you money. You've already thought of it!" said Vautrin. "Because how can you possibly succeed, unless you get paid for love? Ah, my dear student, virtue isn't a now-and-then business: either it's there, or it isn't. They tell us we're supposed to do penance for our sins. What a charming approach, eh? You shed your crimes just by saying you're sorry! Seducing some woman, just to get your foot on such-and-such a step on the social ladder—setting all the children in some family at each other's throats—all those ghastly things we do, either secretly, or just for our own pleasure, or just in our own interest—tell me: do you really think that's all faith, hope, and charity? Why give a dandy two months in prison, for stealing half a child's inheritance in one night's work, but throw the kitchen sink at some poor devil who steals a thousand francs and gets a little rough in the process? But that's your law for you! Every sentence in the whole Code of laws shines with absurdities. The man with a slick tongue, wearing fancy yellow gloves, does some assassinating that doesn't make any blood flow, though blood's been given, all right; the other murderer opens your door with a burglar's jimmy: but they're both operating under cover of night! The only difference between what I'm proposing and what you're surely going to do, someday, is that this time you won't need to shed any blood. How can you possibly believe in anything absolute, in a world like this! You've got to be contemptuous of human beings, and find yourself open spaces, gaps in the law's nets, and crawl right through them. The secret of all great fortunes, when there's no obvious explanation for them, is always some forgotten crime—forgotten, mind you, because it's been properly handled."

"That's enough! I don't want to hear any more, I'll end by doubting myself: the only things I know for sure, right now, are my own feelings."

"Relax, my charming child. I'd thought you were stronger," said Vautrin. "I won't say anything more. Just one final word." He stared at the student fixedly. "You are in on my secret," he said slowly.

"A young man who can turn you down won't have any trouble forgetting it."

"Ah, that's well said, I like that. Someone else, you know, is likely to be less scrupulous. Just remember what I'm prepared to do for you. I'll give you two weeks. Take it or leave it."

"He's as hard as iron, that fellow!" said Rastignac to himself, watching Vautrin walk calmly off, his cane under his arm. "He told me in so many words exactly what Madame de Beauséant said to me, though he put it politely. He was ripping at my heart with steel claws. Why was I planning to call on Madame de Nucingen? He knew what I was up to just as soon as I'd shaped the idea. In a few minutes, this highwayman told me more about virtue than all the men I've known and all the books I've read. If you really can't be virtuous and make exceptions, have I in fact robbed my sisters?" he wondered, first picking up and then dropping his money packages back onto the table. He sat down once more, and stayed where he was, lost in stunned meditation. "To be faithful to virtue is to be a sublime martyr! Nonsense! Everyone believes in virtue, but who's actually virtuous? Freedom is everyone's idol, but where on earth do you find a free people? These youthful years of mine are still as clear as a cloudless sky: if you decide to be great, to be rich, isn't that a decision to lie, compromise, grovel—and then stand tall again? To flatter, to deceive? Haven't you agreed to be a flunky for those who have already lied, and compromised, and groveled? Before you can be their accomplice, you have to be their servant. Hah! No. I want to work nobly, purely; I want to work night and day, I want a fortune I've earned. Maybe it will be the slowest of fortunes, but every night I'll lay my head on my pillow, knowing my conscience is clear. What could be better than to look back at your life and find it as pure as a lily? Life and me, we're like a young man and the girl he's engaged to. Vautrin's made me see what can happen, after ten years of marriage. Damn! I can't make heads or tails of it. I don't want to try thinking it through: the heart's a good enough guide."

He was roused from his reverie by the voice of fat Sylvie, calling that his tailor had arrived; Eugène came in, the packages of money still in his hands, and wasn't a bit sorry to have the man see him thus endowed. After trying on his evening wear, he put on his new morning garments, which completely transformed him.

"I'm every bit as good as Monsieur de Trailles!" he assured himself. "Finally, I really look like a gentleman!"

"My dear sir," said Père Goriot, coming into his room, "you asked me if I know which houses Madame de Nucingen frequents?"

"Yes!"

"Well then! This next Monday she'll be at Marshall Carigliano's ball. If you can be there, do please tell me if my daughters were having a good time, and what they were wearing—and all the rest of it."

"How did you manage to learn all this, my good Père Goriot?" asked Eugène, making the old man sit down near his fire.

"Her maidservant told me. It's Thérèse and Constance who tell me about everything they do," he went on happily. The old man looked much like a lover, still young enough to be delighted by some stratagem that, without her knowing about it, let him stay in touch with his mistress. "You'll see them—but I won't," he said, naively envious.

"Perhaps not," said Eugène. "I plan to ask Madame de Beauséant if she'll introduce me to the Marshall's wife."

He felt a kind of inner satisfaction, thinking of presenting himself at the vicomtesse's home, dressed as from now on he would always be. What philosophers call the abysses of the human heart are no more than self-deceiving thoughts, the involuntary effects of self-interest. Such violent inner swings, such sudden changes, which have been the target of so many diatribes, are in fact calculations we make for the sake of our pleasures. Seeing himself well dressed, with proper gloves and well-fitting boots, Rastignac forgot his virtuous resolution. Youth cannot afford to look at itself in the mirror of conscience, when it begins to bend from the straight and narrow, though people of mellower years have long since seen that reflection of themselves: the whole difference between the two stages of life lies right there.

Of late, the two neighbors, Eugène and Père Goriot, had become good friends. Their secret friendship was based on psychological factors which, in the case of the student and Vautrin, had created quite different feelings. The bold philosopher who will someday formulate just what effects our feelings produce in the material world will find, surely, more than one proof of their effective operation, in that realm, in the links they create between humans and animals. Is there a judge better able to deduce a man's character from his face than a dog who has to decide whether or not a stranger will be friendly? That proverbial expression we all use, "linked atoms," is one of those solid linguistic facts to be found in all languages, giving the lie to the foolish prating of those who love to rummage in the dung heaps of primitive words. People *feel* themselves loved. That sense is visible everywhere, it flits across all boundaries. A letter is like a living soul, such a wonderfully faithful echo of its sender's voice that, for truly sensitive hearts, letters are one of love's richest treasures. Père Goriot, whose unthinking emotion lifted his canine nature almost to sublime levels, had sniffed the compassion, the warm goodwill, the youthful sympathy the student's heart felt for him. This newborn linkage had not, however, led to any exchange of confidences. Eugène might have indicated his interest in meeting Madame de Nucingen, but it had not been because he expected the old man to introduce him; he simply hoped that some indiscretion might assist him. And for his part, Père Goriot had spoken to Eugène about his daughters only in connection with what he'd allowed himself to reveal, the day they had both visited him.

"My dear sir," the old man had said, "why did you suppose Madame de Restaud might have wanted to hear you pronounce my name? My daughters love me. I am a contented father. But my two sons-in-law are not well disposed toward me. I haven't wanted these two dear creatures to suffer because their husbands and I do not get along, so I've preferred to see them only in secret. Other fathers, who can see their daughters whenever they like, couldn't possibly understand how this little mystery affords me a thousand delights. I simply can't do it, do you see? So when the weather's good, first I ask my daughters' maids if they've gone out, and then I go walking along the Boulevard Champs-Élysées. I wait for them to come by, my heart begins to pound as soon as their carriages appear, I admire how they're dressed, and as they go by they throw me a little laugh that splashes gold over everything, just like the rays from some beautiful sun. And then I stay there, because of course they have to come back. And then I see them again! Being out in the fresh air has done them good, they're all rosy. I can hear people saying, all around me, 'Now there's a beautiful woman!' It makes me incredibly happy. She's my own flesh and blood, do you see? I love the horses that pull them; I'd love to be the little dogs they hold on their laps. I get to see their pleasures. We all have our own way of loving, and mine doesn't do anyone any harm, so why is everyone so interested in me? I have my own kind of happiness. Is it against the law for me to go out at night and look at my daughters, just as they leave their houses to go off to a ball? And how disappointing it is if I'm there too late, and they tell me, 'Madame's already left.' One morning I waited out there for almost three hours, to look at Nasie, because it had been two days since I'd seen her. I almost burst with joy!

"Please, only talk about me if you're going to say how nice to me my daughters are. They keep trying to load me down with all sorts of gifts, but I stop them, I tell them, 'Keep your money!' And what *should* I do? I don't need anything. And anyway, my dear sir, what am I? A wicked old corpse whose soul goes wherever my daughters go. Now when you've seen Madame de Nucingen, you can tell me which of the two you like best!" the old man said, after a moment of silence, seeing that Eugène was preparing to take a walk in the Tuilleries, awaiting the proper time to make his visit to Madame de Beauséant.

This walk, however, completed the student's downfall. There were women who noticed him. He was so handsome, so young, and resplendent in such very good taste! And finding himself the object of an attention virtually admiring, he stopped thinking about his sisters or the aunt he'd despoiled, or about his virtuous horror. He'd seen fluttering over his head the speckled wings of that demon so easily mistaken for an angel, Satan, who sprinkles down rubies, who aims his golden arrows at palaces, draping women in imperial purple, casting a foolish glory on thrones (in fact so utterly simple in their origin); he had heard in his ears the sizzling voice of that god of vanity, whose tinsel strikes us as a symbol of power. Vautrin's words, no matter how cynical, had lodged every bit as deep in his heart as, in some ancient virgin's memory, there lies an image of some old saleslady's wretched face, cackling, "Oh, you'll have money and love to spare!"

After loitering lazily about, at about five in the afternoon Eugène presented himself at Madame de Beauséant's, where he fell victim to one of those terrible blows against which youthful hearts are helpless. To that point, he had always found the vicomtesse overflowing with friendly politeness, that sweet-flowing grace conferred by an aristocratic education, and which is never truly there unless it comes, automatically and unthinkingly, straight from the heart.

As he entered, Madame de Beauséant made an impatient gesture and said, in a curt voice,

"Monsieur de Rastignac, I simply can't see you, not at least right now! I'm far too busy . . ."

For anyone who had learned the social code, and Rastignac had absorbed it all in a flash, these words, that gesture, that look, that inflection in her voice, summed up all there was to know about the nature and the ways of men and women of her class. He was vividly aware of the iron hand underneath the velvet glove; the personality, and especially the self-centeredness, under the polished manners; the plain hard wood, under all the varnish. He could finally hear the "I THE KING!" which starts under the plumes waving over the throne and spreads till it hits home under the helmet of the lowest gentleman among gentlemen. Eugène had been entirely too quick to take this woman's word for her own kindness. Like all those who cannot help themselves, he had signed on the dotted line, accepting the delightful contract binding both benefactor and recipient, the very first clause of which makes clear that, as between noble souls, perfect equality must be forever maintained. Beneficence, which ties people together, is a heavenly passion, but a thoroughly misunderstood one, and quite as scarce as true love. Both stem from the lavish nature of great souls. Rastignac badly wanted to attend the Duchess of Carigliano's ball, so he choked back his annoyance.

"Madame," he said in an emotion-laden voice, "if it had not been an urgent matter, I should not have imposed on you. Please be so good as to let me see you later: I will wait."

"In that case! Come have dinner with me," she declared, a bit embarrassed at how harshly she had spoken, for she was in fact quite as good a woman as she was a great lady.

Stung by this sudden reversal, Eugène nevertheless told himself, as he turned and left, "Grovel, take whatever comes. Good Lord, what must the others be like if, at the drop of a hat, the very best of women wipes away her promises and drops you like an old shoe? Every man for himself, eh? On the other hand, it's certainly true that her house is hardly a shop, to which you go when you want to buy something, and it's also true that it's wrong for me to need her so badly. As Vautrin says, you have to turn yourself into a human cannonball."

But these bitter thoughts were soon dissipated, as the student thought of what a pleasure it would be, dining at the viconmtesse's table. It is astonishing how, like a kind of predestination, even life's minor events conspire to push you forward, in that life's work in which, as the terrible sphinx of Maison Vauquer had declared, you find yourself as if on a battlefield, and you kill to keep from being killed, you deceive to keep from being deceived—a battlefield at the gate of which he had no choice but to lay down conscience, and his heart, put on a mask, compete with absolutely no pity for anyone else and, as in ancient Sparta, seize his fortune without anyone seeing him, so he might deserve to have the crown placed on his head.

When he came back, he found the vicomtesse overflowing with that bounteous graciousness she had always shown him. They went to the dining room together; the vicomte was waiting for his wife; and the table shone with that luxury which, as everyone knows, was after the restoration of the monarchy raised to the very highest pitch. Like many of those in the bored upper crust, the pleasures of the table were virtually the only ones Monsieur de Beauséant could enjoy; in fact, he was a gourmand of the same school as Louis XVIII and the Duke d'Escars. The delights proffered by his table, accordingly, were double, embracing both what was eaten and the setting provided for its consumption.

No such spectacle had ever struck Eugène's eye, for this was the first time he had ever dined in an establishment in which social greatness was hereditary. It was no longer the height of fashion to have supper, when a ball was over, as it had been under the Empire, when soldiers needed to fortify themselves, keeping constantly ready for the fighting they had to engage in, both indoors and out. All Eugène had done, so far, was go to a ball. He had already begun to develop that self-assurance which, later, would so clearly distinguish him, and it kept him from gaping and gawking. All the same, seeing this ornate silver, all the thousand elegances of a sumptuously set table, and for the first time in his life witnessing a meal served without a sound being made, it was exceedingly difficult for a man of quick and passionate a temperament not to prefer this life of continual elegance to the life of privation which, that morning, he had been so willing to embrace. His mind took him back, for a moment, to Maison Vauquer, and he experienced such a sense of profound horror that he swore to leave there in the very first month of the new year, quite as much to have himself in some decent establishment as to flee from Vautrin, whose large hand he could feel on his shoulder. And if you stop to think of the thousand forms which corruption takes, in Paris, whether open or unobserved, a sensible man might well wonder by what aberration the State decided to set its schools in that city and bring together so many young men, and how pretty women can be safe, walking Parisian streets, and how on earth the wealth displayed by money changers keeps from sprouting wings and flying right out of their alms-bowls. And yet when you consider how few serious crimes in fact take place—indeed, how few breaches of the peace of any sort these young people actually commit—how admiring must we be of these patient Tantaluses, constantly struggling to control themselves and almost always victorious! Properly drawn, the perpetual struggle between impoverished students and the city of Paris would constitute one of the most dramatic canvases of our entire modern civilization.

Madame de Beauséant kept looking over at Eugène, trying to induce him to participate in the conversation, but in the vicomte's presence he had no desire to say a word.

"Are you taking me to the opera tonight?" she asked her husband.

"Can you doubt the pleasure it would give me to oblige you?" he answered with a sardonic gallantry that quite took in the student, "but I have a previous commitment to meet someone at the vaudeville theater."

"Ah, his mistress," she assured herself.

"You won't be seeing Ajuda tonight?" the vicomte asked his wife.

"No," she said irritably.

"Well then! If you absolutely require an escort, why not rely on Monsieur de Rastignac?"

Laughing, the vicomtesse turned to Eugène.

"Now that might really compromise you," she said to the student.

Eugène replied, inclining his head,

" 'The French love danger,' Monsieur de Chateaubriand has said, 'because that's also where they find glory.' "

It was not too long thereafter that, in a fast gig, he and Madame de Beauséant went rattling toward the fashionable theater, and when he walked into her luxurious box, overlooking the stage, and noted how all the opera glasses had turned to survey him and the vicomtesse at his side (her dress was a thing of wonder), he began to believe in fairy godmothers. He was moving from one enchantment to another.

"You must talk to me," Madame de Beauséant informed him.

"But there's Madame de Nucingen! just three boxes from us. Her sister and Monsieur de Trailles are over on the other side."

While she was speaking, the vicomtesse glanced at the box occupied by Mademoiselle de Rochefide, and when she did not spy Monsieur Ajuda there, her face began to glow with extraordinary pleasure.

"She's quite charming," Eugène declared, after surveying Madame de Nucingen.

"Her eyebrows are white."

"But what a delightful slim figure!"

"Her hands are too large."

"And such beautiful eyes!"

"Her face is much too long."

"But height adds distinction."

"How lucky that must make her. Just see how she fools with her opera glass! Every movement she makes fairly reeks of the Goriot in her," declared the vicomtesse, to Eugène's utter astonishment.

In fact, Madame de Beauséant was surveying the entire theater, apparently paying no attention to Madame de Nucingen, but she noted every gesture the other woman made. The audience was truly a thing of beauty. Delphine de Nucingen was immensely flattered to have so caught the attention of Madame de Beauséant's young, handsome, elegant cousin, for it was clear that he was looking at no one but her.

"If you go on staring at her like that, Monsieur de Rastignac, you'll create a scandal. You'll never accomplish anything, if you throw yourself at people like that."

"My dear cousin," said Eugène, "your assistance has been admirable; if you want to complete the task, all I ask of you is a small service that will cause you very little pain and will do me a world of good. I am smitten."

"So soon?"

"Yes."

"With *that* woman?"

"Is there anyone else with whom I could be successful?" he observed, giving her a knowing look. "Now, the Duchess of Carigliano is devoted to the Duchess de Berry," he went on after a moment. "You will surely be seeing her, so if you'll just be good enough to introduce me and to bring me to the ball she's giving this Monday. I'll meet Madame de Nucingen there, and undertake my first skirmish."

"Gladly," she said. "If you're already so taken with her, your affairs of the heart are going very well indeed. There's de Marsay, over in Princess Galathion's box. Madame de Nucingen is clearly in pain and agony. What better moment for making your approach to a woman, particularly a banker's wife? These women from Chausée d'Antin love their revenge."

"And what would you do, in her place?"

"I would suffer in silence."

Just then the Marquis Ajuda-Pinto appeared in Madame de Beauséant's box.

"I've rather made a mess of things, in order to come to you," he said, "which I tell you so my efforts won't have been entirely in vain."

The glow on the vicomtesse's face showed Eugène what true love looked like, and how to clearly distinguish it from the mere affectations of Parisian coquetry. Impressed, he quietly yielded his place to the marquis.

"What a noble—what a sublime creature is a woman who loves like this!" he sighed to himself. "And this fellow's betraying her for a rag doll! How could *anyone* betray her?"

He felt childishly angry. He could have groveled at her feet, he wished he had some demonic power with which to carry her off, clutched close to his heart, the way an eagle soars up from the plain to its mountain nest, bearing a small white suckling goat.

He was also humiliated, finding himself in such a grand Museum of Beauty without a picture of his own—that is, a beautiful mistress of his own.

"A mistress, and an almost royal post," he said to himself. "That's real power!"

He gave Madame de Nucingen a quick glance, like a man just insulted, glaring at his enemy. Then the vicomtesse turned toward him, a flickering of her eyelids indicating her great gratitude for his discretion. Act One was now over.

"You know Madame de Nucingen well enough, don't you," she said to the Marquis, "to introduce Monsieur de Rastignac to her?"

"She'll be delighted to meet him!" the marquis replied.

Rising, the handsome Portuguese took Eugène's arm—and in the twinkling of an eye, there he was, right in front of Madame de Nucingen.

"My dear Baroness," said the marquis, "I have the honor to present to you the Chevalier Eugène de Rastignac, a cousin of the Vicomtesse de Beauséant. You've made such an extraordinary impression on him that I thought it only right to complete his happiness by bringing him directly to his idol."

He spoke these words in a bantering way which softened a rather coarse notion, but one that, thus gracefully disguised, never makes a woman unhappy. Madame de Nucingen smiled and offered Eugène her husband's place, that gentleman having just left.

"I don't dare suggest that you stay here," she said to Rastignac. "Anyone fortunate enough to be near Madame de Beauséant is sure to stay right where he is."

"Ah," Eugène said softly, "It seems to me that, the better to please my cousin, I ought to stay right here. Before the marquis came," he added in a normal voice, "we were in fact talking only of you, and how well you looked."

The marquis left.

"You really intend to stay with me?" the baroness asked. "We'll have a chance to become acquainted: Madame de Restaud's given me a lively interest in meeting you."

"Then she's not telling you the truth, for she showed me to the door."

"I beg your pardon?"

"Madame, my conscience bids me tell· you the truth, but I must beg your indulgence in confiding such a secret to your ears. I live next door to your father. I had no idea that Madame de Restaud was his daughter. I was sufficiently incautious to speak of him, all innocently, which much angered both your sister and her husband. You wouldn't believe in what bad taste the Duchess of Langeais and my cousin thought this rejection of your father. I told them all about it, and they laughed themselves sick. And then, comparing you and your sister, Madame de Beauséant spoke of you in warm terms, madame, and told me how good you always were to my neighbor, Monsieur Goriot. And indeed, how could you not love him? He adores you so passionately that, in truth, I find myself a little jealous. This morning, in fact, we spent two hours talking about you. And then, tonight, dining with my cousin, still full of all your father and I had been saying about you, I remarked that you couldn't possibly be as beautiful as you were loving. Wanting, surely, to be kind to so warm an admiration, Madame de Beauséant brought me here, informing me with her typical gracefulness that I would see for myself."

"How strange," the banker's wife observed, "that I'm already indebted to you! It won't be long before we're old friends."

"Friendship with you, madame, could hardly be an everyday

affair," said Rastignac. "But to be your friend is not what I could ever long for."

Women are always fond of these amateurish clichés, which only seem inept when one reads them off a page. They take on incomparable weight, decorated with a young man's gestures, his voice, his glances. Madame de Nucingen was charmed by Rastignac. But, like all women, unable to respond when anyone lays it on as heavily as the student had done, she changed the subject.

"I must admit my sister *is* wrong, treating my poor father like that: he's really been virtually godlike to the two of us. I'd never have yielded on this question, myself, except that Monsieur de Nucingen flatly ordered me to see my father only in the morning. But for a long time now that's been making me exceedingly unhappy. It's reduced me to tears. This sort of duress, coming hard on the heels of all the other brutalities of marriage, has been one of the principal difficulties troubling our household. I dare say there's not a woman in Paris who, though she may seem utterly happy, is in fact more miserable. You'll think me an idiot for talking to you like this. But you're my father's friend and for that reason you can scarcely be a stranger to me."

"I don't think you've ever met anyone," Rastignac told her, "who feels so warm a desire to be close to you. What, after all, are you looking for? Happiness," he said, carefully lowering his voice; it struck her to the core. "Well then! If a woman's happiness is to be loved, adored, to have a friend to whom she can confide all her desires, her dreams, her sorrows, her joys; to bare her soul, exhibit her pretty faults and her beautiful virtues, without the slightest fear of being betrayed: believe me, a heart capable of such unchanging devotion, and such unceasing warmth, can only be found in the breast of an overflowingly idealistic young man, one capable of dying at a wave of your hand, a man who still knows nothing of the world and has no interest in knowing it, because, for him, you have become the world.

"You'll laugh at me, I know you will, for all my naïveté, because here I am, fresh from the provinces, as green as grass, having known only good country people, and never expecting to be assaulted by love. I happened to visit my cousin, who's virtually adopted me, and it's she who has made me aware of passion's thousand treasures; like Mozart's Cherubino, I love all women, while I wait until I can devote myself exclusively only to one among them all. And when I saw you, as I came in here tonight, I felt myself swept foward as if by some swift current. And I've already thought so much about you! Not that I dreamed you'd be as beautiful as in fact you are. Madame de Beauséant told me not to stare at you as I was doing. But how can she know how drawn I was, seeing your lovely red lips, your white skin, your soft, sweet eyes. Ah, you see? I too say foolish things. But let me say them!"

Nothing delights women so much as having such sweet words recited to them. The most prudish among them will listen, even when she does not dare reply. Having thus begun, Rastignac fired off round after round, in a voice flirtatiously muffled, and Madame de Nucingen spurred him on with smiles, from time to time glancing over at de Marsay, who was still in the Princess Galathion's box. Rastignac stayed with Madame de Nucingen until just before her husband returned, to bring her home.

"Madame," Eugène told her, "I expect to have the pleasure of calling on you before the Duchess of Carigliano's ball."

"Und zince mine wife eggspecks you," remarked the baron, a heavily built Alsatian whose plump face suggested dangerous subtlety, "denn vill you be vell velcomed."

As Eugène went to say goodbye to Madame de Beauséant, who was just preparing to leave with the Marquis Ajuda-Pinto, he said to himself,

"I've got this well under way, because she didn't seem particularly startled, hearing me say, 'And you? will you love me too?' The mare's got my bit between her teeth: now we need to jump on and make her go where we want." The poor student did not realize that the baroness had barely been listening to him, waiting as she was to receive from de Marsay one of those decisive letters that tear up your soul. Delighted with this quite unreliable success, Eugène walked with his cousin until they got to the inner archway where people waited for their carriages.

"Your cousin scarcely seemed the same man," said the marquis, laughing, as soon as Eugène had left them. "I dare say he'll break the bank. He's as flexible as an eel: he'll go far, I'm sure he will. And who but you could have picked out a woman for him, just exactly when she'd be needing consolation."

"Yes," said Madame de Beauséant, "but first we have to find out if she's still in love with the one who's jilting her."

EUGÈNE WALKED HOME to New Saint Geneviève Street, building all sorts of fairy castles in his head. He was well aware of how Madame de Restaud had been watching him, whether in Madame de Beauséant's box or Madame de Nucingen's, and he thought it likely that the countess's door would no longer be closed to him. And since he expected to do equally well at the Carigliano ball, he had now established four major connections, all right at the heart of Parisian high society. Without bothering to know exactly how he knew, he already understood that, to rise to the top in this world's complex play of forces, he needed to hitch himself to some vehicle in motion.

"If Madame de Nucingen does indeed take an interest in me, I'll teach her how to handle her husband. The fellow's a major speculator, he's fairly rolling in golden opportunities, so he could help me rake in a fast fortune."

Nor did he say this to himself crudely; he was still too inexperienced to quickly evaluate a situation, weighing and balancing it in precise terms: his ideas drifted along the horizon like fast-moving clouds but, though they were nowhere near so hard and blunt as Vautrin's, had they been scrutinized in the test-tube of conscience, they would have yielded nothing of remarkable purity. A few transactions of this sort, and men come to acquire the loose moral standards of our time, in which straightforward, clearly moral characters are scarcer than ever before—those fine spirits never bent out of shape by evil, to whom indeed the least deviation from clean-handed directness seems positively criminal: magnificent portraits of truth and honesty displayed for us in masterpieces like Molière's *Alceste* and, more recently, in the persons of Jenny Deans and her father, in Walter Scott's novel *The Heart of Midlothian*. Perhaps works of a very different nature may succeed in being no less magmificent, and no less dramatic, despite the fact that they depict the turning and twisting by which an ambitious man of the world, who wants to reach his goal but still preserve appearances, manages to get around his conscience.

By the time he reached his doorstep, Rastignac had developed a warm passion for Madame de Nucingen, who seemed to him slender and slim, as delicate as a swallow. The intoxicating sweetness of her eyes, the silky softness of her skin (under which it seemed to him he could see the blood flowing), the enchanting sound of her voice, her blond hair—he remembered everything, and perhaps his long walk, which kept his own blood circulating vigorously, helped his fascination develop.

He banged loudly on Père Goriot's door.

"Neighbor," he said, "I saw Madame Delphine."

"Where?"

"At the opera."

"Was she happy? Come in, come in." And the good man, who had come to the door dressed only in his nightshirt, threw it open and quickly retreated to his bed.

"So tell me all about her," he asked.

Finding himself for the first time a visitor in Père Goriot's room, Eugène could not entirely disguise his shock, seeing the hovel in which the father dwelled, having so recently admired the daughter's clothing and jewels. The window was bare and curtainless; wallpaper was peeling off the walls, unglued, in spots, by the dampness, then curling up to reveal bare plaster, dingy and yellow from smoke. The old man was lying on a wretched mattress, covered by only a single thin blanket and a bedspread padded out with good-sized strips torn from Madame Vauquer's old dresses. The floor was damp and exceedingly dusty. Across from the window stood one of those squat old rosewood chests of drawers, its copper handles twisted like vines and embellished with leaves and flowers; a jug of water sat in the basin of an old woodblock washstand, along with shaving utensils. The old man's shoes sat on the floor, in a corner; there was a night table at the head of his bed, plain bare wood covered by no marble and with no door to swing on its hinges; in the chimney corner (there wasn't the slightest sign of a fire) was the square walnut table whose lower bar had enabled Père Goriot to twist his silver serving pieces into ingots. The room's miserable furnishings also included a shabby writing desk (on which lay the old man's hat), an armchair with a straw seat, and two plain chairs. The poorest of poor message-boys, holed up in his attic, was clearly better off than Père Goriot, here in Maison Vauquer. Looking like the worst cell in a prison, the room was a chilling, heart-knotting sight. Luckily, Goriot did not see the expression on Eugène's face, as he set his candle on the little night table. The good old man turned on his side, his covers pulled up around his chin.

"So! Who do you like better, Madame de Restaud or Madame de Nucingen?"

"I prefer Madame Delphine," the student replied, "because she more truly loves you."

At these words, passionately spoken, the old man stuck out both arms and grasped Eugène's hand.

"Thank you, thank you," he said, obviously deeply moved. "So what did she say about me?"

The student repeated the baroness's remarks, not without improving on them, and the old man listened as if hearing the very Words of God.

"What a dear child! Oh yes, yes, she does love me! But don't believe what she told you about Anastasie. You know, my girls are jealous of each other. But that's just another proof of their affection. Madame de Restaud loves me just as much. I know it. A father knows his children the way God knows us, he can penetrate right into their hearts, he can understand what they're thinking. They love me equally, believe me. If only I'd had decent sons-in-law, then I'd be happier than I can tell you! But you know as well as I do, there's no such thing as perfect happiness in this world. If I could have lived in their houses—just to hear their voices, just to know they were there, just to see them going out, the way I watched them before they were married, oh that would set my heart jumping! Were they both well-dressed?"

"Certainly," said Eugène. "But tell me, Monsieur Goriot: having daughters who lead lives of such luxury, how can you possibly live in a hovel like this?"

"Oh Lord," said the old man, with an air of absolute indifference, "what good would it do me to have anything better? I can't really explain these things; I don't have a tongue that can put together two consecutive words in proper style. But it's all in here," he went on, tapping at his heart. "For me, life is my two daughters. If they're having a good time, if they're happy, if they're all dressed up, if they get to walk on carpets, what difference does it make what kind of clothes I wear and what sort of room I lie down in? Their being warm doesn't make me cold; if they're happy and laughing, then I'm never bored. Their troubles are the only ones I have. When you get to be a father, when you'll say to yourself, listening to your own children babbling, 'That's my flesh and blood!' when you'll feel these tiny creatures clutching at every drop of your blood, of which they're the final, finest flower— because that's what they are!—you'll find yourself almost living in their skins, you'll feel as if it's you moving when they take a step. I hear their voices everywhere. One sad look from them, and my blood congeals. Someday you'll understand how their happiness makes you happier than your own. How can I explain it to you? It's as if something moves around inside you, and spreads peace and contentedness all over.

"What shall I say? I lead three lives. Shall I tell you something really funny? So! When I got to be a father, I understood God. He's everywhere, because the whole creation was born of Him. And that's how I am with my daughters. But I love my daughters better than God loves the world, because the world isn't as lovely as God is and my daughters are lovelier than I am. They're so much a part of me that, really, I felt as if you'd see them tonight. Oh Lord! if someone would make my little Delphine as happy as a woman is when she's really loved—Lord! I'd shine his shoes, I'd run his errands for him. Her maid's told me about this little de Marsay fellow, I know he's a dirty dog. I've felt like breaking his neck. Not to love such a jewel of a woman, with a voice like a nightingale, and a figure like a model! What on earth was she thinking of, marrying that fat Alsatian blockhead? They both de- served handsome young fellows, nice young fellows. Well, they've done what they wanted to do."

The old man was exalted. It was the first time Eugène had ever seen him, lit by the fires of his paternal passion. It's worth noting how powerfully emotion can work on us. No matter how gross we may be, the moment we breathe some strong, lively feeling it's as if that emotion emits a magical liquid that changes our face, quickens our movements, colors our voice. The stupidest man in the world, thus gripped by passion, can rise to absolute heights of eloquence—not perhaps in his actual words but certainly in his thoughts—and seem to move as if in some utterly luminous sphere. Goriot's voice, his every gesture, contained the communicative power of some great actor. For, after all, what are beautiful feelings but the soul's poetry?

"Well then! In that case, perhaps you won't be sorry to hear," Eugène told him, "she's clearly planning to break with this de Marsay. That Beau Brummel's thrown her over for the Princess Galathion. For my part, tonight, I've fallen in love with Madame Delphine."

"No!" Père Goriot exclaimed.

"Yes. She didn't dislike me, either. We made some pretty love-talk for an hour or so, and I'm to call on her Saturday afternoon, the day after tomorrow."

"Ah, how I'd love you, my dear sir, if you made her happy! You're a decent man, you wouldn't torment her. And if you betrayed her, why, I'd just break your neck. You see, a woman can't be in love with two men. But Lord! I'm babbling, Monsieur Eugène. And it must be too cold in here for you. Dear God! Since you were talking to her, what did she want you to tell me?"

"Nothing," Eugène said to himself.

"She told me," he said aloud, "that she sends you a good daughter's kiss."

"Goodnight then, neighbor, sleep well, have good dreams; you've already given me mine with that lovely message. May the

Good Lord smile down on you in whatever you do! You've been like a good angel to me, tonight: you've brought me the very likeness of my daughter."

"The poor old man," said Eugène to himself, as he lay down in his own bed. "It's enough to wring a heart of marble. His daughter no more thought of him than she did of the Grand Turk."

From that point on, Père Goriot saw his neighbor as an unexpected confidant, and a friend. The ties between them were the only ones by which the old man could have been attached to any other human being. Nor does strong emotion ever mislead us. Père Goriot foresaw that he would be somewhat closer to his daughter Delphine, and more welcomed by her, if she became fond of Eugène. And, besides, in his conversation with the student he had confessed one of his chief sorrows. Although he wished happiness for Madame de Nucingen a thousand times every day, she had yet to know the sweetness of love. And Eugène certainly was (to borrow the old man's own words) one of the nicest young men he had ever met; it seemed clear that the student would bring Delphine all those pleasures of which, till now, she had been deprived. So Goriot began to feel a constantly increasing friendliness for his neighbor—a sentiment, in fact, without which we would be in no position to set down the final outcome of this tale.

The next morning, at breakfast, the other boarders were surprised to see the affection with which Père Goriot looked at Eugène, next to whom he seated himself, and how the two conversed together, and above all how changed was the old man's face, usually so like a plaster mask. Vautrin, seeing the student for the first time since their little conference, seemed to be trying to plumb the young man's soul. Before he'd fallen asleep, Eugène had lain in the darkness, thinking of the vast fields opening out in front of him, and remembering the fellow's scheme he couldn't help thinking of Mademoiselle Taillefer's hypothetical dowry, nor could he keep himself from looking at Victorine as even the most virtuous young man in the world might look at a wealthy heiress. By pure chance, their eyes met. The poor girl could not help but find Eugène charming, in his new elegance. The glance they exchanged was quite significant enough for Rastignac to feel sure he was the subject of one of those vague longings that overcome all young girls and which they attach, helplessly, to the first tempting man who comes along. It was as if he heard a voice crying, "Eight hundred thousand francs!" But then his mind leaped back to its memories of the previous night, and it seemed to him that his overriding passion for Madame de Nucingen would provide an antidote for all such involuntary but evil notions.

"They were doing Rossini's *The Barber of Seville* at the opera last night," he declared suddenly. "I've never heard such delicious music. Oh Lord! what happiness it would be, having a box at the opera!"

Père Goriot seemed to snatch this remark right out of the air, as a dog might leap at its master's command.

"You're all a lot of fighting cocks," said Madame Vauquer, "all you men: you do whatever you want to."

"How did you get home?" Vautrin inquired.

"On foot," replied Eugène.

"Me," declared the Tempter, "I don't care for halfhearted pleasures: I'd go to the opera in my own carriage, and sit in my own box, and I'd come home again as comfortably as I went. All or nothing! That's my motto."

"And it's a very good one," declared Madame Vauquer.

"Perhaps you'll be seeing Madame de Nucingen," Eugène whispered to Goriot. "She'll surely welcome you with open arms; she'll probably ask you a thousand little questions about me. I happen to know she'd do anything to be received at my cousin's house, the Vicomtesse de Beauséant. Don't forget to tell her I love her far too well not to ensure exactly that gratification."

Rastignac left for the Law School as soon as he could, wanting to remain in that odious house as short a time as possible. But he spent almost the entire day walking here and there, as if in testimony to the brain fever experienced, to be sure, by all young men afflicted with exceedingly vivid hopes and expectations. Vautrin's arguments led him to thoughts of the entire social order, and he was thus deeply enmeshed when, in the Luxembourg Park, he bumped into his friend Bianchon.

"Where does that exceedingly solemn look come from?" the medical student wondered, taking his arm so they could walk on together.

"I've been tormented by evil thoughts."

"Of what sort? Ideas can cure you, you know."

"They can?"

"If you give in to them."

"You're laughing, but you don't know what you're talking about. Have you read Rousseau?"

"Certainly."

"Remember that passage where he asks his reader what he would do if, without ever leaving Paris, he could turn himself into a rich man simply by willing the death of some old Mandarin way off in China?"

"Yes."

"And?"

"Bah! I'm up to my thirty-third Mandarin."

"I'm not joking. Look, if you knew for a fact it was possible, and all you had to do was nod your head, would you do it?"

"Is he really good and old, this Mandarin? But, hey! young or old, paralyzed or still walking around, my Lord . . . Damn! Anyway, no."

"You're a good fellow, Bianchon. But now suppose you loved a woman, loved her to desperation, and she didn't have the money she needed, lots of money for her clothes, for her carriage—for everything she's always dreamed about?"

"Ah, but you're trying to sweep away my rationality, and then you ask me to give you reasoned arguments."

"So! Bianchon, I'm out of my head: cure me. I have two sisters, both of them angels of beauty, of innocent artlessness, and I want them to be happy. How do I spend five years getting them each a dowry of two hundred thousand francs? And you know very well there are times when you have to gamble big, when you can't risk using up all your luck just for the sake of pennies."

"But that's exactly the question everyone has to answer, when they start out, and you want to cut the Gordian Knot with a sword. But for that, old boy, you have to be Alexander, or else you go to jail. Me, I'll be satisfied with the petty life I'll make for myself in the country, where I'm destined to go clomping around in my father's shoes. Men can find what they want in the tiniest of circles, you know, just as easily as they can in some enormous circumference. Even Napoleon couldn't eat dinner twice, and he couldn't enjoy any more mistresses than a medical student acquires as a lowly hospital intern. Our good luck, my good friend, is always to be found somewhere between the soles of our feet and the occipital bone at the top of our head, and what's more, the internal perception is the same whether the experience costs us a million a year or a hundred francs. I vote for the Chinaman's life."

"Thank you, Bianchon! You've done me good. We'll always be friends."

"Then tell me," the medical student went on, as they emerged from Couvier Court and entered the Zoological Garden, "I've just seen the Michonneau woman and the Poiret man, seated on a bench and chatting with a man I remember seeing, last year, when we had all that rumpus around the Parliament Building—a man who looks to me like a policeman trying to disguise himself as just another honest middle-class citizen. So: let's keep our eyes on those two: I'll explain later. Goodbye. Right now, I have to run to my four o'clock class."

When he got back to Maison Vauquer, Eugène found Père Goriot waiting for him.

"Here," the old man said, "here's a letter from her. Ah, what a wonderful handwriting, eh?"

Eugène opened the letter and read:

> *Monsieur, My father tells me you love Italian music. It would please me if you would accept a place in my box at the opera. This Saturday we'll be hearing the soprano, Fodor, and the bass, Pellegrini, so I'm sure you won't say no. My husband joins with me in asking you, also, to come dine informally with us. If you can come, you'll make him very happy indeed, relieving him of his marital obligation to escort me to the theater afterwards. Don't bother to reply: simply come, and accept, please, my very best wishes,*
>
> D. de N.

"Let me see it," the old man said to Eugène, once the letter had been read. "You'll go, won't you?" he went on, after having sniffed at the paper. "Ah, that smells good! Right there, her fingers touched it right there!"

"But a woman doesn't throw herself at a man's head like that," Eugène said to himself. "She wants to use me to get de Marsay back. Spite's the only thing behind all this."

"Well? well?" said Père Goriot. "So what are you thinking?"

Eugène was quite unaware of the deliriums of vanity afflicting certain women, just then, having no idea that, to obtain a foothold in the Faubourg Saint-Germain, a mere banker's wife was capable of virtually any sacrifice. In that era, fashion put at the very top of the social heap any and all women who were recognized by the small world of the Faubourg Saint-Germain, known as "the Ladies of the Royal Circle," the leaders of whom were Madame de Beauséant, her friend the Duchess of Langeais, and the Duchess of Maufrigneuse. Only someone so isolated as Rastignac could have been ignorant of the absolute frenzy with which ladies of the Chausée-d'Antin clamored for entry into that superior circle where the very stars of their sex glittered and gleamed. But his wariness was useful, arming him with the coolness and the gloomy capacity to set conditions rather than simply accepting them.

"Yes, I'll go," he finally answered.

So it was curiosity which led him to Madame de Nucingen's, though had the lady spurned him, it might perhaps have been passion which took him there. All the same, he looked forward rather impatiently to the hour when he would finally set off. For a young man, his first intrigue probably has almost the same high interest as his first love. Guaranteed success creates a thousand pleasures that men are loath to admit; indeed, it constitutes the very charm of certain women. It is not the difficulties of a conquest which give rise to desire so much as its ease. Certainly, men's passions are either excited or sustained by one or the other of these two causes, which between them entirely divide up love's imperial realm. Arguably, this is a division founded in the whole great question of temperament—and no matter what anyone says, that is the key to all of human society. If melancholy types need coquetries to spur them on, nervous or sanguinary sorts are equally likely to pack up and run, when resistance lasts too long. Or, to put it differently, elegies are quite as essentially lymphatic as dithyrambs are bilious.

Dressing for the occasion, Eugène relished all those little

pleasures which young men don't dare talk about, for fear of being teased, but which for all that stimulate a young man's confidence. He combs his hair while fancying some pretty woman's gaze running over the dark ringlets. He allows himself some of the same infantile idiocies practiced by young girls, dressing themselves for a ball. Self-satisfied glances survey his trim figure, as he smooths out his outfit. "Certainly," he tells himself, "there'll be lots of men who won't look half as good!" And then he goes downstairs, just when all the lodgers are seated at dinner, and is the happy recipient of all the mocking cheers evoked by his elegant garb. Nobody sitting around that table can see a new suit without putting in his two cents worth.

"Giddyup, giddyup, giddyup!" called Bianchon, clicking his tongue on the roof of his mouth, as if spurring on a horse.

"Here comes a duke and peer of the realm!" said Madame Vauquer.

"You're off for a night of flirting?" noted Mademoiselle Michonneau.

"Co-co-ri-co!" crowed the painter.

"Give my best to the lady you're marrying," said the Museum employee.

"He's married?" cried Poiret.

And Vautrin called out,

"A wife with a smoking compartment, seaworthy, with just the right complexion, available for anywhere from twenty-five to forty francs, very latest design, easy to clean, long-wearing, part linen, part cotton, part wool, completely free of all dental disease and all other maladies approved by the Royal Academy of Medicine! And what's more, very good for children! Even better for headache, indigestion, and all other ailments of the throat, eyes, and ears!" He went on, with all the easy, comic volubility of a sideshow barker: "Now for this marvel, gentlemen, what am I bid?

Two sous? Not on your life. This is the genuine article, left over from the household of Genghis Khan, once owned by all the sovereigns of Europe, not to mention the Grrrrrrand Duke of Baden-Baden! Step right in, gentlemen! Get your tickets over here! Ah, and the music! One, two, three, four, one, two, three, four! Oh-ho, clarinetist, that was a wrong note," he growled huskily. "I'll have to crack you on the hands!"

"Lord, Lord! What a splendid man!" sighed Madame Vauquer, turning to Madame Couture. "I could never get bored, not with him around."

Amid all the laughter and jokes called forth by this comic speech, Eugène spotted a furtive glance from Mademoiselle Taillefer, who was leaning close to Madame Couture and whispering something in her ear.

"Cab's here," called Sylvie.

"And where's he going?" asked Bianchon.

"To Baroness de Nucingen's."

"Monsieur Goriot's daughter," Eugène added.

Hearing his name, they all turned to look at the former vermicelli maker, who was himself watching Rastignac enviously.

The Nucingens lived on Saint-Lazar Street, in one of those flighty houses, with thin columns and shabby porticoes, that people in Paris find "pretty," a real banker's house, resplendent with expensive affectation, with stuccoed walls, with staircase landings set in marble tile. He found Madame de Nucingen in a small room decorated with Italianate paintings, in a style much like that seen in cafés. The lady was despondent. Her attempts to hide her sadness piqued Eugène all the more because it was clearly not something put on for his benefit. He had expected to find a woman overjoyed to see him, but he found her truly miserable. He was somewhat offended.

"I know I have little claim on your confidence, madame," he

finally said, after a bit of teasing about her self-absorption, "but if in fact I'm somehow interfering, I count on you to simply say so, frankly and openly."

"Stay, stay," she said. "If you went away I'd be all alone. Nucingen's eating in town, and I don't want to be alone, I need to be distracted."

"But what's wrong?"

"You'd be the very last person I'd tell!" she exclaimed.

"Then I'd really like to know," he continued, "since I apparently do have something to do with it."

"Maybe! No, no," she went on, "it's one of those petty family arguments you have to bury right at the bottom of your heart. Didn't I say as much, the other day? I'm not as happy as I may seem. Golden chains are the heaviest of all."

When a woman tells a young man she's unhappy, and the young man is lively, and well dressed, and has fifteen hundred francs lying around in his pocket, he has no choice but to think as Eugène thought, and to do as Eugène did.

"What can you possibly want?" he replied. "You're beautiful, you're young, you're well-loved, you're rich."

"Let's not talk about me," she declared, shaking her head ominously. "We'll have dinner together, just the two of us, and then we'll hear the most enchanting music. How do I look?" she continued, standing up and displaying her white cashmere dress, decorated with sea-green figures of an obviously costly elegance.

"I wish you belonged to me," said Eugène. "You're utterly charming."

"You'd be acquiring a wretched property," she said with a bitter laugh. "You can't see my misfortune but, all the same, no matter how I look, I'm utterly miserable. My worries keep me awake at night, and soon I'll be an ugly witch."

"Impossible!" declared the student. "But I'm still curious to find out if a devoted love might somehow wipe away these troubles."

"Oh, but if I told you, you'd run off and leave me," she said. "Whatever affection you think you feel for me is simply typical male gallantry, but if you really did love me, you'd be crushed by the same horrible misery. You see, I have to keep it to myself. So please," she went on, "let's talk about something else. Come see my rooms."

"No, let's stay here," replied Eugène, dropping onto a small sofa in front of the fire, right next to Madame de Nucingen, and taking her hand with bold self-confidence.

She allowed him to hold her hand, and even pressed his, with one of those sudden, concentrated movements which indicate strong emotion.

"Now look here," said Eugène, "if you really have problems, you must tell me all about them. Give me the chance to prove I love you only because you're you. Either tell me your troubles, so I can deal with them, even if I have to kill half a dozen men in the process, or I'll get up and leave, and then I'll never come back."

"All right!" she cried, gripped by a wave of despair that made her strike her own forehead, "I'll put you right to the test. Yes," she said as if to herself, "there's no longer any other way."

She rang for the servant.

"Is my husband's carriage ready?"

"Yes, Madame."

"I'm taking it. Give him mine, and my horses. Don't serve dinner until seven.

"Come, let's go," she said to Eugène; when he was driving along in Monsieur de Nucingen's carriage, with Monsieur de Nucingen's wife beside him, the young man felt as if he were in a dream.

"To the Palais Royal," she directed the coachman, "near the Théâtre Français."

As they drove along, she seemed upset, refusing to answer the thousand and one questions Eugène asked, unable to understand this mute, dense, thick-headed resistance.

"Another minute and she'll have escaped me," he told himself.

When the carriage finally stopped, the baroness sat studying the student with a look that silenced his silly words; he was half beside himself.

"You really love me?" she said.

"Yes," he answered, disguising the sudden fear that took hold of him.

"You won't think badly of me, no matter what I ask of you?"

"No."

"Are you willing to do as I say?"

"Gladly."

"Have you ever gambled?" she asked, her voice trembling.

"Never."

"Ah, I can breathe again. You'll be lucky. Here's my purse," she went on. "Take it! It holds a hundred francs, which is all the money this happy woman has. Go into a gambling house, I don't know exactly where they are, but I know there are some here. Bet this money in a game they call roulette, and either lose it all or else bring me back six thousand francs. And when you come back, I'll tell you my troubles."

"The devil take me if I have any idea what I'm doing, but I'll do it," he said happily, because to himself he was saying, "Now she's compromised herself, she'll never be able to refuse me a thing."

He took the pretty purse, stopped only to ask a clothes peddler where the nearest gambling house might be, and then ran to number nine. He went in, handed his hat to a servant, and asked where he might find the roulette wheel. Veteran gamblers, looking on, were astonished when he was promptly guided through the room to a long table. They followed after, gawking; without the slightest embarrassment, Eugène asked if someone would show him how to make a bet.

"If you put a coin on any one of these thirty-six numbers," a respectable-looking white-haired old man told him, "and it turns up, then you'll have thirty-six coins."

Eugène tossed his hundred francs on the number representing his own age, twenty-one. Then there was an astonished cry, though he did not understand it. He had won without knowing it.

"Take your money," said the old man. "You can't win twice in a row, not the way you're doing it."

The old man handed him a small rakelike instrument, and Eugène pulled in three thousand six hundred francs and, still not understanding what he was doing, dropped it all on the red. The audience stared at him enviously, seeing that he was going on. The wheel turned, he won again, and the banker threw him another three thousand six hundred francs.

"Now you have seven thousand two hundred francs," the old man whispered in his ear. "If you'll take my advice, you'll leave right now, because this is the eighth time in a row red has turned up. And if you've a kind heart, you'll be grateful for this good advice and make life a little easier for this poverty-stricken old soldier, who fought with Napoleon, but finds himself completely down on his luck."

In a stupor, Eugène let the old fellow help himself to fifteen francs, then went out with his remaining seven thousand, still not understanding the game he'd played, but stunned by his good luck.

"So, here you are!" he said to Madame de Nucingen, showing

her the seven thousand francs the moment the carriage door had closed behind him. "Now where are we going?"

Delphine wrapped him in a wild embrace, and kissed him fervently, though without passion.

"You've saved me!"

Tears of joy ran freely down her cheeks.

"My friend, I'm going to tell you everything. You'll be my friend, won't you? You think I'm rich, rolling in money, I lack absolutely nothing—or, at least, I look as if I lack nothing! Well! Let me tell you, Monsieur de Nucingen never lets me have a cent. He provides the house, my carriages, my theater boxes; he gives me a tiny allowance for my clothes, he's deliberately making me a secret beggar. But I'm too proud to beg. I would have been the lowest creature in the world, wouldn't I, if I bought his money at the price he wants me to pay for it? With a fortune of seven hundred thousand francs, how could I have let him skin me alive! Precisely by being proud, by being indignant. We're so young and foolish, when we begin our married lives! The begging words he wanted me to use, to ask for money, would have torn my lips to shreds, I couldn't say them; I managed to save a little here and a little there, and I used the money my father'd given me, and then, pretty soon, I was in debt. Marriage is the worst trick in the world, believe me, I can't tell you how bad it is: it's enough just to tell you I'd throw myself out the window, if I had to live with this man without having separate rooms of my own.

"Well, when it came to the point where I had to tell him all my young woman's extravagances, my debts for jewels and all the other little things I'd wanted (because my poor father had gotten us accustomed to having anything our hearts desired), I suffered like a martyr, but I finally got up the courage and I told him. Didn't I have a fortune of my own? Nucingen flew into a rage, he said I'd ruin him—he said horrible things! I wished I was buried a hundred feet under the ground. But, since he'd taken my dowry, he finally paid, but only on condition that all my personal expenses had to come from an allowance he'd give me, and I agreed, just to have some peace.

"And then, later on, well," she said, "I wanted to match the vanity of someone you know. Maybe he did deceive me, but I can't deny he has a genuinely noble character. But he finally left me, and shamefully! *No* one should ever desert a woman to whom, once when she needed it, he's tossed a pile of gold! You *have* to go on loving her, forever and forever! You, you blessedly fine youngster, just twenty-one, so young, so pure, perhaps you wonder how a woman could possibly accept money from a man? But Good God! Isn't it only natural to share everything with the person to whom you owe your happiness? Once you've given all of yourself, who can worry about giving just some part of all that? Money only matters once love has vanished. But don't we bind ourselves for our whole lives? Does anyone who thinks she's well loved ever think she won't be loved? Men swear eternal love to us, so how do we come to each have a separate pocketbook?

"You can't imagine what I suffered, earlier today, when Nucingen absolutely refused to let me have six thousand francs, when he gives that much to his mistress, some girl at the opera, every single month of the year! I felt like killing myself. The stupidest ideas were going through my head. I actually envied people who were nothing but servants, even my own maid. To ask my father would have been a fool's errand! Anastasie and I have eaten him alive: my poor father would have sold himself, if he could find someone to pay him six thousand francs.

"But you, you've saved me from shame, and from death; I was overwhelmed with misery. Ah, monsieur, monsieur, I owed you this explanation, I've been wild and foolish with you. When you left me, earlier, when I couldn't see you any longer, I felt like running away, all by myself, on foot . . . where? I don't know. This is how half the women in Paris live: the outside is all luxury, but their soul's full of cruel worries. I know some poor creatures even more miserable than I am. But there are some women who have to have merchants give them pretend bills for nonexistent purchases. There are others who have to steal from their husbands: some men believe hundred-franc cashmeres can be had for five francs, and some that a five-franc cashmere costs a hundred. There are women who starve their children, and scrounge and scrimp, just so they can buy a dress.

"I'm innocent of such horrible frauds. And this will be the last of my agonies. There are women who sell themselves to their husbands, so they control them, but at least I'm free! I could get Nucingen to absolutely drown me in gold, but I'd rather simply weep, with my head leaning against the heart of some man I can look up to. Oh, after tonight Monsieur de Marsay won't be able to think of me as a woman he's bought."

She lowered her head to her hands, to keep Eugène from seeing her tears, but he uncovered her face and stared at it: she was truly sublime, like this!

"Mixing money and feelings, isn't it awful? You won't be able to love me," she said.

This jumbling of real emotion, which always makes women seem larger than they are, and the offenses that the social order forces them to commit, overwhelmed Eugène, who murmured soft, soothing words to console this beautiful woman, so innocently heedless in her cry of misery.

"You won't let this keep you from loving me," she said. "Promise me that."

"Ah, madame! I couldn't if I wanted to," he said.

With a grateful, gracious gesture she took his hand and held it to her heart.

"Thanks to you, I'm free again, and I'm happy. I've been living under the weight of an iron hand. And now I will live simply, and spend nothing. You'll like me just as I am, my friend, won't you? Now you keep this one," she said, taking only six of the seven banknotes. "I owe you a thousand, in all conscience, because I planned to go half and half with you." Eugène defended himself as if he'd been a virgin. But when the baroness said, "If you're not my accomplice, I'll have to look on you as my enemy," he accepted the money.

"I'll save this for an unlucky day," he said.

"That's exactly what I was afraid you'd say!" she cried, turning pale. "If you want me to mean anything to you, swear to me," she said, "that you'll never go back and gamble again. My God, if I were to corrupt you! I'd die of grief."

The carriage reached her home. The contrast between her misery and the opulence in which she lived was stunning, and Eugène kept hearing Vautrin's words, repeated over and over.

"You sit there," directed the baroness as they entered her bedroom; she seated herself on a small sofa near the fire. "Now I'm going to write a very difficult letter! Help me."

"Don't write anything at all," said Eugène. "Just put the money in an envelope, address it, and let your maid bring it to him."

"But what a love you are!" she said. "You see? That's what it means, being well-bred from the start! That's the pure Beauséant showing through," she added, laughing.

"She's charming," Eugène said to himself, more and more smitten. He looked around the room, which fairly breathed the voluptuous elegance of some rich courtesan.

"Do you like it?" she asked, ringing for her maid. "Thérèse, bring this directly to Monsieur de Marsay, and hand it to him and to him only. If he's not there, bring it back to me."

As she left, the maid shot a wicked glance at Eugène.

Dinner was announced. Rastignac gave Madame de Nucingen his arm, and she led him to a delightful dining room, where he found set out, once again, the same luxury he'd admired at his cousin's house.

"Whenever they're giving an opera," she said, "you'll come and dine with me, and then you'll escort me to the theater."

"I could easily get used to such a life, if only it would last," he said, "but I'm simply a poor student who has yet to make his fortune."

"Oh, it will be made," she replied, laughing. "You'll see: these things take care of themselves—but I never expected to be so happy."

It is the nature of women to let the possible demonstrate the impossible and to destroy facts by sheer intuition. When Madame de Nucingen and Rastignac walked into their box at the theater, she was wrapped in an air of contentment, making her so radiantly beautiful that everyone who saw her indulged in those petty insults against which women are defenseless and which, often, can make imaginary licentiousness, invented as a mere joke, seem entirely credible. Once you know Paris, you believe nothing that is said there, just as you say nothing about what is really happening.

Eugène clasped the baroness's hand, and as the music moved them they communicated their responses by increased or diminished pressure. It was, for them, an intoxicating evening. They left the theater together, in her carriage, Madame de Nucingen wanting to carry Eugène as far as Newbridge *[le Pont Neuf]*, and as they drove she defended herself against even one of those kisses with which, at the Palais Royal, she had been so prodigal. Eugène reproached her for such inconsistency.

"Back then," she answered, "it was simply gratitude for a quite unexpected sacrifice, but now it would be a promise."

"And you won't make me any, you ingrate."

He was annoyed. With one of those impatient gestures that thrill a lover, she let him have her hand to kiss, and he took it with such bad grace that, in turn, she was enchanted.

"Until Monday, at the ball," she said.

As he walked on, alone, by moonlight, Eugène found himself engaged in some very serious thinking. He was at one and the same time both happy and dissatisfied—happy with an adventure likely to end by giving him one of the prettiest and most elegant women in Paris, a woman he deeply desired, but dissatisfied to see how his fortune-making plans had miscarried, for this reversal made him feel the true weight of the hesitating thoughts that, for two days now, had been burdening his mind. Failure always emphasizes the strength of our pretensions. The more Eugène relished Parisian life, the less he wanted to live in poverty and obscurity. He crumpled the thousand-franc note in his pocket, and offered himself a thousand specious reasons why he ought to keep it for himself.

He reached New Saint Geneviève Street, at last, and as he climbed the stairs saw a light. Père Goriot had left his door open, and his candle burning, so the student wouldn't forget to "tell him all about his daughter," as he had put it. Eugène concealed nothing.

"Oh," Père Goriot exclaimed, in a fit of violent jealousy, "do they think I'm ruined? I still have thirteen hundred francs a year! Oh, the poor child, why didn't she come to me? I would have mortgaged my income, I would have gone into my capital, I could have bought myself an annuity with what was left. Why didn't *you* come and tell me the problem, my good young neighbor? And how could you have had the heart to risk her poor hundred francs! It breaks my heart. You see what those sons-in-law of mine are like! Ah, if I had them right here, I'd break their necks, both of them! My God—crying? she was crying?"

"With her head on my vest," said Eugène.

"Let me have it!" cried Père Goriot. "What! My daughter's tears, my dear Delphine, were spilled right here, though when she was a little girl I never let her cry! Oh, I'll buy you another vest, don't wear it again, let me have it. According to the marriage contract, she's entitled to her own property. Ah, tomorrow I'm going to hunt up my old lawyer, Derville. I'll demand an accounting of her fortune. I know the law, I'm an old wolf, I'll go find my teeth again."

"Take this," the student said. "It's the thousand francs she wanted me to have for my share. You keep it for her, take care of it."

Goriot stood looking at Eugène, then reached out and took his hand, onto which a tear fell.

"You'll succeed," said the old man. "Remember, God is just. I know honesty when I see it, so let me tell you, there aren't very many men like you. Would you like to be my dear child, too? But go to bed. You can sleep, you're not a father yet. She was crying, I understand that—and there I was, quietly eating like some idiot, while she was suffering—me, though I'd sell the Father, the Son, and the Holy Ghost to keep either one of those girls from shedding a single tear!"

"By God," said Eugène to himself, as he lay down, "I think I'm going to be an honest man the whole rest of my life. Following your conscience certainly has its rewards."

Perhaps only those who truly believe in God can do good and keep quiet about it, and Eugène truly believed. The next day, when it was time to go to the ball, Rastignac went to Madame de Beauséant, who took him there with her, in order to present him to the Duchess of Carigliano. The great lady welcomed him graciously, and there in her house he once again saw Madame de Nucingen. Delphine had dressed herself with great care, wanting to please everyone so she could best please Eugène, whose glance she awaited impatiently, though she thought she hid her anxiety quite well. For those who understand a woman's emotions, this is an especially delightful moment. What man can say he hasn't deliberately held back on his judgment, teasingly disguising his approval and pleasure, in order to hunt for the promises that might be forthcoming from the anxiety he's caused, playing on fears he could wipe away with a single smile?

All during the ball, the student tried to calculate just where he stood, finally understanding that as Madame de Beauséant's openly acknowledged cousin he did indeed enjoy significant status. His conquest of the Baroness de Nucingen, which that status had already given him, made him stand out from the crowd so clearly that, as he was now aware, all the other young men were staring at him enviously—and, in intercepting some of their glances, he relished the first fruits of complacency. As he went from room to room, and from group to group, he was deliberately boasting about his good luck. The women predicted, with a unanimous voice, that he would be a great success. Delphine, suddenly worried about losing him, promised not to refuse him, later, the kiss she had so strongly resisted, two nights before. In the course of the evening, Rastignac was offered a number of invitations. His cousin introduced him to a number of women, all of whom had pretensions to elegance, and whose houses were said to be pleasant enough; he could see himself being propelled toward the greatest, the most beautiful things in Parisian life. For him, the evening had all the charms of a debutante's brilliant coming-out ball, something he would remember till the day he died, exactly as a woman's mind will return to the ball where she first had her successes. And the next day, when, over breakfast, and for all to hear, he told Goriot how everything had gone, he could see Vautrin smiling diabolically.

"And do you really believe," demanded this fierce logician, "that a fashionable young man can live on New Saint Geneviève Street, at Maison Vauquer? A thoroughly respectable establishment, certainly, and in every conceivable way, but for all that something less than fashionable. It's prosperous, it's overflowingly abundant, it's fiercely proud of being, temporarily, home to someone like de Rastignac, but when all's said and done it's still New Saint Geneviève Street, and it's hardly luxurious, because it's one hundred percent *patriarcharama*. My young friend," Vautrin went on with an air of paternal jesting, "if you really want to be somebody, here in Paris, you've got to have at least three horses, with a light carriage for the morning and a covered gig at night—in a word, roughly nine thousand francs, and that's just for the wheels. You'll be totally unworthy of your great destiny if you don't spend, say, three thousand francs on your tailor, six hundred francs on perfume, a hundred at the boot-maker's. And as for your laundress, why, she should cost you another thousand francs. Fashionable young men simply can't spend too much on their linen, you know: isn't it precisely there that they're most frequently inspected? Love and the Church both like handsome napkins on their altars. So we're up to fourteen thousand. For the moment, I'll say nothing about how much you can lose on gambling, here in Paris; you've got to have at least two thousand francs in your pocket. I've led that life, I know how much it costs. Then you've got to add, on top of these initial expenses, three hundred francs for pastry, another thousand for a place to hang your hat.

"So you see, my boy, just for all this fiddle-faddle we need twenty-five thousand a year, or else we fall into the mud and they all make fun of us, and our whole bright future evaporates—all our successes, all our mistresses! Ah, but I forgot about our valet, and our groom, too! Is Christopher delivering your love letters? And are you writing them on the right kind of paper? It could be the death of you, you know. Take the word of an old boy with lots of experience!" he continued, letting his bass voice boom out. "Either find yourself some virtuous attic roof you can live under, and marry yourself off to hard work—or else find some other road to follow."

Here Vautrin winked and shot a glance at Mademoiselle Taillefer, as if to remind Eugène and sum up in that one quick look all the seductive arguments he'd already planted in the student's heart, with the clear intention of corrupting him.

For the next few days Rastignac led the most dissipated life imaginable. He dined with Madame de Nucingen virtually every night, and was her escort when she went out. He would return at three or four in the morning, get up at noon to dress, and then, when the weather was good, walk in the Park with Delphine, squandering day after day without realizing how much it all cost, breathing in the whole social whirl, all the seductive possibilities of a luxurious life, with the impatient excitement of a flowering female palm tree, yearning toward the life-giving spray of her mate's pollen. He gambled for high stakes, winning or losing hugely, and was soon accustomed to the extravagant life young men lead in Paris. From his first winnings, he sent fifteen hundred francs to his mother and his sisters, and handsome presents along with his repayment. He had announced his intention of leaving Maison Vauquer, but by the end of January he was still there, and had no idea how he would ever leave. All young men seem to be subject to an inexorable law, though in fact they are simply driven by their youth and the wild fury with which they fling themselves into pleasure. Whether rich or poor, they never have enough money for life's necessities, though they can always find enough for any whim that strikes them. Lavish in anything they buy on credit, they are absolute misers when it comes to paying out cash, taking revenge for what they don't have by wasting whatever they can get their hands on. To put it still more bluntly, a student takes better care of his hat than his suit. Because his tailor's charges are immense, they're basically left unpaid for as long as possible, while the comparatively modest sums owed his hatmaker make the latter one of the least tractable of all those creditors who must be dickered with. While the opera glasses of pretty ladies may be trained, high in a theater box, on a young man's dazzling waistcoat, the same young man is probably doing without stockings, for the hosier too is one of the boll weevils eating at his purse. And that was Rastignac's state. Madame Vauquer always saw his hand empty, while that same hand poured out money for anything his vanity required, his purse deflating and then wildly inflating totally out of harmony with basic natural laws. Before he could actually leave the stinking, unworthy *pension* where his aspirations met frequent humiliation, wouldn't he have to pay his landlady a month's rent and buy furniture for his more sophisticated lodgings? And that was always exactly what he could not afford to do. To fund his gambling, Rastignac might be perfectly capable of using his winnings to buy expensive watches and gold chains which, later, he could take to the pawnbroker—that sober and close-mouthed friend of all young people—but when it came to paying for his food, his board, or simple utensils without which his elegant existence could not be properly enjoyed, he found himself utterly unable either to lay his hands on the wherewithal or even to brazen out his shortages. Debts contracted for needs already satisfied were mere vulgar necessity; they could no longer be a source of inspiration. Like most of those who have lived so chancy an existence, he'd wait to the very last moment before paying bills that, to any middle-class eyes, are matters of sacred obligation—as Mirabeau always did, settling the account for the bread he ate only when the charge reached him in the militant form of a bill of exchange.

And then Rastignac lost all his money and fell into debt. He began to understand that, without fixed and reliable resources, he could never continue this new existence. All the same, although the precarious situation left him groaning under its stinging blows, he felt completely unable to give up his extravagant pleasures; he was determined to maintain them, no matter what it might cost. The luck he'd counted on, to win him his fortune, had faded into chimeras, and the all-too-real obstacles had swollen to immense size. As he became aware of the domestic secrets of Monsieur de Nucingen and his wife, he realized that, to transform love into an instrument of fortune, he had to swallow all sense of shame, he had to abandon those noble ideals which, for young men, serve as absolution for their sins. He had thrown himself into this new life, on the surface so great and grand, but riddled with the tapeworms of remorse, this life whose fleeting pleasures insisted on being paid for by constant, piercing pain, and in rolling around and around in it he had made himself, like La Bruyère's Absent-Minded Man, a bed at the bottom of a very muddy ditch—though, like that Absent-Minded fellow, all he had soiled, as yet, had been his clothing.

"So we've murdered that Mandarin?" Bianchon asked him, one day, as they rose from the table.

"Not quite," Eugène answered, "but I can hear his death rattle."

The medical student took this as a witty remark, but it was a terribly serious one. Dining at the *pension* for the first time in a long while, Eugène had eaten in a moody silence. Instead of rising and taking his leave, when dessert was served, he had stayed where he was, sitting near Mademoiselle Taillefer and, from time to time, looking at her most attentively. Other lodgers were still sitting there, cracking nuts, while still others strolled about, continuing conversations begun during the meal. As usual, people left when they felt like leaving, according to the degree of interest they took in the conversation or to how lightly or heavily digesting their food pressed down on them. During the winter the dining room was rarely completely empty until eight o'clock, by which point the four women would be left alone and could make up for the silence that their sex bound them to, in such an assembly of men.

Struck by Eugène's obvious preoccupation, Vautrin too remained in the dining room, though he'd seemed on the verge of taking his leave; he kept himself as well-concealed as possible, so Eugène might perhaps think he had in fact gone. Then, instead of joining the last of the lodgers as they straggled out, he slyly posted himself, next door, in the *salon*. He had read deep in the student's soul and sensed a decisive development.

And, indeed, Rastignac faced the same perplexing situation many young men have experienced. Whether she herself was in love or only flirting, Madame de Nucingen had put Rastignac through all the torments of true passion, deploying for his benefit all the resources of Parisian feminine diplomacy. Having compromised herself, as far as public attention was concerned, by closely attaching Madame de Beauséant's cousin to herself, she held back when it came to actually giving him the rights which he seemed already to enjoy. For an entire month she had so cleverly whipped up Eugène's senses that, in the end, she had conquered his heart as well. The student might well have thought himself the master, in the early stages of their relationship, but Madame de Nucingen had become definitely the stronger, helped by a stratagem which stirred up in Eugène all that variety of feelings, good or bad, which simultaneously coexist in any young Parisian male, who are really two or three men at the same time.

Was she acting entirely consciously? No: women are always

sincere, even in the midst of their most shocking duplicities, because it is always some natural emotion which dominates them. Perhaps, having given this young man such a hold on her, by having openly demonstrated her affection for him, Delphine was merely responding to a sense of personal dignity, which led her either to revoke any concessions she might have made or, at least, to enjoy suspending them. Even at the very moment when passion seizes her, it is perfectly natural for a Parisian woman to delay her final fall, as a way of testing the heart of the man into whose hands she is about to deliver herself and her future!

Madame de Nucingen's dreams had been deeply betrayed, the first time, and her faithfulness to a young egotist had earned her nothing. She had good reason to be mistrustful. Perhaps she could sense, in Eugène's conduct towards her, a certain lack of respect, for his rapid rise had made him conceited, and in addition theirs had certainly been a strange situation. Certainly, she wanted a man of his age to find her imposing, and without any question she wanted to feel herself grand in comparison to him, having for so long felt herself small and insignificant in comparison to the man who had so recently abandoned her. She did not want Eugène to think her merely an easy conquest, precisely because, as she knew only too well, that was exactly how de Marsay had seen her. In short, having given herself to the degrading pleasures of someone young but virtually monstrous in his licentiousness, she was now tasting the sweetness of strolling in love's flower-strewn regions, and finding it charming to relish everything she found there, listening slow and lingeringly, feeling herself softly caressed by chaste breezes.

Thus true love is forced to pay for the less satisfactory sort. This is bound to be a common reversal, so long as men refuse to understand how many flowers fall to the ground, in a young woman's soul, as soon as deceit strikes. In any case, whatever her reasons, Delphine found Eugène thoroughly delightful and took enormous pleasure in playing with him, knowing all the while, surely, that she really was loved and that, in the end, she would cure him of his suffering—but only when it was her royal pleasure as a woman to do so. Eugène's own self-respect would not permit this very first combat to end in a defeat, so he kept on, persistently, rather like a young hunter absolutely determined, in his first season, to kill a partridge before he put up his gun. All his anxieties, all his wounded pride, his despair (whether real or false), clung more and more exclusively to this one woman. Paris had long since given him Madame de Nucingen, but he was no nearer to possessing her now than when he had first laid eyes on her. Too young to understand that, sometimes, a woman's flirting is a good deal kinder than her cold and unsatisfying love, he fell into frequent blind rages. If this season in which a woman still worries about yielding to love offered Rastignac the fruits of its freshness, for him those became quite as costly as they were green, tart, and wonderfully delicious to the taste. Sometimes, seeing himself penniless and with no future, he would think of the roads to fortune Vautrin had shown him and, in spite of his conscience, he would wonder about a marriage with Mademoiselle Taillefer. When poverty yammered most forcefully in his brain, he'd find himself almost involuntarily succumbing to that sphinx's plans: even Vautrin's very looks sometimes almost hypnotized him. And now, as Poiret and Mademoiselle Michonneau went up to their rooms, Rastignac thought himself alone with Madame Vauquer, Madame Couture—who was knitting some wool sleeves, her head nodding in the warmth of the stove—and her young charge, and looked at Victorine with such interest that the girl felt obliged to cast her eyes down.

"Is something worrying you, Monsieur Eugène?" she asked after a long, silent moment.

"Is there a man who hasn't got his worries!" Rastignac replied. "But if we young fellows were sure of being well and truly loved, with a devotion that would repay us for the sacrifices we're always ready to make, perhaps we wouldn't ever have any worries."

Mademoiselle's Taillefer's only response was a glance that could never have been considered equivocal.

"And you, mademoiselle," he went on, "you think you know your own heart, right now, but can you be certain you won't ever change?"

A smile flickered across the poor girl's lips, like a ray shining straight out of her soul, and her face became so radiant that Eugène was frightened he might have released a veritable explosion of emotion.

"Really!" he persisted. "Suppose tomorrow you were to become rich and happy, and some immense fortune came falling out of the clouds, would you still love the poor young man who wept for you, in your days of distress?"

She nodded her head prettily.

"Even a very unfortunate young man?"

She nodded once more.

"What kind of nonsense are you talking over there?" called Madame Vauquer.

"Leave us alone," Eugène replied. "We understand each other perfectly well."

"Ah? Do we have a promise of marriage between Chevalier Eugène de Rastignac and Mademoiselle Victorine Taillefer?" demanded Vautrin in his great bass voice, as he suddenly appeared in the dining room doorway.

"Oh! How you frightened me!" exclaimed Madame Couture and Madame Vauquer at exactly the same time.

"I could have done a lot worse," Eugène answered, laughing,

though Vautrin's words had made him feel the cruelest, throbbing emotion he'd ever experienced.

"That will be enough of your wicked jokes, gentlemen," declared Madame Couture. "My dear, we will go upstairs now."

Madame Vauquer went up right after her two lodgers, so she could save on candles and the cost of a fire by spending the rest of the evening in their rooms. Eugène found himself quite alone with Vautrin, and very much face to face.

"I knew you'd get there," the man said to him, though with perfect calm. "But listen here! I'm just as sensitive as anyone else, you know what I mean? Don't decide right now, you're not on the steadiest ground. You're in debt. If you do decide to join up with me, I want it to be because you're making a rational choice, not because you've been pushed by passion or despair. Perhaps you're a couple of thousand short. Here, would this help?"

He pulled a wallet from his pocket, this demon of a man, and took out three thousand-franc banknotes, which he proceeded to wave in front of Eugène's face. For the student it was cruelly difficult, He owed the Marquis Ajuda-Pinto a hundred francs; he owed Monsieur de Trailles another hundred; he had given his word of honor to them both. But he did not have the money, which was why he had not gone to Madame de Restaud's, where he was expected. It was one of those informal gatherings where one nibbles on little cakes and drinks tea, but can easily lose six thousand francs at whist.

"Monsieur," said Eugène, barely able to conceal a convulsive trembling, "after the confidences you've placed in me you must understand, surely, that I cannot possibly allow myself to be under obligation to you."

"Well! I'd have been shocked had you said anything else," the Tempter replied. "You're a good young fellow, you're sensitive, you're as proud as a lion and as nice as a young girl. Oh, the

Devil would be delighted to nab your soul. I like that in young men. Another two or three rounds of hard political thought, and you'll learn to see the world as it really is. Playing out a virtuous scene or two gives the superior man the sense of fulfilling his dreams, to the immense applause of all the idiots in the cheap seats. It won't be long before you're one of us. Oh, if you want to apprentice yourself to me, I'll teach you all there is to know! Anything you long for will be yours at once, no matter what it may be: honor, fortune, women. You'll drink civilization to the dregs, and all in ambrosia. You'll be our favored child, our Benjamin, we'll cheerfully wipe ourselves off the face of the earth, if you want us to. Any obstacle in your path will be removed. But if you retain your scruples, are you going to think me a rascal? Well, a man who thought he was just as honest as you do, Monsieur de Turenne, had *his* little dealings with bandits, and didn't think he'd been particularly compromised.

"You don't want to be obligated to me, eh? Why should that hold you back?" Vautrin went on, letting himself smile. "Take these pieces of paper, and right down there," he instructed, pulling out a tax stamp, "there, on the other side, you write, 'Accepted and acknowledged, for the sum of three thousand francs, payable in one year.' Then you date it! The interest is quite enough to remove any lingering scruples for you; you can think of me as a Jew, and feel entitled to cut me in the street. I haven't any objection to your thoroughly despising me, right now, because I'm convinced you'll come to love me. You'll find I have some tremendous abysses, some huge, focused emotions that fools think of as vices, but you'll never find me lazy, and you'll never find me ungrateful. In a word, I'm neither a pawn nor a bishop, my young friend, but a castle."

"What in God's name are you?" cried Eugène. "You were put on this earth to torment me."

"Oh no, I'm a very good man who's willing to get his hands dirty so you'll be out of the mud for as long as you live. And do you wonder why I'm so devoted to your cause? Well! someday I'll tell you the whole story, I'll whisper it right in your ear. I've startled you right from the start, haven't I, showing you how the social machine runs and all the noises it makes? But you'll get over that fright, just the way a drafted soldier does when he finds himself out on the battlefield, and you'll get used to thinking of people as if they were soldiers, determined to sacrifice themselves for the sake of those who've been self-anointed as kings. Things have really changed. In the old days, they used to tell a courageous man, 'Here's a hundred francs, kill that fellow over there for me, if you please,' and then they'd all go and peacefully eat their dinners, having finished someone off just because he said yes, or else because he said no. And here I am, proposing to give you a handsome fortune, and all you have to do is nod your head, which won't and can't cost you a thing—and you're hesitating! We've gone soft, that's what's happened."

Eugène signed the I.O.U.'s, and exchanged them for the banknotes.

"So! Well, now look here, we have to talk sensibly," Vautrin went on. "I plan to leave here in a couple of months, headed for America; I'm going to go plant my tobacco. I'll send you some cigars, for old times sake. If I get to be rich, I'll help you. If I don't have any children (and it's more than likely I won't, because I haven't much interest in taking a cutting and replanting myself down here), well! I'll leave you my fortune. Is that being a real friend? But I'm very fond of you, I really am. I have a positive passion to dedicate myself to someone else. I've already done it, you know. You see, my young friend, I live on a plane far more exalted than other men are even aware of. For me, deeds are nothing more than methods, procedures, because all I see is the goal they're aiming toward. What does a man more or less matter to me? This much!" he exclaimed, snapping his thumbnail on a tooth. "A man's everything, or else he's nothing. If his name is Poiret, he's less than nothing: you can wipe him away like a bed-bug, he's worthless, and he stinks. But a man like you is a god, not just a machine covered with skin, but a theater where fine feelings sprout and grow—and feelings are all that matters, as far as I'm concerned. Is a feeling anything but an entire world poured into a thought?

"Consider your Père Goriot: for him, his two daughters are the entire universe, they're the thread by means of which he guides himself through the world. And as for me! Well, for a man like me, who's dug around in the world as thoroughly as I have, there's only one real emotion, and that's the friendship of one man for another. I know *Venice Preserved*,❧ by heart, and Pierre and Jaffier, in that play, they're absolutely my passion. Have you seen a lot of men so tough that when one of their buddies says, 'Let's go bury a corpse!' they just go and do it, without a sniffle, without getting upset? I've done that, I have, yes.

"And I don't talk like this to everybody, believe me. You, damn it, you're a superior man, I can tell you anything, you can understand it all. You don't go mucking around in marshes, like the shit-faced toads we've got all around us. So! That's that. You'll get married. Let's each shove in our swords! Hey, but mine's made of iron, and it never goes slack, oh no!"

Vautrin left, not waiting to hear the student's negative response, but wanting to make things easier for Eugène. The man seemed to understand the little shows of resistance, the inner struggles men use to make themselves look and feel better, and to justify to their consciences the unworthy things they do.

❧ 1685 play by Thomas Otway.

"He can do whatever he wants," Eugène told himself, "but I'm certainly not marrying Mademoiselle Taillefer!"

Once he had beaten back the queasiness, the interior fever it gave him even to contemplate a pact with this man for whom he felt such a horror—this man who nevertheless grew ever larger and more powerful in the student's eyes, both because of his unabashed cynicism and the boldness with which he attacked the entire social order—Rastignac got himself dressed, called for a cab, and went off to Madame de Restaud's. For some time now, this lady had been increasingly solicitous of our young friend, whose every step seemed to lead him more directly into the very center of the fashionable world, and whose influence, someday, seemed sure to be formidable indeed. Eugène paid his debts to de Trailles and the Marquis Ajuda-Pinto, played whist for a while, and won back everything he had lost. Like most men who haven't yet made their way, and who are inclined to be more or less fatalistic, he was distinctly superstitious and saw this good luck as Heaven's reward for his constancy in remaining on the virtuous road. One of the first things he did, the next morning, was ask Vautrin if he still had the I.O.U.'s from the night before. The reply being in the affirmative, he was of course delighted to instantly repay the borrowed three thousand francs.

"You're doing well," responded Vautrin.

"But I'm not your accomplice," said Eugène.

"I understand, I understand," Vautrin went on, cutting him off. "You have your little childish games to play. You're still hanging around the doorway, just fooling around."

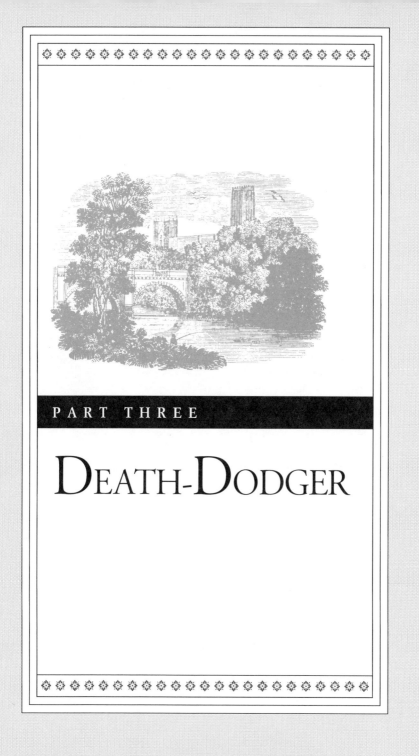

PART THREE

DEATH-DODGER

TWO DAYS LATER, POIRET AND MADEMOISELLE MICHON-
NEAU WERE SEATED ON A BENCH ALONG A DESERTED
LANE IN THE PARK, ENJOYING THE SUNSHINE AND
CHATTING WITH THE MAN WHO HAD SEEMED SUSPICIOUS, AND
RIGHTLY SO, TO EUGÈNE'S MEDICAL STUDENT FRIEND.

"My dear lady," this Monsieur Gondureau was saying, "I find it hard to understand your hesitation. His Excellency, the Chief Inspector of the Royal Police . . ."

"Ah," repeated Poiret, "His Excellency the Chief Inspector of the Royal Police."

"Exactly, His Excellency is much concerned about this business," Gondureau went on.

It may perhaps seem to you not quite natural that Poiret, an old workman, surely a died-in-the-wool bourgeois (no matter how devoid of any ideas, bourgeois or not), would go on listening to the pretended businessman after hearing, from the man's own mouth, the word "police," thus revealing that under the mask of an honest man he in fact bore the face of a policeman. But it was, I assure you, completely natural—and so that you, and all of you, may better understand the specific species to which Poiret in fact belongs, in the great and large family of fools, I am now going to inform you of something said by certain scientific observers and, to this very moment, never publicly revealed. There is, you see, a nation of pen-pushers, forever locked in to a budgetary slot between the degree of latitude marked off at roughly twelve hundred francs a year—you might say, a sort of administrative Greenland —and the third latitude up, at which point somewhat more torrid salaries begin, say from three to six thousand a year, which nation dwells in a fairly temperate climate, where tips occur so naturally that, in spite of all difficulties, they flourish quite nicely, thank you. One of the most obvious signs of the limp and narrow rigidity of these bureaucratic creatures is a sort of involuntary, mechanical, instinctive respect for that Grand Lama of any and all Ministries, who is made known to each and every employee thereof by an utterly indecipherable signature and the fearsome title, HIS EX-CELLENCY, THE CHIEF MINISTER, five words fully as potent as, in Boieldieu's opera, *The Caliph of Baghdad*, the sultan's formula of secret power, "Il Bondo Cani" [The Great Khan]—words that, to these flattened-out insects, represent an absolutely sacred Force, above and beyond any appeal or other recourse. Like the Pope for Catholic Christians, this Chief Minister is in the eyes of all his employees completely infallible; the luster he sheds upon each of his actions, and all of his words, is communicated to these underlings by the mere mention of his name; his golden braid drapes itself over everything, conferring total legality on any order he gives; his very name—"His Excellency"—not only attests to the purity of his motives and the sanctity of his wishes, but serves as a password for ideas otherwise wholly unacceptable. Anything these miserable men would never do, in their own interest, is instantly hurried into motion the very moment the sacred words are intoned: "His Excellency wishes . . . His Excellency has decided . . ." Bureaucracies have their ways of passively resisting, of course, just as the Army does, and any other system which stifles the conscience, crushing a man's humanity, and ending, in time, by adapting him—like a vise or a machine-screw—to his proper place in the governmental machine. Plainly experienced in these matters, Monsieur Gondureau immediately recognized Poiret for one of these bureaucratic idiots and so brought out his *Deus ex machina*, the talismanic name "His Excellency," exactly when, in openly revealing his position, he needed to dazzle and overwhelm Poiret, who struck him as the male version of Michonneau, just as Michonneau seemed the female form of Poiret.

"Ah! His Excellency Himself is very concerned, the Chief Inspector of. Ah! that's a very different affair," murmured Poiret.

"Now you understand what your friend here has just been saying," went on the pretend businessman, turning to Mademoiselle Michonneau, "your friend in whom you place such absolute trust and reliance. Well then! His Excellency is now quite sure that this so-called Vautrin, who lodges at Maison Vauquer, is in fact an escaped convict from Toulon Penitentiary, where he's known as 'Death-Dodger.' "❂

"Ah!" said Poiret. "Death-Dodger! He's done very well, if he deserves such a name.

"Indeed," the detective continued. "He's earned that name because, no matter how bold a business he's been up to, he's

❂ Trompe-la Mort.

always been lucky enough to end with his head still on his shoulders. But he's a very dangerous fellow, believe me! He's capable of extraordinary things. Indeed, even his being sentenced to jail in the first place is something he actually yielded to because of his immense sense of honor . . ."

"So he's a man of honor?" Poiret interrupted.

"After a fashion. He agreed to answer for a crime actually committed by someone else, a mistake made by a singularly handsome young man of whom he was very fond, a young Italian with a taste for gambling, who has since gone into the Army and behaved himself extremely well.

"But if His Excellency is convinced that Monsieur Vautrin is this Death-Dodger, why does he need my help?" asked Mademoiselle Michonneau.

"Well, now, yes!" said Poiret. "If indeed His Excellency has, as you say, done you the honor of telling you that he is quite quite certain . . ."

"Certainty is not the right word; rather, he feels very sure. Let me explain. Jacques Collin, also known as Death-Dodger, has the absolute trust of every convict in three different penitentiaries; they've all picked him to be their agent and their banker. He earns a good deal from this sort of business, which plainly requires a man of marked talent."

"Oh ho!" exclaimed Poiret. "Do you get the joke, Mademoiselle? He's calling Vautrin a marked man, because he's certainly been marked, hasn't he?"

"This so-called Vautrin," the detective went on, "handles all the convicts' money, and invests it, and takes care of it, using it also for anyone else who manages to escape, or their families (when that is they have so instructed him to dispose of it, at need), or their mistresses, for whose benefit also they sometimes draw on him, as on a bank."

"Their mistresses! said Poiret. "Do you mean to say, their wives?"

"No indeed. For the most part, convicts do not have legitimate spouses, but only what we call concubines."

"You mean, they all live with women they're not married to?"

"Inevitably."

"Well, well!" said Poiret. "These are terrible things, and His Excellency really shouldn't encourage them. And since you have the honor to be admitted into His Excellency's presence, it strikes me it's your job—because I can see you have properly charitable notions—to explain to His Excellency all about this immoral behavior, which sets a very bad example for the rest of society."

"Monsieur, it's hardly the government's job to set itself up as a model of virtue."

"That's true, yes. But if you'll allow me, sir . . ."

"Let him go on, my dear, let him go on," urged Mademoiselle Michonneau.

"So you see, mademoiselle," Gondureau continued, "the government is very much interested in seizing such an illicit horde, which is said to add up to quite a lot of money. Death-Dodger can command very large sums, for he acts as an illegal receiver not only for his convict friends, but also for the members of the League of Ten Thousand . . ."

"Ten thousand thieves!" exclaimed Poiret, startled.

"No, the League of Ten Thousand is an association of thieves on a truly large scale, men who are involved only when truly significant sums are at stake: they won't bother with anything worth less than ten thousand francs. These are the most distinguished people who come before the criminal courts. They know the law, so when they're caught it's never a question of the death penalty. And this Collin fellow is their confidant, their adviser. With the help of his immense resources, this man is known to have established a kind of private police force, a whole series of connections and interconnections wrapped around him like some impenetrable mystery. For the past year or so we've had spies swarming all around him, but we've never been able to nab him red-handed. So both his money and his talents are constantly bolstering the forces of crime, supplying them with capital, and raising up a whole army of evil-doing men perpetually at war with society. If we can grab Death-Dodger and get hold of his treasure chest, we'd be striking right at the root of all this evil. So, you see, we're dealing with a serious affair of state, a matter of high politics, and anyone who helps us succeed will earn the very highest honors. You yourself, my dear sir, could find yourself working for the government again, perhaps you'll become private secretary to a police commissioner—occupations which, of course, won't in any way stop you from collecting your retirement pension."

"But why," asked Mademoiselle Michonneau, "hasn't Death-Dodger simply taken all this money and run off?"

"Ah!" said the detective. "The moment he started, he'd be followed by a man who'd kill him for trying to rob their bank. You can't steal a treasure chest as easily as you can a girl from a decent home. In any case, Collin just isn't that sort, he'd couldn't do anything like that: he'd think himself dishonored."

"Indeed," said Poiret, "you're absolutely right, he would be completely dishonored."

"But that still doesn't tell us why you don't just grab him," said Mademoiselle Michonneau.

"Indeed," said the detective, "I'll explain that, too. But," he bent and whispered in her ear, "you'd better keep your gentleman friend from interrupting me, or I'll never get to the end of it. He'll have to pay pretty handsomely, to get people to sit and listen to him." And then, aloud, he continued: "When he came to Paris, this Death-Dodger took on the role of an honest man—he made himself into a good respectable citizen, he took lodgings in a quiet boardinghouse, because, oh, he's a sly one! you'll never catch him napping. Our Monsieur Vautrin's a quiet, respectable fellow, a man who does some pretty substantial business."

"Naturally," Poiret said to himself.

"And suppose we arrest somebody and he turns out to be a genuine Monsieur Vautrin: the Minister wants to be careful not to set all the businessmen in Paris against him, nor public opinion, either. And the chief of police is in a pretty shaky position; he's got lots of enemies. If he makes a mistake, the people who are after his job will take advantage of all the noise and the do-gooder whining and throw him out of office. What we have to do, in this case, is what we did in the Cogniard affair, that fake Count Saint-Hélène: if he'd been a real Count Saint-Hélène we'd have been in a real mess. Everything has to be verified."

"Ah, yes, and you'll need a pretty woman's help," Mademoiselle Michonneau said with lively interest.

"Death-Dodger would never let a woman get anywhere near him," said the detective. "Let me tell you a secret: he can't stand women."

"In that case," replied Mademoiselle Michonneau, "what good would I be to you, in making a positive identification, supposing I were willing to do it for two thousand francs?"

"Nothing could be simpler," the detective said. "I'll bring you a flask containing a special potion, something that will send him into a harmless fit, one that looks exactly like apoplexy. It works equally well in wine or in coffee. Quick as a wink, you'll pop your man into a bed, and to make absolutely sure he's not dead you'll pull off his clothes. And as soon as you're alone with him, give him a good slap on the shoulder and that'll do it! You'll see the convict letters branded right there."

"That no trick at all," said Poiret.

"All right then! Will you do it?" Gondureau asked the old girl.

"But just suppose," said Mademoiselle Michonneau, "just suppose there aren't any letters branded on his shoulder, what then? do I still get two thousand francs?"

"No."

"What will I get?"

"Five hundred francs."

"To do such a thing, and for so little! Wicked deeds are all the same to your conscience, you know, and I'll have my conscience to deal with."

"And I can tell you," said Poiret, "that this lady has a lot of conscience, in addition to being a very nice person, and someone who knows what's what."

"Oh well!" Mademoiselle Michonneau went on. "Let me have three thousand francs if it is Death-Dodger, and nothing at all if he's just some ordinary fellow."

"Fine," said Gondureau, "but on one condition: it's got to be done tomorrow."

"Ah, but first I have to consult my religious confessor."

"You're really something!" exclaimed the detective, standing up. "All right, then: until tomorrow. And if you need to speak to me, come to lower Saint-Anne Street, at the corner of Saint-Chapelle. There's only one door under the archway. Ask for Monsieur Gondureau."

Bianchon, coming back from medical school, heard the strange name, "Death-Dodger," and was struck by it; he also heard the famous detective saying goodbye to the old couple.

"Why don't we just do it," Poiret said to Mademoiselle Michonneau. "Three thousand francs would bring in three hundred a year for the rest of your life."

"Why?" she replied. "Let's just think about all this. If Vautrin is in fact Death-Dodger, maybe we could do better cutting a deal with *him*. On the other hand, trying to get money out of him would let him know just what's going on, and he's the sort who'd skip off and leave us empty-handed. And wouldn't that be a pain!"

"But if we warned him," Poiret added, "didn't the man say they were watching him all the time? And then, you'd lose everything."

"Anyway," Mademoiselle Michonneau mused, "I don't much like him, this Vautrin! Whenever he talks to me, he always says nasty things."

"And you could do better," said Poiret. "This man who's been talking to us, I think he's all right, in addition to being pretty well dressed, and what he said makes sense: it's just being a good citizen, helping society get rid of a criminal, no matter how virtuous he might be. Leopards don't change their spots. But what if Vautrin decides to kill all of us? Good God, we'd be guilty of all those murders, not to mention that we'd also be the victims!"

But Mademoiselle Michonneau was so deep in thought that she could not pay attention to the words tumbling out of Poiret's mouth, falling much like drops trickling out of an imperfectly closed faucet. Once the old man lurched into speech he'd go right on jabbering, unless she stopped him, like a wind-up clock ticking away on the wall. Once he'd begun, on no matter what subject, he'd proceed sideways, parenthetically, saying just the opposite of whatever he'd said at first, without ever coming to any conclusion. By the time they got back to the *pension*, he was working his way through a long sequence of quotations and legal citations that had led him to narrate his testimony in the case of a certain Ragoulleau and Lady Morin, in which case he had been summoned as a witness for the defense.❖ As they entered Maison Vauquer, Poiret's companion could not help noticing Eugène de Rastignac and Mademoiselle Taillefer so quiveringly wound in intimate conversation that neither of them so much as noticed the two elderly lodgers walking across the dining room.

"It had to end like that," said Mademoiselle Michonneau to Poiret. "They've been tugging at each other's souls for a week now."

"Yes," he answered. "And she was convicted, too."

"Who?"

"Madame Morin."

"I talk to you about Mademoiselle Victorine," said Michonneau, who without thinking about it walked right into his room after Poiret, "and you answer me about Madame Morin. Who on earth is *she*?"

"What might Mademoiselle Victorine be guilty of?" asked Poiret.

"She's guilty of falling in love with Monsieur Eugène de Rastignac, and plunging right on, the poor innocent child, without any awareness of where it's leading her!"

That afternoon, Madame de Nucingen had reduced Eugène to despair. In his heart of hearts, he had completely surrendered to Vautrin, not stopping to inquire why that extraordinary man felt so friendly to him or where such an association might lead. Only a miracle could have pulled him back from the abyss into which he had stepped, an hour earlier, exchanging the sweetest possible vows with Mademoiselle Taillefer. Victorine felt as if she'd

---

❖ An 1812 criminal prosecution in which the lady was found guilty of trying to kill the man. Balzac uses their real names, both here and in another novel, *Une Ténébreuse Affaire (A Shady Affair)* (1841), in which Vautrin also figures.

been hearing some angelic voice floating down to her out of the clouds above, and to her eyes Maison Vauquer had taken on the fantastic colors decorators love to splash all over public theaters: she loved, she was loved (or at least thought she was)! And what woman would not have believed Rastignac, seeing him, hearing him during that long hour when all the Argus-eyes of the *pension* were closed? As for Eugène, who was struggling against his conscience, knowing he was doing wrong and wanting to do wrong, assuring himself that a woman's good fortune would redeem this venial sin, his despair actually heightened his charms, he positively glittered from all the hellish fires burning in his heart. Luckily for him, the miracle occurred: Vautrin came bounding in and at once saw right into the souls of these two young people, wedded by the schemes his infernal genius had concocted, but disturbing them in their job by suddenly starting to sing, in his great mocking voice,

"Oh I love my Fanchette,
Who's never arty . . ."

Victorine fled, but she carried with her a sense of good fortune outweighing all the ill winds that, from the moment she'd been born, had been blowing her way. Poor child! A clasping of hands, her cheek caressed by Rastignac's curly hair, a word spoken so close to her ear that she felt the warmth of his lips, the pressure of a trembling arm around her waist, a kiss stolen from against her neck—these were the testaments of her love, made more burningly tender, more passionately alive, more captivating by far than the most rapturous love words spoken in all the most famous love stories, because there in the kitchen next door lurked fat Sylvie, liable at any moment to come bursting into that radiant dining room. These "tiny prayers," as our ancestors so charmingly called them, seemed serious crimes indeed, to a pious young girl who went to confession every second week! In that single hour she had been more lavish with the treasures of the soul than, later in life, happy, rich, she could possibly have been even in surrendering her very self.

"It's all arranged," Vautrin told Eugène. "Our two dandies have gone at it. Everything went perfectly. Straightforward difference of opinion. Our pigeon insulted my falcon. It's for tomorrow, at Fort Clignancourt. By about eight-thirty in the morning Mademoiselle Taillefer will become heir to her father's love, and also to his fortune, even while she's sitting here and quietly dunking bits of freshly buttered bread in her coffee. That's something to think about, eh? Her little brother's really very good with a sword, so he's as cocky as if he held a royal flush, but he's going to get it all the same, because I invented a brand-new maneuver just for him, a way of suddenly raising the sword and getting your man right between the eyes. I'll show you how it works, because it's stupendously useful."

Rastignac listened to him, stupefied, unable to reply. Just then Père Goriot, Bianchon, and several other boarders walked in.

"That's exactly right," Vautrin assured him. "That's just how you ought to take the news. Oh, you know what you're doing. Very good, my little eagle! You'll be a governor of men, you're strong, straight, you've got guts; I admire you."

He wanted to take Eugène's hand. Rastignac quickly pulled it back and fell into a chair, turning pale; he felt as if a pool of blood were spreading in front of him.

"Ah, so we're still wrapped in some virtuous baby clothes," Vautrin murmured. "Papa Oliban is worth three million, I've counted up his fortune. The dowry will turn you spotless white like a wedding dress, even in your own eyes."

Rastignac could vacillate no longer. He made up his mind that, tonight, he would go and warn Monsieur Taillefer and his son. Just then, Vautrin having left him, he heard Père Goriot whispering in his ear:

"You're sad, my child! But I'll cheer you up."

And the old vermicelli maker lit his candle at one of the lamps. Eugène followed after him, caught up in a sudden curiosity.

"Let's go in your room," Père Goriot said, having gotten the student's key from Sylvie. "Ha, this morning you were convinced she didn't love you, eh?" Goriot went on. "She threw you out of the house, didn't she, and it drove you wild, it made you desperate. You silly goose! She was expecting *me*. Me, do you understand? We had to finish arranging for a real jewel of an apartment, and you'll be living there, you'll be moving there in just three days. But don't give me away. She wants to surprise you, but I can't keep a secret from you, not for very long. You'll be on Artois Street, just a hop and a skip from Saint-Lazare. And you'll be living like a prince. We've furnished it as if for a pair of newlyweds. We've been at it for a whole month, too, without saying a word. My lawyer's been at work, and my daughter's going to get her thirty-six thousand francs a year, which is the interest on her dowry, and I'm going to make sure her eight hundred thousand francs is invested in good solid property."

Silent, his arms crossed over his chest, Eugène paced up and down from one end of his small, untidy room to the other. Père Goriot took advantage of a moment when the student's back was turned to put on his mantel a red morocco box, with the de Rastignac arms printed on it, in gold.

"My dear child," the poor old man said, "I'm in this all the way up to my neck. But listen, I wasn't a disinterested party, I was deeply concerned about your changing your lodgings. So if I ask you something, eh, you won't turn me down?"

"What would you like?"

"Up above your apartment, on the fifth floor, there's another room that goes with your place, so how about if I live there, eh? I'm getting old, I'm too far from my daughters. I won't bother you. I'll just be there. Every night you can tell me about her. That won't bother you, will it? When you come home, there I'll be in my bed, and I'll hear you, and I'll say to myself: he's been to see my little Delphine. He's taken her to a ball, he's made her happy. If I wasn't feeling well, it would be like taking medicine for my heart, hearing you come back, or moving around, or going out again. There'll be so much of my daughter in you! And I'll just be a step from the Champs-Élysées, where they go driving every day, and I'll always see them, even if sometimes I'm not right on time. And then sometimes, maybe, she'll even come to your place! And I'll hear her, in the morning I'll see her in her nice soft bathrobe, scampering around, walking like a pretty little pussycat.

"She's just the way she used to be, this last month, she's a girl again, happy, all spick and span. Her soul's recovered, and she owes her happiness to you. Oh, I'd do impossible things for you! You know, as we were coming back, she said to me, 'Papa, I'm so happy!' When they say to me, all formal-like, 'My dear father,' they freeze my heart, but when they call me 'Papa' it feels as if I can still see them like little girls, they bring back all my memories. It makes me really feel like their father. I feel as if they still don't belong to anyone else!"

The good old man wiped his eyes, but went on weeping.

"It's been a long time since I've heard them call me that, a long time since she's walked alongside me and held my arm. Oh yes, it's a good ten years since I've been able to walk along next to one of my daughters. And how nice it is, feeling her dress brush against me, being careful to fit my steps to hers, taking in her warmth!

"Well! This morning, I took Delphine everywhere. I went

into all the shops with her. And then I took her home again. Oh, just keep me near you! You'll need someone, sometimes, to do something for you, and I'll always be there. Oh, if this fat Alsatian blockhead would only die, if his gout would decide to climb up into his stomach, how happy my daughter would be! Then you'd be my son-in-law, you'd really be her husband. Lord! She's been so miserable, knowing nothing of worldly pleasures, that I forgive her for everything. Our Father in Heaven must smile down on fathers who really love their children. How much she loves you!" he exclaimed after a moment, shaking his head. "When we were going there, she kept talking to me about you: 'He's so good, father, isn't he? He has such a good heart! Does *he* talk to you about *me*?' I tell you, from d'Artois Street all the way to Panorama Arcade, she told me all about it! She's finally poured out her heart, right into mine. I wasn't an old man any more, the whole morning long, I didn't weigh as much as an ounce. I told her how you'd given me the thousand francs. Oh, the sweet darling, she was moved to tears!

"But what's that over there, on your mantel?" Père Goriot finally remarked, dying of impatience as he saw how Rastignac remained frozen in place.

Still stunned, Eugène stared dazedly at his neighbor. The duel that Vautrin had said would take place the very next day clashed so violently with this fulfillment of all his dearest hopes that he felt himself caught up in some living nightmare. He turned toward the mantel and saw the little box, opened it, and found inside a sheet of paper lying across a magnificent Bréguet watch. There was a message written on the paper:

> I want you to be thinking about me all the time, *because* . . .
>
> DELPHINE.

That last word, he thought, surely referred to something they had said, some argument, perhaps. His eyes grew damp. He saw his family arms enameled onto the box's gold lining. This beautiful watch he'd been wanting for so long, the gold chain, the key, the fine workmanship, the engraving, were like an answer to all his prayers. Goriot stood there, radiant. Obviously, he had promised his daughter to tell her every last detail of how Eugène had reacted to her present, for he was as swept up by youthful emotions as they were, nor did he seem the least excited and happy of the three of them. He already loved Rastignac, both on his daughter's and on his own account.

"You go see her tonight, she's waiting for you. That fat blockhead of an Alsatian is dining at his dancer's place. Oh ho, but was he ever embarrassed, when my lawyer told him off! Didn't he pretend to love my daughter to distraction? Let him lay a hand on her and I'll kill him. Just knowing that my Delphine . . ." He drew a deep sigh. "It would make me commit a crime, it would, but it wouldn't be murder: he's just a calf's head on a pig's body. You'll let me live there, won't you?"

"Yes. My good Père Goriot, you know perfectly well I love you . . ."

"I see it, you're not ashamed of me, not a bit! Let me give you a hug." He folded the student in his arms. "Promise me you'll make her happy! You'll go there tonight, won't you?"

"Certainly! But first I have to go and do something that can't be put off."

"Can I help?"

"Oh Lord, yes! When I go off to see Madame de Nucingen, go to Monsieur Taillefer—not the young one, the father—and tell him I need an hour of his time, tonight, to tell him something of absolutely urgent importance."

"But is it true, young man," said Père Goriot, his face changing, "that you've been courting his daughter, the way those idiots down there have been saying? By all that's holy! You don't know what it's like, when Goriot hits you. And if you're playing us fast and loose, it'll be a hammer blow! Ah, but it can't be true."

"I swear there's only one woman in the world I love," replied the student, "and I've only just realized it."

"Ah, that's good, that's very good!" Père Goriot cried.

"Still," Eugène went on, "Taillefer's son is fighting a duel tomorrow, and I've been told he'll be killed."

"Is that any of your business?" said Goriot.

"But he has to stop his son . . ." Eugène exclaimed.

He was interrupted, just then, by the sound of Vautrin singing, just outside Rastignac's door,

"Ah, Richard, ah my king,
The world's abandoned you now . . .

Boom! Boom! Boom! Boom!

I've been around and around the world
And everyone knows my name . . .

Tra la, la, la, la . . ."

"GENTLEMEN!" called Christophe. "The soup's waiting for you, everyone else is at the table!"

"Just a minute," said Vautrin, "bring down a bottle of my good Bordeaux."

"Do you like the watch, eh?" asked Père Goriot. "Oh, but she's got good taste!"

Vautrin, Père Goriot, and Rastignac went down together and found themselves, because they had come late, sitting next to one another. All during the meal, Eugène treated Vautrin as coldly as possible, though this same Vautrin—in Madame Vauquer's eyes the most amiable of men—had never been so enthusiastic and lively. He was fairly crackling with witty remarks, and knew just how to whip up the other boarders. This confidence, this absolute self-assurance, staggered Eugène.

"What's happened to you, today?" Madame Vauquer asked Vautrin. "You're twittering like an excited sparrow."

"I'm always happy when I've done some first-rate business."

"Business?" observed Eugène.

"Oh yes, business. I've sold some goods that'll bring me a fine commission. Now, Mademoiselle Michonneau," he remarked, noticing how the old maid was staring at him, "is there something about my face that bothers you? You're looking me over like an American Indian. Tell me, tell me! And just to be nice to you, whatever it is I'll change it, I will.

"But you and I won't fight about that, will we, Poiret?" he added, leering at the retired old civil servant.

"The devil with that!" exclaimed the young painter. "You ought to pose as Hercules the Practical Joker!"

"Well now, I might just do that! If, that is, Mademoiselle Michonneau will pose like one of these lovely stone Venuses you find in the cemetery."

"What about Poiret?" asked Bianchon.

"Oh, Poiret has to pose as Poiret!" cried Vautrin. "He'll be the God of Gardens, because that's where you grow *poires* [pears] . . ."

"Oh, that's a feeble one!" Bianchon cut in. "Because there you'll be, somewhere between the pears and the cheese."

"This is all a lot of nonsense," announced Madame Vauquer, "and you'd do better, Monsieur, to let us have some of your good Bordeaux, because I can see the bottle sticking up its nose! Now *that* will make everybody happy, in addition to being good for the stomach."

"Gentlemen," said Vautrin, "our Madame Chairman quite rightly calls us to order. Madame Couture and Mademoiselle Victorine will not be offended by our merry chatter—but please, respect Père Goriot's utter innocence. So: let me propose to you a little bottle-rama of Bordeaux, rendered doubly illustrious by the noble name of Laffitte❀—though that is emphatically *not* a political allusion. Let's go, Chinaman!" he called, seeing that Christophe had not moved. "Over here, Christophe! Hey—don't you even recognize your own name? Chinaman, bring on the liquid refreshment!"

"Here it is, monsieur," said Christophe, handing him the bottle.

Having filled Eugène's glass, and Père Goriot's, while his neighbors drank he carefully poured out a few drops for himself, rolled them around on his tongue, then suddenly grimaced.

"Damn! Damn! It tastes of cork. Keep this one for yourself, Christophe, and go get us another. The stuff on the right, remember? There are sixteen of us, so bring down eight bottles."

"Since you're making a splash," the painter declared, "I'll pay for a hundred chestnuts."

"Ha hah!"

"Whoa!"

"Ooooh!"

The catcalls shot out like the exploding spokes of a firecracker-wheel.

"All right, Momma Vauquer!" cried Vautrin. "Let's have a couple of bottles of champagne!"

❀ Château Lafite = fine wine; Jacques Laffitte (1767–1844) = banker/politician.

"Wouldn't that be something! Why not ask for the whole house? Two bottles of champagne! Lord, but that'd cost a full twelve francs! I wouldn't make a cent on it! But if Monsieur Eugène will pay for it, I'll give you some blackberry liqueur."

"Ah, that stuff works like an emetic," murmured the medical student.

"Shut up, Bianchon," Rastignac called to him. "Every time I hear that word my heart goes . . . All right, yes, go get the champagne, I'll pay for it."

"Sylvie," instructed Madame Vauquer, "set out biscuits and some little cakes."

"Ah, your little cakes have all grown up," said Vautrin, "they've got beards. But bring out the biscuits, yes."

Soon the Bordeaux was making its rounds, everyone grew lively, and the laughter sounded louder and louder. It was savage laughter, mixed with the cries of assorted wild animals. When the Museum employee emitted a well-known Parisian street cry, patterned on the meowing of an amorous tomcat, eight voices bellowed simultaneously:

"Knives sharpened!"

"Bird feed, bird feed!"

"Ice cream, ice cream!"

"Fix your china!"

"Fresh fish, fresh fish!"

"Beat your carpets, beat your wives!"

"Old clothes, old lace, old hats, sell 'em all!"

"Cherries, cherries, sweet and ripe!"

But Bianchon outdid them all, with a perfect nasal imitation: "Um-be-REL-las!"

And then there was a wild, head-splitting racket, full of stuff and nonsense, a regular opera of an uproar, which Vautrin conducted as if they'd been an orchestra, while closely watching Eugène and Père Goriot, who looked as if they must be drunk already. Leaning back in their chairs, the two of them were gravely contemplating this unaccustomed disorder, and drinking virtually nothing; they were both totally preoccupied with what lay ahead of them, that evening, yet neither of them felt able to stand up and walk away. Shooting quick glances at them, and noting every change in their faces, Vautrin took the opportunity, just as their eyes flickered and they looked as if they were falling asleep, to lean down and murmur in Rastignac's ear:

"Young fellow, we're not sly enough, not by a long shot, for fighting with Papa Vautrin, and he loves you too much to let you do anything stupid. When I've decided to do something, only God Himself is strong enough to bar the door against me. Ho ho, we wanted to go warn Père Taillefer, didn't we? Like a naughty schoolboy. The oven's warm, the dough's kneaded, the loaf's in the pan; tomorrow we'll chew it up and the crumbs will fly all over . . . So do we really want to stop it from baking? No, no, let it get done to a turn! If there're any leftover bits of regret, digestion'll take care of 'em. Because while we're having our little nap, my friend, Colonel Count Franchessini will invite you, courtesy the point of his sword, to share in the inheritance of Michel Taillefer. As the new heir, Victorine will have a cool fifteen thousand a year. I've been snooping around, and let me tell you, what she'll inherit from her mother comes to more than three hundred thousand francs . . ."

Eugène could hear these words, but he could not reply: he felt his tongue sticking to the roof of his mouth, and sensed that some irresistible somnolence had him in its grip; he could still see the table and his fellow diners, but only as if through a kind of gleaming fog. The noise gradually subsided, the lodgers drifted out, one by one. And when the only ones left were Madame Vauquer, Madame Couture, Mademoiselle Victorine, Vautrin, and

Père Goriot, Rastignac could just make out, as if she were someone in a dream, Madame Vauquer taking the half-empty bottles and pouring their contents into other half-empty bottles, making herself a set of full ones.

"Oh, they're wild, these young fellows, they're wild!" she was saying.

These were the last words Eugène could still hear and understand.

"There's no one like Monsieur Vautrin for having fun," said Sylvie. "Let's go: Christophe, over there, is snoring like a top."

"Goodnight, Momma Vauquer," said Vautrin. "I'm off to admire the splendid Monsieur Marty perform *The Savage Mountain*, a play based on that gr-reat novel, d'Arlincourt's *The Hermit*. I'll take you with me, if you like, and these two ladies as well."

"No, thank you," said Madame Couture.

"My dear lady!" cried Madame Vauquer. "You turn down the chance to see a play based on *The Hermit*, a novel written by the great Atala de Chateaubriand, a book we so much enjoyed reading that we cried all over it, don't you remember, last summer, out under the *leendens*, because it's really such a virtuous book that your young lady there might very well profit from it."

"We don't go to the theater," replied Victorine.

"We might as well leave these two," said Vautrin, giving first Père Goriot's head, and then Eugène's, a faint, comical push.

And then, arranging the student's head on the back of the chair, so he could sleep more comfortably, he gave him an affectionate kiss on the forehead, singing,

> *"Sleep, sleep, my sweet little darlings!*
> *I'll always watch over your sleep."*

"I'm afraid he might be sick," said Victorine.

"Then stay and take care of him," Vautrin went on. "After all," he whispered in her ear, "it's your duty as a good wife. He adores you, this young fellow, and you'll be his little wife, you just wait and see." And then, in his normal voice, he declared, " 'They lived happily ever after, were highly respected, and had lots of children.' That's how all good romances end, isn't it? So, let's be off, Momma Vauquer," he said, turning and giving her a hug, "get your hat on, and your pretty dress with all the flowers, and that shawl worthy of a countess. Me, I'm going to hunt you up a cab."

And out he went, singing,

"Oh the sun, the sun, the beautiful sun,
You who ripen the lemons . . ."

"My Lord, Madame Couture! I could live on the rooftops and be happy, with a man like that. So," she added, turning to the vermicelli maker, "there's Père Goriot, out like a light. The old miser never thought of taking me *nowhere*, not him. But watch out, he's going to roll off his chair and onto the floor! It isn't right for a man his age to get himself blind and deaf and dumb drunk! And you'll tell me he can't lose what he hasn't got. Well, Sylvie, bring him up to his room."

Sylvie took the old man under the arms, made him walk, and then threw him like a package, dressed exactly as he was, across his bed.

"Poor young man," murmured Madame Couture, pushing back a lock of hair that had dropped over Eugène's eyes, "he's just like a girl, he's not used to this sort of thing."

"Let me tell you," said Madame Vauquer, "in the thirty-one years I've run this establishment a lot of young men have passed through my hands, after a manner of speaking, but I've never seen anyone as nice, as distinguished, as Monsieur Eugène. How handsome he is, sleeping like that! Let his head rest on your shoulder, Madame Couture. Hah! He's falling onto Mademoiselle Victorine: God looks after little children, all right. Pretty soon, he'll bang his head on the chair knob! But they'd make a mighty fine couple, these two."

"Be still, neighbor," said Madame Couture. "You're saying things . . ."

"Nonsense," Madame Vauquer scoffed. "He can't hear a thing. So let's go get me dressed, Sylvie. I'm going to wear my big corset."

"Oh, your big corset, right after supper, Madame," said Sylvie. "No, get somebody else to lace you up, because I'm not going to be the one who kills you. That would be a real dumb thing, and it might cost you your life."

"Who cares? I have to do right by Monsieur Vautrin."

"You're that crazy about your heirs?"

"Come on, Sylvie," starting out of the room, "no more arguments."

"At her age," observed Sylvie, looking at Victorine and gesturing toward her mistress.

Madame Couture and her ward (on whose shoulder Eugène slept) were now all alone in the dining room. Christophe's snores echoed through the silent house, in striking contrast to Eugène's peaceful slumber, for he slept as gracefully as a baby. Happy to allow herself one of those loving acts which evoke all a woman's emotions, for under these circumstances she felt no guilt, feeling the young man's heart beating against hers, Victorine's face displayed something very like the pride of a protective mother. And among the thousand thoughts flowing through her heart, there arose, as she shared the pure, young warmth of his body, a piercing sense of voluptuousness.

"You poor sweet girl!" said Madame Couture, pressing her hand.

The venerable lady stared thoughtfully at Victorine's simple, patient face, upon which the blessed light of happiness had descended. The girl looked like one of those primitive medieval paintings in which the artist has neglected all the subordinate parts, concentrating the magic of his calm, proud brush on his subject's yellow skin, but with the sky overhead glittering in gleaming bright gold.

"He didn't drink more than two glasses, Momma," said Victorine, running her fingers through Eugène's hair.

"But if he'd been a libertine, my daughter, he'd have managed that as easily as the others did. His drunkenness sings his praises."

A carriage could be heard, out in the street.

"Here's Monsieur Vautrin, Momma," said the girl. "Let Monsieur Eugène's head rest on your shoulder. I don't want that man to see me like this, sometimes he says things that make me feel all soiled, and when he looks at a woman, he seems to be taking her dress off."

"Oh no," said Madame Couture, "you're quite wrong! Monsieur Vautrin's a good man, something rather like the late Monsieur Couture—a bit brisk, but nice, rough but well-meaning."

Stepping softly, Vautrin came in, and looked down at the picture made by the two young people, caressed by the lamplight.

"Ah," he said, crossing his arms, "this is a charming sight, one that would have inspired our good Bernardin de Saint-Pierre, author of *Paul and Virginie*,❖ to write some lovely pages. How beautiful youth is, Madame Couture. Poor boy," he said, looking at Eugène, "sleep, because sometimes good things come to us while we're sleeping. Madame," he said, turning to the widow,

❖ Sad, sentimental, highly moral tale, published in 1787.

"what attracts me to this young man, what moves me about him, is my knowledge that the beauty of his soul matches the beauty of his body. Just look, isn't this the very picture of a cherub leaning on an angel's shoulder? Oh, he's worthy of love, that one! If I were a woman, I'd want to die—no, I wouldn't be so stupid—I'd want to live for him. And in admiring them both as I am, madame," he said, lowering his voice and bending to the widow's ear, "I can't help thinking that the good Lord has created them expressly for each other. God works His wonders in mysterious ways," he declared, raising his voice once more. "He sees straight to the bottom of our kidneys and our hearts. And as I see you thus united, my children, joined by your shared purity, I declare that you cannot ever again be separated. God is just. And as for you," he said to the young woman, "it seems to me I can see prosperity hovering just over your head. May I have your hand, Mademoiselle Victorine? I'm a good fortune-teller, I have foretold some very pleasant things. Don't be afraid of me. Ah: what's this I see? By my faith as an honest man, one of the greatest fortunes in all Paris is going to come to you. You'll heap happiness on the man you love. Your father is going to call you to him. And you'll be married to a young man with a title, young, handsome, someone who absolutely adores you."

Just then, the heavy steps of their coquettish landlady were heard on the stairs, interrupting Vautrin's prophecies.

"Ah, here comes Momma Vauquerrrrrr, just as lovely as starrrrrs in the skies, and tied up like a carrot. But can you still breathe?" he asked, setting his hand at the top of her corset. "These briskets are a bit squeezed, Momma. If you weep, there'll be an explosion—but never fear, I'll gather up all the pieces with the care of a true collector."

"Oh, he talks just the way a gallant Frenchman ought to!" exclaimed the happy widow, bending to Madame Couture's ear.

"So goodbye, children," Vautrin continued, turning back to Eugène and Victorine. "You have my blessing," he declared, placing his hands on their heads. "And do believe me, mademoiselle, an honest man's prayers aren't just empty words, they're bound to bring you good luck, because God listens to them."

"Goodnight, my dear friend," said the landlady to Madame Couture. "Do you think," she added in a whisper, "that Monsieur Vautrin might really have designs on me?"

"Ahem! Ahem!"

"Ah, Mother dear," sighed Victorine as soon as the two women were alone, looking down at her hands, "if only the good gentleman were right!"

"But there's only one thing necessary, and then he would be," replied the older lady. "Your monster of a brother just has to fall off his horse."

"Oh, Mother!"

"Good Lord, maybe it's sinful to wish your enemy evil," Madame Couture went on. "Oh well. I'll do penance. But truth to tell, my heart would be smiling as I laid flowers on his grave. He's a wicked young man! He isn't even brave enough to speak up for his own mother, and he's schemed to have everything she left for himself, and keep you from having any. Your mother had a nice fortune. Unluckily for you, the marriage contract didn't say a thing about disposing of her dowry."

"My own good luck would be painful indeed, if it came to me at the cost of someone else's life," said Victorine. "If the only thing that could make me happy were for my brother to disappear, then I'd rather spend the rest of my life right here."

"My Lord, as that nice Monsieur Vautrin says, because you can see he's as religious as he could be, he really is," Madame Couture went on, "and he's no unbeliever, as I've had the pleasure of finding out, the way all these others are, because they talk about

God with less respect than they show the Devil. Ah! But who can possibly know what paths it pleases Providence to guide us along?"

With Sylvie's help, the two women finally got Eugène up to his room, and lay him in his bed, after which the cook loosened his clothes so he could sleep more comfortably. Before leaving, and when her protectress's back was turned, Victorine kissed Eugène on the forehead, deriving quite as much pleasure as she deserved from this criminal act. She looked all around his room, as if collecting all the joys of that day and compressing them, as it were, into a single thought and composing it into a picture she could contemplate over and over, and then she went to sleep, the happiest creature in all Paris.

The little party which had enabled Vautrin to get both Père Goriot and Eugène to drink his opium-flavored wine was also the man's undoing. Bianchon, faintly tipsy, had forgotten to ask Mademoiselle Michonneau about Death-Dodger. Had he so much as pronounced that name, it would certainly have put Vautrin on guard—Vautrin, or, to let him assume his real name, Jacques Collin, one of the most famous of all convicts. And when he'd called her a "graveyard Venus," Mademoiselle Michonneau had made up her mind to betray the ex-convict, though until then, knowing how open-handed Collin could be, she'd been wondering if it mightn't really be better worth her while to warn him and let him escape during the night. With Poiret at her side, she went to lower Saint-Anne Street, hunting Vidocq, the equally famous chief of police, still thinking she was doing business with one of his detectives, a man named Gondureau. Vidocq gave her a gracious welcome. And after a conversation in which all the little details were spelled out, Mademoiselle asked for the potion by means of which she was to effect her verification of the convict's branding mark. Watching this great policeman sigh contentedly, as he rummaged in his file cabinet and extracted a small bottle, Mademoiselle Michonneau understood that there was something about this particular arrest that involved more, much more, than the recapture of some ordinary jailbird. Thinking as hard as she could, she guessed that, operating on information provided by traitorous convicts, the police expected they would sooner or later lay their hands on assets of very considerable value. But when she voiced these suspicions to Vidocq, that sly fox began to smile, then tried to distract the old maid.

"No, you're wrong," he told her. "Collin is the most dangerous college professor who's ever been on the criminal side of things. And that's all there is to it. All the crooks know it, too: he's their flag, their banner, the one who keeps them going, even their Bonaparte; they all adore him. This is one sly dog who's never going to have his pumpkin rolling on the pavement, under the guillotine."

Mademoiselle Michonneau not understanding, Gondureau explained to her that "college professor" and "pumpkin" were two lively expressions in thieves' language, criminals primarily viewing the human head as an "off and on again" proposition. A "college professor" was the living brain in its "on" position, its ability to think, to plan. But a "pumpkin" was their disdainful way of referring to the human head as essentially worthless, once it had been cut off.

"Collin likes to toy with us," he went on. "When we have to deal with men like him, hard and tough as Sheffield steel, we prefer to kill them if, when we make our arrest, they make the least show of resistance. We expect that tomorrow morning we'll be able to take care of Collin that way, somehow or other. Then we avoid all the legal fuss, the expense of watching over him, feeding him, which makes everything a lot easier for the entire community. All the legal procedures, subpoenas for witnesses (and we have to pay them, too)—the whole business of handling these crooks legally is a lot more expensive than the thousand francs you're going to get. And we save time, this way. One swift flick of a bayonet in Death-Dodger's stomach, and we stop a hundred crimes before they're committed, not to mention that we also keep fifty doubtful characters from going wrong—the sort of fellows who'll behave very sensibly as long as they're tiptoeing past a courthouse. Such police procedures make a good deal of sense, you know. According to those who understand what real charity involves, when the police take these measures they are truly preventing crime."

"They're simply serving their country," said Poiret.

"Exactly!" Vidocq answered. "Tonight you're making a lot of sense, my friend. Yes, of course we're serving our country. But the world doesn't want to see us in that light. Society refuses to recognize it, but we perform immense services for them. In any event, a superior man needs to rise above prejudice, and a Christian needs to accept the evils that follow along in the wake of good, when it's effected in unconventional ways. Paris is Paris, you know what I mean? The word explains my whole life.

"And so good-day to you, mademoiselle. I'll be with my men, tomorrow, at King's Gardens. When you want me, send Christophe to Buffon Street, to the same address as before, and ask for Monsieur Gondureau.

"Monsieur, I'll say farewell to you, too. If anything's ever stolen from you, please count on me to get it back for you. At your service."

"Well!" said Poiret. "There are idiots who come apart, just hearing the word 'police.' This fellow's very friendly, and what he's asking you to do is as easy as saying hello."

The following day, surely, must be considered one of the most extraordinary in all the recorded history of Maison Vauquer. The most remarkable event ever to rock its peaceful existence, before then, had been the meteoric appearance of the so-called Countess of Ambermesnil. But nothing could possibly compare to the upheavals of this greatest of all days, which figured forever afterward in Madame Vauquer's conversation.

In the first place, both Père Goriot and Eugène de Rastignac slept until eleven o'clock. Having returned from the theater at midnight, Madame Vauquer herself had stayed in bed until ten-thirty. Christophe's long slumbers had created considerable delays in the *pension*'s daily routines, for he had drained the bottle Vautrin gave him. Neither Poiret nor Mademoiselle Michonneau complained about having to wait for their breakfasts. As for Victorine and Madame Couture, they slept away the whole morning. Vautrin had gone out, before eight o'clock, but then returned just as the meal was finally being served. No one made any fuss, accordingly, when at about eleven-fifteen Sylvie and Christophe went knocking on all the doors, announcing that breakfast was waiting. While Sylvie and the other servant were thus engaged, Mademoiselle Michonneau was the first to come down, quickly pouring her policeman's potion into Vautrin's silver goblet, set like all the others in the double-boiler on the sideboard and heating the milk for his coffee. The old maid had counted on this way of doing things, at Maison Vauquer, to assist her in striking her blow. Nor was it an easy matter, getting all seven of the lodgers to the table, that morning. Just when Eugène, the last of all to come down, appeared yawning and stretching himself, a messenger brought him a letter from Madame de Nucingen. It went as follows:

> *My friend, I won't stand on silly pride, or be angry with you. I waited for you until two in the morning. Waiting for someone you love! Anyone who has experienced this torture would never impose it on anyone else. I understand perfectly that this is the*

first time you've ever been in love. But what happened? I've been worried. If I hadn't been afraid of betraying my heart's secrets, I'd have come to see if whatever you were involved in was something good or something bad. But to go out at that hour, whether on foot or in my carriage, would have been the ruin of me, wouldn't it? I was terribly aware of what a misfortune it is, being a woman. Reassure me, tell me just why you didn't come, after what my father surely told you. I'll be angry, of course, but I'll forgive you. Are you sick? Why do you live so far away? Oh send me a word, please. And soon, yes? If you're very busy, one word will be enough, I assure you. Tell me: I'm coming right away, or else: I'm in pain, and I can't come. But if you were sick, my father would have come and told me! What happened? . . .

"Yes, yes, what happened?" Eugène cried, rushing into the dining room, waving the letter without having read it to the end. "What time is it?"

"Eleven-thirty," said Vautrin, putting sugar in his coffee.

The escaped convict looked at Eugène with that coldly fascinating stare which wonderfully magnetic men are able to muster and which, they say, is capable of calming raving lunatics in insane asylums. Eugène was trembling all over. Then a cab could be heard, from out in the street, and one of Monsieur Taillefer's servants (Madame Couture recognized him at once) came rushing in, flustered and frightened.

"Mademoiselle," he called to Victorine, "your father wants you, right now! Something horrible has happened. Monsieur Frederick's been in a duel, and he's been stabbed in the forehead, and the doctors despair of saving him—you'll barely be able to say farewell to him, he's no longer conscious."

"The poor young fellow!" exclaimed Vautrin. "Why should you get into fights when you have thirty thousand solid francs a year to live on? My Lord, but young people simply don't know what they're doing."

"Monsieur Vautrin!" Eugène said loudly.

"What, what, you great baby?" said Vautrin, calmly finishing his coffee, a procedure which Mademoiselle Michonneau watched far too closely to be in any way affected by the extraordinary event which had stupefied everyone else. "In Paris, they fight duels all the time, don't they?"

"I'll go with you, Victorine," said Madame Couture.

Both ladies rushed out, not bothering to put on either hat or shawl. Before she disappeared, Victorine, her eyes brimming with tears, gave Eugène a look which said, I wouldn't have believed our good fortune could make me weep like this!

"Hah!" said Madame Vauquer. "So you really are a prophet, Monsieur Vautrin."

"I am anything and everything," replied Jacques Collin.

"It's really amazing," Madame Vauquer continued, stringing together a meaningless chain of commonplace comments. "Death never warns us he's coming. Young people often get taken before old ones. We're very lucky, we women, not being vulnerable to duels, but we have other problems men don't suffer from. We bear children, and the pangs of childbirth last for a long, long time! What a bonanza for Victorine! Now her father can't help but take her under his wing."

"You see?" Vautrin remarked, glancing at Eugène. "Yesterday she didn't have a penny, and today she's worth millions."

"So then, Monsieur Eugène," Madame Vauquer exclaimed, "it's all turned out very well for you, hasn't it?"

This made Père Goriot look at Eugène, at which point he saw the crumpled letter in the student's hands.

"But you haven't finished reading it! What's going on? Are you turning out like all the others?" he asked bluntly.

"Madame," announced Eugène, turning to the landlady and speaking with such obvious horror and disgust that everyone in the room was shocked, "I will never marry Mademoiselle Victorine."

Père Goriot clasped his hand and embraced him. He would have liked to kiss him.

"Ah?" said Vautrin. "Well, the Italians have a word for it: *col tempo*, in time, in time."

"I'm to wait for your reply," Madame de Nucingen's messenger said to Rastignac.

"You may say I'll be there."

The man left. Eugène was in such a state of anger and fury that he could not mind his tongue.

"What should I do?" he said aloud, though speaking to himself. "I haven't any proof!"

Vautrin began to smile. Just then the poison in his stomach began to act. But the convict was a man of such strength that, despite this, he rose, stared straight at Rastignac, and said, his voice suddenly hollow,

"Young fellow, sometimes good things happen to us while we're asleep."

Then he dropped to the ground, like a corpse.

"It's divine justice," said Eugène.

"My God, what's happened to poor Monsieur Vautrin?"

"He's having a fit," exclaimed Mademoiselle Michonneau.

"Sylvie, go girl, get the doctor," ordered Madame Vauquer. "Ah, Monsieur Rastignac, run and fetch Monsieur Bianchon, because Sylvie will never find our own doctor, Monsieur Grimprel."

Happy for any excuse to get him away from that den of horrors, Rastignac went running out.

"Christophe, hurry up, go to the pharmacy and ask for something to cure a fit."

Christophe too went out.

"Now, Père Goriot, help us get him up to his room."

They lifted Vautrin, got him up the stairs, and put him on his bed.

"I'm of no further use to you," said Goriot. "So I'm going to see my daughter."

"You selfish old dog!" cried Madame Vauquer. "Go, and I hope you die in the street!"

"See if you can find some ether," Mademoiselle Michonneau instructed Madame Vauquer, as she and Monsieur Poiret pulled off Vautrin's outer clothing.

Madame Vauquer went downstairs at once, leaving Mademoiselle Michonneau mistress of all she surveyed.

"All right, hurry up and get his shirt off and right back on again! That way you can be good for something," she informed Poiret, "by keeping me from seeing him naked. You're standing there with your mouth hanging open!"

They turned Vautrin over, Mademoiselle Michonneau gave the unconscious man a hard slap on the shoulder, and the two fatal letters, white surrounded with red, could be seen perfectly clearly.

"There you are, you've just earned yourself a neat three thousand francs," Poiret exclaimed, turning Vautrin back again, while Mademoiselle Michonneau put on his shirt. "Oof! He's heavy," he went on, letting the unconscious man fall flat.

"Shut up. Maybe he has a moneybox?" the old maid said swiftly, her eyes seeming to pierce right through the walls, while she eagerly investigated every stick of furniture in the room. "Can we open his writing desk, for some reason or other?" she continued.

"That might not be a good idea," Poiret answered.

"Why not? Stolen money, which used to belong to God

knows who, no longer belongs to anybody. But there isn't time," she concluded. "I hear the old lady coming back."

"Here's some ether," said Madame Vauquer. "I tell you, this is a day for extraordinary happenings! Lord! But this man can't really be sick, he's as white as a chicken."

"As a chicken?" echoed Poiret.

The landlady set her hand over Vautrin's heart.

"And his heart's beating nice and even."

"Even?" exclaimed Poiret, stunned.

"So he's fine."

"You think so?" Poiret wondered.

"Yes, by God! He looks like he's just sleeping. Sylvie's gone for a doctor. Is he sniffing the ether, Mademoiselle Michonneau? Ah, it's just a se-pasm. His pulse is fine! He's as strong as a Turk. Just look, mademoiselle, just see how his stomach's all covered with fur: oh, he'll live a hundred years, he will! Even his wig's still right in place. Ah, it's glued on, his hair's fake, look here, it's really red. They say they're either good as gold, redheads, or rotten to the core! This must be a good one, eh?"

"Good for hanging," said Poiret.

"You mean, on some pretty girl's neck!" Mademoiselle Michonneau exclaimed quickly. "You go away, Monsieur Poiret. It's our business, we women, to take care of you men when you're sick. Besides, for as much use as you are, you might as well go out for a walk," she added. "Madame Vauquer and I, we'll take care of dear Monsieur Vautrin."

Monsieur Poiret went off without making a sound, like a dog that's been kicked by its master.

Rastignac had gone out for a walk, he needed the air, he felt he was suffocating. He had meant to stop it, this crime that had been committed a few hours ago, at the agreed-upon time. What had happened? What should he do now? He trembled at the thought of being accomplice to a murder. Vautrin's calm still horrified him.

"But suppose he dies and never says a word?" Rastignac said to himself.

He walked up and down the back alleys, as if a pack of bloodhounds were sniffing on his trail, and in his mind he could hear them baying along behind him.

"Ah ha!" he suddenly heard Bianchon saying. "Have you read the morning paper?"

It was *The Pilot*, a radical rag edited by Monsieur Tissot,❂ which appeared later than the regular morning newspapers, setting out the day's news for provincial readers a full day before the other rags got around to it.

"It's got a wonderful story," said the medical student. "Taillefer's son fought a duel with Count Franchessini, of the Old Guard, and got two inches of iron planted in his forehead. And now our little Victorine's one of the richest women in Paris. Hey, if only we'd known in advance! Oh, how death turns things upside down! Is it true, by the way, that the little lady used to smile on you?"

"Shut up, Bianchon. I'll never marry her. I love a magnificent woman, she loves me, I . . ."

"You sound exactly like someone who's kicking himself for not being unfaithful. Just show me the woman, would you, who'd be worth sacrificing old Taillefer's fortune for!"

"Are all the demons in Hell after me?" cried Rastignac.

"What the devil's the matter with you? Are you crazy? Let me have your hand," Bianchon instructed, "so I can take your pulse. You're running a fever."

❂ Pierre-François Tissot, formerly a professor at the Collège de France, dismissed when the monarchy was restored.

"Go to Madame Vauquer's place," Eugène directed. "That rascal Vautrin's had a fit."

"Oh ho!" said Bianchon, turning away, "you're confirming my suspicions, but I'll go confirm them for myself."

The law student's walk was a solemn one. Indeed, it was something like a tour of his conscience. But though he hesitated, though he grilled himself, though he wavered, at least his sense of his own honesty finally emerged from this harsh, horrible debate truly tested, like an iron bar that no one can bend. He remembered the things Père Goriot had confided in him, the night before, he remembered the apartment Goriot and his daughter had picked out for him, on d'Artois Street, near Delphine. He took out her letter, re-read it, kissed it.

"Love like this is my anchor, my salvation," he told himself. "This poor old man's heart has really suffered. He doesn't talk about his troubles, but who can't figure them out! Well then, I'll take care of him as if he were my own father, I'll make sure he experiences a thousand sorts of happiness. If she loves me, he'll come to my place all the time and spend the day near her. This other great lady, this Countess de Restaud, is a wretch, she'd turn her father into a janitor. But dear Delphine! She's better for him, she's really worth loving. And how happy I'll be, tonight!"

He pulled out his watch and admired it.

"Everything's gone right for me! When you love each other, and you're faithful, it's all right to help each other, I can certainly accept this from her. Besides, there's no doubt I'm going to be successful, so I'll be able to give it back, a hundred times over. There's nothing criminal about this relationship, nothing even the most moral person in the world could frown at. How many completely moral people live exactly like this! We're not deceiving anybody: what degrades people is lying and cheating. When you lie, that's when you're unworthy, right? She's been separated from her husband for a long time. Anyway, I'm simply going to tell him, this Alsatian, to let me have this woman, because he can't possibly make her happy."

Rastignac's struggle went on for a long time. And even though the victory finally went, as it had to, to youth's strengths and virtues, still, by four-thirty, with dusk starting to fall, an ungovernable curiosity led the student back to Maison Vauquer, which he had now silently vowed to leave for good. He wanted to know if Vautrin was dead.

Having first decided to give the unconscious man a stomach-emptying drug, Bianchon had carried some of what Vautrin vomited back to his hospital, to have a chemical analysis performed. Seeing how insistently Mademoiselle Michonneau wanted simply to throw it all away, his doubts had gotten even stronger. And then Vautrin was so quickly and easily entirely himself again that the medical student couldn't help suspecting a plot against the man who was surely the *pension*'s gay life of the party. By the time Rastignac returned, Vautrin was back on his feet, standing near the dining room stove. Having heard the news about young Taillefer's duel, the lodgers—except for Père Goriot—had congregated earlier than usual, curious to hear all the details of the affair and what effect it had had on Victorine's destiny, and were busy chatting about the whole adventure. As Eugène came in, his eyes met those of the imperturbable Vautrin, and the escaped convict's glance pierced so deeply into the student's heart, plucking so powerfully at wickedly-tuned strings, that the young man shook all over.

"So, my dear young fellow," Vautrin observed, "the Grim Reaper's going to wait a long time before he gets me. According to these ladies, I've come through a fit that would have killed an ox."

"Ho—you'd do better to say a bull," called out Madame Vauquer.

"Could you be sorry to see me still alive?" Vautrin murmured in Rastignac's ear, convinced he could read the student's very thoughts. "You'd have to be stronger than the Devil himself!"

"Well, it seems to me," said Bianchon, "that when Mademoiselle Michonneau was talking about someone called Death-Dodger, the other day, she used a name that fits you like a glove."

The name hit Vautrin like a bolt of lightning; he turned pale, staggered for a moment, and his magnetic glance glittered at Mademoiselle Michonneau like a shaft of sunlight, a powerful gust of hatred that cut her legs right out from under her. The old maid half fell into a chair. Poiret immediately stepped between her and Vautrin, realizing that she was in danger, for the escaped convict's face dropped the benign mask behind which his true nature had been hidden, revealing a wild savagery. Utterly flabbergasted, no one else had yet figured out what was going on. Then they heard the sound of men approaching, and the ring of rifles being set against the pavement. And just as Collin was automatically surveying the walls and windows, hunting some way out, four men appeared in the doorway. Vidocq came first, and three detectives followed after him.

"In the name of the law, and the name of the King," announced one of the officers, though there was such a loud murmur of astonishment that no one could hear him.

But silence quickly descended once again, as the lodgers moved aside, making room for three of the men, who came forward, their hands in their pockets, and loaded pistols in their hands. Two uniformed policemen stepped into the doorway they'd left, and two others appeared in the other doorway, near the stairs. Soldiers' footsteps, and the readying of their rifles, echoed from the pavement outside, in front of the house. Death-Dodger had no hope of escape; everyone stared at him, irresistibly drawn. Vidocq went directly to where he stood, and swiftly punched Collin in the head with such force that his wig flew off, revealing the stark horror of his skull. Brick-red, short-clipped hair gave him a look at once sly and powerful, and both head and face, blending perfectly, now, with his brutish chest, glowed with the fierce, burning light of a hellish mind. It was suddenly obvious to them all just who Vautrin was, what he'd done, what he'd been doing, what he would go on to do; they suddenly understood at a glance his implacable ideas, his religion of self-indulgence, exactly the sort of royal sensibility which tinted all his thoughts with cynicism, as well as all his actions, and supported both by the strength of an organization prepared for anything. The blood rose into his face, his eyes gleamed like some savage cat's. He seemed to explode into a gesture of such wild energy, and he roared with such ferocity that, one and all, the lodgers cried out in terror. His fierce, feral movement, and the general clamor he'd created, made the policemen draw their weapons. But seeing the gleam of cocked pistols, Collin immediately understood his peril, and instantly proved himself possessor of the highest of all human powers. It was a horrible, majestic spectacle! His face could only be compared to some steaming apparatus, full of billowing smoke capable of moving mountains, but dissolved in the twinkling of an eye by a single drop of cold water. The drop that doused his rage flickered as rapidly as a flash of light. Then he slowly smiled, and turned to look down at his wig.

"This isn't one of your polite days, is it, old boy?" he said to Vidocq. And then he held out his hands to the policemen, beckoning them with a movement of his head. "Gentlemen, officers, I'm ready for your handcuffs or your chains, as you please. I ask those present to take due note of the fact that I offer no resistance."

The astounding swiftness with which this human volcano had cooled and absorbed molten lava and flames produced an admiring murmur.

"That stops you, eh, Mister Copper?" the convict went on, staring at his celebrated captor.

"All right, get your shirt off," the gentleman from lower Saint-Anne Street ordered.

"Why?" said Collin. "There are ladies present. I'm denying nothing, I'm surrendering."

He paused, looking around like an orator contemplating some stunning revelations.

"Papa Lachapelle," he directed, speaking to an old, white-haired man who, after pulling the arrest-report form out of his briefcase, had seated himself at the end of the table, "write it all down. I admit to being Jacques Collin, known as Death-Dodger, sentenced to twenty years behind bars—and I've just proved that I've earned my nickname. Had I so much as lifted my hand," he explained to the lodgers, "these three stool pigeons would have emptied my veins right onto Momma Vauquer's nice clean floor. These jokers love to cook up ambushes!"

Hearing these words, Madame Vauquer grew faint.

"My God, it's enough to make you sick: just yesterday I was at the theater with him—me!" she said to fat Sylvie.

"Just consider what you're saying, Momma," Collin went on. "Did it do you any harm, being in my box at the theater, yesterday?" He had raised his voice. "Are you any better than we are? There's less shame branded on our shoulders than there is in your hearts, you limp links in a gangrenous social chain: the best of you never said no to me." His eyes lingered on Rastignac, at whom he smiled graciously, the pleasant glance contrasting sharply with the harsh, rough expression on his face. "We've still got our bargain

going, my little angel, if you want to take me up on it! You know
what I mean?"

And he began to sing:

"*Oh I love my Fanchette,*
Who's never arty . . ."

"And don't you worry about it," he continued, "I know how
to collect what's due me. They're too afraid of me to try any swin-
dles, let me tell you!"

Prison language and prison ways, with their brusque transition from pleasant to horrible, their ghastly grandeur, their easy
familiarity, their vulgarity, suddenly shone out in the man's biting
remark—although in truth he was no longer a man, but the em-
bodied representative of a degraded people, a savage, logical nation, brutal, flexible. In an instant Collin had been transformed
into a kind of hellish poem which depicted all human emotions
except one, remorse. He looked the very image of the fallen arch-
angel, forever militant. Rastignac lowered his eyes, accepting this
criminal kinship as if in expiation for all his evil thoughts.

"So. Who turned me in?" Collin inquired, letting his terrible
glance roam around the room. And then he stopped at Mademoiselle Michonneau. "It was you," he said to her, "you old slut,
you set off that fake fit, you busybody! All I'd have to do is say
two words and in another week your head would be off. But I
forgive you, I'm a Christian. But it wasn't you who really ratted
on me. So, who was it?—Oh ho, you're digging around up there!"
he exclaimed, hearing the policemen opening his bureau drawers
and going through his things. "The birds all left the nest, they flew
off yesterday. You won't learn a thing. Here's where I keep my
account books!" he said, hitting himself in the forehead. "But now

I know who did the trick. It was that son of a bitch, Silk-Thread. It was him, wasn't it, Daddy Man-Catcher?" he said to Vidocq. "That fits perfectly with keeping our cash upstairs there. But there's nothing left any more, my little stoolpigeons. And as for Silk-Thread, it won't be two weeks before he's eating dirt, even if you get your whole police force watching over him.

"How much did you pay her, that Michonette?" he asked the policemen. "A couple of thousand francs? I'm worth more than that, you putrefied old Ninon,✿ you worn-out Madame Pompadour, you graveyard Venus. Had you warned me, instead, you'd have gotten six thousand francs. Ah! that never occurred to you, did it, you old fleshmonger, or else you'd have held out your hand in my direction. Yes, I'd have paid that, easily, to keep from taking this little trip, which just makes trouble for me, and costs me money," he observed, as they fastened handcuffs around his wrists. "Now these fellows are going to have their fun, making my life difficult until the cows come home. If they send me right to jail, it won't be long before I'll be doing what I usually do, in spite of every little flatfoot alive. Down there, they'd all turn themselves inside-out to spring their boss, this fellow they call Death-Dodger, from behind bars! Is there a single one of you who could call on more than ten thousand comrades, the way I can, to do anything and everything for you?" he demanded proudly. "There's good in there!" he called, clapping himself on the chest. "I've never betrayed anyone! Hey, you old bitch, look at all these people!" he said, addressing Mademoiselle Michonneau. "I scare them silly, but you, you make them feel like throwing up. Go collect on your lottery ticket!"

He paused, looking at the lodgers.

"What are you, a bunch of dumb animals? Haven't you ever

✿ Ninon de Lenclos (1620–1705), famous Parisian hostess.

seen a convict before? A convict like this one, like Jacques Collin, standing right here, is not only a man but he's less of a coward than the rest of you, because he stands up and fights against the incredible lies of this so-called social contract—as Jean-Jacques❖ called it—and I lay claim to being one of his disciples. Anyway, it's just me against the government and its whole pile of courts and cops, and its heaps of money, and I say screw them all."

"Damnation!" said the painter. "What a portrait subject he'd be!"

"So tell me, you hangman's bootlicker, you Watchman for the Widow-maker (the potent poetical word we use for the guillotine)," the convict went on, turning toward Vidocq, "be a good fellow, eh, and tell me if it really was Silk-Thread who turned me in! I don't want him to pay for what someone else did; it wouldn't be right."

The agents who'd been opening everything, and writing everything down, came back into the room and, in a low voice, said something to their chief. The official report was ready.

"Gentlemen," Collin said to the lodgers, "now they're going to take me away. You've all been pleasant to me, during my time here, and I'm grateful. Allow me to say farewell. Accept, please, the gift of some figs that I'll send you from Provence." He took several steps, then turned and looked straight at Rastignac. "Goodbye, Eugène," he said, his voice gentle, sad, utterly unlike the brusque, harsh tone he'd been using. "If you get into trouble, I've left you a devoted friend you can turn to." In spite of the handcuffs, he assumed a dueling posture and, moving like a fencing master, called out, "One! Two!" and lunged. "If you run into bad luck, call on him. Money and man—they'll both be at your disposal."

❖ Jean-Jacques Rousseau (1712–1778), French social reformer.

And the remarkable fellow conveyed this final message so clownishly that no one but Rastignac and himself could possibly have understood it. When the house was finally free of all the policemen, and soldiers, and detectives, Sylvie, who had been rubbing her mistress's temples with vinegar, stared around at the lodgers, stunned,

"Well!" she said. "All the same, he's a good man."

Like a charm, this observation broke the spell under which they'd all been held, gripped as they were by a whole battery of excited emotions. And after a quick glance at each other, the lodgers turned as one and stared at Mademoiselle Michonneau, cowering next to the stove, as thin, dried-out, and frigid as a mummy, her eyes cast down, as if she feared that the eyeshade she had on might not be enough to conceal their looks. They had felt uncomfortable with her for a long, long time, but now they suddenly understood why. A heavy murmur reverberated through the room, its absolute unity of sound indicating an equally absolute unanimity of disgust. Mademoiselle Michonneau heard it, but did not move. The first to speak was Bianchon, who leaned toward the man next to him.

"I'll be leaving," he said softly, "if that old maid keeps eating with us."

They all heard him and, except for Poiret, they all winked to register their approval, after which, strengthened by the general agreement, the medical student went over to the old man.

"Since you're so friendly with Mademoiselle Michonneau," he said to Poiret, "tell her, make her understand that she's got to leave, and right away."

"Right away?" Poiret repeated, stunned.

He went over to Mademoiselle Michonneau and whispered in her ear.

"I've paid my rent!" she exclaimed, glaring like a viper at the other lodgers. "I pay my way, just as you all do!"

"That needn't keep you here," said Rastignac. "We'll all chip in and pay you back."

"You're on Collin's side," she declared, scowling at him venomously, with a particularly knowing sneer, "and it's not hard to figure out why."

Hearing this, Eugène jumped up, as if intending to throw himself on the old maid and strangle her. That knowing sneer, the treachery of which he understood only too well, burned in his soul with a horrible light.

"Leave her alone," the lodgers called out.

Rastignac crossed his arms over his breast and stood absolutely still.

"That's got to be the end of this Mademoiselle Judas," said the painter to Madame Vauquer. "If you don't get rid of her, the rest of us will leave your stable, and we'll tell everyone the only people who can stand it here are spies and convicts. If you show her to the door, however, we'll shut our mouths about this whole affair, because, after all, something like this could happen in the best of circles, as long as convicts are branded on the shoulder and not on the forehead, and they're not forbidden to disguise themselves like Parisian bourgeoisie and act as stupid as they all are."

Madame Vauquer, hearing this, suddenly recovered her strength and sat up, crossing her arms and opening her clear eyes, in which there was no trace of tears.

"My dear sir, then you plan to ruin me? That Monsieur Vautrin . . . but oh Lord!" she interrupted herself. "I can't keep from calling him by the honest name he used here! Anyway," she went on, "that makes one room empty, and now you want me to have two more I'll need to rent, just when the whole world's all settled in and nobody's looking to move."

"Gentlemen," announced Bianchon, "get your hats and we'll all take our meal on Sorbonne Place, at Flicoteaux's."

It took Madame Vauquer no more than the twinkle of an eye to figure out the best side to take, and turning to Mademoiselle Michonneau, she said,

"Now, my pretty little one, you don't want to ruin me, do you? You can see for yourself how hard on me these gentlemen are being: you go on up to your room, for tonight."

"For good, for good!" the lodgers all cried. "We insist that she leave right now."

"But the poor girl hasn't even eaten," whined Poiret.

"Let her go eat wherever she wants to," several voices declared.

"Out, you stool pigeon!"

"Out, both stool pigeons!"

"Gentlemen," cried Poiret, standing up, suddenly infused with the courage love lends to a rutting ram, "show some respect for her sex!"

"Stool pigeons don't have any sex," said the painter.

"Celebrated sexorama!"

"Out the doorarama!"

"Gentlemen, this is highly improper! Before you can turn people out, there are procedures to follow. We've paid our rent, we're staying," declared Poiret, jamming his hat down on his head and sitting in a chair alongside Mademoiselle Michonneau, to whom Madame Vauquer was preaching a sermon.

"Naughty boy," the painter said to Poiret. "Go away, naughty boy!"

"All right, if you're not going, then all the rest of us are," said Bianchon.

And they rose as one and started out of the room.

"What are you doing to me, mademoiselle?" screamed Madame Vauquer. "I'll be ruined! You *can't* stay here, they'll resort to violence."

Mademoiselle Michonneau stood up.

"She's going!"

"She's not going!"

"She's going!"

"She's not going!"

This aggressive chant, and all the hostile remarks beginning to be aimed at her, left Mademoiselle Michonneau no choice but to leave, though in a low voice she first made the landlady agree to a number of stipulations.

"I will go to Madame Buneaud's," she said threateningly.

"Go wherever you like, mademoiselle," said Madame Vauquer, who understood this choice of a rival establishment, for which she naturally felt a keen dislike, as a direct insult to herself. "Go to Buneaud's, you'll drink wine that would make a goat hop up and down, and you'll eat secondhand scraps."

Without a sound, the lodgers formed two lines. Poiret looked so yearningly at Mademoiselle Michonneau, showing himself so simple-mindedly indecisive, not certain whether to go or stay, that the delighted boarders, overjoyed that Mademoiselle Michonneau was going after all, began to laugh at him, too.

"Yip, yip, yip, Poiret!" the painter called. "Let's go, hop, hop, hop!"

The Museum employee began to sing, in his best comic style, a well-known ballad:

"Young and handsome Dunois,
Leaving for the East . . ."

"Go on already," cried Bianchon, "you're bursting to go, *trahit sua quemque voluptas*❖ [Do what makes you happy]."

"Everybody has his own girlfriend—a free translation of Virgil," explained the assistant school-master.

Mademoiselle Michonneau glanced at Poiret, and made as if to take his arm, and he could not resist so direct an appeal: he came to lend the old maid his support. Applause rang out, plus a veritable explosion of laughter:

"Bravo, Poiret!"

"Good old Poiret!"

"Poiret as Apollo!"

"Poiret as Mars!"

"Brave old Poiret!"

Just then, a mailman came in, handing Madame Vauquer a letter; after reading it, she let herself fall into a chair.

"All that's left is to burn my house down! Let it be hit by lightning! Taillefer's son died at three o'clock. Well, I'm being punished for wishing well to those women, at that poor young man's expense. Madame Couture and Victorine ask me to send on their things, they're going to live at her father's house. Monsieur Taillefer will allow his daughter to keep the old widow with her, as a companion. So now I have four apartments empty, and five lodgers are gone!"

She sat there, looking ready to weep.

"Oh, misery's falling on me!" she cried.

Suddenly the sound of a carriage approaching, then stopping, could be heard outside.

"Another thunderbolt!" said Sylvie.

Suddenly Goriot appeared, his face shining with such happiness that it was enough to make you believe in regeneration.

❖ Virgil, *Ecloques*, 2, 65.

"Goriot in a cab," the lodgers murmured. "It's the end of the world."

The old man went right up to Eugène, who had been sitting, self-absorbed, off in a corner, and took the young man's arm.

"Come, come," he said joyously.

"Don't you know what's happened?" Eugène asked. "Vautrin was an escaped convict, and they came and arrested him. And Taillefer's son is dead."

"Well! What's all that to us?" replied Père Goriot. "I'm having dinner with my daughter, at your place, you know what I mean? She's waiting for you, come on!"

He pulled so forcefully at Rastignac's arm that, like it or not, the young man had to walk out with him, carried off as if Goriot had been reclaiming his mistress.

"So let's eat!" called the painter.

They all scrambled into their places around the table.

"Bless my soul!" said fat Sylvie, "everything's going wrong today: now my stew's all stuck to the pan. Bah! Too bad, you'll eat it burned and that's that!"

Seeing only ten instead of eighteen diners gathered at her table, Madame Vauquer, disheartened, couldn't say a word, so they all tried to think of consoling topics and make her feel better. But though those who came to Maison Vauquer only to dine were, at first, satisfied to discuss Vautrin and the day's events, they quickly yielded to sly, roundabout temptation, chattering on about duels, prisons, criminal justice, what laws needed amending, and what jail was like. They were soon a thousand miles distant from Jacques Collin, from Victorine and her dead brother. There may have been only ten of them, but they babbled and shouted like twenty—indeed, there seemed to be more of them than usual, which constituted the entire difference between that night's dinner and the one the night before. The casual indifference of this egotistic little world which, the next day, would need to have some new prey to devour, drawn just like this one from Paris's daily doings, inevitably took over, and Madame Vauquer herself allowed soothing hope—which spoke with fat Sylvie's voice—to creep up once more.

For Eugène that whole day, from morning to night, could not help but be phantasmagoric, because in spite of his strength of character and the goodness of his heart, when he found himself sitting in the cab, next to Père Goriot, he could not sort out all the thoughts whirling through his head. The old man's words fairly shone with happiness, lapping at the student's ears, after what he had seen and felt, like phrases heard in a dream.

"It was all fixed up this morning. The three of us will eat together every night—together! Understand? It's been four years since I've sat down to dinner with my Delphine, my little Delphine. And now I'll have her to myself for a whole evening. We've been at your apartment all morning. I've been working like a sailor, with my coat off. I helped them move all the furniture. Oh, oh, you have no idea how sweet she can be, at the dinner table, she kept fussing over me, 'Take some of this, Papa, eat some of this, it's good.' And then I can't eat at all. Ah, I haven't been so at peace with her as I am right now, not for a long, long time!"

"So today," Eugène observed, "the world's gone upside down?"

"Upside down?" answered Père Goriot. "The world's never been so right side up! Every face I pass in the street is smiling, people are all shaking hands and hugging each other—as if they were all going to have dinner with their daughters, gulping down a nice little dinner that she ordered, right in my presence, from one of the best chefs in Paris. But oh! Put it near her and bitter aloes would turn as sweet as honey."

"I think I'm coming back to life," said Eugène.

"Hurry up, coachman!" Père Goriot called out, yanking open the little window in front of him. "Faster, faster! I'll tip you a hundred sous if you get us where we're going in less than ten minutes!"

Hearing this, the coachman began to clatter across Paris at the speed of light.

"He just won't drive, this fellow," Père Goriot muttered.

"But where are you taking me?" Rastignac wondered.

"Home, to your own apartment," Père Goriot replied.

At d'Artois Street, the carriage stopped. Père Goriot was the first one out, tossing ten francs to the coachman, throwing his money around like a widower who, caught up in a paroxysm of pleasure, can't be bothered worrying about anything.

"Come on, let's go up," he urged Rastignac, hurrying him through a courtyard and then leading him right to the door of a third-floor apartment, located at the back of a handsome new building. There was no need to ring the bell. The door was opened for them by Thérèse, Madame de Nucingen's chambermaid. Eugène found himself in a delightful bachelor's apartment, consisting of a hallway, a small living room, and a bedroom that had a dressing room overlooking a garden. And in the living room, furnished and decorated in the handsomest and most gracious taste, he saw in the candlelight Delphine, as she rose from a small sofa near the fireplace, set her veil on the mantel, and said to him, her voice radiating tenderness,

"So we had to hunt you out, you who understand nothing whatever."

Thérèse left the room. The student took Delphine in his arms, holding her tight and crying with happiness. This final contrast between what he was seeing and what he had just come from, all in a single day during which one vexation after another had wearied both his heart and his head, left him utterly overwrought.

"I knew all along he loved you, I did," Père Goriot said softly to his daughter, as Eugène lay stretched out on the sofa, so limp that he could neither speak nor quite understand how this ultimate magic wand had been lifted and waved.

"But come see, come see," Madame de Nucingen urged him, taking him by the hand and leading him into a room designed as an exact replica, though on a smaller scale—curtains furniture, everything—of Delphine's bedroom.

"There's no bed," Rastignac said.

"Quite so, monsieur," she replied, blushing and squeezing his hand.

Eugène, looking at her, suddenly understood, young as he was, all he needed to know about the true modesty of a woman in love.

"You are one of those creatures meant to be eternally adored," he whispered in her ear. "Yes, let me tell you, since we understand each other so well: the more vibrant and honest love is, the more it must be veiled, hidden, mysterious. We won't share our secret with anyone."

"Ah, so I'm not anyone, is that it?" Père Goriot grumbled.

"You know perfectly well that you're one of *us*, that's what . . ."

"Ho, that's what I wanted to hear! Just don't pay any attention to me, all right? I'll come and I'll go like some good fairy who's everywhere, someone you know is always around even if you don't see him. So! My little Delphine, my Ninette, my little one! Wasn't I right to tell you, 'There's a nice apartment on d'Artois Street, let's furnish it for him!' You didn't want to. You see? I'm the author of your happiness, as I'm also the author of your days. To be happy, fathers must always be giving, and giving. Always giving: that's just what you do, when you're a father."

"What?" Eugène wondered.

"Yes, yes, she didn't want to, she was afraid they'd say all sorts of stupid things, as if happiness meant anything to the world! But every woman alive dreams of doing exactly what she's done . . ."

But Père Goriot was speaking to himself, for Madame de Nucingen had drawn Rastignac into the dressing room, from which, softly but very audibly, one could hear the sound of a kiss. The dressing room too was as elegant as the rest of the apartment, for absolutely nothing had been omitted.

"Did we really guess what you'd want?" she asked, going back into the living room and sitting at the table.

"Perfectly," he said, "more than perfectly. Oh, but this utter luxury, all these dreams made true, all this youthful poetry, so elegant, I'm only too well aware that I simply don't deserve it— and how could I accept it from you, poor as I am . . ."

"Ah! Ah! You're already resisting me, are you?" she said, pretending prettily to be scolding him, while simultaneously pouting deliciously, the way women always do when they want to make fun of some scruple, the better to clear it out of their path.

But all day long Eugène had been questioning himself, probing terribly seriously, and Vautrin's arrest, in particular, had shown him into what a deep abyss he had almost fallen; his high-minded sentiments, his refinement, were thus too recently and too thoroughly reinforced to let him give in to this caressing dismissal of his noble ideals. He felt a profound sadness descending over him.

"Really?" exclaimed Madame de Nucingen. "You'd really refuse? Do you understand what that would mean? You're unsure of the future, you don't dare link yourself to me. You're afraid you might betray my love, aren't you? If you love me, if I . . . but I do love you, so why shrink from such insignificant debts? If you only knew the pleasure I've had, arranging everything for this bachelor household, you wouldn't hesitate, and you would tell me you were sorry. I had some money that belonged to you, I made good use of it, and that's all. You think you're being noble, but you're being extremely petty. You're asking for too much. Ah!" she murmured, seeing Eugène's passionate glance, "and you're making such a fuss over nothing. But if you don't love me, oh! refuse it all. My fate hangs by your word: speak! Father," she went on after a moment of silence, turning to Père Goriot, "please, give him some good reasons. Does he think I'm any less sensitive about our honor than he is?"

Watching, listening to this interesting quarrel, Père Goriot's face wore the fixed smile of an opium addict.

"You child!" Delphine went on, taking Eugène's hand. "You're standing right at life's entrance, and there in front of you is a barrier many men can never overcome, and a woman's hand reaches out to open the door for you, and you refuse! But you'll triumph, you'll make yourself a magnificent fortune, success is written right across your handsome forehead. So why won't you be able to pay me back, then, what I'm lending you today? In the old days, didn't ladies give their knights armor, and swords, and shields, and coats of mail, and horses, so they could go and fight in tournaments in their lady's name? Well then! What I'm offering you, Eugène, are today's weapons, the tools required of anyone who wants to be anybody. Oh, it must be lovely, that attic you're living in, if it looks anything like Papa's room. Aren't we going to eat our dinner? Are you trying to upset me? Answer me!" she declared, giving his hand a shake. "My God, Papa, make him agree, or I'll leave and you'll never see me again."

"I'll make you agree," said Père Goriot, pulling himself out of his enraptured state. "My dear Monsieur Eugène, you'll be borrowing money from the Jews, won't you?"

"I'll have to," was the reply.

"Fine, so I'll lend it to you," the good man went on, pulling out his battered wallet. "I've turned myself into a Jew, I've paid all the bills, here they are. You don't owe a cent for anything you'll find here. It wasn't such a huge sum, just a little more than five thousand francs. So I'm lending it to you—me! You're not going to say no to me, I'm no woman. You'll take a piece of paper and write me out an acknowledgment, and later on you'll pay me back."

Eugène and Delphine both shed tears, at the same time, as they looked at one another, surprised. Rastignac held out his hand to the good man, who took it.

"After all!" said Goriot. "Aren't you both my children?"

"But oh, my poor father," said Madame de Nucingen, "how did you do it?"

"Well, there we are!" he replied. "When I talked you into letting him be near you, and then I saw you buying things, as if for a bridegroom, I said to myself, 'It's going to be too much for her!' The lawyer tells me the lawsuit against your husband, to make him give you back your fortune, will take more than six months. Fine. So I sold my thirteen hundred and fifty franc lifetime annuity; then I took fifteen thousand francs and got myself an annuity for twelve hundred francs, well secured, and then, my children, I took the rest of my capital and paid for everything you bought for this apartment. I've got myself a room, up there, for fifty francs a year, I can live like a prince on forty sous a day, and all the rest is my own. I don't spend much, I virtually never need to buy clothes. So for the last two weeks I've been laughing in my beard, telling myself, 'Oh, are they going to be happy!' So—you're happy, aren't you?"

"Oh, Papa, Papa! cried Madame de Nucingen, throwing herself on him; he held her on his lap. She showered him with kisses, her golden hair caressed his cheeks, and she shed a few tears on his grinning, beaming face. "My dear father, you really are one of a kind! No, there isn't another father like you, not anywhere. And since Eugène already loves you, how is he going to feel now?"

"But, children," said Père Goriot, who had not in ten years felt his daughter's heart beating against his, "but, my little Delphine, my Delphinette, you're going to make me die of happiness! My poor heart will break. So there, Monsieur Eugène, we're already even!"

And the old man hugged his daughter so savagely, so deliriously, that she gasped,

"Oh, you're hurting me!"

"Hurting you!" he exclaimed, turning pale. He looked at her with a kind of superhuman sadness. To properly represent his appearance, this Paternal Christ, we'd have to hunt through all the masterpieces ever painted of our Savior's Passion, as He suffered for all mankind. Père Goriot bestowed a tender kiss on the waist his hands had squeezed too tightly. "No, no, I didn't hurt you, no," he went on, smiling quizzically at her, "it's you who hurt me by crying out like that. It actually cost more," he whispered in his daughter's ear, kissing her with great care, "but we have to lie to him a little, or else he'll be angry."

Stupefied by the man's inexhaustible devotion, Eugène stood looking at him with that innocent admiration which, in the young, is faith.

"I'll make myself worthy of all that," he declared.

"Oh, my Eugène, what a lovely thing to say."

Madame de Nucingen kissed the young man's forehead.

"On your account," said Père Goriot, "he turned down Mademoiselle Taillefer and her millions. Oh yes, she loved you, that girl—and with her brother dead, she'll be as rich as Croesus."

"You shouldn't have said that!" cried Rastignac.

"Eugène," Delphine whispered in his ear, "now I have something to feel sad about, tonight. Oh, but how I'll love you! And for ever and ever!"

"This is the best day I've had since you girls were married," exclaimed Père Goriot. "The good Lord can make me suffer as much as He likes, now—except not on your account—and I'll be able to say to myself, 'This past February, even if for just a moment, I was happier than most men are able to be in their entire lives.' Look at me, Fifine!" he said to his daughter. "Ah, she's really beautiful, isn't she? Just tell me, have you seen many women with a complexion like hers—and those little dimples! No, you haven't, you haven't. Well, I'm the man who created this stunning woman. Still, because you've made her so happy, she's become a thousand times lovelier. Now I could go right to Hell, neighbor," he said. "I give you my place in Heaven, if you need it. But let's eat, let's eat!" he continued, no longer knowing what he was saying. "The world is ours!"

"My poor father!"

"If you only knew, my child," he said, rising and walking over to her, then clasping her head and showering a thousand kisses in the middle of her braided tresses, "how little it costs you to make me happy! Just come see me sometimes, I'll be up there, you won't have to walk more than a step. Promise me you will, promise!"

"Oh yes, dear Papa."

"Say it again."

"Yes, my good, dear Father."

"Enough, I'd make you say it a thousand times, just to hear it. Eat, let's eat!"

The evening went by in an orgy of childishness, nor was Père Goriot the least crazy of the three of them. He lay down at his daughter's feet, and kissed them; he stared hard and long into her eyes; he rubbed his head against her dress; and in a word he did such things as the very youngest and tenderest lover might well do.

"You see?" Delphine said to Eugène. "When my father's with us, everything has to revolve around him. But that may be a little bothersome, sometimes."

Having several times felt the stirrings of jealousy, Eugène could not criticize her remark, though it contained the very essence of ungratefulness.

"And when will the apartment be finished?" Eugène asked, looking around the room. "Will we have to leave here, tonight?"

"Yes, but tomorrow you'll have dinner with me," she said delicately. "There'll be an opera, tomorrow."

"I'll get an orchestra seat, I will," said Père Goriot.

It was midnight. Madame de Nucingen's carriage was waiting. Père Goriot and the student went back to Maison Vauquer, their more and more excited talk of Delphine producing an odd sort of contest in how they voiced their violent passions. Eugène couldn't keep himself from admitting that the good man's fatherly love, untainted by any hint of personal interest, exceeded his own, both in its strength and in its dimensions. The father's idol was forever pure and beautiful, and his adoration encompassed everything that had been as well as what was yet to come.

They found Madame Vauquer sitting by the stove, with Sylvie on one side of her and Christophe on the other. Like Marius sitting in the ruins of Carthage, the old landlady was waiting for the only two lodgers she had left, moaning to Sylvie. Lord Byron may have lent Tasso some singularly handsome lamentations, but they had none of the profound truth of those emitted by Madame Vauquer.

"Sylvie, there'll only be three cups of coffee to make, tomorrow morning. Oh God, my house so empty, it's enough to break your heart. What's left of my life, without my lodgers? Nothing,

nothing at all. Here's my house with everything that filled it simply taken away. They furnished my life, and without them, now, it's all unfurnished. What have I done to Heaven to bring down on me all these disasters? We've laid in a stock of beans and potatoes for twenty people. The police, right here in my house! We're going to be living on potatoes and nothing but potatoes. And I'll have to send Christophe away!"

Suddenly awake, Christophe said,

"Madame?"

"Poor fellow! He's just like a dog," said Sylvie.

"An entire season ruined, because everyone's already found lodgings. Where am I going to find myself any more lodgers? I'll go mad. And that witch Michonneau stole Poiret from me! What's she done to him that he's so attached to her, following her around like a pet puppy?"

"Ah, yes!" exclaimed Sylvie, wagging her head, "these old maids, they know a trick or two."

"And poor Monsieur Vautrin, they've turned him into a convict," the landlady went on. "Well, Sylvie, it's too much for me, I still can't believe it. A lively fellow like him, a man who had brandy in his coffee, for only fifteen francs a month, and who always paid cash, right to the last penny!"

"And who was very generous!" echoed Christophe.

"There must be a mistake," said Sylvie.

"No, no, he admitted it himself," Madame Vauquer continued. "And to think that all these things happened right here in my house, in a neighborhood where you never even hear a cat walking! By my soul as an honest woman, I must be dreaming. Because, remember, we saw Louis XVI's disaster, we saw Napoleon's fall, then we saw him come back and get sent away again, and all that was perfectly possible—but there shouldn't be any risk in running a *pension*: people can do without a king, but they always have to eat, and when an honest woman, born a Conflans, offers meals with all sorts of good things, well, at least until the end of the world comes . . . But that's it, it's the end of the world."

"And just think that Mademoiselle Michonneau, after doing all these horrible things to you, is supposed to be getting a thousand francs a year!" exclaimed Sylvie.

"Don't tell me about it, she's just a scheming scoundrel," said Madame Vauquer. "And on top of everything else, she's going to Buneaud's! But she's capable of anything, she's surely been guilty of ghastly things, in her time—murders, thievery. She ought to be the one to go to jail, instead of that poor dear man . . ."

Just then Eugène and Père Goriot rang the bell.

"Ah!" sighed the widow. "There are my only faithful ones."

The two faithful ones, who had virtually forgotten Maison Vauquer's disasters, immediately and bluntly informed their landlady that in the future they would both be living in the Chausée-d'Antin district.

"Ah, Sylvie!" said the widow. "That's the end of me. You've given me my death's blow, gentlemen! That one got me right in the pit of the stomach. It feels like an iron bar in there. I've aged ten years or more, in just this one day. I'll go out of my mind, by God! What am I going to do with all those beans? Well then, well then, if I'm going to be alone here, you can leave tomorrow, Christophe. Farewell, gentlemen, good night."

"What's the matter with her?" Eugène asked Sylvie.

"What's wrong with her! After what happened, everyone's left. Her head's going around and around. Just a minute, I'll go see if she's crying. That'll be a tearjerker, sure enough. And in all the years I've been in her service, it'll be the first time she's ever cried."

But the next day Madame Vauquer was, as she put it, "reasonable." She may have looked the part of a woman who has lost all her lodgers, a woman whose entire life had been turned upside down, but her mind was clear, and the sadness she displayed was the true sorrow, the profound sorrow, of hurt feelings, of shattered ways and habits. No lover, going away from the place where his mistress lives, and looking longingly back, could have appeared more dismal than Madame Vauquer, gazing at her empty table. Eugène consoled her, saying that Bianchon, who would soon be finishing his internship at the hospital, would surely be coming to take his place, and that the Museum employee had often said how much he'd like to have Madame Couture's rooms, and that, surely, in a very few days she'd have her house filled once again.

"May God hear your words, my dear sir! But the damage has been done. You'll see, Death will be visiting here in just a few days," she moaned, looking lugubriously around her dining room. "And who will he be carrying off?"

"It's good we're moving out," Eugène said to Père Goriot.

"Madame," said Sylvie, running in wildly, "it's three days since I've seen Mistigris!"

"Oh Lord, if my cat's dead, if he's left us, I'll . . ."

The poor widow couldn't finish, she clasped her hands and fell back into her armchair, overwhelmed by this terrible prophecy.

Toward midday, which is when the mailmen reach that neighborhood, Eugène received a letter in an elegant envelope, bearing the Beauséant seal. It contained an invitation, addressed to Monsieur and Madame de Nucingen, for the great ball at the vicomtesse's home, scheduled a full month earlier. Along with the invitation was a short note for Eugène:

> *It seemed to me, my dear sir, that you would be very glad to carry my best wishes to Madame de Nucingen; here then is the invitation you requested, for I will be truly pleased to meet Madame de Restaud's sister. Bring that pretty lady to me, and be*

> *careful she does not use up all your affection, since in return for*
> *the regard in which I hold you, you owe me my share as well.*
>
> Vicomtesse de Beauséant

"Ah," said Eugène to himself, rereading this letter, "but Madame de Beauséant makes it perfectly clear that she does not want to see the Baron de Nucingen."

He went directly to Delphine, delighted to have won her a pleasure for which, without much doubt, he would be amply repaid. Madame de Nucingen was in her bath. He waited in her boudoir, suffering from the natural impatience of a hot-blooded young man, anxious to take possession of a mistress he has been craving for two long years. There are certain emotions a young man experiences once and once only. The first real woman with whom he establishes a connection, who comes to him in all the splendor that goes with Parisian society at its best, never has any rival in his heart. For love, in Paris, is unlike love anywhere else. In Paris, neither men nor women are taken in by the elaborate flowering of commonplaces draped, for the sake of decency, over attachments which are supposed to be disinterested. In that world, a woman's responsibility is not only to satisfy her heart, and her senses, but—perfectly plainly—also to gratify the thousand and one vanities of which Parisian life is composed. In Paris above all love is basically boastful, shameless, wasteful, an ostentatious fraud. If all the women at the court of Louis XIV were jealous of Mademoiselle de la Vallière, on account of the sweeping passion which led that great prince to forget that his cuffs had cost a thousand francs apiece, when, in order to hasten the Duke of Vermandois's entrance into this world, he recklessly let them be torn to shreds, what can one expect of the rest of humanity? Be young, rich, have titles, be even loftier still, if you can: the more incense you burn before your idol, the more she will shine favorably on you—if you have an idol. Love is a religion, and of necessity its cult is costlier than any other; it goes by quickly, like a child of the city streets who likes to show where he's been by all the havoc he leaves behind him. The luxury of emotion is the poetry of garrets and attics—for without that wealth, what would become of love in such locations? There may be exceptions to these draconian laws, formulated in Paris's iron code, but they're only to be found in lonely places, among souls who refuse to let themselves be carried away by society's rules and regulations, people who dwell close by some source of pure clear water, evanescent but also forever flowing—people who, loyal to the green shade under which they live, constantly rejoice at the sound of infinity speaking, a voice which they see written in everything, and which they learn to find in themselves, waiting patiently for their wings, feeling only tender sorrow for those who are more worldly.

But Rastignac, like most young men who have had a preliminary taste of grandeur, meant to enter the world's jousting tournament fully armed; he had caught the fever of it, perhaps aware that he was strong enough to prevail, even dominate, but not yet knowing either how or to what end such ambition might lead him. Without some pure and sacred love that fills all of life, this thirst for power can become a good thing: it strips away merely personal concerns and, instead, makes national grandeur its object. But Eugène had not yet reached the point at which a man can truly contemplate and judge life's course. In fact, he had not yet entirely shaken off the charm of all the fresh and fragrant ideas that, like foliage, surround and envelop young people raised in the provinces. He had hesitated, still, at crossing this Parisian Rubicon. Despite his burning curiosity, he had clung to fundamental reservations based on the happy life led, on his country estate, by the true gentleman. All the same, his final scruples had vanished the previous night, when he'd found himself in his own apartment.

Relishing the material advantages conferred by fortune, as he had for so long enjoyed the moral advantages conferred by his birth, he had sloughed off his provincial skin, taking up his stance, comfortably, in a position from which the future looked very good indeed. And as he lolled on a soft chair, waiting for Delphine in her pretty boudoir that had become partly his, too, his image of himself was so unlike that Rastignac who had come to Paris, a year before, that as by a process of psychological optics he contemplated himself he wondered if, in truth, he was seeing the same man.

"Madame is in her room," Thérèse came to tell him, and he shivered at the news.

He found Delphine stretched out on the sofa, next to the fire, looking cool and refreshed. Seeing her displayed on the billowing muslin, he couldn't keep from being reminded of one of those Indian plants, the fruit of which grows deep in the heart of its flowers.

"Ah! So here we are!" she exclaimed, her voice full of emotion.

"Guess what I've brought you," said Eugène, sitting on the sofa and taking her arm, so he could kiss her hand.

Reading the invitation, Madame de Nucingen gestured happily. Her eyes, damp with sudden tears, turned to Eugène, and she threw her arms around his neck, drawing him to her in an ecstasy of satisfied vanity.

"And it's you (oh you darling," she whispered in his ear, "but Thérèse is in my dressing room, and we must be careful!) to whom I owe such happiness! And oh, that's true happiness. Obtained through you, it's far more than mere selfish pleasure. No one else was willing to introduce me into that world. Seeing me there for the first time, you may think me petty, frivolous, empty-headed like a typical Parisian woman, but do not forget, my friend, that

I remain ready to sacrifice everything for your sake, and if I wish even more passionately than ever to find myself in the Faubourg de Saint-Germain, it's because you're there."

"Doesn't it seem to you," Eugène observed, "as if Madame de Beauséant is trying to tell us she's really not expecting to see Baron de Nucingen at her ball?"

"Indeed yes," the baroness answered, giving him back the letter. "Those women have a positive genius for insolence. But it makes no difference, I'm going. My sister will surely be there, I know she's planning a beautiful outfit. Eugène," she went on, her voice lowered, "she's going so she can dispel some horrid suspicions. You haven't heard what they're saying about her? Nucingen told me, just this morning, they were talking about it quite openly at the club. My God, just imagine what a woman's honor, and a family's, can depend on! I feel myself attacked—wounded— through my poor sister.

"According to certain people, Monsieur de Trailles signed notes for more than a hundred thousand francs, and most of them have gone unpaid, and he was going to be sued. Faced with this disaster, my sister apparently sold her diamonds to a Jew, those beautiful diamonds I'm sure you've seen her wear, which she got from her mother-in-law. You can imagine, for the past few days that's all people have been talking about. I suspect Anastasie's having a gold-spangled dress made, so everyone at Madame de Beauséant's ball will look at her, and then she'll show herself absolutely shining with every single one of her diamonds. But I don't want to make any less of an impression. She's always tried to walk all over me, she's never been nice to me, and I've done so much for her, I've always given her money when she hasn't had any. But let's not talk about all that, today I just want to be happy."

At one o'clock in the morning Rastignac was still there, and when Madame de Nucingen was lavishing on him a lover's farewell, that "goodbye" so full of pleasures still to come, she said to him, her expression tinged with melancholy,

"I'm so fearful, so superstitious, just call these feelings of mine anything you like, but I fairly quiver at the thought of paying for my happiness by some frightful catastrophe."

"What a child you are," murmured Eugène.

"Oh—so tonight *I'm* the child!" she laughed.

Eugène went back to Maison Vauquer, knowing that the next day he would leave it for good, and as he walked he surrendered himself to those lovely dreams that all young men cherish, while the taste of happiness lingers fresh on their lips.

"Well?" said Père Goriot, when Rastignac went by his door.

"Well!" exclaimed Eugène. "I'll tell you all about it, tomorrow."

"Everything, mind you!" cried the good man. "Go to sleep. Tomorrow our happy new life begins."

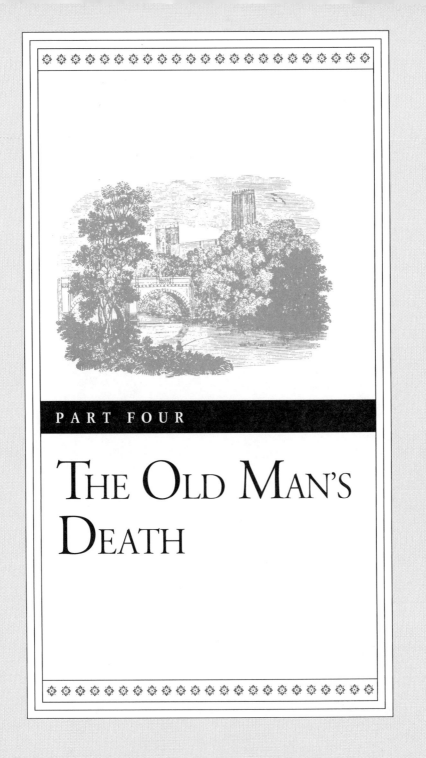

PART FOUR

THE OLD MAN'S DEATH

THE NEXT DAY, GORIOT AND RASTIGNAC WERE ONLY WAITING FOR THEIR MOVING MAN TO APPEAR, TO SAY GOODBYE TO THE *PENSION*, WHEN TOWARD NOON THE SOUND OF A CARRIAGE STOPPING RIGHT IN FRONT OF MAISON VAUQUER ECHOED UP AND DOWN NEW SAINT GENEVIEVE STREET. Madame de Nucingen stepped out and asked if her father was still there. When Sylvie answered in the affirmative, she went slowly up the stairs.

Although his neighbor did not know it, Eugène too was in his room. At breakfast, he had asked the old man to take his things to the new apartment, telling him they would meet, at four o'clock, in d'Artois Street. Then, while Goriot went looking for porters, Eugène ran to answer the roll call at the law school, then hurried back without anyone seeing him, so he could settle his accounts with Madame Vauquer, unwilling to leave that for Goriot, who, carried away by his all-consuming zeal, would surely have paid the student's bill for him. But the landlady having gone out, Eugène went back up to his room, to make sure he'd left nothing behind, and was very glad he'd thought of so doing when, in the table drawer, he found the blank I.O.U. he'd given Vautrin, which Vautrin had blithely tossed in there the day he'd been paid off. There being no fire in the empty room, he was just about to tear it to bits when, hearing Delphine's voice, he decided to stay as quiet as he could, so he could hear what she'd say, thinking she ought not to have secrets from him. And then, once he'd heard her first words, he found the conversation between father and daughter so fascinating that he could not help but listen to it all.

"Oh, Father," she said, "thank God you had the idea of demanding an account of my fortune, before I could be ruined! Is it safe to talk?"

"Yes, the house is empty," answered Père Goriot, his voice sounding suddenly different.

"Father, what's wrong?" Madame de Nucingen went on.

"You're here," said the old man, "to knock me over the head with an axe. May God forgive you, my child! You don't know how much I love you, for had you'd known you'd never have so bluntly said such things to me, especially if the situation isn't desperate. And what could have happened, what could be so urgent that you had to come looking for me here, when in just a few minutes we'd have been in d'Artois Street?"

"Oh, Father! Can one be so rational as that, when a catastrophe strikes? I've been out of my head! Your lawyer has uncovered a bad problem, one that's sure to fall on our heads. Your long business experience is going to be absolutely essential, so I came running to find you just the way a drowning man clutches at a branch. When Monsieur Derville saw Nucingen putting a thousand and one difficulties in our way, he countered by threatening a court order that it wouldn't be at all hard to obtain. So Nucingen came to see me, this morning, asking if what I really wanted was both his ruin and mine. I told him I didn't know anything about it, except that I knew I had a fortune, and I ought to be in possession of that fortune, and everything having to do with this whole nasty business should go through my lawyer, because I was a complete ignoramus and couldn't possibly understand the least little thing about it. Isn't that what you would have wanted me to say?"

"That's fine," Goriot answered.

"Well!" Delphine went on. "Then he brought me up to date on his affairs. He's invested every penny he owns, and every penny of mine, in some enterprises just barely off the ground, and so he's necessarily very short of cash. If I forced him to produce my dowry, he'd have no choice but to go into bankruptcy, but if I'll just wait a year he promises on his honor that, by investing my capital in these real estate operations, he'll be able to give me twice or even three times as much and I'll be in full control of the whole thing.

"He's telling the truth, Father, and he's frightened me. He begged me to forgive him, he's set me completely free, I have his permission to do exactly as I please, but on condition that I leave him entirely free to manage everything in my name. As a sign of good faith, he promised to send for Monsieur Derville whenever I wanted, to verify that the deeds executed in my name have been drafted properly. In short, he's tied his hands and feet together and put himself completely in my power. He wants control of the house for another two years, and I'm not to spend more on myself than he gives me. He's made it clear that keeping up appearances is the best he can do, he's gotten rid of his dancer, and in the future he'll be bound to the strictest but very secret penny-pinching, so his speculations can ripen without his credit going under. I made it as difficult as I could, questioning everything and making him sweat, so I could get more information: he even showed me his books, and then he broke down and cried. I've never seen a man in such a state. He completely lost his head, he talked about killing himself, he was positively raving. He made me feel sorry for him."

"And you believed all this nonsense?" cried Père Goriot. "He's a real comedian, your husband! I've done business with these Germans: they're almost all men of absolute good faith, as frank and open as you please, but when they turn malicious and scheming, under that air of honesty and goodwill, they're even worse than all the others. Your husband's been taking advantage of you. He feels himself hard-pressed, he conjures up death, but he intends to be more completely in control, in your name, than he ever was in his own. He'll use this opportunity to shield himself from risk. He's as subtle as he is treacherous; he's a rotten customer.

"Oh no, I'm not going to my grave and leave my daughters stripped of everything they own. I still know a little bit about business. So he tells you he's got his cash all tied up, does he? Well! His investments are worth something, he has documentation—receipts, contracts! Let him produce them, and settle up your share. We'll pick the best investments, we'll take the risks ourselves, and we'll have everything in your name: 'Delphine Goriot, married to but living apart from, and holding her property separately from, Baron de Nucingen.' Does he think we're idiots, that fellow? Does he imagine I could even contemplate the idea of leaving you without your fortune, without so much as a crust of bread? Not for a single day—not for a night—not for two hours! If anything like that happened, I wouldn't survive it. What!

I'd have worked for forty years, carried great sacks of flour around on my back, sweated through one adversity after another, I'd have deprived myself my whole life long, and for you, my angels, for whose sake every labor, every burden, seemed light, and then today my fortune, my very life, would just go up in smoke! I'd die like a mad dog.

"By all that's most sacred on earth, and in Heaven, we're going to clear this all up, we're going to verify his books, his bank accounts, everything he has a hand in! I won't sleep, I won't lie down, I won't eat until I've determined that your fortune is intact. My God, you and he lead separate lives; Maître Derville will always be your lawyer and, thank God, he's an honest man! Mother of God! You'll keep that nice little million of yours, your fifty thousand a year, for as long as you live, or I'll kick up such a rumpus right here in Paris—ah, ah! If we don't get justice in the courts, I'll go straight to the legislature. Knowing that you were in peaceful, secure possession of your money, that you wanted for nothing, was enough to cure all my ills and take away all my sorrows. Money is *life*. It can do everything.

"What does he think he's up to, that fat Alsatian idiot? Delphine, don't you let that fat pig get a quarter of a penny out of you—that one, him, who's chained you up, who's made you suffer. If he needs you, we'll tie him up all right, we'll make him walk straight. Lord, Lord, my head feels as if it's on fire, I can feel something burning right in my skull. My Delphine in want! Oh! My Fifine, You! God damn it, where are my gloves? Let's go, let's go! Hurry up, I want to see everything, all his account books, his cash on hand, his correspondence—everything! And right now! I'm not going to rest until I know absolutely positively that there's no more risk to your fortune—until I see it with my own eyes."

"My dear father! Let's not get all excited. If you let the slightest hint of vengeance get into this business, if you show yourself this hostile, I'll be lost. He knows you, he knows that, at your prompting, I'm worried about my fortune, but, I swear to you, he's got it and he means to keep it. He's the kind of man who'll run off with all his money, and leave us holding the bag, scoundrel that he is! And he knows me, he knows I'd never dishonor the name I bear by prosecuting him. But at the same time as he's strong, he's also weak. I've already looked into everything. If we push this too far, I'm ruined."

"Then he's a crook?"

"Well, Father, yes, he is," she exclaimed, throwing herself into a chair and bursting into tears. "I didn't want to admit it to you, I wanted to spare you the pain of knowing you'd married me to a man like that! His secretive ways and his conscience—body and soul—oh, he's all of one piece! It's horrible. I hate him, I loathe him. Yes—after everything he's told me, I have no respect left for this disgusting Nucingen. Any man who can throw himself into business dealings like those he described hasn't any sensitivity at all, and I'm afraid precisely because, now, I understand him so perfectly. He's blithely proposed—my own husband—that he'd give me absolute freedom—do you know what that means?—if, in return, I'd let him make use of me, if he was in trouble and he needed to—in a word, if I'd let him make me his strawman, his dummy."

"But we have laws! There's a gallows right here in Paris for a son-in-law like that!" cried Père Goriot. "And if there's no executioner handy, I'll guillotine him myself!"

"No, Father, there are no laws stopping him. Just listen to what he told me, without any of his fancy language: 'Either you're ruined, you haven't got a cent, everything's gone, because you're the only accomplice I can think of, or else you let me run my business properly.' Is that clear enough? I'm still important to him. My feminine integrity gives him confidence: he knows I'll let him keep his fortune, I'll be satisfied with my own. It's a dishonest, a criminal association, and I have to agree to it, under penalty of being ruined. He's buying my conscience and paying for it by letting me feel happy as Eugène's wife. 'I let you misbehave, so you let me commit crimes and ruin other people!' That's pretty clear, too, isn't it?

"And do you know what he calls 'running his business'? He buys undeveloped land in his own name, and then builds houses on it, but in the name of straw men. These straw men make all the construction arrangements, though the builders are not to be paid for a long time, and then, for some nominal sum, they transfer title in the houses to my husband, after which they settle with the poor deluded builders by going into bankruptcy. Using the Nucingen name is enough to dazzle these unfortunate construction people. Oh, I've understood the whole thing. I also understand that, just in case he needs to underwrite the payment of enormous sums, Nucingen has transferred extensive assets to Amsterdam, London, Naples, Vienna. How are we to lay our hands on them all?"

Eugène heard the heavy sound of Père Goriot's knees, as he fell to his knees on the hard tiles.

"My God, what have I done to you? My daughter bound to this wretch, he'll get anything he wants out of her. Forgive me, my daughter!" the old man cried.

"Oh yes," said Delphine, "if I'm in something of an abyss, it may well be your fault. We understand so little, when we get married! What do we know about the world, and business, and men, and how things are done? Our fathers have to do our thinking for us. But my dear father, I'm not reproaching you, not at all, forgive me. The fault, here, is mine and mine alone. Oh no, no, don't cry, Papa," she said, kissing her father's forehead.

"Don't *you* cry any more, my little Delphine. Let me have

your eyes, let me clean them with kisses. Now! Let me clear my head and untangle this mess your husband's made."

"No, let me do it; I'll know how to handle things. He really cares about me, so I'll use my leverage with him to get some of my fortune invested in my own name. Maybe I can get him to buy me the old Nucingen estate, in Alsace, he likes the place. You just come tomorrow and have a look at his books, and what he's up to. Monsieur Derville really doesn't understand business matters. But no, don't come tomorrow. I don't want to go through all that. Madame de Beauséant's ball is the day after tomorrow, I want to take care of myself so I look pretty, and well rested, and do honor to my dear Eugène! Let's go have a look at his room."

There was the sound of another vehicle stopping, out in New Saint Geneviève Street, and then the sound of Madame Restaud's voice could be heard on the staircase, asking Sylvie,

"Is my father in?"

This was enough to save Eugène, who had already decided to throw himself down on his bed and pretend to be asleep.

"Ah, Father! Has anyone told you about Anastasie?" said Delphine, recognizing her sister's voice. "Some very strange things have apparently been happening in her house, too."

"Good God!" exclaimed Père Goriot. "This will be the end of me. My poor head can't endure yet another misfortune."

"Hello, Father," said the countess, as she entered the room. "Ah, you're here, Delphine."

Madame de Restaud was plainly embarrassed, meeting her sister.

"Hello, Nasie," said the baroness. "Is it so strange to find me here? I see my father all the time, you know."

"Since when?"

"If you came yourself, you'd know."

"Don't torment me, Delphine," said the countess in a pathetic voice. "I'm quite sufficiently unhappy, I'm lost, oh my poor father! Oh, this time I'm really lost!"

"What's the matter, Nasie?" cried Père Goriot. "My child, tell us everything."

Madame de Restaud grew pale.

"Delphine, come, help her, be good to her, and—as if it were possible—I'll love you even more!"

"My poor Nasie," said Madame de Nucingen, helping her sister to a chair, "tell us. We two, you know, we're the only people in the world who'll always love you enough to forgive you, no matter what. You see? Family feelings are the safest of all."

She administered a dose of smelling salts, and the countess got hold of herself.

"It's going to kill me," said Père Goriot. "Over here," he went on, stirring up his peat-block fire, "come over here, both of you. I'm cold. What's wrong, Nasie? Tell me, quick, you're killing me . . ."

"Well then!" said the poor woman. "My husband knows everything. Can you believe it, Father, a while ago, you remember that overdue note of Maxime's? Well, it wasn't the first one. I'd already paid a lot of them. Toward the beginning of January, Monsieur de Trailles was in a very bad mood. He wouldn't tell me anything, but it's easy enough to read right into someone's heart, when you love them, anything will do it—and, besides, there were warnings. Anyway, he was more loving, more tender than I'd ever seen him, and I was so very very happy. Poor Maxime! He thought of saying goodbye to me, he told me; he felt like blowing his brains out. And so I positively tormented him, I begged and I begged, I knelt down in front of him for two solid hours. And then he told me he had to have a hundred thousand francs! Oh, Papa, a hundred thousand francs! I went out of my head. You wouldn't have it, I've eaten up everything . . ."

"No," said Père Goriot, "I couldn't have done it, unless I went and stole back the notes. But that's what I should have done, Nasie! I'll go now."

Hearing this mournful cry, sounding for all the world like a dying man's death rattle, and making brutally clear the agony of fatherly love reduced to hopelessness, the two sisters hesitated. What egotism could possibly have been immune to this cry of despair, flung out like a pebble thrown into an abyss, only to show how deep it was?

"I got them back, Father, by selling what didn't belong to me," said the countess, dissolving in tears.

Delphine too was moved, and set her head against her sister's neck.

"So it's all true," she said.

Anastasie kissed her sister's head, Madame de Nucingen threw her arms around Anastasie, kissing her tenderly, and lowering her head on her breast.

"Here, here you'll always be loved, and never judged," said Delphine.

"My angels," said Goriot, his voice weak, "why does it have to be misery that brings you two together?"

"To save Maxime's life, indeed, to preserve my own happiness," the countess went on, encouraged by these signs of warm, palpitating tenderness, "I went and I took to that usurer, you know him, a man born in Hell, absolutely unmovable—I brought him the family diamonds that mean so much to Monsieur de Restaud —all of them, his, mine, I sold them all! I sold them! Do you understand? I saved him. But me, I'm dead. Restaud found out everything."

"Who? How? I'll kill him!" Père Goriot cried.

"He called me into his room, yesterday. I went in. . . . 'Anastasie,' he said to me, in such a voice (oh, his voice was enough, I understood everything), 'where are your diamonds?' "

" 'In my room.' "

" 'No,' he said, looking at me, 'they're over there, on my dresser.' And then he showed me the jewel case, which he'd covered with a handkerchief. 'Do you know where I got them?' he asked me. I fell to my knees . . . I cried, I asked him just to say how he wanted to see me die."

"You said that?" cried Père Goriot. "In the sacred name of the Lord, anyone who hurts either one of you, so long as I'm alive, can be absolutely sure I'll grill him alive! Oh, I'll cut him up like . . ."

Père Goriot's voice faded, choked deep in his own throat.

"And then, my dear, he asked me for something even harder to give than my life. May Heaven keep other women from hearing the words I heard!"

"I'll kill the man," said Père Goriot calmly. "But he only has one life, and he owes me two. Anyway, what then?" he went on, watching Anastasie.

"Then!" said the countess, after hesitating for a moment. "Then he looked at me. 'Anastasie,' he said, 'I'll keep all of this completely quiet, we'll stay together, we have children. I won't kill Monsieur de Trailles, I might miss him, and to get rid of him by some other means could get me into trouble with the law. To kill him in your arms would be to dishonor all the children. But in order to preserve those who are yours, and whoever may be their father, and me myself, I require two things of you. First, answer me: are either of the children mine?' I said yes. 'Which?' he asked. 'Ernest, the oldest.' 'Fine,' he said. 'Now, you must swear to do one more thing.' I swore I would. 'You will sign over your income to me, whenever I ask you to.' "

"Don't, don't!" cried Père Goriot. "Don't ever sign that! Oh, oh, Monsieur de Restaud, you have no idea what it means to make a woman happy, she'll go hunting happiness wherever she can find it—and you think you're going to punish her, with your stupid impotence? . . . Oh ho, I'll be there, me, and I'll make you stop! You'll find me standing in your way. Rest easy, Nasie. Ah, his heir's important to him! Fine, fine. I'll kidnap his son, because, by God, that's my grandson. Don't I have a right to see the brat? I'll hide him away in a village somewhere, I'll take care of him, don't you worry. I'll make him knuckle under, this monster, I'll tell him, 'It's just you and me! If you want your son back, give my daughter what belongs to her, and let her do as she pleases.' "

"Father!"

"Yes, I'm your father! Oh, I'll be a real father. This joker of a grand lord's not going to mistreat *my* daughters. By God! I don't know what this is, flowing in my veins. There's tiger blood in there, I feel like tearing both these fellows to pieces. Oh, my children! Is this what's happened to your lives? Oh, for me it's death. What will become of you when I'm no longer here? Fathers need to be alive for as long as their children. Oh Lord in Heaven, how Your world's gotten out of hand! But You Yourself had a Son, they tell us. You've got to keep us from suffering through our children. Oh, my sweet angels! It's only your sadness that brings you to me. You only let me see your tears. Well, but you love me! Yes, I see you love me. Come, come to me, cry on me! My heart's big enough, it can hold everything. Oh yes, you'll have done a good job of breaking it, but even the little pieces still turn into fathers' hearts. I wish I could take all your pain, suffer for you. Oh, when you were little, how happy, how happy you were . . ."

"Those were the only happy days we ever knew," said Delphine. "Where have they gone to, those times when we used to go tumbling down the sacks in the big warehouse?"

"But Father! That isn't everything," Anastasie whispered in Goriot's ear, making him start. "I only got a hundred thousand francs for the diamonds. So they're suing Maxime. But all we have left to pay is twelve thousand francs. He's promised me he'll be sensible, he won't gamble anymore. His love is all I have left in the world, and it's cost me too much not to kill me, if he ever escapes me. I've sacrificed my fortune for him, my honor, my peace of mind, my children. Oh, Father, let Maxime at least be free, respectable, let him live in the world where he best knows how to make something of himself. All he owes me, now, is happiness; we have children who will grow up penniless. If he goes to jail, everything will be lost."

"I have nothing, Nasie. Nothing more, nothing, nothing more! It's the end of the world. Oh, the world's tottering, it's falling. Run away, save yourself! Ah, but I still have my silver buckles, and I have six sets of silverware, the first ones I ever got. But really, all I've got left is an annuity, just for my life, it's twelve hundred francs a year . . ."

"What happened to all the unlimited annuities?"

"I sold them, I kept just this little bit of income, to stay alive. I had to have twelve thousand francs to fix up an apartment for Fifine."

"In your house, Delphine?" Madame de Restaud asked her sister.

"Oh, what difference does it make?" Goriot went on. "The twelve thousand francs are gone."

"I quite understand," said the countess. "For Monsieur de Rastignac. Ah, my poor Delphine, don't do it, be careful. You can see where it's led me."

"My dear, Monsieur de Rastignac is a young man who would never ruin his mistress."

"Thank you, Delphine. In this crisis of mine, I expected better of you—but then, you've never loved me."

"Yes, yes, she loves you, Nasie," cried Père Goriot, "she's always telling me so. We talk about you, she keeps telling me how beautiful you are and that she's never been more than pretty."

"She!" the countess echoed. "She's beautiful, but she's cold."

"That may be," said Delphine, turning red, "but how have you always treated me? You've rejected me, you've made sure that everywhere I want to go the doors are shut in my face, although I've never given you the slightest reason to make me suffer so. And have I ever come squeezing poor Papa, a hundred thousand francs at a time, milking him of his whole fortune, and reducing him to the state he's in now? It's all your doing, my sister. I've come to see my father whenever I possibly could, I haven't shoved him out the door and then come licking his hands when I needed his help. I didn't even know he'd spent that twelve thousand francs on me. I was making all the arrangements myself—it was me! Do you understand? Anyway, when Papa did give me presents, it wasn't because I came asking for them."

"You've been happier than I have: your Monsieur de Marsay was rich, you knew just what you were doing. You've always been a miser. All right, goodbye, I have no sister, I have no . . ."

"Enough, Nasie!" cried Père Goriot.

"Only a sister like you could go on saying what no one else still believes," said Delphine. "You're a monster."

"My children, my children, stop, or I'll kill myself right here and now."

"All right, Nasie," said Madame de Nucingen. "I forgive you, you always were unlucky. But I'm better than you. For you to say such things to me, just when I was feeling I could do anything to help you—anything—even go to my husband's bedroom, which I wouldn't do even for myself, not even for . . . But that's just the way you've always mistreated me, ever since I was nine."

"Oh children, children, kiss and make up!" cried their father. "You're both angels."

"No, no, let go of me!" cried the countess, struggling to be free of him, Goriot having taken her by the arm. "She has less pity for me than my husband has! Oh, she's the very image of virtue, she is!"

"I'd rather have it said that I owed money to Monsieur de Marsay than admit that Monsieur de Trailles cost me more than two hundred thousand francs," replied Madame de Nucingen.

"Delphine!" shrieked the countess, taking a step toward her.

"Insult me, and I'll speak the simple truth," the baroness replied coldly.

"Delphine! you're a . . ."

Père Goriot lunged toward her, pulling her away and stopping her from continuing, his hand over her mouth.

"Fah! My God, Father, what on earth have you had your hands in, this morning?" cried Anastasie.

"Well, it was wrong of me, yes," said the poor father, wiping his hands on his trousers. "But I'm moving, I didn't know you were coming."

But how happy it made him, getting her to turn her anger on him.

"Ah!" he went on, sinking into a chair. "You two have broken my heart. I'm dying, children! My skull's burning up, there's a fire in there! Please, be nice to each other! You'll kill me. Delphine, Nasie, all right, you're both wrong, you're both right! See, Dedel, see!" he went on, turning to the baroness, his eyes filled with tears, "he needs twelve thousand francs, let's try to find it. Don't look like that." He knelt down in front of Delphine. "Ask your sister to forgive you, do it for me," he whispered in her ear, "because, after all, isn't she the one who's unhappy?"

"My poor Nasie," said Delphine, shocked by the wild, lunatic expression his sadness had spread across her father's face, "I was wrong, kiss me . . ."

"Ah!" cried Goriot. "That's like putting medicine on my heart! But where shall we find twelve thousand francs? Maybe I could take somebody's place in the military draft?"

"Oh no, Father, no!" both daughters exclaimed, embracing him.

"May God repay you for even thinking of that," Delphine declared. "We couldn't pay you even with our lives, could we, Nasie?"

"And even then," the countess observed, "my poor father, it would be just like a drop in the bucket."

"But can't I do *anything* for my own flesh and blood?" cried the desperate old man. "I swear I'll save you, Nasie! I'll kill someone for you. I'll do what Vautrin does, I'll go to jail, I'll . . ." He stopped, as if suddenly struck by lightning. "No more!" he cried, tearing at his hair. "If I knew where to go, to steal the money, but it's not easy to find the right place to rob! To get into a bank, ah, that would take more than one man, and it would take time. All right, so I have to die, the only thing I can do is die. Yes, I'm no good anymore, I'm not a father! No. She comes and asks me, she needs my help! But me, miserable wretch, I have nothing left. Ah ha, you kept some lifetime payments for yourself, you old rascal, and you have daughters! Don't you love them anymore? Oh die, die like the dog you are! Yes, I'm lower than a dog, even a dog wouldn't act like that! Oh, my head! It's boiling!"

"Papa, don't," cried both young women, trying to stop him from beating his head against the wall, "Papa, don't!"

He was sobbing. Horrified, Eugène picked up the note he'd signed for Vautrin, which had a stamp good for a much larger sum; he changed the amount, quickly turning it into a note for twelve thousand francs, payable to Goriot, and hurried into his neighbor's room.

"Here, here's the money you need, madame," he said, giving the note to the countess. "I was asleep, your conversation woke me, and I remembered how much I owed Monsieur Goriot. You can use it, I'll pay every cent."

Frozen in her tracks, the countess stood holding the slip of paper.

"Delphine," she said, pale, trembling with anger, with fury, with an insane rage, "as God is my witness I'd have forgiven you everything, but this! What, he was there all the time, and you knew it! You'd stoop so low as to take revenge on me like this, letting me tell everything, my secrets, my whole life, my children's lives, my shame, my honor! Leave me, you're no longer anything to me, I hate you, I will do anything I can to hurt you, I . . ." Anger withered her throat, she stopped in mid-sentence.

"But he's my son," cried Père Goriot, "our child, your brother, your savior! Throw your arms around him, Nasie! All right, I'll do it," he went on, hugging Eugène in a frenzy. "Oh, my child! I'll be even more than a father to you, I'll be your whole family. I'll be God, I'll throw the entire universe down at your feet. Kiss him, Nasie! He's not a man, he's an angel, a real-life angel!"

"Leave her alone, Father," said Delphine. "She's out of her head."

"Out of my head! Out of my head! And what about you?" cried Madame de Restaud.

"My children, if you go on like that I'll die," cried the old man, falling back on his bed as if struck by a bullet. "Oh, they're killing me!" he muttered.

The countess stared at Eugène, who had not moved, stunned by the violence of this scene.

"Monsieur?" she said to him, questioning him with a gesture, with her voice, with her glance, and paying no attention whatever to her father, as Delphine was quickly unbuttoning the old man's vest.

"Madame," replied Eugène, not waiting for her to finish the question, "I'll pay it, and I'll never breathe a word."

"You've killed our father, Nasie!" said Delphine to her sister, pointing to the unconscious old man as the countess swiftly made her escape.

"It's all right, I forgive her," said the good man, opening his eyes, "she's in a horrible mess, enough to upset a better head than hers. Comfort Nasie, be good to her, promise your poor father, who's dying, you'll do that," he asked Delphine, squeezing her hand.

"What's wrong with you?" she asked, terrified.

"Nothing, nothing," her father answered. "I'll get over it. Something's pressing on my forehead, it's a migraine. Oh poor Nasie, what she has to look forward to!"

Just then the countess returned and threw herself down, clasping her father's knees.

"Forgive me!" she cried.

"Enough," said Père Goriot, "you'll make me even sicker."

"Monsieur," said the countess to Rastignac, her eyes streaming with tears, "sorrow made me unfair to you." She grasped his hand. "Will you be like a brother to me?"

"Nasie," said Delphine to her sister, hugging her, "my little Nasie, let's forget all this."

"Oh no!" responded Madame de Restaud. "I'm going to remember every word of it!"

"My angels," cried Père Goriot, "you've pulled the curtain away from my eyes, your voices re-awakened me. So kiss and make up. So, Nasie! That note will save you?"

"I think so. But, Papa, don't you have to sign it?"

"Ah, how stupid of me, to forget that! But I'm not feeling well. Nasie, don't be angry at me. Let me know when you're out of trouble. No, no, I'll come myself. But I won't come, no, I can't ever see your husband again, I'd kill him on the spot. But if he tries to get at your fortune, I'll be there. So go, quickly, my child, and tell Maxime to be more sensible."

Eugène stood immobile.

"Poor Anastasie," said Madame de Nucingen, "she's always been violent. But she has a good heart."

"She only came back so he could sign it," he whispered in Delphine's ear.

"You think so?"

"I wish I didn't have to. Watch out for her," he said, raising his eyes as if to confide in God what he did not dare actually say.

"Indeed, she's always been something of an actress, and my poor father lets himself be fooled by her pretenses."

"How are you feeling, my good Père Goriot?" Eugène asked the old man.

"I need to sleep," he answered.

Eugène helped him settle down. Then, once the good man fell asleep, holding Delphine's hand, his daughter rose to go.

"Tonight, at the opera," she said to Eugène, "you'll tell me how he's doing. And tomorrow you're moving, monsieur! Let's have a look at your room. Oh, how ghastly!" she exclaimed, walking in. "You've been worse off than my father. But you behaved very well, Eugène. If it were possible, I'd love you even more, but let me tell you, my dear child, if you really intend to make your fortune you'd better not go throwing twelve thousand francs out the window! The Count de Trailles's a gambler. My sister doesn't want to admit it. He should have been looking for his money right where he knows how to win or lose whole mountains of gold."

Goriot suddenly moaned, though they'd thought him asleep, but when the two lovers came over to him they heard these words:

"They're not happy!"

Whether he was asleep or awake, the way he said this so clutched at his daughter's heart that she bent over the straw mattress on which her father lay and kissed him on the forehead. He opened his eyes, saying,

"It's Delphine!"

"Ah! And how are you?" she asked.

"Fine," he said. "Don't worry, I'll be all right. Go on, go on, children, go and be happy!"

Eugène went with her, as far as the Nucingen house, but he refused to stay to dinner, worried by the state in which he'd left Goriot, and went directly back to Maison Vauquer. He found Père Goriot already back on his feet and quite ready to go down for dinner. Bianchon seated himself so that he could carefully watch the old man's face. And when the medical student saw how Goriot picked up his bread, feeling it to see of what sort of flour it had been made, he noted that the old man moved with a complete absence of conscious volition, and shook his head ominously.

"Come sit next to me, Mister Doctor-to-Be," said Eugène.

Bianchon did so, and more willingly than he'd done when he approached the old lodger.

"What's wrong with him?" Rastignac asked.

"Unless I'm much mistaken, his goose is cooked! Something extraordinary must have happened, internally: I'd guess a serious cerebral event isn't far off. Although the lower part of the face seems quiet enough, note how the upper portions are being involuntarily drawn up toward the forehead—see? His eyes, too, look as if there's already been some perfusion of serum in the cerebellum. Doesn't it seem as if there's a fine dust spread all through them? I'll know more by tomorrow morning."

"Is there anything to be done?"

"Nothing. It might be possible to somewhat delay death, if we could find some way to induce a reactive movement, out toward the extremities, to the legs, perhaps, but if these symptoms haven't disappeared by tomorrow night the poor fellow's as good as dead. Do you happen to know what might have caused this? He must have experienced some violent shock, to so crumple his whole mental state."

"Yes," replied Rastignac, recalling how relentlessly Goriot's daughters had been pounding on the old man's heartstrings. "At least," the law student said to himself, "at least Delphine really does love her father!"

At the opera, later that evening, Rastignac was careful not to unduly alarm Madame de Nucingen.

"Oh, don't worry," she said, after Eugène had spoken only a few words, "my father's strong. It's just that we upset him a bit, this morning. Our fortunes are in danger: do you have any idea what a disaster we might be facing? It will be hard for me to live on, if your affection can't keep me from feeling what, until now, I've always thought of as a kind of fatal anguish. But the only fear I have left, the only disaster I worry about anymore, is that I might lose the love that has made me feel what a joy life can be. Apart from that feeling, everything else has become utterly unimportant to me, I no longer care about society. You are everything to me. If being rich makes me at all happy, it's simply because it lets me make *you* happy. I'm ashamed to admit that I haven't felt such an intense love since I was a girl. Why? I don't know. My whole life is in you, now. My father gave me a heart, but it's you who've made it beat. The whole world can say anything it wants of me, none of that matters just so long as you—and you have no right to begrudge me this—forgive me for the sins which an irresistible feeling condemns me to commit!

"Do you think I'm an unnatural daughter? No, no, how could anyone not love a father as good as ours? Could I possibly keep him from seeing, finally, the natural consequences of such deplorable marriages as those we made? Why did he allow us to go ahead with them? Wasn't it his job to think on our behalf? Now, yes, I know he suffers as much as we do, but could we have done anything? Make him feel better! We can't make him feel even a tiny bit better. All our complaining and scolding couldn't do him as much harm, couldn't make him as sad, as the fact that we're resigned to it. Sometimes life is simply bitter, bitter all through."

Eugène could not reply, overwhelmed by tenderness at her naive expression of true feeling. Parisian women may often be deceitful, drunk with vanity, self-centered, flirts, frigid, but when they're truly in love they surrender themselves to their passions far more completely than most women; they transcend all their pettinesses, they become sublime. Eugène was struck, too, by the fine, profound good sense a woman can bring to bear on the most natural and universal of feelings, when some special emotion allows her to isolate it and see it as from a distance. Madame de Nucingen was troubled by his silence.

"What are you thinking?" she wondered.

"I'm still hearing what you just said. Till now, I thought I loved you more than you loved me."

She smiled, bracing herself against the rush of pleasure, so she could keep their conversation within the bounds set by propriety. It was the first time she had ever heard the vibrant expression of youthful, honest love. Just a few more such words, and she could not have controlled herself.

"Eugène," she said, carefully changing the subject, "don't you know what's going on? Everyone in Paris will be at Madame de Beauséant's, tomorrow. The Rochefide family and the Marquis d'Ajuda have agreed to keep things quiet, but tomorrow the King will sign the marriage contract—and your poor cousin still knows nothing about it. She cannot help but receive her guests, but the marquis won't come to her ball. No one's talking about anything else."

"And society finds such infamy amusing, and helps it along? Don't *you* realize this will kill Madame de Beauséant?"

"No," answered Delphine, laughing, "you don't understand such women. Still, all Paris will come to her house, and I'll be there, too! And I owe my good fortune to you."

"In any event," said Rastignac, "mightn't this be one of those absurd rumors Parisians are always creating?"

"Tomorrow we'll know the truth."

Eugène did not go home to Maison Vauquer. He couldn't keep from enjoying the delights of his new apartment. If he'd been obliged to leave Delphine, the night before, an hour after midnight, this time it was Delphine who left him, returning home at about two in the morning. He slept late, the next day, waiting for Madame de Nucingen to come to lunch with him, at about noon. Young men so relish such pretty pleasures that, indeed, Eugène had almost forgotten Père Goriot. Growing accustomed to each of his elegant new furnishings was, for him, like a long holiday celebration. And having Madame de Nucingen there with him made everything even more glowingly wonderful. But shortly before four o'clock, remembering the happiness Père Goriot had been looking forward to, after he too had moved to this house, the two lovers' minds turned to thoughts of him. Eugène noted that they had to bring the good man there without any delay, in case he got sick, and left Delphine, hurrying back to the *pension*. But neither Père Goriot nor Bianchon were in the dining room.

"Well!" the painter told Rastignac. "Père Goriot's in bad shape. Bianchon's upstairs with him. One of the old man's daughters has been here, the Countess of Restaudarama. Then he wanted to go out and things got worse. Society is about to be deprived of one of its handsomest ornaments."

Rastignac bolted toward the staircase.

"Wait, Monsieur Eugène!"

"Monsieur Eugène," called Sylvie. "Madame wants to speak to you."

"Monsieur," the widow said to him, "you and Monsieur Goriot were to leave on February fifteenth. It's now three days past that, we're at the eighteenth, so I have to be paid an additional month for each of you, but, if you'll guarantee to take care of Monsieur Goriot's rent, your word will be good enough."

"Why? Don't you trust him?"

"Trust him! If he's never again right in the head, and he dies, his daughters won't let me have a cent, and all his old clothes put together aren't worth ten francs. He got rid of the last of his silver this morning, I don't know why. He's gotten dressed like a young man. God have mercy on me, but I think he put rouge on his cheeks, he looked really rejuvenated."

"I'll be responsible for everything," said Eugène, shivering with horror and anticipating dreadful things still to come.

He went up to Père Goriot's room. The old man was stretched on his bed, Bianchon near him.

"Greetings, Père," Eugène said.

The good man smiled sweetly at him and, turning his watery eyes toward the student, replied,

"How is she?"

"Fine. And you?"

"Not bad."

"Don't tire him," said Bianchon, leading Eugène into a corner.

"And?" Rastignac said to him.

"Only a miracle can save him. There's been a serious stroke,

I've used mustard plasters and, luckily, they had some effect, they did some good."

"Can he be moved?"

"Absolutely not. He must remain here, he can't be allowed any activity, he has to be kept from all emotion . . ."

"My dear Bianchon," said Eugène, "you and I can surely take care of that."

"I've already had a visit from the chief physician of my hospital."

"And?"

"He'll tell us tomorrow night. He promised to come again, after hours. Unluckily, this morning our good old idiot, here, did something utterly stupid, nor will he explain why on earth he did it. He's as stubborn as a mule. When I ask him, he pretends he doesn't understand, and makes believe he's sleeping so he doesn't have to answer, and when his eyes are open he just whines and moans. Early this morning he went out, he walked all over Paris, who knows where. He carried off everything he owned that was worth anything—it was like some sacred mission, and even though it was too much for him he just went and did it! One of his daughters was here."

"The countess?" asked Eugène. "A tall brunette with bright eyes, good figure, willowy, beautiful feet?"

"Yes."

"Leave me alone with him for a moment," said Rastignac. "I'll get him to tell me the whole story, and he will, he will."

"I'll take the time to have lunch. But try not to get him upset: there's still a chance."

"Don't worry."

When they were alone, Père Goriot said,

"They'll have a good time, tomorrow. They're going to a great ball."

"So what did you do this morning, Papa, that tonight you're sick and have to stay in bed?"

"Nothing."

"Anastasie was here?" Eugène asked.

"Yes," Père Goriot replied.

"All right! Don't hide anything from me. What was she asking for this time?"

"Ah!" the old man answered, gathering his strength so he could speak, "she's had such bad luck, oh my child! After this business with the diamonds, Nasie doesn't have a penny. For this ball, she'd ordered a spangled dress, which on her will glow like a jewel. Her dressmaker, the wretch, wouldn't let her have it on credit, and her maid's already put up a thousand francs on account. My poor Nasie, having come to that! It breaks my heart. But then, seeing that Restaud no longer trusted his wife, the maid was afraid she'd lose her money, so she fixed it up with the dressmaker that the dress wouldn't be delivered unless she got her thousand francs back. The ball's tomorrow, the dress is ready, and Nasie is in despair. So she wanted to borrow my silver, to pawn it. Her husband wants her to go to this ball, so she can show all Paris the diamonds she's supposed to have sold. Can she possibly say to this monster, 'I owe a thousand francs, pay it?' No. I could understand that, easy enough. Her sister Delphine will be there, wearing a superb gown. Anastasie shouldn't have to take a back seat to her little sister. And she was crying so, oh, my poor daughter! I was so humiliated, yesterday, not having those twelve thousand francs, that I'd have given the whole rest of my miserable life to make amends for that wrong. Don't you see? I've been strong enough to bear anything and everything, but this final lack of money has broken my heart. Oh, oh! so I didn't give it a second thought, I just pulled myself together, I spruced myself up, and I sold the silver plate and the buckles for six hundred francs, and I mortgaged one year of my annuity to Papa Gobseck, in return for a lump payment of four hundred francs. Bah! I'll eat bread! It was enough for me when I was younger, and it's still enough. At least, my Nasie will have a fine party. She'll be all spick and span. The thousand-franc note's right here, under my pillow. That perks me up, having something that will make poor Nasie so happy right underneath my head. She can just show that wicked maid of hers to the door. Can you imagine, servants not trusting their masters! I'll be better tomorrow, Nasie's coming at ten o'clock. I don't want them to think I'm sick, or they won't go to the ball, they'll stay here and take care of me. Tomorrow, Nasie will hug me the way she hugs her child, and her caresses will cure me. Anyway, Eugène, wouldn't I have had to spend a thousand francs at the pharmacy? I'd rather give it to my Universal Healer, my Nasie. At least, I can make her feel a little better, ease her misery a bit. That makes it all right to mortgage my annuity. She's down at the bottom of the abyss, and I'm not strong enough to pull her out. Ah, I'll go back to business. I'll go to Odessa and I'll buy grain there. Russian wheat's worth three times what ours is. You can't import raw cereals, but the smart fellows who drew up those laws never thought of prohibiting things mostly made of wheat! Oh ho, I discovered that, this morning! You can do some fine business with starch and wheat paste, let me tell you."

"He's gone mad," Eugène said to himself, looking down at the old man. "All right, you just rest, don't talk . . ."

Eugène went down, so he could eat, while Bianchon went back upstairs. Then they spent the night taking turns watching over the sick man, while one of them read his medical texts and the other busied himself writing to his mother and his sisters. The next day, according to Bianchon, the sick man gave signs of improvement, but they still had to attend to him as carefully as possible, doing things which cannot be fully described without offending against our time's linguistic prudery. They set leeches on the good man's shrunken body, along with mustard plasters, footbaths, and used a variety of other medical techniques which required all the strength and devotion of two young men. Madame de Restaud did not come, but she sent a messenger to collect her money.

"I thought she'd be coming herself. But that's not a bad thing, she'd only be worried," her father said, seeming to be cheered by the thought.

At seven that night, Delphine's maid arrived, bearing a letter for Eugène.

> *So what are you up to, my friend? Barely introduced to love, am I now to be neglected? In our heart-to-heart exchanges of confidence, you've shown far too beautiful a soul not to be someone who remains forever faithful, understanding that emotions have their subtle shades and tints. As you yourself said, when you heard the prayer in Rossini's* Moses, *"Some people hear only the same notes, over and over, but others are listening to the infinite expressed in music." Recollect that I'll be waiting for you, so we can go to Madame de Beauséant's ball. Monsieur d'Ajuda signed the marriage contract, this morning: that's definite, and the poor vicomtesse only heard about it at two o'clock. Everyone who's anyone in all Paris is going to come to her ball, the way people crowd into the square when there's an execution. Isn't it awful, going to watch that woman hiding her sadness, even as she knows she'll die of it? I certainly wouldn't go, my friend, if I had ever been to her house before, but this is surely going to be the last reception she has, and all the trouble I went to would just be wasted. So my situation is different, you see, from other people's. Besides, I'll also be going there on your account.*

I'll be waiting for you. If you're not at my side in less than two hours, I'm not sure if so grave a crime could ever be forgiven.

Rastignac picked up a pen and wrote the following reply:

I'm waiting for a doctor, who'll tell me whether your father is to live or die. He's dying. I'll come and bring you the verdict, but I'm afraid it can only be a death sentence. You'll be able to decide for yourself if you can still go to the ball.
A thousand tendernesses.

The doctor came at eight-thirty and, though he did not make an optimistic pronouncement, did at least say that death was probably not imminent. He predicted there would be ups and downs, and both the good man's life and his sanity would depend on the course things took.

"But it would be better if he died right away," was the doctor's final word.

Leaving Père Goriot in Bianchon's care, Eugène went to bring Madame de Nucingen this latest somber news, for to him, his spirit still imbued with familial obligations, these developments necessarily took precedence over any pleasurable activities.

"Tell her she should go and have a good time anyway," Père Goriot called out, though he had seemed asleep, sitting bolt upright just as Rastignac was leaving.

He came to Delphine with his heart full of sorrow, and found her with her hair ready, and her shoes, and only the ball gown still to be put on. Rather like the final brushstrokes by which a painter finishes a canvas, these last measures seemed to take even longer than the whole rest of her preparations.

"What? You're not dressed?" she said.

"But your father . . ."

"My father, always my father!" she cried, interrupting him. "But I don't need you to teach me what I owe my father. I've known my father for a long long time. Don't say a word, Eugène. I won't listen to you until you're dressed. Thérèse has gotten everything ready for you; my carriage is ready, so take it; then come back. We'll talk about my father as we drive to the ball. We've got to be on time; if we ever get caught up in a long line of carriages, we'll be lucky to get inside by eleven o'clock."

"But . . ."

"Go! Not another word," she said, dashing into her dressing room in search of a necklace.

"Just go, Monsieur Eugène," said Thérèse, "you're making Madame angry." She pushed him toward the door; he stumbled out, horrified by this elegant form of patricide.

He went and dressed for the occasion, tormented by the saddest, most discouraging thoughts. He saw the world as an ocean of mud into which a man would fall, right up to the neck, if he ever stepped in at all.

"It's one shabby crime after another!" he said to himself. "Vautrin's better than this."

Now he knew society's three great formulations: Obedience, Struggle, and Revolt; or, put differently, the Family, the World, and Vautrin. He hadn't dared enroll himself under any of these banners. Obedience was boring, Revolt impossible, and the Struggle at best uncertain. His mind wandered back to the security of his family. He could still remember the pure emotions engendered by that calm existence, he could recall days spent in the midst of beings who loved him. Adapting themselves to the natural laws of domesticity, these dear creatures had found a simple, sustained, uncomplicated happiness.

But for all these good thoughts, he lacked the courage to

proclaim to Delphine the faith of those pure souls, summoning her to Virtue in the name of Love. His education had already begun to bear its fruits. His love was a selfish one. He had enough insight so he could understand Delphine's heart. He had the sense that, in order to get to this ball, she was capable of walking right over her father's body, and he lacked the strength to try to be her guide, just as he lacked the courage to displease her, and the valor to simply leave her.

"She'd never forgive me for being right in this, when she was wrong," he assured himself.

And then he thought about what the doctors had been saying, and to convince himself that Père Goriot wasn't really as sick as he'd believed; in a word, he piled up all the murderous reasons he could think of to justify Delphine. She didn't really know the condition her father was in. The good man himself would have sent her to the ball, had she come to see him. Our social laws, no matter how inflexibly formulated, frequently pass judgment in cases where what may seem to be a crime is excused by endlessly variable factors introduced, even in the same family, by character-ological differences, divergent interests, and different situations.

Eugène was anxious to deceive himself, he was quite prepared to sacrifice his conscience to his mistress. In the last two days his whole life had changed. Womankind had injected her chaotic influence, downgrading the influence of family, grasping at everything and turning it to her own advantage. Rastignac and Delphine had met under the exact right circumstances for each to provide the other with the most intense pleasure. Their well-seasoned passion had been heightened by that which sometimes kills passion, namely, possession. For only in possessing this woman had Eugène realized that, till then, he had simply desired rather than loved her: happiness had created love, since love is sometimes nothing more than the acknowledgment of pleasure. She might be infamous, she might be sublime, but for the delights of the flesh he had brought her as his dowry, and for those she had showered upon him, he adored this woman, just as Delphine loved him the way Tantalus would have loved an angel, coming to satisfy his hunger or quench the thirsting of his parched throat.

"Now then!" Madame de Nucingen said to him, when he reappeared, dressed for the ball, "how's my father?"

"Bad, very bad," he replied, "and if you want to show me just how much you care, let's quickly go see him."

"We will, yes," she said, "but after the ball. Be nice, my good Eugène, don't preach at me, just come along."

They left. For the first half of the carriage ride, Eugène did not say a word.

"What's wrong?" she asked.

"I keep hearing the death rattle in your father's throat," he said sourly. And then he began to tell her, with a young man's passionate eloquence, the savagery to which Madame de Restaud's vanity had led her, the mortal crisis brought on by Père Goriot's final act of devotion, and how much Anastasie's spangled dress had cost. Delphine wept.

"This is going to make me ugly," she said to herself. Her tears dried up. "I'll go take care of my father," she went on. "I won't leave his bedside."

"Ah! That's what I was hoping you'd say!" he cried.

The streets leading to the Beauséant Mansion glowed with the lights of five hundred carriages. A mounted policeman swaggered at each side of the brightly-lit gate. The denizens of high society had come flocking in such immense numbers, each eager to behold the great woman at the moment of her downfall, that by the time Madame de Nucingen and Rastignac drove up the ground-floor rooms were already full. Since the day when the entire court had come rushing to La Grande Mademoiselle's❖ house, after Louis XIV changed his mind about allowing her to marry and threw her lover into prison, there had not been such a brilliant love affair as Madame de Beauséant's.

But the last daughter of the quasi-royal house of Burgundy rose above her misfortune and, to the very last moment, dominated Parisian high society, having accepted its vanities only insofar as they had let her indulge her true passion. The most beautiful women in all Paris enlivened her house with their dresses and their smiles. The most distinguished gentlemen of the royal court, ambassadors, ministers, illustrious men of all sorts, bedecked with medals and decorations, with ribbons of many colors, thronged around the vicomtesse. The orchestra's melodies rang out under the gorgeous ceilings of this palace—which for its queen might just as well have been an unpopulated desert. Madame de Beauséant stood, calmly upright, at the door of her *salon*, receiving her supposed friends. Dressed in white, her hair in simple braids without any ornament, she seemed totally self-possessed, displaying neither sadness, nor pride, nor any merely pretended pleasure. No one could possibly have read her soul. Seeing her, you might have said she was a Niobe† carved in marble. The smile she showed her close friends was sometimes mocking, but to one and all she seemed completely herself, every bit what she had been when happiness draped its rays over her, so that even the most boorish admired her, as young women in Rome used to applaud a gladiator

❖ Louise d'Orléans (1627–1693), Duchess of Montpensier, Louis XIV's aunt. After years of hoping to marry royalty, at age forty-two she proposed to marry an adventurer.

† Proud Greek mother, turned to stone but still weeping for the death of her children, killed as punishment for her excess of pride in them.

who knew how to smile as he died. It almost seemed as if the world had been made beautiful so it could say a fitting farewell to one of its queens.

"I was afraid you wouldn't come," she said to Rastignac.

"Madame," he said, his voice quivering with emotion, for he took her words as a reproach, "I came so that I might be the last one to leave you."

"Excellent," she said, grasping his hand. "You may very well be the only one here I can trust. My friend, only love a woman you can love forever. Never abandon a lover."

Taking Rastignac's arm, she led him to a sofa, in the room where people were playing cards.

"Go to the marquis for me," she said, when they were seated. "Jacques, my servant, will bring you there and give you a letter I've written to Monsieur Ajuda. I've asked him to return my letters. I suspect there'll be no difficulty and he'll give you all of them. Once you have my letters, come to my room. I'll be notified."

She rose, going to meet her best friend, the Duchess of Langeais, who was coming toward her. Rastignac left, seeking the Marquis d'Ajuda-Pinto at the Rochefide mansion, where he was supposed to be spending the night, and where in fact the law student found him. The marquis led him to a private room and handed him a box, saying,

"They're all there."

He looked as if he wanted to say something to Eugène, perhaps to question him about what had happened at the ball, or about the vicomtesse, or perhaps to confess that he was already unhappy about his marriage, as later he definitely was, but his eyes glowed with a proud light and he had the lamentable courage to keep his noblest feelings to himself.

"Say nothing to her about me, my dear Eugène."

He pressed Rastignac's hand, with a sad, affectionate movement, then signaled him to leave.

Rastignac went back to the Beauséant mansion and was shown directly to the vicomtesse's bedroom, where he could clearly see a departure was being prepared. He sat down near the fire, contemplating her cedar jewel box, and fell into a profound melancholy. For him, Madame de Beauséant had the stature of one of the goddesses in the *Iliad*.

"Ah, my friend," said the vicomtesse, coming in and placing her hand on his shoulder.

His cousin, he could see, was in tears, her eyes uplifted, one hand trembling, the other raised. She snatched up the box, set it in the fire, and watched it burn.

"How they dance! They've arrived right on time, though death will be very late. Oh! My friend," she said, seeing Rastignac about to speak and setting a finger against his lips, "I'll never see Paris again, nor the world, either. At five o'clock, tomorrow morning, I'm leaving, to bury myself in the farthest depths of Normandy. Since three this afternoon I've been making all my preparations, signing documents, taking care of business, and I couldn't send anyone to Monsieur . . ."

She stopped, once again overwhelmed by grief. At such moments suffering is everything, and there are words one simply cannot say.

"In any case," she went on, "I was counting on you, tonight, to do this last service for me. I wanted to give you some pledge of my friendship. I've been thinking of you a good bit, for you struck me as good and noble, young and honest in the midst of a world where such qualities are exceedingly hard to find. I should like you to think of me, sometimes. Here," she said, looking quickly around the room, "here's the little box which used to hold my gloves. Every time I've taken it out, before going off to a ball or to the theater, I felt myself beautiful, because I was happy, and that was the only reason I ever touched it, and I always left it filled with some graceful thought: there's really a great deal of me in there—a whole Madame de Beauséant who no longer exists. Take it, please. I'll make sure someone brings it to you, in d'Artois Street.

"Madame Nucingen's very lovely, tonight: love her well. And if I never see you again, my friend, you may be sure I'll say prayers for you, and prayers have always helped me.

"So: let's go back down. I don't want them thinking I'm up here crying. I've got all eternity in front of me, I'll be completely alone, and there'll be no one to worry about my tears. Stop: one more look at this room."

She stood very still. And then, after quickly covering her eyes with her hand, she wiped them dry, bathed them in cool water, and took the student's arm.

"Let's go, then!" she declared.

Rastignac had never before felt any emotion so violent as that produced by this nobly restrained grief. Once they had returned to the ball, Eugène made the rounds with Madame de Beauséant, a final, delicate attention from this gracious lady. His eye was soon caught by the two sisters, Madame de Restaud and Madame de Nucingen. The countess was magnificent in her display of diamonds, which surely gleamed brilliantly for her, too, because she was wearing them for the last time. For all her pride, and the strength of her love, it was hard for her to bear her husband's glance. It was not a spectacle likely to make Rastignac's thoughts more cheerful. Underneath both sisters' diamonds, he could see the straw pallet on which their father was lying. His obvious melancholy deceived the vicomtesse, and she withdrew her arm.

"Go on!" she said, "I don't want to deprive you of your pleasure."

Delphine at once reclaimed her possession, delighted at the effect she'd been producing, and anxious to credit him with all the signs of recognition she'd been receiving in this great world, where she hoped to make her own way.

"How did you think Nasie looked?" she asked him.

"She's discounted everything," he said, "up to and including her father's death."

By four in the morning, the crowding in the *salons* began to ease. Soon thereafter, the sound of music was heard no longer. Rastignac and the Duchess of Langeais found themselves alone in the very largest of all the rooms. Then the vicomtesse came in, after saying goodbye to her husband, thinking the student was the only one she'd find there; Monsieur de Beauséant had gone off to bed, repeating as he went, "It's the wrong thing, my dear, to shut yourself away at your age! Stay here with us."

Seeing the duchess, Madame de Beauséant couldn't keep from an exclamation of surprise.

"I understood you completely, Clara," said Madame de Langeais. "You're going away, intending never to return, but you're not going to leave without hearing what I have to say and without our coming to terms with one another."

She took her friend's arm and led her into the adjoining room, where, after looking at her for a moment, tearfully, she embraced Madame de Beauséant and kissed her on both cheeks.

"My dear, I don't want us parting coldly; that would leave me with too heavy a weight of remorse. You can rely on me as you would rely on yourself. You've been magnificent tonight, I've felt myself worthy of you, and I want you to see that. I've been guilty of unkindnesses to you, I've not always behaved well, but forgive me, my dear: I repudiate everything that could possibly have hurt you, I wish I could simply take back my words. Our souls have been united in precisely the same sadness, nor can I say which of us is to be the more unfortunate. Monsieur de Montriveau was not here tonight: do you understand? Anyone who saw you at this ball, Clara, will never forget you. For myself, I intend to make one last and final effort. Should it fail, I propose to enter a convent! And you, where will you go?"

"To Courcelles, in Normandy, to love, to pray, until the time comes for God to take me out of this world.

"Go, Monsieur de Rastignac," added Madame de Beauséant, her voice quivering, suddenly remembering that the young man was still waiting. The student made a deep bow, took his cousin's hand, and kissed it. "Goodbye, Antoinette!" she went on. "Be happy. As for you, Eugène, you already are, you're young," she said, "you can still believe. When I leave this world, I will have been surrounded, like the other privileged souls who preceded me, by genuinely honest and pious feelings!"

Rastignac left at about five in the morning, after seeing Madame de Beauséant start off in her heavy traveling coach, and after receiving her last, tear-stained farewell—tears which proved that, no matter how lofty their station, human beings are never able to escape the laws of the heart or to live without grief, as some of those who flatter the masses would like them to believe. He went back to Maison Vauquer on foot, in the cold, wet morning air. His education was almost complete.

"We're not going to be able to save our poor Père Goriot," Bianchon said at once, as soon as Rastignac entered his neighbor's room.

"My friend," Eugène said to him, after staring at the sleeping old man, "go, fulfill the modest destiny which is all you've let yourself want. Me, I'm in Hell, and I have no choice but to stay there. Whatever wickedness you hear the world accused of, it's true, believe it! Not even Juvenal could paint the horror under all the gold and jewels."

Being obliged to go out at two the next afternoon, Bianchon came to wake Rastignac, for during the morning Père Goriot's condition had taken a serious turn for the worse, and the medical student wanted Eugène to watch over the old man.

"The good man hasn't got two days left to live," the medical student observed, "and maybe he won't last more than half a dozen hours, but we can't stop fighting the disease. We'll have to give him some pretty expensive treatment. And we'll be his male nurses, all right—but I'm afraid I haven't got a cent. I've turned his pockets inside out, I've ransacked all the drawers, but I can't come up with a thing. When he was in his right mind for just a minute, I asked him what he could muster, and he told me he didn't have a dime either. What kind of shape are you in, eh?"

"I've got twenty francs left," replied Rastignac, "but I'll go gamble with it and get us more."

"And if you lose?"

"I'll beg money from his sons-in-law and his daughters."

"And what if they won't give you any?" Bianchon replied. "The most urgent thing, right this moment, isn't finding the money but getting the good man wrapped in a boiling hot mustard plaster, from halfway up his thighs down to the bottom of his feet. If it makes him scream, maybe he can still pull through. You know how to do all that. Besides, Christophe will help. Me, I'll go to the pharmacist and sign for the medicines we've been taking. But it's a shame the poor fellow couldn't be brought to our hospital, that would have been a lot better. Come on, I'll get you started, and don't you leave him till I get back."

The two young men went into the room where the old man was lying. Eugène was terrified, seeing the change in Goriot's face, now contorted, white as a sheet, and completely slack.

"How goes it, Papa?" he asked, leaning over the mattress.

Goriot's dull eyes looked up attentively, but did not recognize the student. Eugène couldn't bear the sight, his eyes filled with tears.

"Bianchon, shouldn't we put some sort of curtains over the windows?"

"No. Atmospheric conditions are irrelevant. I'd be delighted if he could be either cold or hot. Still, we will need a fire to brew our concoctions. I'll send up some sticks, and they'll do until we can get real firewood. All day yesterday, and last night, too, I burned everything you and the poor old man had. It was damp, water was rolling down the walls. I could just barely keep the room dry. Christophe swept up, it was a real pig-sty in here. I burned some juniper, it stank so bad."

"My God!" exclaimed Rastignac. "But what about his daughters?"

"Now listen, if he wants anything to drink, give him some of this," said the medical student, pointing out a large white jug. "If you hear him complaining, and his belly's hot and hard, get Christophe's help and give him . . . well, you know. If by any chance he gets all wrought up, and starts to talk a lot—I mean, if he's pretty much out of his head, don't worry about it. That won't be a bad sign. Just send Christophe to our hospital. One of us, either my friend or me, will come and cauterize him.

"While you were asleep, this morning, we had a long conference with one of Doctor Gall's students, and the head doctor at Hôtel-Dieu Hospital, and our chief, too. These gentlemen think they've spotted some strange symptoms, so we're following the progress of the disease very closely, hoping to illuminate some matters of pretty high scientific interest. One of these gentlemen argues that if the brain serum happens to press harder on certain organs than on others, very definite, different results may occur. If they speak to you, listen carefully, so you can tell what sort of difficulties they're talking about: is it the effects on memory, or on mental acuity, or judgment; whether they're concerned about corporeal issues or primarily emotional ones—you know, can he still count, is he living back in the past; and, in a word, just be ready to tell us exactly what these learned gentlemen think. It's entirely possible that the damage has been massive, and he'll die as the idiot he is right this moment. In this sort of sickness, everything is incredibly strange! If the bomb explodes *here*," said Bianchon, pointing to the occipital region of the sick man's head, "we've seen some really weird developments: for example, the brain recovers some of its capacity, and death is considerably delayed. The serous fluids can flow out of the cerebellum, going in directions only determinable later, when we do an autopsy. Over in the Home for Incurables, they've got one stupefied old fellow in whom clearly, the discharge went straight down the spinal column; he's in immense pain, but he's still alive."

"Did they have a good time?" asked Père Goriot, suddenly recognizing Eugène.

"Ah!" said Bianchon. "All he ever thinks about is his daughters. He's already told me, a hundred times, 'They're dancing! She got her dress!' He's been calling for them, saying their names over and over. It's enough to make me cry, God damn it! the way he speaks to them: 'Delphine! My little Delphine! Nasie!' So help me God," declared the medical student, "you simply can't help weeping."

"Delphine!" said the old man. "She's there, isn't she? I know she is."

His eyes became wildly active, looking all across the walls and at the door.

"I'll go tell Sylvie to get those plasters ready," exclaimed Bianchon. "This is exactly the right time."

Rastignac was left alone with the old man, sitting at the foot of the bed, his glance fixed on that frightful, infinitely distressing face.

"Madame de Beauséant's fleeing, and this one's about to die," he murmured. "Beautiful souls can't stay for very long in this world. But really, how can grand passions possibly exist in such a shabby society as ours, so petty, so superficial?"

His mind brought up memories of the great ball he'd just been to, contrasting it with the sight of this grim deathbed. Suddenly Bianchon came back.

"Let me tell you, Eugène, I've just had a word with our head doctor, and I came back here on the run. Now, if he manifests any rational symptoms, if for example he starts to talk, lie him right down on a long poultice, so the mustard absolutely covers him from the nape of the neck all the way down to his kidneys, and then call me at once."

"My dear Bianchon," said Eugène.

"Listen, it's a matter of high scientific interest," the medical student said, with all the enthusiasm of a neophyte.

"Yes," replied Eugène, "so I'll be the only one taking care of this poor old man because I like him."

"Had you seen me this morning," declared Bianchon, not in the least offended, "you wouldn't say that. Doctors who have been out in practice see only the sickness, but me, my dear fellow, I still see the sick man as well."

He left, and Eugène was again alone with the old man, worrying about a crisis—and, in fact, one came soon enough.

"Ah, it's you, my dear child," said Père Goriot, recognizing Eugène once more.

"I hope you're feeling better?" asked the student, taking Goriot's hand.

"Yes, my head's been feeling as though it was squeezed in a

vice, but that's going away. Have you seen my daughters? They'll be here soon, they'll come running as soon as they know I'm sick, they used to take such good care of me, when we lived on Jussienne Street! But my Lord! I wish my room were fit to receive them. There was a young man here, and he burned up all my peat."

"I hear Christophe coming," Eugène told him. "He's bringing some wood this same young man sent you."

"Fine! But how are we going to pay for it? I haven't a cent left, my child. I've given it all away, all of it. Now I'm a charity case. Was the spangled dress pretty, at any rate? (Oh, my God, how it hurts!) Thank you, Christophe. May God repay you, my boy, because me, I've got nothing left."

"I'll take care of you, you and Sylvie too," Eugène whispered in the boy's ear.

"My daughters told you they're coming, didn't they, Christophe? Go call them again, I'll find a dollar for you. Tell them I don't feel good, I want to hug them, I want to see them one last time before I die. Tell them that, but don't tell them too much, don't frighten them."

Rastignac signaled to Christophe, and the boy left the room.

"They'll come," the old man continued, "I know my girls. That good Delphine of mine, how unhappy she'll be, if I die! And Nasie, too. I could wish I'd never die, so I didn't make them shed tears. What death means, my good Eugène, is never seeing them again. It's going to be good and boring, there where I'm going. For a father, Hell means being without his children, and I've already served my apprenticeship in that, since they've been married. Jussienne Street was Heaven, for me. I tell you, if I ever get to Paradise, I'll be able to come back in spirit and be where they are. I've heard people talk of things like that. Is it true? It seems to me I can see them, right now, just the way they were when we lived on Jussienne Street. They used to come downstairs, in the morning. 'Good morning, Papa,' they'd say. I'd take them on my lap, I'd tease them and play with them, all sorts of little games. We'd always have breakfast together, we'd have dinner—and, in a word, I was a real father, I took pleasure in my children. When they were still on Jussienne Street, we never argued, they knew nothing about society or the rest of the world, they really loved me. Oh Lord! Why can't they always stay little? (My God, how it hurts, how my head hurts!) Ah! Ah! forgive me, my children. It's hurting me terribly, and this must be real pain, because you've toughened me against any ordinary suffering. My God! If I only had their hands in mine, it wouldn't hurt so much. Are they really coming? Christophe is such an idiot! I should have gone there myself. But he's going to see them, he will.

"But you were at the ball, yesterday. Tell me how they were, will you? They don't know I'm sick, isn't that it? They wouldn't have danced, if they had, the poor little things! Oh, I don't want to be sick anymore. They still need me too much. Their fortunes are in danger. And the husbands they're tied to! Cure me, cure me! (Oh, how it hurts. Ah! ah! ah!) Don't you see, I've got to get better, because they have to have money, and I know where to go to get it. I'll go make spaghetti and macaroni in Odessa. I've got a head on my shoulders, I'll make millions. (Oh! it hurts, I can't stand it!)"

Goriot fell silent for a moment, apparently summoning up all the strength he had left, to endure the pain.

"If they were here," he said, "I wouldn't be complaining. So why am I carrying on like this?"

He fell into a light doze, and did not wake for a long time. Christophe came back. Thinking Père Goriot asleep, Rastignac let the boy tell him, in his normal voice, exactly what had happened.

"Monsieur," he said, "first I went to the countess's house,

but I couldn't get to see her, she was having some big business with her husband. When I insisted, Monsieur de Restaud came out to speak to me, and this is what he told me: 'Monsieur Goriot's dying, fine! It's the best thing he can do. Right now I need Madame de Restaud, we have important things to do, and she'll come when we've finished them.' He was pretty angry, he was. I was just going to leave, when Madame de Restaud came in, through a door I hadn't noticed, and she said, 'Christophe, tell my father I'm negotiating with my husband and I can't break away; these are life-and-death matters for my children; but I will come, just as soon as all this is over with.'

"But as for the baroness, well, that was another story! I never got to see her, and I never got to talk to her. 'Ah,' her maid told me, 'my mistress came home from the ball at a quarter past five in the morning; she's asleep; if I wake her up before noon, she'll have a fit. When she rings for me, I'll tell her that her father's not doing so well. When it comes to bad news, there's always plenty of time to tell her.' I begged her and begged her! Nothing doing! So I asked if I could speak to the baron, but he'd gone out."

"Neither of his daughters is coming!" Rastignac exclaimed. "I have to write to both of them."

"Neither one of them," echoed the old man, sitting up in bed. "They're busy, they're asleep, they're not coming. I knew it. You have to die to understand what children are! Ah! my friend, don't get married, don't have children! You give them life, and they give you death. You bring them into the world, they chase you out of it. No, they're not coming! I've known that for ten years. I told myself as much, sometimes, but I didn't dare believe it."

A tear came out of each eye, hanging motionless on the red rims, falling no further.

"Ah! If I'd been rich, if I'd kept my fortune, if I hadn't given them everything, they'd have been here, they'd be polishing my cheeks with their kisses! I'd be living in a mansion, with beautiful rooms, with servants, with my own warm fire, and they'd be here, all in tears, and with their husbands, and with their children. I'd have had all that. But—nothing. Money brings you everything, even daughters. Oh! my money, where has it gone? If I were rich and I could leave it to them, they'd have taken care of me, they'd have looked after me; I'd hear them, I'd see them. Oh, my dear son, my only child, I prefer being miserable, being deserted! At least, when you're unlucky and you're loved, you know you're really loved. But I'd still rather be rich, because then I'd see them. My God, who knows? They have hearts like rock, both of them. I loved them too much for them to love me at all. A father's got to be rich, he's got to keep his children on a tight rein, like sneaky horses. And there I was, down on my knees in front of them. What scoundrels! Oh, they were so courteous to me, for the first ten years after their marriages. If you only knew how solicitous they were, back then! (Oh, my God, it hurts, it's cruel how I'm suffering!) I'd just given each of them almost eight hundred thousand francs, they couldn't be impolite to me, nor their husbands either. They'd welcome me: 'Oh, Father, come over here; oh dear Father, come over there.' There was always a place set for me at their table. I'd have supper with their husbands, who really put themselves out for me. I still seemed to be worth something. And why? Because I hadn't told them anything about my business. A man who gives eight hundred thousand francs to each of his daughters is a man you want to look out for. So they made a fuss over me, but it was just for my money. It's not a nice world. I've seen it, oh, I've seen it! They'd take me to the theater in their carriage, and when they had parties I'd come whenever I felt like it. In a word, they let everyone know they were my daughters, and they admitted to everyone I was their father. I still knew what I was doing, in those days, and nothing got past me, let me tell you. It was just scheming, all of it, and it pierced me right to the heart. I could see perfectly well it was all make-believe, but it was too late, there was nothing I could do about it. I wasn't as comfortable, eating in their houses, as I was sitting at the table downstairs, here. And, you know, when some of those society people would whisper in the ears of my sons-in-law, 'Who is that gentleman?' 'That's my rich father-in-law, he's rolling in money.' 'Well, what do you know!' they'd answer, and then they'd look at me with the respect money deserves. But if I got in their way sometimes, I had to pay for my shortcomings! Besides, who's perfect? (My head's sore all over!) Then I'd suffer just the way you suffer when you're dying, my dear Monsieur Eugène—but really, it wasn't as bad as the first time Anastasie looked at me and I knew that something I'd just said had humiliated her: the way she looked at me was like opening every one of my veins. I wished I could understand it all, but what I really understood was that there was no place for me anymore, not on this earth. And the next day I went to Delphine's house, to cheer myself up, and what do you know, I did something there, too, and made her angry at me. I went crazy. The whole next week I didn't know what to do. I didn't dare go see them, for fear they'd scold me. And then there I was, not allowed into my own daughters' houses.

"Oh Lord! since You understand how I've suffered, since You know how unhappy I've been and everything I've had to endure—since You've known every time they've stuck a knife into me, all these years which have turned me old, and changed me, and turned me gray, and killed me, why are You making me suffer like this, today? I've done more than enough penance for loving them too much. They've taken right and proper vengeance for my love, they've torn me to pieces like executioners. But fathers are so stupid! I loved them so much that I kept coming back for more, like a gambler who can't stay away. My daughters, they were my vice; when all's said and done, they really were like my mistresses! They were always needing something, some piece of finery, both of them; their maids would come and tell me, and I'd give them whatever they needed, so they'd let me come and see them! Just the same, they gave me some good lessons about what I was supposed to do, when I was in society. And they didn't wait till the day after, let me tell you! They began blushing for me. So that's what happens, when you educate your children. But me, at my age, how could I go back to school! (My God, how it hurts! Help, Doctors! Help! Cut open my head and it won't hurt so much!)

"Oh my daughters, my daughters! Anastasie, Delphine! I want to see them. Let the police go find them and bring them here! Justice is on my side, all on my side, and so is Nature, and the Law. This is all wrong! If fathers are trampled underfoot, the whole nation will perish. Anyone can see that. Human society— the whole world—it all turns on fatherhood, and everything will collapse if children stop loving their fathers. Oh, just to see them, just to hear them, it doesn't matter what they say as long as I hear their voices, that will make it hurt less, especially Delphine's voice. But tell them, when they come, not to look at me coldly, the way they've been doing. Ah! my good friend, Monsieur Eugène, you don't know how it feels, having those golden looks turned leaden and gray. From the day their eyes no longer shone on me, I've lived in eternal winter; all I've had to eat has been misery, and I've stuffed myself with it! I've lived so I could be humiliated, so I could be insulted. I love them so much that, whatever the insults, I swallowed them all, I accepted everything for the pitiful, shameful little pleasures they granted me in return. For a father to have to sneak around, hiding himself, so he can see his daughters! I gave them my entire life but, now, they won't give me a single hour of their time. I'm thirsty, I'm hungry, my heart's on fire, but they won't come and refresh me in my final agony, for this is the end, I feel it. But they don't understand what it means to trample on your father's corpse! There's a God in Heaven, He wreaks vengeance, no matter whether we want Him to or not, we other Fathers.

"Oh! they'll come, they'll come! Come, my sweet ones, come give me one more kiss, one last kiss, your father's last sacrament, your father who'll intercede with God on your behalf, who'll tell Him you've been good daughters, who'll plead for you! After all, you're nothing but innocents. That's what they are, my friend, they're innocents! Make sure everyone knows that, so no one bothers them on my account. It's all my fault, I got them used to walking all over me. I liked that, I really did. No one should pay any attention, it's not a matter for human justice, or for divine justice, either. God Himself would be unjust if He condemned them because of me. I didn't know how to behave, I committed the stupidity of abdicating my own rights. I would have utterly degraded myself, anything for them. What can you do! Some of the most beautiful, best-endowed souls in the world have succumbed to the corruption of such paternal indulgence. And now I'm miserable, I've been properly punished. All this chaos in my daughters' lives, I'm responsible for it all, I spoiled them, I ruined them. All they want, now, is pleasure, just the way they used to want candy. I always let them have whatever their girlish minds wanted. Think of it: when they were fifteen, they had a carriage! They got everything. It's all my fault, but it's a loving fault. Their voices simply opened my heart.

"I hear them, they're coming. Oh, yes! yes, they'll come. The law requires them to come see their father die, the law's on my side. They only have to come this once. I'll pay for the trip. Write to them, tell them I have millions to leave them! On my word of honor. I'll go to Odessa, I'll make the best Italian pasta. I know how. I can see it, there's millions to be made out there. No one else has thought of it. Because that stuff won't spoil in transit, the way wheat will, or flour. Hey, hey, pasta? There's millions in it! So you won't be telling lies, tell them it's millions and millions, and even if it's just greed that brings them, I'd rather be fooled, at least I'll see them. I want my daughters! I made them! They're mine!" he exclaimed, sitting bolt upright once again, the snowy hair on his head disheveled, his face glaring at Eugène with all the threatening menace it could muster.

"Now, now," said the student, "lie down again, my good old Goriot, I'll write to them, yes. And if they still haven't come, as soon as Bianchon gets back I'll go fetch them myself."

"If they still haven't come!" the old man repeated, his face turning purple. "But I'll be *dead*, I'll be dead in a fit of fury— fury! I feel it swirling all over me! And right now I can see my whole life. I've been a fool! They don't love me, they've never loved me! That's obvious. If they haven't come by now, they won't ever come. The more they hesitate, the less willing they'll be to let me have this last pleasure. I know them. They've never understood anything of my unhappiness, my suffering, my needs, and they'll understand my death even less; they haven't the slightest idea how I feel about them. But I understand, oh yes, all this cutting myself open means that, for them, nothing I do is worth anything anymore. If they'd asked to put out my eyes, I'd have said, 'Out with them!' I'm so stupid. They think all fathers are like theirs. You have to value yourself for what you're really worth. But their children will avenge me. So it's the best thing for them to come. Warn them, they're risking their own final hours. This one crime is equal to all the criminal acts there are. Go, tell them, if they don't come, it's like killing their father! They've committed enough crimes already, they don't need to pile up more. Call to them, the way I do: 'Hey, Nasie! Hey, Delphine! Come see your father who's been so good to you, and who's in such pain!' But there's no one, no one. Am I going to die all alone, like a dog? That's my reward: desertion. They're both unspeakable, they're scoundrels! I hate them, I despise them; I'll come out of my coffin, at night, so I can curse them all over again, because, really, my friends, did I do anything wrong? It's them, they're behaving terribly! Right? What am I talking about? Didn't you just tell me Delphine's there? She's better than her sister. You're like my son, Eugène, you are! Love her, be a father to her. Her sister's the unlucky one. And their fortunes! Ah, my God! I'm dying, I can't stand it! Cut off my head, all I need is my heart."

"Christophe, go find Monsieur Bianchon," Eugène cried, terrified by the turn the old man's complaints and exclamations were taking. "Bring him back in a cab!

"And I'll go find your daughters, my dear Père Goriot, I'll bring them for you."

"Drag them here, drag them! Call out the police, the Navy, the Marines, everyone! everyone!" the old man declared, staring at Eugène with the last flickering gleams of rationality. "Tell the government, tell the attorney general, just so they bring them, I want them!"

"But you cursed them."

"Who says so?" the old man responded, dumbstruck. "You know how much I love them, I worship them! If I could see them I'd be cured . . . Ah, my good neighbor, my dear child, how good you are, yes, you; I wish I could show you how grateful I am, but the only thing I can give you is a dying man's blessing. Ah, but I wish I could at least see Delphine, so I could tell her to pay my debt to you. If her sister still can't come, bring me Delphine. Go, tell her you won't love her anymore if she doesn't come. She loves you so much that she'll surely come. Give me water, my insides are on fire! Put something on my head. My daughter's hand, that would save me, I know it would . . . Oh God! Who'll get back their fortunes if I'm not here? I'll go to Odessa for them, Odessa, I'll make pasta out there."

"Take a sip of this," said Eugène, raising the dying man and holding him erect with his left hand, while with the other offering him a cup of barley-tea.

"You love your father and your mother, I know you do!" gasped the old man, clutching Eugène's hand with his feeble fingers. "Do you understand—I'm going to die, and I'm not going to see them. My daughters. These last ten years I've lived, always thirsty, never allowed to drink . . . My sons-in-law, they've killed my daughters. Yes—once they were married, I didn't have any daughters. All you fathers, get the legislature to pass a law governing marriage! Better still, if you love them, don't ever marry off your daughters. Sons-in-law are scoundrels, they ruin daughters, they pollute everything. No more marriages! We're the ones who raise our daughters, and then, when we die, we don't see them. There has to be a law about fathers dying. It's shocking, that's what it is! Vengeance! It's my sons-in-law, they're keeping my daughters from coming. Kill them! Kill that Restaud, kill that Alsatian, because they're killing me! Either they die or they give me back my daughters! Ah! It's all over, I'm dying without them. Without them! Nasie, Fifine, come, come, please come! Your father's going away . . ."

"My good Père Goriot, be calm, be quiet, don't get excited, don't think about things."

"Not seeing them—that's true pain!"

"You'll see them, you'll see them."

"Yes!" the old man cried, his eyes wild. "Oh, I'll see them! I'll see them, I'll hear their voices. I'll die happy. Yes, that's enough, I won't ask to go on living, it doesn't matter any more, it was all too much. But seeing them, touching their dresses, ah! just their dresses, that's little enough, just to feel something of theirs! Just let me touch their hair . . . I want . . ."

His head toppled to one side, as if he'd been hit by a club. His hands twittered under the blanket, as if he were grasping his daughters' hair.

"I bless them," he said with an effort, "I bless them."

And then, suddenly, he was still. Bianchon came in.

"I met Christophe," he said, "he's getting you a carriage."

Then he glanced down at the sick man, lifted Goriot's eyelids with his thumbs; the two students saw a dull glance, utterly without vitality.

"He won't come out of this one," said Bianchon, "I don't see how he possibly can."

He took the old man's pulse, then put his hand over Goriot's heart.

"The machine just keeps going, but that's no advantage, not in his state; he'd be better off dead!"

"Oh God, yes," Rastignac answered.

"Hey, what's the matter with you? You look as pale as death."

"My friend, I've been listening to his screams, his groans. There's definitely a God. Oh yes, yes! Either there's a God, and He's made a better world for us, or this world of ours makes no sense at all. If it weren't so tragic, I'd be dissolved in tears, but even as it is my heart, my stomach, they're tied up in knots."

"Listen, we're going to need a lot of things. Where do we find the money?"

Rastignac pulled out his watch.

"Take this, go on, pawn it. I don't want to have to stop on the way, I'm afraid of losing a single minute—and there's Christophe, I hear him. I don't have a cent, we'll have to pay the fare when I get back."

Rastignac virtually threw himself down the stairs, then left immediately for Helder Street, where Madame de Restaud lived. As he rode along, deeply impressed by the ghastly spectacle he had just witnessed, his indignation grew more and more heated. When he got to the house and asked for Madame de Restaud, he was told that she could not be seen.

"But I'm here on behalf of her father, who's dying," he told the servant.

"Monsieur, the count himself has given us the very strictest orders."

"If Monsieur de Restaud is indeed at home, please tell him the state his father-in-law is in and inform him that I absolutely must speak to him, and this very moment."

Eugène waited a long time.

"He may very well be dying right now," he thought.

He was escorted into a room, where Monsieur de Restaud, himself standing in front of a fireplace in which no fire burned, received him without asking that he be seated.

"Monsieur," said Rastignac, "at this very moment your father-in-law is dying in a ghastly hovel, without so much as a penny with which to quench his thirst; he is at the very point of death and asks to see his daughter . . ."

"My dear sir," the Count de Restaud answered him coldly, "you yourself are quite aware that I feel no particular affection for Monsieur Goriot. He has thoroughly compromised his character with Madame de Restaud, he has ruined my life, and I can only see him as the enemy of my peace and tranquility. Whether he dies, or whether he lives, is to me a matter of complete indifference. And there you have the sum of my feelings about him. The world might choose to hold them against me, but I scorn any such opinion. Right now, as it happens, I am engaged in matters far more important to me than any idiots or totally inconsequential persons. As for Madame de Restaud, she is in no condition to venture forth. What's more, I do not wish her to leave her home. Tell her father that, just as soon as she has fulfilled her obligations to me, she will come to see him. If indeed she loves her father, she could be free in a matter of moments . . ."

"Monsieur de Restaud, it's not my business to judge your conduct, you are the master of this household, and of your wife; but may I count on your sense of fairness? Fine! Simply promise me to tell her that her father will not live another twenty-four hours, and has indeed already cursed her for not being at his bedside!"

"Tell her yourself," replied Monsieur de Restaud, impressed by the obvious signs of indignation in Eugène's voice.

Led by the count, Rastignac went to the room the countess usually occupied, and found her there, drowning in tears, buried in an armchair like a woman who wished herself dead. He felt sorry for her. Before noticing Rastignac's presence, she looked at her husband so fearfully that, it was clear, she was the victim of complete prostration, all her strength wiped out by physical and psychological tyranny. Her husband gave her head a shake, which seemed to impart to her enough energy to speak.

"I've heard it all. Tell my father that, if he understood the situation I'm in, he'd forgive me. I did not expect such torture, such agony, and I am not strong enough to endure it—but I will resist until the end," she threw at her husband. "I'm a mother. So tell my father that, no matter how it may seem, I'm guilty of nothing in my behavior to him!" she cried to the student, despairingly. "Nothing!"

Understanding the terrible crisis in which the woman was caught, Eugène said farewell to them both and, stupefied, left them. Monsieur de Restaud's manner made it clear that he'd come in vain; he understood perfectly that Anastasie was no longer free to do as she chose. So he ran to Madame de Nucingen, and found her still in bed.

"Oh, I'm so sick, my poor friend," she told him. "I caught cold, going to the ball, I'm afraid I'm developing pneumonia, I'm just waiting for the doctor to come . . ."

"Even if you were at death's door," he cut her off, "you'd have to drag yourself to your father's side. He's calling for you! If you could hear even the least harrowing of his cries, you wouldn't think yourself sick at all."

"Eugène, my father may not be as sick as you say, but it would fill me with despair to do anything you might think wrong, so I'll do whatever you want me to. But I know my father, and he would absolutely die in misery if going out like this made me fatally ill. Well! I'll go just as soon as my doctor comes. Oh! why aren't you wearing your watch?" she exclaimed, not seeing the chain. Eugène blushed. "Eugène! Now if you've already lost it, Eugène . . . oh! that would be bad, very bad."

He leaned over her bead and whispered in her ear.

"You really want to know? Well, I'll tell you! Your father hasn't got a cent to pay for the shroud we'll be putting him in, tonight. I had to pawn your watch, I didn't have anything else."

Delphine leaped out of bed, ran to her desk, took her purse, and handed it to Rastignac. She rang for her maid, crying out,

"I'm coming, I'm coming, Eugène. Just let me get dressed— but I'll look monstrous! You go on, I'll get there before you do! Thérèse!" she called to her maid, "Tell Monsieur de Nucingen to come up, I need to speak to him right away."

Pleased at being able to tell the dying man that one of his daughters, at least, was coming, Eugène returned to New Saint Geneviève Street almost gaily. He dug around in the purse, so he could quickly pay off the cab driver. All this young woman, so rich, so elegant, had in her purse was seventy francs. When he'd climbed up the stairs, he found Bianchon holding up Père Goriot, while the hospital surgeon worked on him, under the supervision of the hospital doctor. They were cauterizing his back with flaming mustard plasters—science's final, futile remedy.

"Do you feel that?" the doctor asked.

But Père Goriot, having caught sight of Eugène, only replied, "They're coming, aren't they?"

"Maybe he can still make it," said the surgeon. "He's talking."

"Yes," Rastignac answered. "Delphine's following right behind me."

"My God!" said Bianchon. "He's been talking about his daughters all along, crying out for them the way a man being burned at the stake is supposed to cry for water."

"Stop," the doctor instructed the surgeon, "there's nothing more to be done, he can't be saved."

Bianchon and the surgeon lay the dying man back on his dirty mattress.

"But no matter," said the doctor, "we still have to change his bed linen. There may be no hope, but we must respect him as a human being. I'll be back, Bianchon," he told the medical student. "If he's still in pain, rub some opium on his diaphragm."

The surgeon and the doctor left.

"Well, Eugène my boy, be brave!" said Bianchon, as soon as they were alone. "What we've got to do is get him into a clean shirt and change his bed. Go tell Sylvie to bring up some sheets and give us a hand."

Eugène went down and found Madame Vauquer and Sylvie busy setting the table. As soon as he opened his mouth, the widow came over, looking at him sourly, the way a shopkeeper will when he wants neither to lose his money nor anger his customer.

"My dear Monsieur Eugène," she told him, "you know quite

as well as I do that Père Goriot hasn't got a penny to his name. To supply sheets to a man who's about to turn up his eyes is to throw them away, not to mention that there'll be at least one needed for his shroud. It's like this, you already owe me a hundred and forty-four francs, so add to that forty more for sheets, plus other little things, and the candle Sylvie will be giving you, and it all adds up to at least two hundred francs, which a poor widow like me can't afford to lose. Lord! Be fair, Monsieur Eugène, I've lost quite enough, these last five days, ever since bad luck came to sit at my table. I'd have laid out ten francs, I would, if that man had been gone all this time, the way you said he would. This is hard on my lodgers. I feel like having him carted off to the hospital. Just put yourself in my place. For me, after all, this is my whole life."

Eugène raced back up the stairs.

"Bianchon, where's the money from the watch?"

"Right there on the table, the three hundred and sixty-odd francs we have left. They gave me enough so I could pay up all our debts. The pawnshop receipt's under the money."

"Here, Madame Vauquer," Rastignac said, after rattling back down the stairs, half sick to his stomach, "let's get it all taken care of. Monsieur Goriot won't be with you much longer, and me . . ."

"Oh yes, he'll be leaving feet first, poor old man," she said, as she counted out two hundred francs, looking half cheerful, half carefully melancholy.

"Let's get it over with," said Rastignac.

"Let him have some sheets, Sylvie, and go help these gentlemen, upstairs."

"Don't forget to take care of Sylvie," Madame Vauquer whispered in his ear, "she's been up two nights in a row."

But the moment Eugène turned his back on her, the widow ran over to her cook.

"Take the patched-up sheets from number seven. They're more than good enough for a dead man, by God," she whispered in Sylvie's ear.

Already on his way up the stairs, Eugène did not hear a word of this.

"All right," said Bianchon, "let's get his shirt off. You sit him up."

Eugène lifted the dying man, while Bianchon took off his shirt; the old man's hands twitched, as if to protect something on his chest, making plaintive, incoherent sounds, like an animal trying to express immense pain.

"Ah! Ah!" exclaimed Bianchon. "He wants that little chain of woven hair, and the tiny locket we had to take off a minute ago, so we could get the plasters on him. Poor man! He's got to have them back. Take a look on the shelf over there."

Eugène fetched a chain into which strands of ash-blond hair, surely Madame Goriot's, had been woven. On one side of the locket he read, "Anastasie," and on the other, "Delphine." A representation of his heart, which had always lain against his heart. The ringlets inside the locket were so fine they must have been cut when his daughters were little more than babies. The moment the locket touched his chest the old man sighed so profoundly, with such evident satisfaction, that it was a frightening sight. It was one of the last echoes of human feeling, all of which seemed to be retreating down into that unknown center from which instincts and emotions first come. His face was contorted by a kind of morbid joy. Both students, struck by the incredible force of an emotion which survived even reason itself, found themselves shedding hot tears, which fell on the dying man and drew from him a shrill, bitter cry of pleasure:

"Nasie! Fifine!"

"He's still alive," said Bianchon.

"And what good does it do him?" Sylvie said.

"It lets him suffer," Rastignac responded.

Signaling to his comrade to follow suit, Bianchon knelt down so he could get his arms under the sick man's knees, and then, from the other side of the bed, Rastignac slid his hands under Goriot's back. Sylvie stood ready to pull off the dirty sheets, when they lifted the dying man, and replace them with the clean ones she had brought. Their tears having deceived him, Goriot summoned his last strength and stretched out his hands, which on either side of the bed met with the students' heads, which he clutched at, tugging at their hair, and murmuring, feebly, "Ah! My angels!" Just two words, two faint sounds emphasized by the soul which flew up and away as he spoke.

"The poor, poor man," said Sylvie, moved by this exclamation, which breathed the noblest of all feelings, evoked for the last time by the most awful, unintended delusion.

Père Goriot's final sigh on earth was thus a murmur of joy. It summed up his life: he had been deceived this one last time. They laid him reverently back on his mattress. From now on, all that could be seen on his face was the miserable result of the struggle between death and life, waged in a machine no longer capable of that mindful consciousness which produces, in all human beings, sensations of pleasure and of pain. His end was only a matter of time.

"He'll be like this for a while, and then he'll die without anyone knowing it; there won't even be a death rattle. The brain's absolutely broken down."

Just then they heard a young woman, breathless, hurrying up the stairs.

"She's too late," said Rastignac.

It wasn't Delphine, but Thérèse, her maid.

"Monsieur Eugène," she said, "there was a violent scene between my mistress and the baron, because the poor lady wanted money for her father. She fainted, the doctor came, they had to bleed her, and she was screaming, 'My father's dying, I want to see Papa!' It was heart-rending."

"All right, Thérèse. It wouldn't do any good for her to come, now, because Monsieur Goriot wouldn't know her."

"Oh the poor dear man, is he that sick!" exclaimed Thérèse.

"You won't need me anymore, I have to go serve dinner, it's already four-thirty," said Sylvie, who as she reached the head of the stairs almost ran into Madame de Restaud.

The countess was like some somber, awful specter. She looked down at the deathbed, dimly lit by a single candle, and shed tears, seeing her father's deathmask, on which still throbbed the final shuddering signs of life. Discretely, Bianchon left the room.

"I couldn't get away in time," she told Rastignac.

The student acknowledged her with a sad motion of his head. Madame de Restaud took her father's hand, and kissed it.

"Forgive me, Father! You used to say my voice could call you out of the grave, so come back to life, just for a moment, and bless your repentant daughter. Listen to me. This is awful! But yours is the only blessing I can still receive, here on earth. Everyone hates me, I even hate myself. Even my children will hate me. Take me with you, I'll love you, I'll take care of you.

"But he can't hear me, I'm out of my mind."

She dropped to her knees, staring wildly at her father's remains.

"My misfortune's complete," she said, turning and glancing up at Eugène. "Monsieur de Trailles has run off, leaving immense debts behind him, and I've finally understood he was lying to me. My husband will never forgive me, and I've surrendered my fortune to his hands. I have no illusions left. Ah! I've betrayed the only heart"—and she gestured toward her father—"which loved me, which adored me! I never appreciated him, I drove him away, I wronged him a thousand times over, wretch that I am!"

"He knew it," Rastignac said.

Just then Père Goriot opened his eyes, but it was simply the effect of a convulsion. This movement, for a brief instant making the countess hopeful, was no less ghastly a sight than the dying man's eyes.

"Did he hear me?" she cried. "No," she answered herself, sitting down next to the bed.

Since she wanted to watch over her father, Eugène went downstairs, intending to take a bit of food. The regular dinner guests were already at their places.

"Well," the painter remarked, as Rastignac came in, "apparently we're going to have a little deatharama, up there?"

"Charles," Eugène replied, "it seems to me you might make less morbid jokes on this subject."

"Aren't we even allowed to laugh in here?" the painter answered. "What could be wrong, since Bianchon says the old man's no longer conscious?"

"Well!" the Museum employee took it up. "He'll die exactly the way he lived."

"My father's dead!" the countess screamed.

Hearing this terrible cry, Sylvie, Rastignac, and Bianchon ran up the stairs, where they found that Madame de Restaud had fainted. After restoring her to consciousness, they brought her out to the cab, which was still waiting. Eugène left her in Thérèse's care, directing her to take Anastasie to Madame de Nucingen's house.

"Oh yes, he's as dead as they come," said Bianchon, coming back down.

"To the table, gentlemen," declared Madame Vauquer. "The soup will get cold."

The two students sat next to one another.

"What has to be done now?" Eugène asked Bianchon.

"What indeed. I've closed his eyes, and I've laid him out properly. Once the city coroner's verified the cause of death, he gets sewn into a shroud, and then he'll be buried. What do you think ought to happen?"

"He won't go sniffing his bread anymore," said someone, imitating Goriot's gesture.

"Good Lord, gentlemen," exclaimed the assistant schoolmaster, "leave Père Goriot alone, let's stop chewing on his corpse, because he had the last sauce applied a full hour ago. One of the privileges of this great city of Paris is that you can be born here, and live here, and die here without anyone paying the slightest attention to you. Let's take advantage of what civilization offers us. There'll probably be sixty deaths in this city, today alone: would you like to mourn for the slaughter of the faithful, here in Paris? If Père Goriot's dead, so much the better for him! On the other hand, if you want to worship him, go up and pray over the corpse, and let the rest of us eat our meal in peace and quiet."

"Oh, yes!" the widow declared. "It is indeed better for him that he's dead! When he was alive, the poor man experienced more than enough unpleasantness."

And this was the only funeral oration spoken over a being who, to Eugène, represented Paternity incarnate. The fifteen diners began to chat exactly as they always did. When Eugène and Bianchon had eaten, they felt their blood frozen by the clatter of knives and forks, the sound of casual laughter, and all the easygoing, gluttonous, uncaring faces around them. They went out in search of a priest who could sit up with the dead man, that night, and pray over him. Having very little to spend, they had to measure out the last respects they could pay Goriot. By about nine o'clock, the corpse was laid out in that bare room, on a cheap mat, a candle burning on each side, and a priest had come to sit beside the old man's body. Before going off to bed, Rastignac had asked the priest how much it would cost to have a mass said, and to carry the corpse to its burial, then wrote notes to Baron de Nucingen and to Count de Restaud, asking them to send someone who could see to such expenses. He dispatched Christophe with these messages, then lay down and immediately fell asleep, absolutely exhausted.

The next morning, Eugène and Bianchon were obliged to personally register the old man's death, and by noon an official certificate had been issued. But still, two hours later, neither of Goriot's sons-in-law had sent the necessary funds, nor had anyone made an appearance in their name, and Rastignac had no choice but to pay the priest himself. And after Sylvie said she'd need to have ten francs for sewing the old man into his shroud, Eugène and Bianchon calculated that, without any help from the dead man's relatives, they'd barely have enough to cover all the costs. So the medical student took it upon himself to have the body laid in a pauper's coffin, which he had brought over from the hospital (where it could be had for less).

"Let's do a number on these jokers," Bianchon suggested. "Let's buy him a grave site, for five years, and arrange a third-class mass and the cheapest possible funeral. If neither his sons-in-law nor his daughters offer to pay you back a cent, just carve on his gravestone: 'Here lies Monsieur Goriot, the Countess de Restaud and the Baroness de Nucingen's father, buried here at the expense of two university students.' "

Which was what Eugène did, but only after he'd made one last, futile attempt to see both the Nucingens and the Restauds. He was not admitted at either house. The doormen had been given strict orders.

"My master and mistress," they both said, "are receiving no one: their father having died, they've been thrown into the deepest, most profound mourning."

Eugène knew enough about Parisian high society to realize that any protest would be pointless. It made his heart contract, realizing he would not be able to see Delphine.

"Sell some trinket," he wrote, standing there, "and let your father go decently to his final resting place."

He sealed this brief note, and asked the baron's doorman to hand it to Thérèse, so she could give it to her mistress, but the doorman brought the note to Baron Nucingen, who threw it in the fire. Having done what he could, all the arrangements completed, Eugène came back to Maison Vauquer at about three o'clock, and could not keep back a tear when he saw the coffin in front of the house, out in the deserted street, barely covered by a black sheet, and resting on two chairs. A singularly ugly dispenser lay, untouched, next to a silver-plated bowl of holy water. No one had bothered to drape black cloth across the door: this was a pauper's funeral, without any fuss, with no one to follow the corpse to its grave, nor any friends, nor any family. Bianchon, who had been called to the hospital, had left Rastignac a hasty note, explaining what had been arranged with the church. The price of a mass, he reported, was simply out of their reach, so they'd have to be satisfied with a less expensive vespers service; Christophe had been sent to the undertakers with this information. Just as Eugène finished deciphering this scribbled message, he saw that Madame Vauquer had in her hands the golden chain, interwoven with the hair of Goriot's two daughters.

"How could you have the nerve to take that?" he exclaimed.

"Why not! Does he have to be buried with it?" Sylvie replied. "It's made of gold."

"He certainly does!" Eugène declared indignantly. "Let him at least bring with him the only thing that could remind him of his daughters."

When the hearse arrived, Eugène had them lift the coffin into place, then open it, and he set on the good man's chest an image out of that time when Delphine and Anastasie were young, innocent and virginal, and *they didn't know anything about anything*, as he'd cried out in his last agonies. Only Rastignac and Christophe followed the hearse, along with two hired mourners, as it carried the poor man to Saint Étienne of the Mountain Church, which was not far from New Saint Geneviève Street. When they got there, the corpse was brought into a small, dark chapel, around which the student peered, in vain, for a glimpse of either Goriot's daughters or their husbands. He was alone with Christophe, who felt obliged to pay his last respects to a man who had helped him earn some good tips. While they waited for the priests to arrive, together with the choirboy and the sacristan, Eugène grasped Christophe's hand, unable to say a word.

"Yes, Monsieur Eugène," said Christophe, "he was a good, honest man, who never raised his voice, never did any harm to anyone, and never did anything bad."

The two priests, the choirboy and the sacristan came and gave everything one can have for seventy francs, in an era when religion isn't wealthy enough for prayers to be free. The ecclesiastics chanted a psalm, the Prayer for the Dead, and the *De Profundis* ["Out of the depths of despair . . ."]. The service took twenty minutes. There was only one carriage for mourners, intended for one of the priests and the choirboy, but the driver agreed to take Eugène and Christophe.

"No one's following after us," said the priest, "we can drive fast, so this doesn't take too long, because it's already five-thirty."

But just when the corpse was lifted into the hearse, two fancy carriages drove up, both of them empty, one belonging to Count de Restaud, the other to Baron de Nucingen, and they followed the funeral procession to the cemetery. At six o'clock, Père Goriot's body was lowered into its grave, while his daughters' coachmen watched, both of them disappearing (along with the priest) just as soon as the short prayer the student had paid for was recited. When the two grave-diggers had thrown enough earth on the coffin to hide it from sight, they climbed back out of the grave and one of them, addressing himself to Rastignac, asked for their tip. Eugène rummaged in his pocket, found nothing, and was obliged to borrow a couple of francs from Christophe.

This detail, in itself so insignificant, left Rastignac feeling an overwhelming sadness. The sun was setting, a damp mist grated on his nerves; he looked down at the grave and dropped the last youthful tear he would ever shed—a tear tugged out of him by the pious emotions of a pure heart, and one of those tears that, the moment it falls to the ground, goes flying straight up to Heaven. He stood there, his arms crossed, staring up at the clouds, and, seeing this, Christophe left him there.

Left alone, Rastignac walked to the highest part of the cemetery and looked down at the heart of Paris, winding tortuously along both banks of the Seine, where night lights were beginning to gleam. His glance settled almost greedily, there between the high column in the Place Vendôme and the roof of the Hôtel des Invalides, the center of that great aristocratic society into which he'd wanted to move. He looked at that swarming beehive, his very glance seeming to suck out its honey, and then declared, grandly, "Now it's just the two of us!—I'm ready!"

And then, for the first challenge he hurled at Society, Rastignac went to have dinner with Madame de Nucingen.

Saché, September 1834